DOWN IN THE WOODS

DOWN IN THE WOODS

A Carlow Valley Mystery

James Bowring

First published in Great Britain in 2023 by
The Book Guild Ltd
Unit E2 Airfield Business Park,
Harrison Road, Market Harborough,
Leicestershire. LE16 7UL
Tel: 0116 2792299
www.bookguild.co.uk
Email: info@bookguild.co.uk
Twitter: @bookguild

Copyright © 2023 James Bowring

The right of James Bowring to be identified as the author of this
work has been asserted by them in accordance with the
Copyright, Design and Patents Act 1988.

All rights reserved. No part of this publication may be
reproduced, transmitted, or stored in a retrieval system, in any form or by any means,
without permission in writing from the publisher, nor be otherwise circulated in
any form of binding or cover other than that in which it is published and without
a similar condition being imposed on the subsequent purchaser.

This work is entirely fictitious and bears no resemblance to any persons living or dead.

Typeset in 12pt Adobe Jenson Pro

Printed and bound in Great Britain by 4edge Limited

ISBN 978 1915603 210

British Library Cataloguing in Publication Data.
A catalogue record for this book is available from the British Library.

To Barney
Without whose contributions this book would
have been completed much sooner.

One

Carlow Valley is not the sort of place where murders usually happen. It is situated on the historical border between England and Wales, is a designated area of outstanding natural beauty and, as such, is a popular destination for holidaymakers, weekenders and day trippers. In truth, the two main towns of the area, Morstock and Stowbrook, are small, faded market towns of limited appeal, offering no great attraction to the itinerant visitor save for a smattering of small hotels, mediocre restaurants and understocked convenience stores, but the surrounding countryside more than makes up for their shortcomings. Rolling hills, lush and peaceful in the summer, harsh and threatening in the winter, cascade into verdant valleys while the River Carlow meanders gently through the landscape, providing a tranquil home to countless waterfowl and several families of otters, and the occasional iridescent flash of a darting kingfisher for the keen-eyed birdwatcher. Small picturesque villages like Swincroft, Buckham and Crowdale straggle along the valleys, offering pleasant clusters of picture-postcard, whitewashed cottages for the delight of photographers and artists and the occasional welcome hostelry for walkers and passing motorists. In addition, a number of grand country houses like Chartfield Castle, Wickmorstead Hall and Hackmoor Manor stand like impervious guardians of the area, seemingly protecting it from all manner of potential invaders, while offering some conveniently packaged history and a welcome refuge when the inevitable rains come.

Though Carlow Valley's main attractions appeal primarily to ramblers, cyclists, climbers, canoeists and those with a fondness for the great outdoors, it also has a smattering of cultural attractions, including a renowned symphony orchestra, and a burgeoning reputation as a centre for the arts; indeed, its biennial Arts Festival attracts considerable interest and critical acclaim from all parts of the country and, occasionally, beyond.

Clive Walsingham wiped some condensation from the window with the back of his hand and stared out glumly. On this particular morning, a grey pall of cloud hung over the valley, partially obscuring the tops of the auburn-tinted trees that sprawled across the hillside above the River Carlow. Steady rain was falling diagonally from the sombre clouds, clattering loudly onto the wooden terrace outside. Across the extensive, soggy lawn, the last of the summer blooms hung their heads miserably as the cascading rain pounded their heavy petals.

More than twenty years spent as a police detective had sucked a great deal of emotional sensitivity from him, but, as he stared languidly out at the moody, dispiriting weather, Clive felt listless and sluggish. When he made the decision to leave the police force, he and his new wife, Clare, invested virtually all of their savings into the purchase of the Follycombe Hotel on little more than a whim. When they bought it, it had been losing money for years and it had been an uphill struggle to transform it into a successful and popular base for holidaymakers and peripatetic business people, but the hotel business was a fickle, precarious one, subject, as it was, to economic vicissitudes, government policy, changing tastes and climatic fluctuations and the summer had been a bad one. July had been cool, blustery and dull and August had been wet – so wet in fact that the normally benign River Carlow had threatened to burst its banks, while occasional flash floods had caused disruption to residents and visitors alike.

Clive and Clare's decision to open the bar and dining room to non-residents had partially insulated them against the worst fluctuations of the British summer and the fickleness of fair-weather tourists, and those guests who had booked in advance continued to enjoy the best hospitality that they could offer in difficult meteorological conditions. But there was no hiding the fact that a lot of potential guests, those who would normally have booked at the last minute, had stayed away and their income had, as a result, fallen significantly. In addition, a major coach operator which had provided them with regular bookings throughout the summer was, according to Clare's inside information, in financial difficulties and unlikely to survive the winter.

Clive thrust his hands deep into the pockets of his red trousers and pursed his lips as he continued to peer out of the window. If the calculations on his financial spreadsheet were correct, a slack winter followed by another dismal summer could force the Follycombe Hotel out of business. He knew he should tell Clare – she would expect to know – but, after all the hard work she had put into making the hotel a success, and in the face of her unerring enthusiasm, he couldn't quite bring himself to do so. After all, their fortunes could change – it might need a small miracle but it could happen – and then he would have worried Clare unnecessarily.

For Clive, mid-September was always a seasonal watershed, bringing with it an uneasy mix of emotions. Normally, the end of the high season offered some welcome relief from weeks of unrelenting hard work catering for a hotel full of often demanding, sometimes unreasonable, guests. On this occasion, however, there seemed nothing much to look forward to, except the prospect of long, quiet winter months stretching interminably before him, offering little more than bleak days, dark, cold nights, high expenditure and low income.

Clive sighed. He needed an infusion of coffee. As he wandered through the entrance foyer on his way to the kitchen, his hands still thrust deep into his pockets, he had to step quickly aside as Debbie Oxton bustled breathlessly in, brushing some raindrops from her coat as she did so. She had short, dyed blonde hair, neatly parted in the centre, round, black-framed glasses and alert, pale blue eyes. She had a pear-shaped figure, due in no small part to her unbridled enthusiasm for the chef's exotic, rich desserts, and normally wore an unflattering black skirt which was so tight around her legs that, when she walked, she was forced to take small, waddling steps. She ran the reception area, over which she presided with an assured but occasionally self-important manner and a tendency for brusqueness when faced with a recalcitrant guest.

"I'm so sorry I'm late," she gasped as she pattered across the foyer. "The police have closed the road up by Carlow Woods and I had to come the long way round through Crowdale."

A desperate hotelier has probably committed suicide, Clive mused to himself as he glanced casually at his watch. "No problem, Debbie," he replied amiably. "I'm sure Clare and Beth have coped. We're not exactly rushed off our feet this morning."

Minutes later, as he wandered slowly back through the entrance foyer, his long, bony hands clasped firmly around a hot mug of coffee, Clive saw a figure standing at the reception desk that he recognised. The man was of average height but his gaunt physique and perpetually hunched shoulders made him seem smaller. He had short, dark hair, liberally flecked with silver-grey strands and, Clive noticed for the first time, a small bald patch. The man had heavily lidded brown eyes and a mouth that turned down at the edges, giving him a permanently crestfallen expression. He was wearing a dark grey suit which was showing clear signs of heavy, regular wear. The trousers were creased and wrinkled and the cuffs of the jacket were frayed. A couple of unidentifiable dark stains down the front of the jacket attested to the man's habit of eating his food quickly and messily.

As Clive was discreetly studying his visitor with the practised eye of a former detective inspector, his arm was suddenly grabbed from behind and he was led forcibly into the office.

"What the hell is he doing here?" Clare Walsingham hissed, her grey-green eyes burning with indignation. "You promised me that you'd finished being an amateur detective. You promised me you weren't going to help Dick with any more of his unsolved cases! You promised me you'd devote all your energies to running this hotel profitably."

"That's right," Clive replied while sucking some slopped coffee from his thumb and fingers. "I promised you I wouldn't let myself get involved again and I meant it. So, no, I don't know what he's doing here. Maybe it's got something to do with whatever is going on at Carlow Woods, or maybe he's just come round for coffee and cakes. You know how he likes your cakes!"

Clare was slim and elegant with short, light brown hair, piercing eyes and an expressive face. Being several inches shorter than her husband, she had to crane her neck upwards to look him in the eyes.

"Well, you'd better find out what he wants," she rasped, "apart from cakes of course! I suppose I'll have to go and raid our supply."

Clive held out a reproving hand. "Hang on a minute, darling. I'll find out what he wants and try to get rid of him."

"Huh, that's going to be easier said than done. You know that man clings like a limpet!" Clare turned smartly on her heels and flounced off towards the kitchen.

Curious and more than a little uneasy about his visitor's unannounced arrival, Clive walked back into the entrance foyer to find the man's back turned towards him. He coughed self-consciously. "Dick! How nice to see you. I suppose you're hungry again."

The man turned slowly to face him. Although only a few months had passed since their last encounter, he seemed to have aged. His face was more lined, his hair was greyer and his shoulders more drooped.

"Er, it is Detective Inspector Beauregard, if you don't mind, and I'm here on official business," he announced pompously.

Clive half turned away as he felt an inappropriate smile spreading across his face. Whenever Caspar Beauregard talked pompously, which he often did, Clive could never take him seriously. When he had first come across Acting Inspector Caspar Beauregard, as he was then, he couldn't understand why everyone called him "Dick". Now he was better acquainted with his methods, he knew.

"Oh, I see, I'm sorry," Clive mumbled as he looked quizzically at the inspector. "You'd better come into the office and..."

"And I'll need to speak to Mrs Walsingham as well so..." The inspector failed to finish his sentence as though all verbal energy had drained from him. It was an irritating habit that Clive recalled from their previous encounters.

"Er, well, in that case, we'd better go into the bar – there's more space in there. You know the way. I'll go and fetch Clare."

The bar room had been designed with practical considerations rather than aesthetic ones in mind and was furnished with solid sofas and chairs, upholstered in a shiny, claret material, arranged neatly around a number of low tables. A few unremarkable prints and pictures, mainly of sanitised rural life, adorned the pale maroon walls and a television, which was hardly ever switched on, occupied one corner of the room. Clive pulled out three chairs from one of the low tables and he and Clare sat down opposite the morose-looking inspector.

"Congratulations on your appointment, by the way," Clive began amenably. "You're a permanent detective inspector now!"

"Yes, that's right."

Clive studied his visitor again, noting the well-worn dark grey suit and scuffed black shoes.

"You didn't come on your bike today?" Clive asked impishly as he recalled with some amusement the occasion when Dick Beauregard had been caught in sudden torrential rain while cycling to the hotel and had to change into some ill-fitting clothes left behind by a previous guest while Clare did her best to dry his T-shirt and snug-fitting Lycra cycling shorts.

"No!"

Perplexed by the inspector's strangely monosyllabic responses and heavy formality, Clive exchanged tense glances with Clare and fell silent. He couldn't understand why the inspector was behaving so coldly. Perhaps he suspected that Clive and Clare were guilty of some hitherto unannounced crime, or maybe the inspector was harbouring some resentment for whatever reason. Clive scratched his head and shifted uneasily in his chair. He had, he reminded himself, always been at great pains to allow the inspector to take full credit for their previous successes, even when his contribution had been minimal, so there was no obvious reason that Clive could think of for harboured resentment of any kind. As the oppressive silence continued, Clive slowly raised both hands in front of his thin face, pressed the tips of his fingers together, narrowed his eyes and peered at the inspector.

"So, er, how can we help?"

The inspector cleared his throat. "We, erm, found the body of a woman, yesterday afternoon, in Carlow Woods. She had been badly beaten around the head and partially buried beneath some scrub. A dog walker found her."

"Ah, we were wondering what the police were doing there," Clive replied casually. "Have you identified the woman?"

"She didn't have any personal possessions with her when we found her but there was a vehicle in the car park at the entrance to the woods. The registered owner of the car is Olivia Farringdon, aged 48. We're still awaiting the results of the full post-mortem, of course, but the pathologist reckons she'd probably been dead around five days."

"So that means she was murdered around 4th September," Clive interjected, his curiosity already aroused. "Do you think she was actually murdered in Carlow Woods or murdered elsewhere and dumped there?"

Detective Inspector Beauregard gave an involuntary nod before lapsing into solemn, conventional police-speak. "Obviously, I can't say too much at the moment – we're still examining the site – but it does look as though Olivia Farringdon drove herself to the woods; as I said, we found her car in the car park. So, yes, we think that she was murdered there on 4th September. In the pocket of the jeans she was wearing, we found a receipt, dated 4th September. It was for three nights' accommodation at the Follycombe Hotel."

"What?" Clare Walsingham exclaimed incredulously. "You mean, she'd been staying at this hotel and, on the day she checked out, she got herself murdered? Bloody hell!"

"It certainly looks that way," Inspector Beauregard responded guardedly. "So as someone here in the hotel may have been the last person to see her alive, we're going to have to talk to whoever—"

"Hang on a minute," Clive interrupted. "I hope you're not regarding us as suspects. We're not in the habit of murdering our guests – it's not very good for repeat business."

The inspector shrugged. "You know the procedure. At this stage, we're keeping an open mind but, first of all, I wonder if you could check your records to confirm that Olivia Farringdon did in fact stay here between 1st and 4th September, and, if she did, we'd like to know more about her. What was the purpose of her visit, what did she get up to while she was here, did she say if she was going to meet anyone, did anyone come to see her, did you or any of your team find out anything about her that might be helpful…?"

Her cheeks flushed with excitement, Clare leapt to her feet. "I'll get on to it straight away. Actually, I think I might remember her – we don't get that many women staying here on their own – she was quite small, with tight curls and a miserable expression," she called over her shoulder as she bustled out of the room. The inspector gave another barely perceptible nod.

Clive waited until Clare was out of earshot. "Do I get the feeling that you don't know much about her?" he asked conspiratorially.

"We know that she had a flat in Brookbank and worked as a solicitor's secretary but…" The inspector shrugged again.

"And are there no clues at the site?"

"We're still combing the site but it's going to be very difficult with all the rain we've had. There are some tyre tracks in the car park but it's quite well used and very muddy and…" Belatedly remembering that Clive could be a potential suspect and that he had already imparted more information than was wise, the inspector changed the subject. "So anyway, I'm going to need a list of the guests who were staying here at the same time as Olivia Farringdon and I'll need to talk to those members of your team with whom she may have come into contact. Perhaps you can give me some names." Inspector Beauregard produced a dog-eared notebook and pen from his jacket pocket, opened the notebook and looked expectantly at Clive.

"Er, yes, yes, er, of course," Clive replied hesitantly as he ran his hand through his thinning brown hair. "Well, there's Debbie Oxton who runs the reception desk. You'll have met her before.

She doesn't miss much so she can probably tell you quite a bit about what Olivia Farringdon got up to. And there's Beth Wroxham; she hasn't been here very long so we don't know that much about her. She used to work at a big hotel in London and came with excellent references. She may have cleaned Olivia Farringdon's room – I don't know what rota she was on – so she might have seen something important. And then there's Jamie Coulton, of course."

"Ah, yes, Jamie Coulton," the inspector replied with a knowing smirk. "He's the man who's done time for stealing from old ladies."

"That was some years ago and he's a reformed character these days. As I'm sure you know, he's now in a relationship of sorts with Alison, er, sorry, Detective Constable Pawlett, so I don't think he'll have much opportunity to revert to his old ways, do you?"

"Detective Constable Pawlett is about to become a detective sergeant," Inspector Beauregard announced importantly.

"Is she?" Clive whistled quietly to himself. "That'll certainly keep Jamie on his toes."

"And me too, probably," the inspector replied ruefully, while scribbling in his notebook. "You have a chef?"

"We do! We have several people working different shifts in the kitchen now we've opened our restaurant to non-residents, although I doubt they'll have come into contact with your murder victim. They're mainly part-time and some are seasonal – just a few hours here and there."

"Nevertheless…"

"Our head chef's name is Gary Beechwood. He hasn't been here that long, either. He was recommended by your old mate Richard Edgton." Clive noticed the pen slip from Inspector Beauregard's hand at the mention of Richard Edgton's name. His misguided belief that Richard Edgton had been responsible for a series of major crimes on his patch continued to be a source of acute embarrassment to him. "Gary will also be able to tell you who else was on duty in the kitchen during Olivia Farringdon's stay."

"And I imagine you have a new gardener," the inspector continued, once he had recovered his composure and his pen.

"Yes and no," Clive replied enigmatically, recalling the unfortunate fate that befell Simon Verwood, their previous gardener. "After what happened to Simon, erm, we don't employ our own gardener anymore. We use contractors – Harvey and Holford. They usually send Ray, er, Raymond Gulliver, except when he's on leave or poorly. He doesn't come into the hotel, except to use the toilet or make a cup of tea, but he might have seen your murder victim, I suppose – his shed is down by the car park. And there's also Archie, of course." Clive nodded his head in the direction of a mature ginger cat curled up asleep on a chair in the furthest, warmest corner of the room.

At that moment, Clare returned breathlessly, clutching a piece of paper. "You're right," she announced triumphantly. "Olivia Farringdon did stay here for three nights and checked out after breakfast on 4th September. She stayed in room 13! As I recall, she seemed quite preoccupied when she was here. She didn't say much to anyone, apparently, apart from the argument she had with our chef."

Two

Clive gathered together those members of his team who were on duty and briefly explained the purpose of Detective Inspector Beauregard's visit, urging them to co-operate fully with his inquiries. At the end of his chat, he studied the reaction of each individual. Most were clearly shocked by the discovery of Olivia Farringdon's body and keen to help the police, but two individuals seemed more reluctant. Beth Wroxham appeared uncharacteristically nervous and fidgety, avoiding eye contact and constantly fiddling with the buttons on her blouse, while Debbie Oxton looked perplexed, her forehead convulsed into a deep frown and her blue eyes, normally alert and suspicious, distant and preoccupied.

At Clive's suggestion, Dick Beauregard agreed to talk to Gary Beechwood first. The chef had finished clearing away after breakfast and, not being on duty again until late afternoon, was keen to get away. Gary Beechwood was in his late twenties. He was tall and thin with slightly scruffy fair hair, dark brown eyes and an amiable enough expression although the way he kept drumming his fingers on the edge of the table suggested that he was either impatient or nervous and on edge for some reason.

"I'm Detective Inspector Beauregard," the inspector began, solemnly. "We are investigating the murder of a woman called Olivia Farringdon who stayed here between 1st and 4th September and—"

"Yeah, so I hear; at Carlow Woods? I remember her – miserable cow!" Gary Beechwood replied scornfully.

"How do you mean? In what way?"

Gary Beechwood leaned forward and spoke in a conspiratorial whisper as though he was frightened of being overheard. "Well, one evening, she complained about the steak she'd ordered. She said I'd overcooked it. I mean it was just a simple misunderstanding; she told Jamie, er, Mr Coulton that she wanted her steak medium rare but Jamie had written, or at least I thought he had written, 'medium' on his order pad." Gary Beechwood smirked. "I expect he was too busy going through his considerable repertoire of chat-up lines to concentrate on what he was doing. Anyway, she demanded to see the chef so I had to go and listen to her telling me off in front of all the other guests. She ranted on about how she'd specifically asked for her steak to be medium rare and how it was inefficient and incompetent to have got the order so wrong and how she was going to make a formal, written complaint. She said that the hotel had been recommended to her but she was very disappointed by what she had found. And then she moaned about the dressing on her salad, so…"

"And then what happened?"

Gary Beechwood shrugged. "I offered to prepare another steak. I wasn't very happy about it, I'll admit, but Clive and Clare always stress the importance of satisfied customers. And I prepared a fresh salad without any dressing. I've worked in certain, less reputable establishments where we would have put something in her salad, if you know what I mean, but not here." Gary Beechwood winked at the inspector and jabbed his forefinger on the table for emphasis.

"And is that the only contact you had with Olivia Farringdon?"

"You bet!" Gary Beechwood replied with an exaggerated emphasis. "I kept well out of her way after that and, no, I didn't murder her. Any chef who goes around murdering the people who complain about his food isn't going to last very long."

"I'm going to need a list of who else was working in the kitchen when Olivia Farringdon stayed here."

"Yeah, sure, but they kept even more out of the way than I did. They're kids mainly – they just come in for a few hours, assist me and go. I doubt that any of them knew Olivia Farringdon was staying here."

"Nevertheless!" Inspector Beauregard persisted. "Clive, er, Mr Walsingham, said you haven't been here very long."

Gary Beechwood stroked his stubbly chin thoughtfully. "No, that's right. It must be, let me see, about eight months."

"And where did you work before?"

"My last job was in a restaurant in Hampshire. I was the sous chef."

"Why did you leave?"

"I, errm, I didn't get on with the head chef – he was a bad-tempered old sod– and I wanted to move back here. I was brought up around here. I went to school around here and I've still got some friends here."

"So it was a bit of good luck, you getting this job here?"

"Yes, I suppose it was, but I don't see…" With each answer, Gary Beechwood had been sounding more and more belligerent. Now, he folded his arms across his chest and half turned away from his inquisitor.

"So if the hotel started to receive formal complaints about you, it could jeopardise your future employment prospects."

"Now look! I don't think…"

Inspector Beauregard made a point of checking his watch. It was 10.15. "So what time do you normally finish work after breakfast?"

"I'd normally have finished by now, only you won't let me go yet!"

"So you might have been leaving the hotel around the time Olivia Farringdon checked out on the 4th."

"I've no idea! I don't recall seeing her at all, apart from that one evening when she complained."

"Where do you live?"

"What's that got to do with any of this?"

"I'd just like to know what route you would have taken home."

Gary Beechwood sighed, unfolded his arms and drummed his fingers loudly on the table. "I live in Morstock, if you must know. I've got a flat there."

"So your normal route home would have taken you past Carlow Woods?"

"Yes, I suppose so."

"So, on the morning of 4th September, did you see anything unusual when you drove past Carlow Woods? Any strange cars parked there or people behaving oddly?"

"No, nothing! And as you well know, the car park for the woods is up a track. You can't see it from the main road."

"And I'm sorry if we delayed your journey here this morning."

Gary Beechwood looked mystified. "My journey here? Why would you have delayed me?"

"Because we've closed the road at Carlow Woods."

"Ah, errm, have you? Ah, yes of course. Yes, I remember. No, no, it wasn't really a problem. I leave very early and allow plenty of time and there wasn't much traffic about, so, err, no."

*

Jamie Coulton worked at the hotel variously as a porter, handyman, waiter and occasional barman. Tall, thin and darkly handsome, he was blessed with a serene temperament, an exuberant sense of fun, a flashing smile and a lightness of foot that enabled him to glide silently around the hotel, picking up gossip, dispensing cheerful courtesies and, whenever he could, flirting outrageously with the more impressionable female guests. It was an approach that occasionally earned him lavish gratuities but was not one that found much favour with his current girlfriend, Detective Constable Alison Pawlett.

"Err, as I'm sure you will have heard—" Inspector Beauregard began.

"Yes, I've heard!" Jamie Coulton interrupted, nodding vigorously. "Clive, er, Mr Walsingham told me."

"Yes, erm, we're investigating the murder of Olivia Farringdon who stayed at this hotel between 1st and 4th September. So tell me what you can about her."

"There's not much to tell really," Jamie Coulton replied, his broad smile revealing a near perfect set of pure white teeth. "I served her most mornings at breakfast and in the evening at dinner. She hardly said a word – didn't even thank me when I served her, which I thought was a bit rude, and didn't leave a tip."

"Did you try to chat her up? I hear you have a bit of a reputation for chatting up the female guests."

"I, ahem, I try to flatter the female guests a bit. I regard it as part of my job. It usually puts them in a good mood and then they often part with a bit more money, but Olivia Farringdon was completely indifferent to my patter – basically, she just ignored me."

"She complained about her food one evening…"

"Ah yes. She thought Gary had overcooked her steak. Gary tried to blame me for cocking up the order and things got a bit heated for a while but he cooked another steak for her and everything soon calmed down. No real damage was done, although she was very grumpy about the whole thing, complaining about what an awful hotel this was."

"And did you serve her in the bar at all?"

"Well, now you mention it, that was a bit odd. I didn't see her at all in the bar until the last evening before she left. She ordered two large gin and tonics and sat on her own in a corner, just staring at the wall. She seemed to be very nervous about something – I noticed her hand was shaking a bit every time she lifted her glass. She was checking her mobile every few minutes and spent quite a bit of time talking quietly to herself. And on the morning that she left, she hardly ate any breakfast, which was unusual."

"Did you see her check out?"

"No, I don't remember her going. I was probably helping to clear away after breakfast."

"Did you leave the hotel at all that morning?"

"No! Definitely not! I expect I was working all day, as usual. You're not suggesting I had anything to do with her murder, I hope. She was miserable and she didn't leave a tip but that's hardly grounds for murder."

"Where do you live?"

"We've, er, I've got a small place in Crowdale."

"So your normal route home wouldn't take you past Carlow Woods."

"No, I might go that way if I was going to Morstock to the supermarket or something but, no, not normally!"

Jamie Coulton flashed what he firmly believed to be a winning smile at the inspector but it had the same effect on him as it had had on Olivia Farringdon.

*

Beth Wroxham was what used to be called buxom. She was quite short with a shapely, slightly podgy figure. Her face was round with large hazel eyes and her long pale brown hair tumbled down onto her shoulders. When she spoke, she did so with a hint of an accent though Inspector Beauregard couldn't place its origins.

The inspector began with his usual preamble about the purpose of his visit.

"Gosh, yes!" Beth Wroxham exclaimed, her eyes wide with excitement. "Isn't it awful what happened to that poor woman. I mean, here in the Carlow Valley, you don't expect that kind of thing, do you? In parts of London maybe, and one or two other big cities, possibly, but not here. Do you know who murdered her?"

"No, er, not yet," the inspector replied uncertainly. Beth Wroxham's gushing response had distracted him; it was as though she was excessively nervous about something. "Did you see much of Olivia Farringdon while she was here?"

"Gosh, no!" Beth Wroxham exclaimed earnestly. "I was around, I think, when she checked in but Debbie dealt with her. And I didn't really see much of her at all while she was here. She handed her key over a couple of times, I think, in the morning, when she went out but she didn't say anything about where she was going or what she was doing. And I was on duty when she checked out. She didn't really say much then either – she seemed quite, er, quite preoccupied, I suppose. I asked her if she had enjoyed her stay; Mr and Mrs Walsingham always want us to do that, but she didn't really say anything. She just grunted, handed over her key and marched off."

"What was she carrying?"

"Ooooh, now you're asking! Let me think. I think she had a small suitcase on wheels – black, it was – and, ah yes, I remember, she had a camera, quite a big, expensive-looking one which she put down on the desk while she was checking out, but I don't remember anything else. Honestly, it's so difficult sometimes. You see so many people during the day that you can't remember every small detail."

"No, of course! What exactly are your duties here?"

"Ooooh, I do a bit of everything really. My main job is helping on reception but sometimes I help the chef prepare the plates if we're busy and I often help with cleaning the rooms and making the beds and I might do a bit of waiting at tables but only if we're very busy and they're desperate – I can be a bit clumsy sometimes. I don't think Clare's quite forgiven me for the incident with the soup when—"

"Yes, thank you!" Inspector Beauregard interrupted quickly. "Did you clean Olivia Farringdon's room while she was here? She was in room 13, I believe."

"Gosh, yes, I expect I did. Let me think! Yes, I'm pretty sure I did, but I don't remember much about it. It was quite tidy, I think. There was a map on the table and a few papers, I think, but I didn't see what they were. Mr and Mrs Walsingham don't want us nosing at what the guests leave in their rooms, so I try not to look. Oooh, and there was something else too; I've just remembered. There was a piece of paper on the table with one word written on it – 'circus' I think it said – and I remember thinking that was odd because there aren't any circuses around here. And, I mean, why would you just write that one word, 'circus' on a bit of paper?"

"I see, and were you on duty all day on the day Olivia Farringdon checked out? That would be September 4th."

"Oooh, yes. I normally start at 8.30 in the morning and work through till late afternoon – early evening sometimes if we're especially busy."

"And where do you live?"

"I live here in the hotel, I've got a flat on the top floor." Beth Wroxham giggled nervously. "Well, it's not really a flat – it's just a room that Mr and Mrs Walsingham are kind enough to let me use while I'm saving up for a place of my own."

"And how long have you been here?"

"Oooh, not long; only since June. I was working in a hotel in London, near Paddington station, before that. Honestly you wouldn't believe some of things the guests used to get up to there. I remember one night—"

"Yes, yes, I'm sure," Inspector Beauregard interrupted quickly. "Why did you move here?"

"Oh, er, I..." Beth Wroxham hesitated before falling uncharacteristically silent for a few moments. "I, er, wanted to get out of London. I've never really been comfortable in big towns and cities. And, er, well, I know this area, er, that is, I came here a couple of times with my parents when I was a young girl and it seemed a very nice area and then this job came up and I thought I'd like to give it a try."

"Do you have any friends or family around here?"

"What? Me? Oh, err, no, not really. I mean, the people that I work with here are all very nice and friendly but I'm usually so tired when I finish work that I, er, just crash out really. I'm hoping, if we're a bit quieter during the winter, that I might be able to get out and socialise a bit more, not that I've got much money to spend. I'm saving up to, er, get a place of my own and buy a car. You can't get very far by bus around here and there's not much nightlife."

"Do you know Carlow Woods?"

Beth Wroxham's cheeks turned pink and she looked away. "How do you mean?" she asked.

"Do you go there at all? It's where Olivia Farringdon's body was found."

"Oooh, no! I've been past them on the bus, I think, but that's all I know!"

*

Raymond Gulliver was in his mid-forties. He was short and stocky with wavy dark hair, a round, avuncular face, mischievous eyes and powerful, muscular arms. His tanned, leathery skin suggested that he had worked out of doors for many years and the shoulders of his sweat-stained shirt were damp, as a result of having recently been working outside in the rain. To avoid walking mud onto the newly cleaned floors, he had left his gardening boots by the back door and had wandered through the hotel in his socks, one of which had a large hole through which his big toe protruded.

"I understand you work here as the gardener," Inspector Beauregard asked once he had dispensed with the usual formalities.

Raymond Gulliver scratched his head. "I s'pose I do really, although I'm paid by an agency, Harvey and Holford. I normally work here three or four days a week. Not all day, you understand – sometimes I have some other jobs to fit in."

"Did you come into contact with a woman called Olivia Farringdon. She checked out on 4th September."

Raymond Gulliver scratched his head again. "No, no, I'm sure I wouldn't have. I don't have any dealings with the hotel guests, see. I don't normally come into the hotel. I mean, I might say 'good morning' to them if I bumped into them while they were, like, walking to the car park, but otherwise, no, no, I don't think so."

"Were you working here on 4th September; that would have been last Thursday?"

"Last Thursday, last Thursday," Raymond Gulliver repeated uncertainly. "I think I might have been but I'm not too sure, see. One day feels much like another to me. My boss at Harvey and Holford would be able to tell you. What did this Olivia person look like?"

"I'm afraid I don't have any photos of her when she was alive. I've only got this one of her, taken, err, shortly after we found her."

He handed the photograph to Raymond Gulliver who studied it for a few moments. Inspector Beauregard thought he detected a fleeting look of recognition in the gardener's dark eyes but he couldn't be sure. But he was sure that Raymond Gulliver gulped hard a couple of times before he replied.

"Is this her, then – this Olivia women? Poor lass! N-no, no, I don't remember seeing her at all."

*

Debbie Oxton eyed the inspector suspiciously. Her first instinct on meeting someone for the first time was always one of suspicion.

"I remember speaking to Olivia Farringdon when she phoned to make her reservation," Debbie Oxton replied to Inspector Beauregard's initial question. "It was towards the end of July, I think. She sounded quite businesslike, brusque even, when she phoned but she didn't make much of an impression."

"You were on duty when she checked in?"

"Yes I was, but I don't remember much about it. As far as I recall, she just wandered in, completed the necessary paperwork, I gave her the key to her room and off she went."

"And what about when she was here?"

"Ah well, now I think of it, it was all a bit strange. I mean, most of the people who stay here are on holiday – a few days or a long weekend, that kind of thing – and they are here to enjoy themselves so they're usually pretty relaxed and happy. Obviously, we get some guests who are here on business and they can be pretty grumpy sometimes and there are some who are here for a family occasion of some kind, a wedding, a christening, an anniversary, even a funeral, maybe. But I didn't get the impression that Olivia Farringdon was here on business – she didn't dress right and usually had a pretty late, unhurried breakfast – and there was no hint of a family event of any kind. As far as I know, she didn't meet up with anyone, but she just seemed miserable the whole damned time. She never smiled and she hardly said a word, apart from when she had an argument with the chef. Beth dealt with her when she checked out but from what I could see, she looked pretty tense. Now I'm usually a pretty good judge of character – Clive will confirm that – and there was something about her that wasn't right, something that made me suspicious. She seemed very withdrawn, very edgy about something." Debbie Oxton fell silent as though mulling over some further revelations.

"Were you on duty here all day on 4th September?"

"What? Oh, er, yes, I was. Didn't finish until six o'clock," Debbie Oxton replied distantly.

"Was there something else?" the inspector prompted, picking up on Debbie's sudden aloofness.

"No, not really! It's just, I'm sure I've encountered Olivia Farringdon somewhere before but I can't recall where and it's frustrating me. I'm normally so good with faces and names – Clive will confirm that!"

*

Clive stared hard at his computer screen but his brain, normally so methodical, refused to process the information he was seeing. The financial frailty of his hotel venture was bad enough but the thought that one of his team might be involved in a murder was a good deal worse. He was still staring, unblinking, at the screen when Inspector Beauregard put his head around the door.

"Errm, I'm sorry that I've had to make things so formal today," Inspector Beauregard announced as he sat down across the desk on the spare office chair which had only recently been vacated by Archie the cat. "But you've been a detective. You know there are protocols and procedures when it comes to a murder inquiry…"

"Of course," Clive replied amicably enough although the inspector's bristling stiffness still rankled. "You've got your job to do; I understand. Were my team helpful?"

Dick Beauregard hesitated for a moment before he replied. "Up to a point, but they weren't giving very much away and I suspect there are at least a couple of them who aren't telling the whole truth, but I can't be sure. How well do you know them?"

Clive exhaled sharply. "I don't know their life histories, far from it. As you know, Clare and I have only been here for, well, less than three years. Debbie and Jamie were here when we arrived so we know them reasonable well, I suppose, but Gary has only been here a few months and Beth only a few weeks. They came with good references and have done very well while they've been here, but all we know about them is what's written on their CV. And as for Raymond, well, he's employed by Harvey and Holford, so they probably know a good deal more about him than we do."

The inspector nodded. "There are a couple more questions I'd like answers to, if you can."

"I'll try!"

"Well, for a start, were any of the other guests who stayed here at the same time as Olivia Farringdon behaving suspiciously at all?"

Clive scratched his head. "No, I don't think so. Debbie would have been quick to come and tell me if her suspicious nature had been aroused at all. I think it was mainly couples trying to enjoy a late summer break and a couple of businessmen."

"One of your team said that there was a piece of paper in Olivia Farringdon's room with the word 'circus' written on it. Does that mean anything to you?"

"Circus?" Clive repeated with a puzzled frown. "Just the word 'circus'?"

"Apparently."

"No, it means nothing at all, I'm afraid."

"And do all members of your team have their own transport?"

"Nearly all; most live a few miles away and there's precious little public transport early in the morning or after about six o'clock in the evening. Beth doesn't have a car but we're letting her stay in one of the rooms on the top floor that we reserve for any of our team who need to stay overnight for whatever reason. She can stay there until she's saved enough money to get a place of her own and some wheels."

"So could any of them have followed Olivia Farringdon after she checked out?"

"What? What are you saying?" There was more than a trace of irritation in Clive's tense reply.

"I'm just trying to explore every angle."

"Of course, yes, I'm sorry. It's just that I don't think any of my team would… Well, anyway, Gary usually goes home after he's finished breakfast around ten or ten-thirty. He doesn't return until the afternoon when he starts preparing the evening meals. And Raymond's hours are very variable; it depends partly on the weather and any other work that the contractors want him to do. Jamie was almost certainly on duty here all day, unless he was working a split shift. Clare will be able to tell you when he was on duty. Debbie would most definitely have been on duty and Beth probably, as well. Clare can give you the duty roster for the day."

"And you and Clare?"

"I beg your pardon?"

"Did either of you go out on the morning of 4th September?"

"What…?" Clive was about to explode when he reminded himself that Inspector Beauregard was asking exactly the sort of question he used to ask as a detective inspector. "No, I don't think so. I would've tidied up the bar after the previous evening, spent some time in the office keeping up to date with the administration and done whatever else was needed. And Clare would've been supervising the morning routines, tidying up after breakfast, checking that all the rooms were being cleaned – that sort of thing."

"I see, thank you. I'll need the home address of each of your team in case we need to speak to them again."

Or want to search their houses, Clive thought to himself. "And I wonder if I could ask you a couple of questions that are bothering me a bit," he ventured. "You haven't said much about the circumstances under which Olivia Farringdon was found. Was there the possibility, for example, that there was a sexual motive?"

"No, absolutely not," the inspector replied succinctly.

"She checked out of here on Thursday 4th September and, you said, was probably murdered later the same day, but her body wasn't discovered until yesterday, Tuesday 9th September. Hadn't anybody reported her missing?"

Inspector Beauregard hesitated again before replying. "I'm not sure I should be telling you this but, as far as we know, Olivia Farringdon lived on her own. She had booked leave with her employer until Friday 5th September, so it was only when she failed to turn up for work on Monday 8th that her boss got worried. He reported her missing yesterday, just before we found her body."

Three

Joseph Fawley looked and sounded like an old-school provincial solicitor. His wavy, silver hair, thinning on top, was brushed severely back across his scalp, a pair of horn-rimmed spectacles perched precariously on the end of his podgy nose and his dark, pinstriped suit was shiny enough to reflect the light from the Anglepoise lamp on his large, mahogany desk.

"I'm so sorry to have to bother you at a time like this; it must be very difficult for you," Inspector Beauregard began apologetically.

"Yes, well, of course it is," Joseph Fawley replied in a measured, precise voice. "It's strange really. We solicitors spend quite a lot of time meeting relatives of the recently deceased and trying to console them but it's very different when it's one of you own, as it were."

"Yes it must be. How long had Olivia Farringdon worked for you?"

Joseph Fawley slowly opened a buff folder on the desk in front of him, adjusted his spectacles and studied it carefully. "It would have been four years on 1st October. She'd previously worked for a solicitor in London; she came with a glowing testimonial."

"Why did she move here?"

"Ah, er, her marriage had just broken up. Her husband had run off to Spain with his mistress and set up home out there and I think she wanted to make a fresh start. I don't think it was an especially conscious decision to move here – she just wanted to move out of London and I had a suitable vacancy."

"And how well did you know her?"

Joseph Fawley removed his spectacles and massaged the wide bridge of his nose between his finger and thumb.

"Not very well at all, I'm ashamed to say. Olivia was very good at her job – reliable, punctilious, efficient – but she was never one for gossip or idle chit-chat and nor was I. We'd say 'good morning' to each other when we arrived, we'd deal with the business of the day and then, when we left the office, we'd go our separate ways."

"Did she ever speak of family or friends?"

"I knew about her husband, Derek, and his affair, of course; I handled the divorce for her. And I recall she once spoke briefly about her aged mother who was quite poorly and who she wanted to visit but that's about all I know. I'm afraid I'm not what you might call a 'caring employer.'"

"Did she get much money from the divorce settlement?"

"Hardly a penny, as it happens. When Derek fled to Spain, he was in serious debt."

"I'll need the current address of her ex-husband, if you have it."

"Of course." Joseph Fawley opened a drawer in his desk, removed a sheet of paper, took a fountain pen from his inside pocket and began to write, slowly and neatly. When he had finished and allowed the ink to dry, he carefully folded the paper in two and handed it, with great solemnity, to the inspector.

"Thank you. Did she make a will?"

"Well if she did, I had nothing to do with it. I remember her saying, after her divorce, that she intended to make a will but, as far as I know, it never happened."

"Did she talk at all about what she did when she wasn't working? Did she mention any acquaintances?"

"She hardly mentioned anything – certainly, I don't recall any references to friends or acquaintances. I think she used to enjoy walking. She'd often take a few days off to tackle a long-distance walk somewhere – at least, that's what she told me!"

"Is that why she said she wanted a few days off at the start of September?"

"No it wasn't, actually. As I recall, she said something important had come up which she needed to deal with – she didn't tell me what and I didn't ask. Maybe I'm reading too much into it but I thought she looked a bit uneasy."

"But you had no reason to doubt that she'd turn up for work as usual on Monday 8th September?"

"No, absolutely not! She was always so reliable. That's why I contacted the police. I can give you her address, if it's helpful."

"Thank you, but we've already got her address from her vehicle registration records. One of my team is there at the moment."

*

As soon as she heard the doorbell ring, Detective Constable Alison Pawlett strode briskly to the front door and opened it. Inspector Beauregard wandered into the tiny, gloomy entrance hall of the first-floor flat, his shoulders hunched and his hands thrust deep into the pockets of his dark grey trousers. After the most cursory acknowledgement of his colleague's presence, he looked around. The entrance hall was small and square and, on each of three sides, a wooden door led into another room. One door opened into the living room. Although the ceiling was quite high, the room seemed cramped and sombre. The walls were painted in a light fawn colour, a print depicting a tranquil seaside scene hung from the centre of one wall and a two-seater sofa, also in light fawn, ran along the wall beneath the small window which looked out onto the street below. In front of the sofa, there was a low coffee table with several books and a few magazines arranged neatly on it. There was a television in one corner and, on the wall opposite the window, stood a closed wooden bureau, with an upright chair in front of it. A doorway led into a windowless kitchenette with a few, elderly built-in units in light beech, a washing machine, a fridge-freezer, a hob and a microwave oven.

Another door from the hall opened into the bedroom, decorated in salmon pink, with a single divan bed, a wardrobe, a chest of drawers, a dressing table and the usual accoutrements, while a further door led into the grey-tiled bathroom.

Having completed his initial inspection of the premises, Inspector Beauregard turned and faced his colleague. She had dark, almost black hair, cut short, bright red lipstick, which partially disguised the thinness of her lips, and was dressed from head to toe in blue denim.

"Found anything interesting?" the inspector asked, morosely.

"Not as much as I wanted," the constable replied diffidently, immediately sensing her boss's saturnine mood, something with which she was very familiar. "There are a few things I can tell you, though. For a start, Olivia Farringdon was obsessively tidy. If you look around, everything is neatly arranged – the food and crockery in the kitchen cupboards, the books and magazines on the table, the items on her dressing table, the toiletries in the bathroom, the files and folders in the bureau – all tidied and straightened. And I don't think she did much entertaining, if any. There's not much food in the freezer, there's one bottle of unopened white wine and not much crockery in the cupboards. And there's no sign of a mobile phone, or computer or tablet…"

"No," the inspector sighed. "She probably had them with her when she was murdered. There's no sign of them now, of course."

"But there is something quite intriguing," the constable continued. "I've had a good rummage through all the papers in her bureau and checked in her cupboards and there is virtually nothing from her past – no mementoes, no photographs, no letters, no documents, nothing. It's as though she was trying to erase her past."

"Mmm, I got more or less the same story from Joseph Fawley, her boss. Despite having employed her for four years, he claims to know next to nothing about her or her family or her friends…"

Fully aware of the inspector's irritating habit of not finishing his sentence, Constable Pawlett resumed her narrative. "I've found a few official papers – her divorce papers, the lease for the flat, her contract of employment, passport, that kind of thing, and I found some recent bank statements. She had a few thousand tucked away but I don't think she was a particularly wealthy woman."

"So not murdered for her money?"

"Not unless she'd got some more money hidden away somewhere. I don't know what she got from the divorce settlement."

"Mmm, not much, according to her boss, who handled the divorce. Apparently, her ex-husband left a few debts behind when he ran off to Spain."

"Typical!" Alison Pawlett tutted. "Her outgoings are pretty small; a few standing orders, day-to-day expenses but not much more – no expensive holidays or unnecessary luxuries. Her car was twelve years old."

The inspector looked around again, his expression one of antipathy. "Clearly, she didn't lead a lavish lifestyle!"

"In January, she enrolled in an adult education course on photography and, in a collection of old receipts, I found one for a new camera, but I can't find it or any photographs that she might have taken."

"That's interesting," Inspector Beauregard replied with a rare show of animation. "One of the girls who works at the Follycombe Hotel saw her with a camera but there was no sign of it when we found her and it wasn't in her car. Have you found any walking boots? Her boss said she enjoyed walking."

"Yes, there's a pair in the bottom of her wardrobe but they don't look that well used."

"I see. There weren't any boots in the luggage that we recovered from her car so she probably wasn't planning a walking holiday when she stayed at the Follycombe Hotel."

"There was a bit of mail that had accumulated over the last week but, again, nothing very interesting; mainly junk mail and a reminder that her annual car service was due. But I did find an address book of sorts," Constable Pawlett announced proudly, handing the slim volume over to the inspector with due ceremony. "There aren't many names in it, certainly none that I recognise, but, if you want me to, I'd be happy to try and contact some of the people named."

"Yes, okay, but be careful what you say – best not to mention what's happened to the mysterious Olivia Farringdon."

"And I also found a couple of old photographs tucked away at the back of one of the drawers. Unfortunately, there's nothing on the back of either of them that might tell us where and when they were taken and who the people are. One is a formally posed picture of a young girl with fair hair, about eleven or twelve years old, I'd say, probably in school uniform, and the other one appears to be of the same girl with an older man, sitting on a beach somewhere. Did Olivia Farringdon have a daughter?"

Constable Pawlett handed the photographs over to the inspector who emitted a sigh so heavy that his drooping shoulders heaved.

"I have absolutely no idea whether she had any children or whether the man in the picture is her ex-husband, Derek, and that's the really frustrating thing. Hell, I don't even know who her next of kin is! All I know is that Olivia Farringdon had an ex-husband, living in Spain, she may have had an elderly mother living God knows where, she seems to have no close friends and nobody that we've spoken to knows much about her or what she was doing in Carlow Valley. Let's hope your trawl through her address book yields something interesting. Meanwhile, I'll try and speak to her ex-husband."

*

Clive Walsingham wandered, naked, into the bedroom, clutching a few discarded items of clothing which he dropped into a laundry basket behind the door. Clare looked up from the book she was reading – a historical novel by one of her favourite writers, Gina J Brewsom – and smiled; it was a warm, relaxed smile. She could sense that Clive was preoccupied – he was frowning and tugging at his earlobe, a habit he had formed when he was mulling over a particularly difficult problem. He also absent-mindedly dropped his toothbrush into the laundry basket.

"Any word from Dick, today?" she asked innocently.

"What? Or, er, no – nothing at all, you'll be pleased to hear. I expect his inquiries have taken him elsewhere."

"Oh, that's a shame," Clare conceded. "I'd like to know more about Olivia Farringdon, who killed her and why."

"Would you really?" Clive asked with a hint of surprise in his voice. He ambled over to the bed and sat down next to Clare. "I thought you didn't want to hear anything more of Dick Beauregard and his rambling investigations."

"Not when he's involving you in a case I don't know anything about, but this is different. I've met Olivia Farringdon, I've spoken to her. I feel personally involved."

"You know, there are a couple of things bothering me," Clive admitted as he grasped Clare's hand.

"Oh, really? You do surprise me!"

"I mean, the facts that I've been able to glean from the parsimonious detective inspector are that she lived on her own in Brookbank, which is miles away. As far as we know, she has no particular connections with this area and then, in July, she phoned and made a booking here for three nights. And, during her stay, she didn't appear to meet anyone and, although she went out every day, we don't know where she went. No doubt Dick and his team are checking all the CCTV footage that they can lay their hands on and are appealing for information, but it's a bit like looking for a needle in a haystack. And then, after she checked out of here, it appears she drove alone to Carlow Woods where she encountered her killer."

Clare shuddered at the thought of Olivia Farringdon being murdered. "Do you think she knew her killer?"

"Mmmm. It's unlikely to have been a random attack – Dick said there was no sexual attack of any kind and I can't believe that Olivia Farringdon would have driven to Carlow Woods on a whim. No, she must have gone there to meet someone."

"Do you think she met her killer while she was here or did she already know him?"

"My guess is that she'd had some contact with her killer when she phoned to make the booking but whether she'd met him or not…" Clive shrugged. "Maybe she met him, or her, during the three days she stayed here and something went wrong…"

"Maybe it was a blind date that went wrong," Clare speculated. "Maybe it was someone she met over the internet. Or maybe she only arranged to meet someone after she arrived here. Do you think she had other business to attend to while she was here?"

"It's possible, but I've no idea what, of course. Apparently she'd written the word 'circus' on a piece of paper in her room but I've no idea what that means either. But don't forget, she phoned to make the booking towards the end of July so her visit wasn't sudden or spontaneous. But if she was planning to meet someone in Carlow Woods, and that was the only reason she came here, why book into this hotel? Carlow Woods aren't very far away, granted, but there are a couple of hotels that are a bit nearer."

"But she claimed she was recommended to stay here."

"So it's possible that her killer has stayed here, or dined here, or…"

"Omigod! Or is one of the staff!" Clare shrieked.

"Yes, that thought had crossed my mind. But, maybe she just heard of the excellent service we provide."

"Well I've certainly got no complaints," Clare whispered as she leant forward, removed her nightdress, pushed Clive down onto the bed and rolled on top of him.

Four

Clive and Clare Walsingham were members of the Carlow Bridge Golf Club. Although they were both keen, competent golfers, Clive had initially been reluctant to accept Richard Edgton's offer of free membership as a thank-you for establishing his innocence in a couple of cases that Dick Beauregard had been investigating. After all, although innocent, Richard Edgton still enjoyed a certain reputation as a hard-nosed and, occasionally, ruthless businessman and Clive had no wish to be indebted to him in any way.

But the pressures and constraints of running a hotel meant that Clive and Clare had the opportunity to play golf so infrequently that they could not justify paying a substantial membership fee to belong to a club, especially when their future prosperity was far from guaranteed. Furthermore, it had to be admitted that Richard Edgton had utilised the talents of a couple of the very best golf course designers to produce a beautifully sculpted course meandering along the banks of the River Carlow. So, after some initial hesitation, they had accepted his offer of free membership for a trial period.

As luck would have it, there was a lull in hotel bookings. The major coach operator which used the hotel regularly, had, as Clive feared, been forced to cancel its next booking at short notice and, with fewer than normal individual reservations, mainly as a result of climatic vagaries, Clive and Clare found themselves with some unaccustomed free time. So, with an unusually favourable weather forecast for the whole weekend, they had decided to indulge themselves. Once they had helped to clear away after breakfast and on the strict understanding that Debbie would call them if they were needed back at the hotel, they were preparing to set off for a morning's round of golf. As Clive loaded his bag into the boot of his car, he sniffed the air appreciably. It was a crisp, sunny September morning, the sky was clear, the air was still, the seasonal dew was likely to be transient and there was every prospect of an enjoyable and, knowing Clare, a highly competitive round of golf to come. It was then that Clive's phone rang. Cursing loudly, he studied the screen and then cursed even louder.

"Hello, Dick!" Clive spoke through clenched teeth. "What can I do for you on this wonderful Saturday morning?"

"Clive, I'm sorry to trouble you, I really don't want to… errm, is it a convenient time to…?" Dick Beauregard sounded unusually hesitant, even by his own lofty standards.

"No, Dick, actually it's not a convenient time," Clive replied firmly. "Clare and I are about to go…"

"Only there's been a development; potentially a really, really big development. At the moment, we're managing to keep the lid on things but as soon as this goes public, the shit is going to hit the fan. We are going to have the press and television people crawling all over the place and it's going to get impossible. Clive, I really do need your help – it's very important, otherwise I wouldn't ask. I'm coming straight over."

"Dick, hang on a minute, it's not convenient at… Hello? Hello?"

Clive swore again as Dick Beauregard ended the call abruptly. Meanwhile, Clare, who had been standing at the edge of the car park, enjoying the pleasantly warm sunshine and studying

Clive's orange golfing trousers with a look of mild disdain, had wandered over and was now standing no more than a couple of feet away, looking up at him with an intense and angry stare.

"I hope I haven't just heard what I think I've heard," Clare bellowed.

"I'm rather afraid you have," Clive replied limply. "I haven't been given any choice. Dick didn't say what it was that was so obviously urgent – maybe he's coming to arrest me, or you, or somebody else – but, in my experience, when a detective inspector wants to speak to you, he's damn well going to speak to you. If we went over to Carlow Bridge, the chances are he'd follow us over there and then interrupt our game to interrogate us in full view of a load of indignant members."

"I see!" Clare bellowed again, before turning on her heels and heading briskly towards the hotel entrance.

"Where are you going?" Clive called despairingly after her.

"To hide the cakes! And meanwhile, you can change out of those ridiculous trousers!"

*

It was only twenty minutes later that a car screeched into the car park, its tyres squealing on the tarmac.

"Hello, it sounds as though Dick's brought Alison with him," Clive observed gloomily as he and Clare watched from the window as Inspector Beauregard emerged shakily from the car, clutching the passenger door for support. After a moment or two of deep breathing, he slammed the door shut and set off slowly and slightly unsteadily towards the hotel entrance, followed by Alison Pawlett, her stride surer and more purposeful.

"Dick! And Alison! How nice to see you both!" Clive greeted the detectives sarcastically as they announced themselves to Debbie at reception. "I've set up some space for us in the bar –

we won't be disturbed in there. Clare is on her way with some refreshments and I've asked her to join us."

Once he had escorted the detectives through the foyer and into the bar, Clive manoeuvred them towards a low table surrounded by four chairs, positioned neatly beneath a window. Archie the cat, who had been snoozing contentedly in a nearby chair, raised his head and squawked angrily at the unwarranted intrusion before wandering off huffily in pursuit of a quieter billet. As Inspector Beauregard approached his chair and sat down, Clive scrutinised him more closely. He had eschewed his suit and, today, was wearing a faded blue shirt with a crumpled collar and a pair of grey trousers that he might easily have worn while weeding the garden, if he had one. He seemed breathless and edgy, his complexion was strangely sallow and beads of perspiration were forming on his furrowed forehead. Perhaps, Clive reflected, Alison Pawlett's driving had been particularly terrifying that morning.

"Well, I don't think it would be appropriate for your, erm, wife to join us. I mean, this is official…" Inspector Beauregard replied haltingly and with a hint of the pomposity that had so irritated Clive on his previous visit.

"Out of the question! It's all highly confidential!" Alison Pawlett interjected imperiously.

"Well at least we've established this isn't a social call! I'm assuming that you haven't come to arrest either of us for the murder of Olivia Farringdon," Clive responded, as calmly as he could in the face of what he perceived to be an unnecessarily bombastic approach.

"What? Oh, er, no, no! We're following some new lines of inquiry there. No, no, as I said on the phone, I really do need your help and…"

"Ah, well, then I'm afraid we've got a bit of a problem," Clive replied, as he scratched his head. "You see, after last time

I promised Clare that I wouldn't offer you my help again. She reminded me, quite correctly, that my job now is running a hotel and not playing at being a detective. So, if I agree to help you now, then it must be with Clare's knowledge and agreement. She will need to know exactly what help you want, how much help you want and for how long, and she will need to be kept fully informed at all times. I trust her implicitly not to say or do anything that would jeopardise your investigation – whatever it is – but it is very important to me that Clare is in on this. My marriage might depend on it."

Alison Pawlett, who had witnessed Clare's anger first-hand, when Clive had allowed himself to be sucked too deeply into one of Dick Beauregard's previous investigations and put himself in danger without feeling able to explain to her what was going on, exchanged glances with her boss and nodded.

"Alright," the inspector conceded grudgingly. "But if word gets out…"

"It won't," Clive was quick to assure him as Clare appeared holding a tray with a coffee pot and several cups, saucers and plates, followed by a serenely smiling Jamie Coulton, who was holding a well-stocked plate of assorted cakes. He placed the plate on the table immediately in front of Alison Pawlett, deliberately brushing against her shoulder as he did so, smiled broadly and gave a her sly wink.

"Dick and Alison have agreed that you can stay," Clive reassured Clare as she transferred the crockery from her tray to the table.

"Good, I should hope so!" Clare replied as she sat down next to Clive and, without looking at either detective, started pouring the coffee.

Clive looked up at Jamie Coulton who was still standing attentively at Alison Pawlett's shoulder. "Unfortunately, the invitation doesn't extend to you, Jamie."

"Oh, no, of course not!" Jamie replied unctuously. "I've got work to do anyway." He turned and winked at Alison Pawlett again. "See yah later!"

While Jamie drifted silently out of the room, closing the door slowly behind him, Inspector Beauregard nimbly pounced on a large slice of chocolate cake and placed it firmly on the plate that Clare had just positioned in front of him.

"So what the hell is this all about?" Clive asked. "And it had better be good! You've ruined our planned game of golf this morning."

Inspector Beauregard produced a creased, grubby handkerchief from his creased, grubby trouser pocket and mopped his profusely perspiring brow. "The thing is, we've found another body, early this morning, in Stowbrook Forest. He'd been hit over the head several times, just like Olivia Farringdon."

"The same modus operandi?" Clive asked quickly.

Inspector Beauregard nodded grimly. "It certainly looks that way."

"Don't tell me that the victim had recently stayed at this hotel," Clare interrupted, with a look of alarm in her eyes.

"Oh, no, no! The victim was a local man. We've identified him as Keith Draycott, aged 55..."

"Keith Draycott, Keith Draycott... I know that name from somewhere," Clare said, looking perplexed, as she handed round the cups of coffee. She liked to match her husband's impressive memory of names whenever she could and felt frustrated when her powers of recall deserted her.

"He's the Reverend Keith Draycott. He's the vicar of St. Mary's in Stowbrook. He was previously vicar at... err..."

"St. Giles in Crowdale," Alison Pawlett interjected while her boss tried to recover from his own memory lapse.

"Of course, of course, I remember now," Clare replied, triumphantly. "Wasn't he the father of one of those girls who went missing? It was on the news and in all the papers. How long ago was it? It must be seven or eight years."

"Ten, actually," Alison Pawlett corrected, primly.

"Oh God, yes! I remember that!" Clive added. "You're right; it was all over the papers at the time. My force was asked to assist, if I recall."

"Probably – our local force wasn't really equipped to deal with such a major investigation," Inspector Beauregard added apologetically. Ignoring the cake fork that Clare had helpfully provided, he picked up his slice of cake but, as he lifted it towards his mouth, he seemed suddenly to lose his appetite and, after studying it for a moment or two, slowly replaced it on the plate.

"But surely you don't think his death has anything to do with what happened ten years ago?" Clare asked incredulously.

"Ordinarily, perhaps not, but Alison has been looking into Olivia Farringdon's background and working her way through her address book and we've now established that she used to be known as Olivia Edwyn – that was before she married for the second time – and that her daughter was also one of those who disappeared ten years ago…"

"Omigod!" Clare exclaimed, clamping both hands to her mouth. "You don't think…? I mean, how many girls went missing…? Didn't they arrest someone at the time?"

Clive held out a restraining hand. "Hang on, hang on! Let's just work our way through this logically. You said you found Keith Draycott's body in Stowbrook Forest. Who found him?"

Inspector Beauregard swallowed heavily a couple of times before replying. "An early morning jogger found him. His body was partly hidden in some low bracken."

"And he'd been beaten over the head, like Olivia Farringdon."

"That's correct!"

"And was his car abandoned nearby, like Olivia Farringdon's?"

"No, there was no sign of it, but the forest isn't very far from where he lived, so maybe he walked."

"Or met someone who gave him a lift. So you're thinking that Olivia Edwyn, or Farringdon, and Keith Draycott were murdered by the same person and that their deaths are connected in some way to the disappearance of their daughters all those years ago."

"It, err, has got to be a strong possibility. The pathologist is being a bit cagey until she's completed the full post-mortem. She thinks the weapon was the same, although she's not sure what it was yet – probably a hammer of some kind – and we can establish no other link between the two victims."

"Wow, yes!" Clive exclaimed. "I can see why the media would be interested. Have you got any suspects?"

Inspector Beauregard shook his head slowly and closed his eyes. "No, we've got nothing. It looks as though the killer chose his locations very carefully; they're both heavily wooded areas, nobody much uses them on a weekday, apart from the odd dog walker and jogger, and there are no buildings or busy roads nearby. We've got no eyewitnesses and no reports of anything unusual. Our people are still combing the site but they haven't found anything of much interest so far – apart from one thing, something particularly strange about Keith Draycott's murder."

"Do tell!" Clare gasped excitedly.

"You see, the pathologist is almost certain that he was murdered about three days ago and yet, in his breast pocket, we found a newspaper cutting – and it was from yesterday's edition of the *Carlow Valley Gazette*."

Five

Clive flopped back in his chair and exhaled sharply. "Wow! I've never come across anything quite like that before. Let me be absolutely clear about this; you are saying that he was murdered three days ago, that's Wednesday 10th September, the day you came here to interview us about the murder of Olivia Farringdon?"

"Er, yes, that's right," Inspector Beauregard replied.

"And that there was a cutting from yesterday's local paper, dated 12th September, in his breast pocket."

"That's right!"

"And is there any evidence that his body has been moved at all?"

"No, none! We think his body was dragged slightly, just after he was murdered, to conceal it more in the bracken but that's all."

"Wow!" Clive repeated as he took a sip of coffee and tugged his earlobe. "I don't know your pathologist but I can't imagine she could be so badly mistaken about the time of death. So we must assume that either the murderer deliberately went back to the body and, for some reason, put the cutting in Keith Draycott's breast pocket two days after he was murdered or someone else knew where the body was and went to all the trouble of slipping the cutting into his pocket?"

"That's correct! Bizarre, isn't it?"

"I'll say! But whoever put the cutting in his pocket was taking a hell of a risk so it must be important. Any idea what it was about?"

"I'm not sure. The thing is I had to dash out of the office before they'd assembled all the evidence but I think it was something to do with the Carlow Valley Arts Festival which is taking place in a few weeks time. I'll make sure you see a copy of it."

"Was there any mention of a circus, at all?"

"Not that I know of but, as I say, I had to dash…"

"Yes, so you said. So can I assume that you've got no idea why Olivia Farringdon and Keith Draycott have been murdered, and within the space of a couple of days?"

"That's correct!"

"And, if there is a link to the abduction of those girls, you've no idea why a couple of the parents should suddenly and randomly be murdered after a gap of ten years?"

Inspector Beauregard gave a shrug that was so intense that his whole body seemed to shake momentarily. "Correct again!"

Clive rubbed his hands together with relish. "So if the murderer planted the newspaper cutting, the obvious question is why? Clearly, the murderer knew you'd find it, so was it to taunt you – that is, the police – in some way, or mock you by providing a clue and defying you to solve it? Then again, the cutting could have been put there by someone else, someone who knew where the body was and knows who the murderer is, someone who thinks the cutting will provide a clue as to the murderer's identity. But it seems very tortuous and risky to go to all that trouble; why didn't they just inform you? They could have done it anonymously? What is for sure is that someone is laying down a challenge for us and I do so like a challenge."

Inspector Beauregard sat forward in his chair and placed his hands over his eyes. "Oh, God, it's going to be awful – truly awful!" he muttered.

Clive waited for Inspector Beauregard to say something more – some helpful insights into the progress of the investigation perhaps – but he remained silent, his head bowed and his hands covering his eyes.

"So if we are to believe that the two murders are linked," Clive continued after an awkward silence and an exchange of quizzical glances with Clare, "then the only obvious link is that both the murder victims had daughters who disappeared ten years ago."

"Well that certainly seems to be the obvious link – we don't know of another one. God, it's going to be absolutely impossible when the press gets hold of this. We're going to have journalists crawling all over the place, following us everywhere, thrusting microphones up our noses, asking pointed, and occasionally pointless, questions, demanding why we haven't made any arrests. I really don't think I can…" Inspector Beauregard fell silent again as he cradled his head in his hands.

"I think you need to remind us what exactly happened ten years ago," Clive suggested quietly.

"Alison's got all the notes," Inspector Beauregard replied limply as he slumped in his chair.

Alison Pawlett glanced across at her enervated boss, exchanged exasperated glances with Clive and Clare, and opened her notebook.

"Well, as far I can establish, this is what happened ten years ago. Five girls, aged between twelve and fourteen, all disappeared from this area within the space of three months during the summer. The first disappearance was in July and the last in September."

"None of the girls were found, as I recall. No sightings, no concrete leads, no bodies – they just disappeared?" Clive asked.

"That's right. The first to go missing was Emily Ashurst, aged 13. She disappeared on Friday 23rd July. She lived in Stowbrook and left the house one evening to do some babysitting for a friend of her mother who lived about half a mile away. It was something she'd done a couple of times before – it was a useful bit of pocket money for her – so she knew the family and the route she needed to take. Anyway, she never arrived at the friend's house and has not been seen since. There were the usual appeals for witnesses, house-to-house enquiries and a re-enactment of her final walk along the route she would have taken, but no one came forward with anything concrete."

"You say she'd babysat before?"

"Yes, a couple of times, earlier in the year – nothing untoward happened on either occasion. When she first went missing, it was assumed that she'd run away from home. A couple of her friends said that she wasn't happy and implied that she was getting a hard time from her father, but they wouldn't elaborate. And there was one friend, a girl called Maxine Padfield, who thought Emily might have had a secret boyfriend but she couldn't say, or didn't want to say, who it was. The police made an appeal but no one came forward."

Clive exhaled. "I imagine she'd just broken up for the summer holidays when she vanished, which is not normally the time a kid would do a runner, unless she couldn't face spending the next six weeks with her family. What about her family? Did she have any brothers or sisters?"

"No, she was an only child," Inspector Beauregard replied, his hands still covering his eyes. "Her parents, Alan and Tessa, couldn't think of any reason why she would have gone missing or who might have abducted her."

"Do they still live in Stowbrook?"

"No, they moved out not long after their daughter went missing. They still live in the area though – they've got a place in Morstock. Alan is, or was, something in computers and Tessa worked for the local council."

"Were they under suspicion at the time?"

"They were. Alan Ashurst was known to have a quick temper, there was some speculation that he'd been violent to his daughter and that the violence might have gone a bit too far. And he didn't have an alibi for the time she went missing. But Tessa was adamant that he wouldn't harm his daughter and we could find no evidence. And then, of course, another girl disappeared."

"Mmmm. And who was the next girl to go missing?"

Alison Pawlett studied her notebook again. "That was Catherine Duffield, aged 14; she disappeared on Thursday 12th August. She wasn't a local girl. She was staying with her cousins' family in Swincroft. Apparently, she often spent a week or so with them during the summer holidays. Anyway, she and her cousins – an older boy and a slightly younger girl – were planning a picnic and Catherine volunteered to get some provisions from the village store about three hundred yards away. We know that she made it to the store but, on her way back, she disappeared and, like Emily Ashurst, has never been seen since. Now Swincroft is a sleepy little village; there weren't many people around at the time and nobody claimed to have seen anything out of the ordinary. Catherine's route would have taken her past a care home for the elderly and it was hoped that somebody there might have seen something but the staff were too busy and most of the residents were either asleep or taking tea in the lounge or whatever." Alison Pawlett paused while Inspector Beauregard emitted a heavy, plaintive sigh.

"And what do we know about Catherine Duffield's family?"

Alison Pawlett sighed, though not as plaintively as her boss; hers was more a sigh of frustration. "Very little, unfortunately! Oddly, there's nothing very much in the case notes. All I can tell you is that the family lived miles away in Mellingford. Edward Duffield is, or was, some kind of salesman for a central heating company and travelled around the country quite a bit, leaving Sonia, his wife, to bring up their daughter, Catherine. According to the case notes, such as they are, Edward Duffield was away from home when his daughter disappeared and was very evasive about where he'd been, but he was never treated as a serious suspect and we know that Sonia was at home at the time. And that's about all I can tell you."

"Mmmm, well, we definitely need to find out more about Edward and Sonia Duffield. Was there anything that linked the Duffields to the Ashursts?"

"No, there's nothing in the case notes. As far as we know, they'd never met or communicated."

"The thing is," Inspector Beauregard added, while wiping his clammy palms across the thighs of his scruffy trousers. "Edward and Sonia Duffield weren't local. They lived miles away and didn't know their daughter had gone missing until we told them. They were interviewed, of course, but were at a loss to explain what had happened."

"I see," Clive replied doubtfully. "And the family that Catherine Duffield was staying with – anything of interest there?"

"No, she'd stayed there a couple of times before and seemed to get on well with the family. They were all interviewed at the time but there didn't seem to be anything suspicious going on."

Clive drummed the fingers of his left hand on his knee – he was becoming frustrated. "Oh, well, let's continue with the tale of the missing girls for the moment."

"Early on Friday 20th August," Alison Pawlett continued, "Rosemary Edwyn went missing. She was nearly 13. She was holidaying with her parents at a campsite in Corwood. She left their tent to go to the toilet and shower block, no more than two hundred yards away and never returned. It was high season and the campsite was very busy but, as with the other girls, nobody saw anything unusual and there has been no trace of her since."

"I'm surprised her parents let her out of their sight in view of the other disappearances," Clare said with a hint of self-righteousness in her voice.

"Yes, those comments were made at the time," Inspector Beauregard mumbled. "But the family had been camping for nearly two weeks. They liked to get away from everything so they didn't take a radio or television or a laptop with them and may not have heard about Catherine Duffield. The last they probably heard before they started their holiday was that we were treating Emily Ashurst as an isolated runaway rather than as an abduction."

"And Rosemary Edwyn's parents?" Clive asked.

Inspector Beauregard's reply was breathless and rushed. "Okay, well, err, as I recall, Olivia and Howard Edwyn lived in a London suburb with their only child, Rosemary. Howard was a self-employed builder and Olivia did a variety of part-time secretarial work. They seemed to have lived entirely uneventful lives. I suspect they were not particularly wealthy and, each year, their main holiday would be spent camping in some part of the country. I think Rosemary had been cosseted and protected a bit by her mother, whereas her father was trying to give his daughter a bit more freedom as she grew up. It was Howard who encouraged Rosemary to go to the shower block on her own, for example. Needless to say, as a result of what happened, Howard felt responsible for his daughter's disappearance and he never really got over it. Two years later, he walked in front of a train… Olivia tried to make a new life for herself. She married Derek Farringdon, another builder, but the marriage didn't last. As we now know, he ran off to Spain and Olivia tried to make another new life for herself in Brookbank."

"Have you spoken to Derek Farringdon?"

"Ah, er, n-no I haven't. I phoned the number that Olivia Farringdon's boss gave me and spoke to his, er, his lady friend and she told me that he'd done a runner. He left home about two weeks ago and she's not heard from him since. Apparently he was in serious financial trouble; he'd borrowed heavily to pay off his debts and now the loan sharks were after him. She claimed that she didn't know where he'd gone, although I'm not…"

"So he could be back in this country?"

"Yes, I suppose he could…"

Clive tugged at his earlobe again. "So, obviously something or someone drew Olivia Farringdon back here. She booked her stay here in July so it was planned in advance – it wasn't a last-minute whim. It could have been to meet up with her ex-husband Derek, I suppose, but it doesn't make any sense; why would she arrange to meet him here?" Clive briefly fell silent as he mulled over the significance of what he'd been told. "Have you been able to find out anything more about Olivia Farringdon? Did she have any close friends or other family?"

Alison Pawlett shook her head. "Not that we've been able to uncover. She seems to have led a pretty solitary existence. We know that she'd recently enrolled on an adult education course on photography and she'd bought herself quite an expensive camera, which apparently she had with her when she stayed here but which we now can't find. Unfortunately, those who were on the course said that she kept herself to herself and didn't divulge much about her personal life."

"That's a shame!"

"Yes it is. Anyway," Alison Pawlett continued, "the next to go missing was Charlotte Huxton, aged 13. She disappeared some time after school on Tuesday 14th September. She was a pupil at Polbury Manor School—"

"I was a pupil there," Clare interrupted eagerly. "Sadly a lot longer than ten years ago, though."

"So you might have some contacts that could help us?" Alison asked.

"Well, I'm still in touch with a couple of old school friends but, as I say, it was rather more than ten years ago when we left. Still, maybe they know someone…"

"Might be worth contacting them," Clive suggested before noticing Alison Pawlett's censorious expression. "But better to wait until all of this is out in the open."

"Which won't be very long," Alison Pawlett replied stoically. "It seems that Charlotte Huxton probably went missing on her way home from school on the afternoon of the 14th, but her mother thought she was staying with a friend overnight and only discovered that she was missing the following morning when the school phoned. That same morning, Isabel Draycott, aged 14, also went missing. Apparently, Isabel's father, Keith Draycott, dropped her off about two hundred yards from the school gate but she never arrived and, again, nobody saw or heard anything out of the ordinary."

Clive shook his head in disbelief. "So unless she was late, I'm assuming there would have been hundreds of kids making their way to school at the time and yet nobody saw Isabel Draycott talking to anyone or getting into a strange car or running off."

"Apparently not!"

"And her father, fully aware that some other girls had recently gone missing, chose not to drop her at the school gates?"

"Yes, it was questioned at the time but Keith Draycott explained, quite reasonably, that he thought it was safe to do so because of all the other pupils who were making their way to school at the same time. If someone was planning to snatch a schoolgirl, he was unlikely to do so in front of dozens of the other kids. Or so he thought."

"Yes, I suppose…" Clive conceded grudgingly. "I think you'd better tell me what you know about Keith Draycott."

"At the time of his daughter's disappearance, he was the vicar of St Giles in Crowdale," Inspector Beauregard confirmed.

"Ah, yes," Clare interjected. "I know it; it's a lovely little church down by the river – not so far from us here. You, erm, live in Crowdale don't you, Alison?"

"Yes, I have a billet there," Alison Pawlett admitted reluctantly, not particularly wanting to draw attention to her domestic arrangements with Jamie Coulton.

"Anyway," the inspector continued, "Keith Draycott's first wife was killed in a car crash just over twelve years ago and he was trying to bring up his daughter, Isabel – or Issy as she was known – on his own. As Alison said, Issy went to Polbury Manor School and Keith dropped her off every morning and collected her every afternoon. Often, when he was in a hurry, he would drop her off at the corner of the main road. As we've said, he saw no danger in doing so; in fact, he became something of a local hero in the wake of his daughter's disappearance. Instead of sitting around feeling sorry for himself, he made a point of visiting the parents of the other missing girls and tried to comfort them. He made an impassioned plea on television for whoever was holding the girls to get in touch. In a way, he became the unofficial spokesman for the group of anguished parents. He organised special prayer meetings for them and their missing daughters and spoke very publicly and very eruditely against those who wanted to take the law into their own hands and set up local vigilante groups. In fact, he so impressed the bishop that he moved him to St Mary's at Stowbrook, not long after the disappearances. St Mary's is a bigger church with a much larger congregation. I believe Keith Draycott remarried a couple of years ago, but I don't know much about…"

"So two girls disappeared within a few hours of each other, both apparently within close proximity of the school, when everyone knew about the three other girls going missing and would have been on their guard and yet nobody saw or heard anything unusual or suspicious?" Clive asked incredulously. "It beggars belief!"

"We thought it strange at the time," Inspector Beauregard replied apologetically. "We wondered if the girls might have arranged a clandestine meeting with someone, somewhere else, but we just drew a blank."

"And then, after Isabel Draycott and the other girl, Charlotte, went missing, the disappearances stopped?"

"Yes," Inspector Beauregard confirmed. "One of the people we were interested in was a man called Lennie Cave. He was a petty criminal with a long history of offending. He had several convictions for shoplifting, he'd been caught poaching on Lord Westleigh's estate, he'd been fishing without a licence. But what really interested us was that he'd got a bit of previous for child molesting – two ten-year-old girls – and had a reputation in the area for being a bit of a pervert. A couple of parents reckoned they'd seen him hanging around outside Polbury Manor School around the time that Charlotte Huxton and Issy Draycott went missing. We searched his flat and pulled him in for questioning but he denied any involvement and we couldn't get any evidence. We could place him close to the school when Issy Draycott went missing but couldn't link him to the other disappearances. He didn't really have any convincing alibis and was very evasive when we questioned him, but we had nothing definite on him, so we had to let him go. Anyway, a few of the more hot-headed parents formed themselves into an unofficial vigilante group – despite Keith Draycott's best efforts – and Lennie Cave's flat got targeted. They smashed a couple of windows and daubed his front door in graffiti. A few days later, we found his body on the road beneath the block of flats where he lived. It looked as though he'd jumped from the top floor of the block. When we searched his flat again we found a betting slip on the table and on the back of it, he'd written the one word in capital letters – 'SORRY!'. That was all it said. We could never have proved that Lennie Cave was the man responsible for the disappearances but, after his death, no more girls went missing and, eventually, we closed the file."

"But what if Lennie Cave wasn't responsible?" Clive asked.

"Then the person who was responsible is probably still out there somewhere. God, the press are going to have such a field day…" Inspector Beauregard buried his face in his hands again and groaned loudly.

"From what you've said, Dick, you were part of the team that conducted the original investigation into the missing girls?" Clive asked.

"Yes, although I was only a raw detective constable at the time," Dick Beauregard replied defensively. "Me and Superintendant Rushwick are the only officers still serving with Carlow Valley Police that were part of the original investigation. Superintendant Rushwick was a detective inspector then."

"So, who was the officer in charge?"

"That was Chief Superintendant Ian Mencham. He, errm, retired soon afterwards."

Clive sensed that Dick Beauregard wanted to say a lot more about Chief Superintendant Mencham but felt unable or unwilling to do so. "And where is Ian Mencham now?"

"He still lives in the area somewhere but he's a bit reclusive these days. I don't think anyone in the force has had any contact with him for some years. I expect someone will want to speak to him though." Inspector Beauregard mopped his brow again.

"Yes, I'm sure they will," Clive agreed. "So who is leading the present investigation?"

"As of this morning, it's the aforementioned Superintendant Neil Rushwick."

"But you and Alison are part of the team?"

"We are but that's, errm, partly what I wanted to discuss with you. As I've said – more than once probably – when the media gets hold of the fact that Olivia Edwyn and Keith Draycott have both been murdered, they will be swarming all over the place – they'll be camped outside the police station, they'll swarm all over us every time we leave the station, they'll follow us wherever we go, they'll go digging things up, they won't give us a minute's peace... but they don't know you. You can come and go wherever you want and no one would notice you. You could make a lot of enquiries much more discreetly and much more subtly than we could and we'd pay you well, like we've done before, for your time."

"I see!" Clive went thoughtful. "But as soon as the journalists see you with me, my cover will be blown."

Inspector Beauregard leaned forward and spoke in a whisper, as though frightened that he could be overheard. "But the journalists don't really know Alison – I doubt they've ever met her. So I'd like her to work with you – I'll keep my distance. We can keep in touch electronically; we wouldn't have to meet."

Clive took a deep breath. "And would Alison drive me about?" he asked warily.

"There's nothing wrong with my—" Alison Pawlett began to protest before she was interrupted.

"Only when absolutely necessary," Inspector Beauregard was quick to reply with a rare hint of a smile.

Clive turned uncertainly to Clare. "What do you think, darling?"

"Oooh, sounds fun," Clare enthused. "I'd really like to help in some way. I mean, I used to live in the area when I was growing up and, as I said, I have got some knowledge of Polbury Manor School. But we will need to give priority to running this hotel, won't we, Clive?" She looked accusingly at her husband, who nodded meekly.

"Good, that's a deal then!" Inspector Beauregard confirmed. "I'll make the necessary arrangements and..."

Inspector Beauregard broke off as his phone chirruped into life. "Excuse me, this might be important!" Clutching his phone to his ear, Inspector Beauregard stood up and wandered to a distant part of the bar, where he spoke quietly for a few moments before returning. When he did, his face had an ashen appearance and his expression was even more careworn and woebegone than before.

"I'm very sorry," he announced solemnly. "I've just been told that Kate Huxton has disappeared. My colleagues have been trying to contact her and it turns out nobody has seen her or heard from her for over a week; since 5th September in fact."

"Omigod! That's the day after Olivia Farringdon was murdered," Clare exclaimed while the rest of the room fell into a stunned silence. Eventually, it was Clive who spoke.

"Presumably, Kate Huxton is the mother of Charlotte Huxton?" he asked.

"That's right," Inspector Beauregard began to reply before Clive suddenly stopped him. He had been alerted to a noise just outside the door in the corridor.

"Excuse me one moment," Clive said as he leapt to his feet and dashed over to the door. Outside, in the corridor, he could hear footsteps running away. He couldn't be sure who they belonged to but the rapid pitter-patter suggested it was female. He opened the door and looked out into the corridor but, by then, the footsteps had disappeared into the distance and the corridor was empty.

"I'm sorry about that," Clive said as he returned to his chair. "You were saying, Dick."

"Was I? Oh, yes. Kate Huxton had a rough time when her daughter went missing. Knowing that three other girls had already disappeared in the area, people couldn't understand why she simply assumed her daughter was spending the night with a friend without checking – she was widely criticised for being irresponsible and she took it badly. She had two other daughters, one slightly younger than Charlotte and one a bit older and they both got a hard time for a while. Her husband, Robert, was, at the time, a struggling architect and their marriage was going through a bad patch. Not long afterwards, he walked out, leaving her and her two remaining daughters to struggle along on their own. Robert is now Sir Robert Huxton, a highly respected architect who spends much of his time out of the country working on prestigious building projects. Oh hell, excuse me a minute, I'm not feeling very..."

Inspector Beauregard tried to drink from his cup of coffee but his hand was shaking too much and some coffee spilled into his lap where it formed an embarrassing-looking damp patch. Beads of perspiration began to trickle down his forehead, his eyes closed and he rocked gently back and forward in his chair as though unable to comprehend what was happening.

Alison Pawlett quickly intervened. "Look, I think I'd better get Dick, er, Inspector Beauregard back to the station, he's obviously not feeling too well. Everything is happening so quickly and it's bringing back a lot of bad memories. I think he's finding it all a bit difficult. I'll deliver him and then I'll be right back. I won't be long!"

"I'd like to see a copy of the newspaper article that turned up in Keith Draycott's pocket," Clive called after the two detectives as they left the room, Alison Pawlett gently ushering and steering Dick Beauregard through the doorway.

"Well at least he left all the cakes behind," Clare observed wryly after the detectives had left. "What did you make of all that?"

Clive tugged at his earlobe again. "Obviously, I don't want to close my mind to any possibility at the moment, but I'd be astonished if the two recent murders, Olivia Farringdon and Keith Draycott – and possibly a third, Kate Huxton – are not directly linked to the disappearance of those five girls ten years ago, though I've no idea whether it's the same person responsible and what's triggered them after all this time. Dick obviously thinks there's a link too which, I imagine, is why he was behaving so strangely. For some reason, he seemed excessively uneasy about the press digging around. Maybe Alison can enlighten us when she returns. Meanwhile, I suspect that there is somebody out there who is highly dangerous. I get the impression the police were never entirely convinced that Lennie Cave was responsible for the girls' disappearances, so the real villain may still be out there and, for some reason, has started systematically bumping off the parents. Or maybe we're dealing with somebody else who has an axe to grind or…"

"Omigod!" Clare exclaimed, her face alive with a myriad of conflicting emotions. "That means the parents of the other missing girls might be in danger!"

"Very possibly," Clive soothed. "But I expect Superintendant Rushwick and his team are busy trying to track them down to warn them."

"Of course, of course!"

"It's odd, isn't it?" Clive added. "It's strange in a way, don't you think, that the two people who have been murdered, plus the one who has gone missing, could all have been a bit negligent in some way? Olivia Farringdon allowed her daughter to wander off on her own on a busy campsite, Keith Draycott left his daughter to walk the last two hundred yards to school on her own, despite knowing about three other disappearances, and Kate Huxton didn't bother to collect her daughter from school or even check to see if she had arrived safely at her friend's house."

"You mean it's the revenge of the responsible parent?"

Clive chuckled. "It doesn't seem very likely, does it? Not after all these years. And none of this explains the newspaper cutting that turned up in Keith Draycott's pocket two days after he was murdered and there's been no mention of a circus. So, darling, after what you've heard, are you still happy if I help with this investigation?"

"You bet," Clare replied enthusiastically. "I'm looking forward to what we can find out!"

"Mmmm, there must be somebody out there somewhere who knows something, possibly more than is good for them. I think I'm going to have to do quite a lot of digging to try and find out what really happened ten years ago and I fancy I'm going to encounter some strong resistance along the way. Somebody I must try and speak to is ex-Chief Superintendant Ian Mencham – I need to find out more about his investigations – and Dick is hiding something, I'm sure."

"Hang on a minute," Clare announced, snapping her fingers excitedly. "Didn't Debbie have a son who went to Polbury Manor? I remember her talking about him a couple of times. I think he was a year or two younger than the girls but nevertheless…"

"Yes, you're right. Well done! I think your first task is to talk to Debbie!"

Six

Knowing that Debbie Oxton's insatiable curiosity would have been aroused by the sudden, clandestine arrival of Detective Inspector Beauregard and Detective Constable Pawlett, Clare loitered around the reception area, looking busy, adjusting the furniture and replacing the flowers in a vase on the windowsill but, in reality, just waiting for Debbie's inevitable enquiry. She didn't have long to wait.

"What happened to the golf this morning?" Debbie asked, knowing exactly what had happened to the golf.

Clare smiled gently. "Oh, we couldn't make it, I'm afraid. We had a further visit from the police."

"Ah, well, yes, I was here when they arrived," Debbie sounded flustered. "Is everything alright?"

Clare smiled again. Momentarily, she flirted with the idea of winding Debbie up by saying that Clive was under suspicion of murdering a receptionist but quickly thought better of it. "Yes, they were following up on the murder of Olivia Farringdon. There were a few more questions they wanted to ask."

"Were there?" Debbie paused, hoping that Clare would elaborate but she didn't.

"Did you know that Olivia Farringdon was the mother of one of the girls, Rosemary Edwyn, who went missing ten years ago, along with four other girls?"

Debbie thumped her forehead with her open hand. "Of course, of course – I knew I recognised her from somewhere. Yes, that's it, of course. But surely the police don't think her murder was anything to do with what happened all those years ago."

"Oh, I think it's just one line of inquiry," Clare replied dismissively. "Correct me if I'm wrong, Debbie, but weren't a couple of the girls who disappeared pupils at Polbury Manor School?"

"Yes, yes, they were – actually, I think three of them were. Now what were their names? There was, let me think, Charlotte and there was the daughter of the vicar and there was another girl, Emily something. She went missing during the summer holidays, but she was a pupil at Polbury Manor."

"Was she?" Clare asked innocently. "How interesting! Hang on though, wasn't your son a pupil there as well?"

"Danny? Well, er, yes he was but he was a bit younger than the girls so he didn't really know any of them." Debbie sounded surprisingly defensive.

"No, of course not! How is Danny? What's he doing these days?"

"Ah, er, well," Debbie hesitated. "He was never a great scholar. He's still living at home. He works for my brother-in-law Tommy as an electrician. It's a small family firm, 'Finnarts'; you may have heard of them."

"I'm sure Clive will have done," Clare replied diplomatically. "But tell me about Polbury Manor at the time the girls went missing. I bet there were all sorts of stories and rumours flying around about who might have been responsible for their disappearance."

"Oh, there were," Debbie agreed emphatically. "But I thought the police had concluded that the guy who committed suicide, Lennie somebody, was responsible."

"Never proven though, was it?"

"No, no, I suppose it wasn't. It's just that no more girls went missing after Lennie died. So do the police think someone else was responsible?" Debbie asked, her blue eyes alert and sparkling with curiosity.

"They didn't say," Clare stonewalled. "But you said there were plenty of theories flying around at the time."

"Did I? Oh yes, I did, didn't I?"

"So who was the number one suspect?" Clare teased.

"Oh, there were two or three. There was a young, quite dishy art master called Russell, I think. Apparently, he used to flirt quite openly with a lot of the older girls; he'd often give one or two of them a lift home at the end of the day. Some enjoyed the attention but quite a few found him a bit creepy, I think. If I remember correctly, he suddenly left around the time the girls started to go missing and nobody knew why. And then there was the guy who used to maintain the school playing fields – a groundsman, or groundsperson, I suppose you'd call him. I don't remember his name but apparently he was often hanging around when the girls were changing for hockey. He was really spooky."

"You said there were two or three?"

"Did I? Well, yes, I suppose I did. I mean there were a few around who suspected the head teacher, old Mr Highcliffe. He always looked quite innocent to me but there were those who said he enjoyed inviting some of the girls into his office, if you know what I mean. He retired several years ago but I think he still lives locally somewhere."

"How interesting! Still, I expect the police will have spoken to them at the time and eliminated them."

"Possibly," Debbie agreed doubtfully. "Although there were those who didn't think the police were doing all they could. They seemed to spend a lot of time chasing shadows. I tell you someone, though, who might have more information if you're interested. He was in touch with a lot of parents at the time – the Reverend Keith Draycott."

"Really?"

"Yes. I've seen him here in the restaurant a couple of times recently, with a, errm, lady friend so he still lives around here."

*

Clive was in the office, a mug of coffee by his side, trying to attend to some outstanding invoices and confirm a couple of bookings, but his attention kept wandering. To make matters worse, Archie the cat chose that moment to stroll into the office, leap onto the desk and settle down contentedly in the small gap between the computer screen and the keyboard. Reluctant to evict his interloper for fear of the damage his flailing claws might do, Clive was absently shuffling some papers on his desk for the third time and pondering on the two murders when his phone rang. The voice at the other end sounded formal and austere.

"Is that Mr Walsingham?" the voice asked.

"Yes, yes it is," Clive replied apprehensively.

"My name is Neil Rushwick, Detective Superintendent Neil Rushwick. You may have heard of me."

"Ah, yes, I have. Dick, er, Detective Inspector Beauregard mentioned your name when he came to see me earlier."

"Yes, it's about that visit that I've called. You see, unfortunately DI Beauregard isn't, how can I put this? He isn't too well at the moment. You may have noticed he wasn't quite his usual self."

"He didn't eat any of our cakes for a start," Clive replied, more flippantly than was wise.

"Yes, well, whatever," Superintendant Rushwick replied disdainfully. "Anyway, the thing is, I've had to stand him down from the investigation – for the time being at least. Hopefully he'll be firing on all cylinders soon enough. The trouble is that, as I expect he mentioned, we've got a really big, complex, high-profile investigation going on. The Carlow Valley force is not especially big and, with a senior detective off the case, we're really struggling. Now I know you've helped DI Beauregard in the past and produced some very impressive results and I was wondering if you could help us again."

"Well, y-yes," Clive replied with a hint of suspicion in his voice. "I told Dick, er, Detective Inspector Beauregard that I'd be happy to help."

"Excellent, excellent! Only without DI Beauregard to act as a link, we're going to have to formalise the terms of reference a bit. For a start, I'd like you to concentrate your efforts on what happened to the missing girls ten years ago. I'm arranging for you to have a copy of all the relevant case notes and I'd like you to have a good read through them to see if anything was missed at the time or if anything looks a bit suspicious in the light of, er, recent developments. And if you need to go back over any statements that were made at the time or talk to anyone who was involved, that would be a huge help – we've got our hands full just dealing with what's happening at the moment. Of course, you'll need to have an official title – just for the duration of the investigation, you understand. We can't have you barging around talking to people and saying rather limply that you're just helping us out and we can't introduce you as an 'ex-detective inspector' so I'd like you to be our Investigation Liaison Officer."

Clive heard himself laugh out loud. "I beg your pardon?"

"That way you can be an official member of our team and get paid properly for the work you do and…"

"Can I be very clear?" Clive interrupted. "I have no desire whatsoever to be on the police payroll again. I am trying to run a hotel and…"

"Yes, quite," Superintendant Rushwick agreed. "So that's settled then!"

"It most certainly is not…" Clive protested.

"And I'd like you to work alongside Detective Sergeant Pawlett."

"Sergeant?" Clive asked, sounding surprised.

"Yes that's right. She wasn't officially due to take up her new duties until 1st October but, in view of what is happening, the date has been brought forward."

"Well, I'm very pleased for her, of course…"

"And I'd like her to work undercover," Superintendant Rushwick continued remorselessly. "When the press get hold of this story, they'll be swarming all over the place. Now they know me and they know DI Beauregard and one or two other senior officers but they don't know DS Pawlett and that's the way I'd like it to stay. So, assuming that you have a room free, I'd like DS Pawlett to pretend to be a paying guest at your hotel. That way the two of you can work together without raising anyone's suspicions and she can keep in touch with me electronically. We'd pay for the room, of course. And as one of the recent victims stayed at your hotel just before she was murdered, I'd like DS Pawlett to nose around a bit, check out your guests, keep an eye on your staff, you know, to see if anyone's behaving suspiciously."

"Now hang on a minute," Clive protested again. "This isn't what Dick and I agreed…"

"Excellent, excellent," Superintendant Rushwick replied. "DS Pawlett has just gone home to do a bit of packing and then she'll come straight over. And she's got a copy of the newspaper cutting you were asking about."

"Yes but…"

"And one other thing I'd really like you to do is go and see Ian Mencham. He was in charge of the original investigation into the missing girls. He's a bit of a recluse these days and not easy to speak to. I know he won't have anything to do with me or with DI Beauregard or anyone else who was part of his team back then and I don't think he'll want to talk to any serving police officers but he might be more amenable to you."

"Yes but…"

"Oh and by the way, we've just heard that Edward Duffield has gone missing!"

"What?"

*

It was late into the afternoon when Clive heard a familiar squealing of tyres in the hotel car park. "Sounds as though Alison's arrived," he announced as he passed Clare in the foyer. "Have you got her room ready for her?"

"Of course, I've put her in Room 13 – I thought it appropriate. I hope she's not superstitious."

"Huh, I doubt it, touch wood. I suggest you get Jamie to take her luggage upstairs and we'll chat to her in the office."

The hotel office was not big enough to comfortably accommodate three people but, at that time of day, it was the only available space where Clive, Clare and Alison could speak in confidence with little risk of being overheard or interrupted. There were normally only two chairs in the office, one of which was frequently occupied by Archie, so Clare had "invited" the portly cat to sleep elsewhere temporarily, and had liberated a stool from the bar which she had wedged into a small space behind the door. "Clive won't mind using the stool," Clare announced cheerfully when Alison arrived. "He's the only one of us whose feet will still touch the ground."

"Well congratulations, Alison!" Clive tried to sound enthusiastic as they jostled each other before squeezing into their respective chairs. "Detective Sergeant, eh?"

"Thanks." Alison Pawlett smiled uncertainly as she sat down. "But I'd rather the circumstances were a little different."

"You mean Dick?"

"Yes. It sounds as though Superintendant Rushwick has been pretty unsympathetic towards him. According to Dick, er, DI Beauregard, he told him he'd got no time for passengers on this investigation and he sent him home. I was summoned and told to drive him there."

"Yes, Dick didn't look at all well when he was here earlier. Do you know what's troubling him?" Clare asked, with a familiar look of concern.

"No, not really; it was quite difficult to get anything coherent out of him. I'm pretty sure he's bothered by something that happened during the original investigation into the missing girls but he won't say what it is. You know, he frightens me sometimes. He couldn't stop shaking on the journey back to his flat." Alison Pawlett shuddered.

Not entirely surprising, Clive reflected, given the normal standard of Alison Pawlett's driving. "Is he usually like that in your car?" he asked, posing the question as innocently as he could.

"No, I've not seen him this bad, although he does get very depressed. He suffers from quite black moods sometimes."

"Is he on any medication?" Clare asked.

Alison Pawlett shrugged. "None that I'm aware of – I've not seen him take anything. But I'm really quite worried; I'm frightened he might do something, you know…" Alison Pawlett's voice tailed off and Clive fancied that he saw a little moisture in the corners of her eyes.

"Mmmm. Tell me about Superintendant Rushwick. He was part of the original investigation team, wasn't he?"

"Yes, he was a detective inspector at the time. He was young and, by all accounts, ambitious – he's still very ambitious now – and I get the impression that he didn't have a lot of confidence in Chief Superintendent Mencham."

"It was Chief Superintendent Mencham who led the original investigation, wasn't it?"

"Yes, DI Beauregard told me that Superintendant Rushwick thought Chief Superintendant Mencham wasn't really up to the task. He'd never led such a high-profile investigation before and he hid behind rules and procedures to disguise his own failings. I think DI Rushwick, as he was then, got very frustrated. He wanted to be out there kicking arses and banging heads, if you know what I mean, but he was reigned in. But you'll need to be careful. If you do manage to make a breakthrough of any kind, he'll take the credit for it. He wants to make a name for himself."

Clive was taken aback by Sergeant Pawlett's candour and he hesitated for a moment. "Er, your Superintendant Rushwick phoned me earlier."

Alison Pawlett nodded. "Yes, I know. He can be very persuasive, can't he?"

"That's mainly because he doesn't listen," Clive protested.

"He asked me to give you this," Alison said as she reached into her denim bag and produced an official-looking document. "It's your job profile and contract of employment."

"It's what?" Clive asked incredulously.

"Your contract as temporary Investigation Liaison Officer; he said he agreed it with you when he phoned."

Clive exchanged puzzled glances with Clare and grimaced. "He most certainly did not," he protested. "I have no intention of being formally employed by any police force ever again."

"But I'm supposed to return the contract to him with your signature on it," Alison Pawlett complained.

"Well you'll have to tell him that I'm still mulling over his offer and I'll let him know my decision in due course. Meanwhile, we've got work to do."

"You're still prepared to help us then?" Alison Pawlett asked.

"Yes, of course. I promised Dick I would, but only on a strictly informal basis. And I've agreed that you can stay here as a guest. Your room is all ready for you and Jamie has taken your luggage up. It's the room Olivia Farringdon stayed in."

"Oh, thanks!" Sergeant Pawlett replied sarcastically. "Did Superintendant Rushwick tell you that he wants me to work undercover while I'm here?" Alison Pawlett pulled a disapproving face, perhaps recalling the broken nose she'd received on a previous "undercover" mission.

"Err, yes he did," Clive confirmed reluctantly. "Clare and I will treat you like any other guest but what about Jamie? Won't he give the game away? You and he, err, well…"

Alison Pawlett fixed Clive with a stern stare. "Jamie has been lectured. I'm not expecting him to be a problem."

"No, no, I'm sure!" Clive agreed with the hint of a smirk. He imagined Jamie Coulton's fate might be quite painful if he stepped out of line.

"Oh, well," Alison Pawlett sighed. "If I'm to do this job properly, I'm going to need a list of all your guests and their room numbers. I'll need to know when they checked in and how long they're staying for and I'll need a list of your staff, especially those who were on duty when Olivia Farringdon was here. And I'll need a list of the people who stayed here while Olivia Farringdon was here, as well as a list of anyone who booked a table for dinner while she was here."

Clive exchanged glances with Clare and raised a quizzical eyebrow. "Yes, of course! Clare can provide you with the information you need, although it might take a while. And we'll try and give you a prominent table in the dining room so you can see what's going on around you, unless you'd prefer to do your spying a bit more surreptitiously."

"This isn't my idea, you know," Alison Pawlett replied tersely, sensing Clive's antipathy. "I'm just doing what I've been told to do. I don't want my first day as a detective sergeant to be my last!"

"Yes, of course, I'm sorry," Clive soothed. "So what's Superintendant Rushwick's priority at the moment?"

"Well, I expect you've heard that Kate Huxton and Edward Duffield have both been reported as missing and, given what has happened to Olivia Farringdon and Keith Draycott, we're all fearing the worst. So Superintendant Rushwick has got everybody out there combing every bit of woodland, open space and waste ground, looking for bodies."

"I see. Tell me about Edward Duffield."

"Well, we only discovered he'd gone missing when we phoned his home to check that he was okay. His wife, Sonia, said that her husband had gone away for a few days. He left home on Thursday 4th September. He didn't say where he was going, except that it was a business trip, and hasn't been heard from since."

"He left home on the day Olivia Farringdon was murdered?"

"That's right!"

"But his wife didn't report him missing?"

"No. Apparently he often went away for a few days – he's a kind of salesman for a central heating company, so he travels around quite a bit. When he left on 4th September, he said it was on business but Sonia didn't sound too convinced. She did say, though, that it was quite normal for him to go away for a few days and not stay in touch. We got the impression that she wouldn't have been heartbroken if he'd not bothered to return home. When I left the office, they were trying to speak to his boss but, as it's the weekend, it may not be easy…"

"Will you excuse me a moment?" Clare announced suddenly as she stood up, treading on Alison Pawlett's toes as she manoeuvred herself towards the door. "I've just got to check something. I won't be long."

As Clare rushed from the room, leaving Clive looking bemused, Alison Pawlett winced slightly and flexed her toes before continuing her narrative. "We have managed to get hold of Alan and Tessa Ashurst, though."

"The parents of Emily Ashurst?"

"Yes. They are both safe and at home. But Alan Ashurst said that he'd been contacted a couple of times, anonymously by text, by someone who claimed they knew what had happened to their daughter. Alan Ashurst admitted that he was intrigued and continued the dialogue by text. Eventually, he agreed to meet the mystery informant. They were due to meet yesterday at the car park next to Framingford Common but Alan Ashurst hung around for a while and nobody turned up so he assumed it was some kind of cruel hoax and went home again."

"How interesting! I think I'd like to speak to Alan Ashurst as soon as it can be arranged. Meanwhile, have you got a copy of the newspaper cutting that you found on the body of Keith Draycott?"

"I have," Alison Pawlett replied as she rummaged in her denim bag. "But I'm not sure how helpful it is." She produced a sheet of paper and handed it over to Clive who subjected it to detailed scrutiny.

"Well, there's no doubt it's a cutting from yesterday's *Carlow Valley Gazette* – the date is very clear. And the article has been quite carefully and deliberately cut from the paper so it must have been put into Keith Draycott's pocket for a reason. And, as Dick said, it is about the forthcoming Carlow Valley Arts Festival. It mentions a number of activities that are taking place, it refers to the co-ordinator, a Mr Chalbury, oh, and here it mentions that some pupils from Polbury Manor School are taking part. It mentions the Carlow Valley Symphony Orchestra, and it mentions the principal local benefactor and sponsor, a certain

Richard Edgton, but there's nothing that specifically refers to Keith Draycott. I had hoped there might be a reference of some kind to a circus, but sadly…"

Clive broke off as Clare bustled back into the room, flinging the door wide open and causing Clive to take evasive action. Clare's face was flushed and her eyes wide with excitement. "I've found it," she announced triumphantly.

Clive and Alison exchanged puzzled glances. "I don't follow," Clive admitted.

"I knew I recognised the name Edward Duffield from somewhere when you were talking about him earlier." Clare was so excited that she was tripping over words. "He stayed here!"

"What?" Clive exclaimed.

"I've checked our records and he checked out last Monday, 8th September."

"Bloody hell! And when did he check in?"

"On the afternoon of Thursday 4th September and…"

"Hang on. That was the day that Olivia Farringdon checked out and was murdered."

"That's right. And they both phoned to make their reservations on the same day, July 25th. And both stayed in the same room – room 13 – the same room that Alison's in! And Debbie told me earlier that Keith Draycott has dined here a couple of times. Isn't it so exciting?"

Clive grimaced. "You're saying that Olivia Farringdon and Edward Duffield both stayed at this hotel and Keith Draycott dined here? Bloody hell!"

*

The sparsely populated dining room at the Follycombe Hotel occupied the large conservatory, which ran almost the entire length of the rear of the building. Shortly after she and Clive had bought the hotel, Clare had redesigned the space to make dining a cosy, more intimate affair with diners able to enjoy their own space without feeling that they were being observed by the other diners, or having their private conversations overheard. By interspersing the rows of tables with intricately decorated screens and trellis frameworks festooned with climbing indoor plants, Clare had managed to create a series of artificial nooks and alcoves and it was in one of the more centrally positioned alcoves that Alison dined. At Clive's suggestion, she sampled one of the chef's specialities, lemon sole, which was served to her attentively by Jamie Coulton who, apart from a couple of lapses when he had to put his hand over his mouth to disguise a brief fit of the giggles, fulfilled his duties with a detached professionalism.

The news that Olivia Farringdon, Keith Draycott and Edward Duffield had all frequented the dining room added a heightened relevance to Alison Pawlett's new surveillance duties, but she was feeling ill at ease. Rather than observing the smattering of entirely innocent-looking guests enjoying their meals and indulging in convivial small talk, she felt alone and vulnerable, sensing, for some reason, that she was, in fact, the one being observed. Unable to talk to anyone, she fidgeted nervously in her chair, tried to avoid eye contact with Jamie and developed a strange fixation with a climbing bougainvillea. She had also eschewed her favourite denim outfit for a smart summer dress, a metamorphosis that only seemed to add to her discomfiture.

Towards the end of her meal, Clive began to circulate among his guests, as he often did, checking that they had enjoyed their meals and asking whether they would care to have a tea or coffee to finish. As he approached Alison, he gave her an almost imperceptible wink and slight smile.

"How was your lemon sole?" he asked with a commendably straight face.

"Oh, it was very good, thank you," Alison replied while lifting a half-full glass of white wine.

"I told you Gary was good," Clive said with a smirk. "We've got Richard Edgton to thank for recommending him."

Alison, who had raised her glass halfway to her lips, suddenly replaced it firmly on the table. "Must you keep mentioning that man's name – that's twice so far today," she protested. She didn't like to be reminded of her fruitless, obsessive pursuit of Richard Edgton in connection with all manner of crimes that he hadn't committed.

"Sorry!" Clive held up his hands in a gesture of apology though there was still a hint of a smirk on his face. "Can we have a chat in the office when you're ready?" he asked in a low whisper.

"The sooner the better," Alison whispered back. She drained her glass and, keeping a judicious distance behind Clive, followed him into the office, where Clare was waiting with a pot of tea and coffee.

"Alison, how did you get on at dinner? How did the spying go?" Clare asked expectantly once everyone had settled into their cramped environment.

"Huh!" Alison Pawlett wrinkled her nose. "I have never seen a less likely looking bunch of mass murderers than your guests. I didn't notice anything remotely out of the ordinary and the only two members of staff I saw were Jamie and Clive. The meal was nice though."

"You need to come to one of our murder mystery weekends," Clive urged. "You'd be surprised at how devious some of these apparently harmless guests can turn out to be."

"Maybe," Alison replied doubtfully. "I'll have to keep up with this pretence, I suppose – I'd hate to miss anything important – but I think I might bring a good book to the next meal."

"Breakfast can be quite entertaining sometimes," Clive suggested, a little disingenuously. "Meanwhile, Clare, have you got anywhere with Edward Duffield?"

Clare leaned forward in her chair, her grey-green eyes ablaze with a mixture of elation and curiosity. "Not very far, I'm afraid," she confessed. "Beth would have been in some contact with him – she cleaned his room for a start – but I've found it virtually impossible to talk to her. For some reason, every time I broached the subject of Edward Duffield, she burst into tears. I asked her why but she wouldn't tell me – all she'd say was that she was upset about something. I let her go up to her room eventually in the hope that she might be a little calmer in the morning."

Clive narrowed his eyes. "That's odd! What about the rest of the team?"

"Nothing much, I'm afraid. One or two vaguely remember our Mr Duffield. He sat on his own in the dining room looking quite lonely and quite sad but he didn't really say anything much to anyone. We get so many single men staying here on business that he was just one more and nobody paid him much attention. Apparently, he smelled of stale sweat and Debbie thought he looked a bit shifty."

"Debbie would," Clive agreed.

"It is a bit too much of a coincidence though, isn't it?" Clare asked. "That Edward Duffield and Olivia Farringdon both stayed here, that they made their reservations on the same day and that he checked in on the day we think Olivia Farringdon was murdered."

"I doubt that it's a coincidence," Clive agreed. "At the moment, we must conclude that someone is targeting some or all of the parents of the five girls who disappeared. Whoever is doing this, and for whatever reason, lives locally – they know the geography of the area, they know where the most secluded woods are – and they almost certainly know this hotel. I suspect that's why Olivia Farringdon and Edward Duffield were recommended to stay here and probably why Keith Draycott used to dine here. I suspect we have entertained a murderer."

"You mean somebody who had already stayed here recommended it to those poor people and then murdered them?"

"Possibly, or someone who's dined here, but it's going to be a hell of a job going through all of our bookings for the past few months – maybe longer – to track down possible suspects. Then again, of course, the link could be somebody who works here…"

"Omigod! Don't say that, Clive. Surely it can't be any of the staff…"

Clive shrugged. "I have no idea," he replied despondently. "They seem honest enough but some of them haven't been here very long and I certainly don't know what any of them were doing ten years ago. That's partly why Alison is here."

"What about Kate Huxton?" Alison Pawlett asked, neatly changing the subject. "Do you think she stayed here?"

"I don't know," Clive replied, sounding slightly piqued. "But we can check. I only know she's gone missing. I don't know where she lives or who reported her missing."

"Oh, I'm so sorry, I should've said," Alison replied apologetically. "It's just that, what with Dick and everything… Well anyway, she lives in Craigbridge, so I suppose she could get here and back in the day for a rendezvous with a potential killer, so probably didn't need to use a hotel. It was one of her daughters, Rebecca, who reported her missing. She was trying to contact her to meet up but she didn't return her daughter's calls or reply to her emails. Her ex-husband, Sir Robert, is out of the country at the moment."

"Does Kate Huxton have a job?" Clare asked.

"She used to work in the office at Craigbridge school but she left at the end of last term – I'm not sure why."

"What date was that?" Clive asked.

"I'd have to check but it was probably around July 25th."

"The same date that Olivia Farringdon and Edward Duffield made their bookings here."

"Blimey, yes! I hadn't…." Alison Pawlett spluttered.

"Okay, so that's a new line of inquiry for us," Clive replied, warming to his task. "Why did Kate Huxton resign? Had she given any notice or did she just walk out, or did she find another job or was she sacked? When and where was she last seen? Did she talk to her daughter or friends or neighbours about receiving strange texts?"

"I'll speak to my colleagues at HQ," Alison confirmed. "They may have some more up-to-date information."

"And how did you get on with your casual discussion with Debbie earlier, Clare?" Clive exchanged a knowing look with his spouse as he asked the question. "Apart from the revelation that Keith Draycott has dined here."

"Oh, er, quite well, I think. As we suspected, her son Danny was at Polbury Manor when the disappearances occurred but I don't think he knew any of the girls. Debbie recollects that the gossip amongst the parents at the time was that the headmaster, Mr Highcliffe, had a bit of a soft spot for young girls and she mentioned a dodgy groundsman – name unknown – and a trendy art teacher called Mr Russell."

"Is Mr Highcliffe still around?"

"I'm not sure. According to Debbie, he retired not long after the disappearances, but she thinks he still lives around here somewhere. Debbie also said that the person who might have more information – he was in touch with a lot of the parents at the time – was Keith Draycott. She obviously doesn't know what's happened to him."

Clive grimaced. "No, but she soon will." He turned to Alison. "You said that Keith Draycott had remarried."

"Yes, I believe so, about two years ago. I don't know much about his wife though."

"Now tomorrow is Sunday. I imagine Keith Draycott was due to take the morning service at St Mary's, so it might be worth finding out what's going to happen now. If there is going to be a service of some kind tomorrow, I wouldn't mind going along to see who turns up and whether his widow puts in an appearance. In any event, I'd like to pay her a visit. She may know who he was in touch with recently and he may have confided in her about what happened ten years ago and who he thought might have been responsible."

While he had been speaking, Clive had been making some notes on a piece of paper which he handed to Alison. "I know it is a lot to ask, Alison, but these are the people I'd really like to talk to and the sooner the better."

"Blimey!" Alison Pawlett protested as she read Clive's notes. "Is that all? Mrs and Mrs Ashurst, Sonia Duffield, Mr Highcliffe and ex-Superintendant Mencham – what are you doing for the rest of tomorrow?"

"Is there anything I can do?" Clare asked eagerly.

"Yes I rather think there is," Clive replied. "Can I suggest you pack up a food hamper and arrange to go and see Dick. He's bothered about something and the sooner we find out—"

Clive was interrupted by Alison Pawlett's phone ringing. He grinned when he heard that the *Ride of the Valkyries* was still her preferred ringtone.

"Hello, sir," Alison said formally with a pained expression on her face. "Yes, yes, Mr Walsingham is here… no, no, I don't believe he has signed the contract yet… yes, yes, would you like to speak to him?"

With a heavy sigh and an apologetic shrug, Alison handed her phone over to Clive.

"Hello, Clive," a voice boomed at the other end of the phone. "Rushwick here. As I feared, people have made the connection between Olivia Farringdon and Keith Draycott and reporters are starting to crawl out of the woodwork here – by tomorrow we'll be under siege so your help is really needed. But Sergeant Pawlett tells me you haven't signed the contract yet."

"No that's quite right," Clive replied firmly. "And I have no intention of doing so. I do not want to be employed by the police and be part of some kind of chain of command. I'm happy to help but only informally and only when I can spare the time."

"But…"

"Excellent, excellent! So that's agreed then!" Clive chuckled as he hung up.

Seven

News of Keith Draycott's murder had spread rapidly through the compact market town of Stowbrook, spawning a wave of ill-informed gossip and wild speculation. By mid-afternoon on the Saturday, after the bishop first heard the news, it had been decided that the morning service on the following day – Sunday 14th September – would be a special service of prayers and thanksgiving for the life of the Reverend Keith Draycott. A little later, the bishop himself confirmed that he would take the service.

St Mary's Parish Church, a typical example of late sixteenth-century church architecture, was constructed from local limestone and had a squat crenellated bell tower at one end. The body of the church could accommodate around five hundred people – although it rarely did – but, on that particular Sunday morning, it was packed to such an extent that some latecomers had to elbow themselves into the aisles around the perimeter of the church where they were forced to lean uncomfortably against the cold stone walls. Clive and Clare, deliberately sitting slightly apart from Alison Pawlett, had managed to squeeze themselves into a pew towards the rear of the church, from where they could observe the congregation, mainly from behind, and the various arrivals and departures. Sergeant Pawlett recognised a couple of her colleagues from Carlow Valley Police, who were on the same reconnaissance mission, but, in keeping with her reluctant undercover role, paid them no obvious attention. Clive scrutinised the congregation carefully but could not identify anyone who looked especially out of place or behaved strangely. It mainly comprised middle-aged and elderly parishioners, dressed in appropriately sober garb, and a smattering of younger families. He assumed that the diminutive woman sitting in the front row, dressed in black, was Keith Draycott's widow.

Having lamented the tragic, premature and violent demise of the Reverend Draycott, the bishop, an elderly man with thinning grey hair, sharp features and a slight stoop, spoke eloquently, though occasionally falteringly, about his enduring popularity, as demonstrated by the size of the congregation, about how he had continued to serve his parishioners with total dedication, even when he was beset by personal tragedy, and about how he had always been only too willing to offer solace and comfort to those who needed it.

Several hymns, including 'The Lord is My Shepherd' and 'Abide with Me' were sung with gusto and, at the end of the service, members of the congregation drifted silently and slowly away, their photographs being surreptitiously taken by a couple of police officers armed with powerful telephoto lenses, from the back of a police van. Meanwhile, Alison Pawlett's two colleagues, their faces grey and careworn, left in something of a hurry. As she was shortly to find out, another body had just been discovered, battered to death in Lannock Woods. The body was that of a middle-aged male and, although no formal identification had been made, no one doubted that it was Edward Duffield, especially as his car had been found in a nearby car park.

*

The original vicarage, built next to the church and of similar vintage, had proved to be too large, rambling and expensive for the church authorities to maintain so they had sold it to a private individual who had transformed it into a gentlemen's club of dubious reputation called "The Dog Collar". With the proceeds, the church authorities had purchased, in its place, a more modest but still generously proportioned eighteenth-century town house, a couple of hundred yards further down the road. It had a symmetrical facade, typical of houses of that period, regularly spaced sash windows and a canopy over the front door.

Vanessa Draycott was smaller, quieter and more self-effacing than Clive had expected. She was probably in her mid-forties with short, mousey hair, a round face, a wide mouth, dark brown eyes and arched eyebrows that gave her a permanently surprised expression. But despite the dreadful emotional upheaval of the last forty-eight hours, there seemed to be a calm dignity about her as she showed her visitors into the lounge of the vicarage.

Alison Pawlett made the introductions. "I'm Detective, er, Sergeant Pawlett and this is Clive Walsingham, our Investigation Liaison Officer." Clive grimaced and looked away.

"Yes, you told me on the phone. I had two other detectives come to see me yesterday, to tell me about…" Momentarily, Vanessa Draycott seemed to be struggling to hold back the tears.

"Yes, they're required elsewhere today; there's been another development, so we're taking over. This is just a follow-up visit," Alison Pawlett replied, stretching the truth a little.

Clive looked quickly around, as was his custom whenever he entered a room for the first time. The walls were painted in pale yellow and much of the wooden floor was covered by a pair of rugs in a predominantly chocolate brown colour. A beige sofa fitted snugly beneath the sash window and there was another matching sofa at right angles to it. Above the fireplace, the mantelpiece was adorned with photographs – a couple were unmistakeably of Keith and Vanessa Draycott but other older ones, Clive presumed, were of his first wife and his daughter, Isabel.

"It's so very good of you to see us," Clive began, solicitously. "I can't begin to imagine how dreadful the last couple of days have been for you."

Vanessa Draycott spoke quietly and slowly as though reflecting carefully on the appropriateness and significance of each word before she uttered it. "If Keith was in my position, he would carry on stoically, more concerned about other people than himself, and that's what I'm trying to do, although I must admit…" She hesitated and Clive thought he saw her bottom lip quiver but she remained composed as she settled herself neatly into the corner seat of one of the sofas, while Clive and Alison sat down at opposite ends of the other one.

"We glimpsed you at the service this morning," Clive observed.

"Yes, I wasn't sure that I could go through with it, but everyone was so kind and the bishop spoke so well, I thought."

"Your husband was obviously very much loved within the community."

"Yes, I think he was, which is gratifying. You know, Keith was a wonderful man – so charming, so amusing, so articulate, so, so… caring. Everyone spoke so highly of him. I think, for a time, the bishop had him earmarked for greater things – a higher office of some kind – but Keith was quite content being a parish priest although…" Vanessa Draycott paused momentarily, suddenly uncertain whether she should continue.

"Although?" Clive prompted.

"I shouldn't say this, of course, but poor Keith had had so much personal tragedy in his life and his faith tested so often that I really don't think he believed in God anymore; but he kept going for the sake of his parishioners."

"Had he shared his doubts with anyone else – the bishop, for example?"

"Oh, no, no! That wasn't Keith's style. No, no, he just kept his thoughts to himself and soldiered on."

"How long have you known him?"

"Let me see; we first met about five years ago, I suppose. I'd just suffered a bereavement and he was so kind and caring. He came to see me two or three times and we just sat and chatted and we got on so well and things just went from there."

"I'm very sorry to hear about your bereavement," Clive said, quietly.

"Thank you. Yes, that was my first husband, Roderick. He'd been ill for a while with cancer and we knew he hadn't got long but it was still a shock when it happened. He knew Keith professionally, as it were – he used to audit the church accounts – and when he died, Keith came to see me and…" Vanessa Draycott swallowed hard and dabbed at her moist cheeks. "I don't seem to have much luck with husbands."

"I'm very sorry," Clive repeated awkwardly. In such difficult emotional circumstances, he knew that Clare was so much better than he was. She was naturally sensitive and compassionate, knowing instinctively what to say, in a way that Clive found difficult after so many years of having to keep his emotions in check as a detective inspector. "Did Keith, errm, say much about his life before you met? Did he speak much about his personal tragedies?"

"He told me a bit about what had happened before we got married but he didn't dwell on the past and I thought it best not to raise the subject. He did tell me that he lost his first wife, Laura, in a car accident around twelve years ago. He was driving when he lost control on an icy road and hit a tree. He got away with minor injuries but poor Laura was killed instantly. I think he always felt guilty about what happened, you know, because he was at the wheel."

Clive stood up, walked over to the mantelpiece, the floorboards creaking under his feet as he did so, and pointed to one of the framed pictures. "Is this a picture of Laura?"

"Yes, that's right; she's sitting next to Isabel."

"And did he tell you what happened to Isabel?"

"He did although it was a struggle for him and I know he felt very guilty about that too. Laura had been such a wonderful mother that Keith struggled to replace her in Isabel's life. He had a busy and demanding job to do, with uncertain hours, and, although he tried his best, I think he felt that he had rather neglected Issy. He told me that he'd had a bit of trouble with her at the start of the new term – I don't think she'd settled into her new class very well and was going through a rebellious phase. And she had claimed to be poorly for a couple of days, although I don't think Keith thought there was anything wrong with her. Obviously, I don't know what happened on the day she disappeared but, for some reason, Keith didn't take her to the school gates; he dropped her at the main road a couple of hundred yards away. It was only as an afterthought that he phoned the school to check that she'd arrived and that was when they told him…"

Alison Pawlett, who had been diligently making notes and who had a new rank to justify, suddenly decided that it was time she made more of a contribution.

"We're linking your husband's murder to what happened to his daughter ten years ago," she announced importantly. "There have been other developments that make it seem likely. Do you know if anyone had tried to contact him recently about what happened back then?"

Vanessa Draycott shook her head. "I don't know any details, I'm afraid, but I do know that he came home one day, quite, what's the word? Not excited exactly but very animated. He said 'somebody knows what happened' – he repeated that phrase several times – and then he disappeared into his study for a while. I can only assume somebody had contacted him with important information but I don't know who or how and I knew better than to ask. If Keith wanted to tell me something, he would."

"How long ago was this?" Clive asked.

"Oooh, it was back in the summer, sometime in July, I should think."

"And did anything happen afterwards that seemed a bit strange or unusual?"

"No, nothing that I can put my finger on, although Keith did seem a bit on edge, which was not like him, but he didn't tell me why and I'm afraid I didn't ask."

"We think your husband was probably murdered last Wednesday the 10th, although we didn't find his body until yesterday. Yet, as far as we know, you didn't report him missing?" Alison Pawlett asked bluntly.

Vanessa Draycott looked uncomfortable at the directness of the question and swallowed hard a couple of times before answering. "Ah, er, no, that's right. You see, he told me that he'd arranged to go and visit his elderly parents. They're both in their eighties and not in the best of health, but they live in Yorkshire so when he goes – sorry, whenever he went to see them, which was quite often – he normally went for several days. As far as I knew, he intended to set off early last Wednesday morning to visit them and was due to return yesterday, Saturday."

"But you weren't worried when he didn't contact you?"

"Good heavens, no! He'd made the trip a number of times and he never usually bothered to make contact, unless he'd forgotten to do something important or wanted a favour. I had his parents' phone number and his mobile number, although he was always losing his phone so it wasn't necessarily much use.

No, I knew where to contact him if I needed to; that was our normal arrangement."

"And his parents never phoned to ask what had happened to him?"

"No they didn't but, knowing what I know now, I rather think he made up the story about going to see them – they hadn't been expecting him. He'd gone off to meet someone else, hadn't he?"

"It certainly looks that way," Clive agreed. "Though what he was planning to do for three days, we don't yet know." He paused momentarily as he recalled that Olivia Farringdon and Edward Duffield had both checked into his hotel for three days. "Tell me, how did your husband normally travel to Yorkshire? Did he drive?"

Vanessa Draycott shook her head again, more vigorously this time. "No, no, he hardly ever drove anywhere, except when he was in a hurry or it was raining. I think he'd lost confidence as a driver after the accident. He liked riding his bike. He said it helped to keep him fit and it made him a bit more visible when he was travelling around the parish. No, he'd gone before I was up on Wednesday – he was always up and about early. He normally got a taxi to the station and then travelled by train. I assumed that was what he planned to do last Wednesday."

"We found his body in Stowbrook Forest which isn't too far from here. Once he left home that morning, he could easily have walked there," Clive mused.

"Or met someone who drove him there?" Vanessa Draycott made the suggestion with such confidence that Clive began to wonder if she knew more about her husband's clandestine meeting than she had admitted.

"Possibly, but at this stage, we don't know; we're appealing for witnesses. We've had it on good authority that your husband was very supportive of the other parents who lost their daughters and he had a highly visible profile within the community. If anyone had any suspicions about who had taken their daughter, your husband would probably have been told. Did he ever say anything to you?"

There was another emphatic shake of the head. "No, nothing! As I've said, it wasn't a chapter is his life that he wanted to talk about and I certainly had no intention of raising it. I do know, though, that he kept in touch with some of the other parents – he'd phone them occasionally or send a reassuring text or email but that's all I know. Do you think he was murdered because he knew too much?"

"Possibly, but we mustn't jump to conclusions," Clive replied cautiously. "And if he did know too much, then it seems he wasn't the only one."

"Where would your husband have kept his computer and his personal files?" Alison asked, with a sudden sense of urgency. Tiring of the speculative nature of the conversation, she was keen to get her hands on some kind of firm evidence.

"Oh, he had his computer in his study. I can show you if you like."

"And his mobile phone?"

"He must have taken it with him when he left last Wednesday; it certainly isn't here. I've tried calling it but I get nothing. Mind you, as I've said, he was always losing his phone."

"Well, it wasn't with him when we found his body," Alison confirmed.

Vanessa Draycott rose to her feet and slowly led her two guests out of the lounge, across the entrance hall and into Keith Draycott's study. "I've kept it exactly as it was when he left on Wednesday. I've not touched or moved anything," she hastened to reassure them.

The study was a small, cold, gloomy room with one north-facing window. Around the walls were a number of walnut bookshelves, each one cluttered with an assortment of books, mainly of an erudite, worthy nature, often piled untidily, one on top of another, and a miscellany of other unrelated artefacts including a pair of binoculars, a couple of model boats, a camera and a violin in an open case. A solid, walnut desk stood in the middle of the room, with a computer screen placed centrally upon it. To one side, a number of books were placed casually in a heap. In the corner of the room, a grandfather clock ticked loudly.

"We'd like to take the computer away with us," Alison announced. "It might contain information that is relevant to our inquiries."

Vanessa Draycott shrugged. "You're welcome to take a look, of course, but I should warn you that everything on there is what I think they call 'password protected' – Keith always seemed very security-minded – and I have no idea what the password is. This room was Keith's territory. I very rarely ventured inside."

Clive, meanwhile, had made a beeline for the untidy heap of books on the desk. He picked them up, one at a time, glanced at the titles and hastily thumbed through them.

"Are these books on your husband's desk for a reason?" he asked. "Were they what he was currently reading?"

"I should imagine so," Vanessa Draycott replied rather airily. "He had a huge appetite for knowledge. He was always very well read and very curious about almost anything. He often had his head in a book, late at night, when he couldn't sleep."

"Well, there's certainly a wide range here," Clive agreed as he looked at each one in turn. "*A History of Church Architecture*, the *Book of Calendars and Dates*, whatever that is, *Ancient Myths and Legends*—"

"Olivia Farringdon had a book about myths and legends on her coffee table," Alison Pawlett interrupted excitedly. "I'm sure she did. I think she'd borrowed it from her local library. I'll check that out!"

"*Great Sporting Achievements*," Clive continued as though he had not heard, or regarded as important, what Alison Pawlett had just said, but he had made the necessary mental note.

"Oh, he was very sporting when he was young," Vanessa Draycott announced proudly. "He played rugby and cricket, he rowed for his college, he was a good hurdler. In fact, he was a bit of a polymath. He seemed to be pretty good at everything he turned his hand to."

Apart from being a father, Clive reflected ruefully. "Did he still play any sports?" he asked.

"No, not these days! He had too many other things to do and he was getting a bit creaky."

"I see he also had a book on *Wines of the World*," Clive observed, picking up the last volume in the heap and thumbing through the pages. "I notice he's put a tick against some of the vintage wines that are mentioned. Was he a connoisseur?"

Vanessa Draycott laughed. "He liked to think so. He had a small collection of vintage wines which he kept under the stairs. I imagine the ticks were against items he had acquired, or wanted to acquire. Unfortunately, a vicar's salary doesn't go very far when it comes to vintage wine. He would consume the odd one when he was reading late into the night. He said it helped him sleep. Are you a connoisseur, Mr Walsingham?"

It was Clive's turn to laugh. "No, not really although since we've been running a hotel, I've gained a bit of knowledge. I like to have some good wines available for the more discerning guests. I know enough to see that he'd identified some good vintages here. May I borrow these books?"

"Of course! Frankly, they're not much good to me now and we've got no immediate family to pass them on to."

"What do you know about the forthcoming Carlow Valley Arts Festival?" Alison asked, remembering the mysterious press cutting and abruptly changing the subject. "Was your husband involved with it?"

"Oh, he took a great interest. As a matter of fact, he was on the organising committee. He was always dashing off for another meeting. I believe he'd agreed for the church to be used as a venue for a number of concerts by the Carlow Valley Symphony Orchestra – he played the violin a bit himself; he was quite accomplished – and he was planning to attend a lot of the events. He was always very keen to actively support the arts."

*

It was difficult to tell from Dick Beauregard's semi-permanent hangdog expression whether he was pleased to see Clare.

Clare was wearing her best caring expression, her expressive eyes displaying an intensity born of deep concern. "Hello, Dick!" she began heartily as she stared at the inspector's head peering anxiously around his front door. From what little she could see in the sombre light, Inspector Beauregard had not shaved or brushed his hair in the last twenty-four hours. "You said it was okay if I called round?"

Dick Beauregard's heavily lidded eyes blinked slowly. "Oh, yes, of course. You'd better come in."

"I've brought some chocolate cake – your favourite!" Clare announced, cheerfully, as she handed over a white cardboard cake box.

"Oh, y-y-yes, right. I'll put the kettle on."

Dick Beauregard meandered distractedly into the kitchen leaving Clare to scrutinise the living room of his small flat. The walls – or what she could see of them – were painted in a pale lilac, which clashed with the badly stained, bright red rug. The faded blue curtains were half drawn across the window. There were a couple of mismatched arm chairs, one of which was covered in an assortment of papers and magazines, mostly on the subject of cycling. Beneath the window, there was a small table with two folding wooden chairs, one at each end. On the table, there was a dirty plate next to a carton which had once contained a takeaway pizza. Close by was a glass containing the dregs of beer which had been poured from the bottle standing next to it. Around the walls was a haphazard assortment of wooden units, originally assembled, badly, from cheap flat-packs, containing drawers, cupboards and shelves. The shelves were stuffed with an untidy assortment of books and folders. In one corner, there was a modest, rickety table on which stood a computer screen with a number of adhesive "post-it" notes, covered in scribbled writing, affixed randomly around the edges. Through a partially opened door, she could glimpse an unmade double bed.

"Is your, er, partner not here at the moment?" Clare ventured.

"Er, n-n-no," Dick replied from the gloomy interior of his kitchen. "She's, er, she's had to go away for a few days. I'm sorry the, errm, place is in a bit of a mess."

He slowly emerged from the kitchen holding two mugs of coffee. Clare noticed that his hands were shaking as he placed them on the table. "I'll just get the cake," he said softly before disappearing into the kitchen and returning with the chocolate cake on a plate, together with a knife and two side plates.

"So, how are you, Dick," Clare began, getting straight to the point of her visit. "You weren't your usual self when you came to see us yesterday. Clive and I were quite worried."

"Ah, no, that's kind of you, but I'm alright really. I, err…" Dick Beauregard replied unconvincingly as he sat down on one of the chairs at the table and gestured Clare towards the other one. "I'm just a bit, you know, stressed about this case – it's got to me a bit, I'm afraid."

"We understood from Superintendant Rushwick that you'd been, er, taken off the case."

"Is that what he said? I don't think that he's ever had a very high opinion of my abilities…"

Clare narrowed her grey-green eyes. Her fabled powers of empathy were going to be tested. "There's something going on, isn't there? There's something about this case that's bothering you."

Dick Beauregard fiddled with the plate on which he had placed the cake, turning it slowly around on the table while he considered what he should say. "I, er, I made a terrible mistake during the original investigation. I was still a raw constable and we were under terrible pressure… Anyway, I managed to cover it up at the time – Chief Superintendant Mencham wasn't that observant – but when Superintendant Rushwick goes through all the old case notes, which he's bound to do, he'll realise what I did and that'll be the end of my career."

"Ah well, you may be in luck there because, as I understand it, Superintendant Rushwick has asked Clive to go through the old case notes. I'm told Mr Rushwick is far too busy investigating the recent murders to sit in his office going over the old paperwork."

Dick Beauregard gave a wan smile. "That sounds like my superintendant. Mind you, Clive has got one of those sharp, analytical minds that I envy. He'll soon spot what I've done and the outcome will be the same."

"Not necessarily," Clare replied. "Don't forget that Clive isn't employed by the police, so he can choose what he says to your Mr Rushwick. I mean, he might decide, for instance, that he's going to need your help to crack the case and he might, you know, choose to turn a blind eye. And if he were to crack the case, you can bet that Clive will let you take the credit. He's got no need to impress anyone – apart from me, of course."

Dick Beauregard sighed heavily and frowned. "Mmm, but there's Alison, er Sergeant Pawlett. She's newly promoted and will be keen to impress. If she knows, she'll have to inform Superintendant Rushwick and…" His voice tailed off, leaving his sentence unfinished, and he slumped forward.

Clare hesitated for a moment or two before she replied. She was going to have to be pretty astute and maybe just a bit creative to prise anything useful out of Dick. "Alison's worried about you, Dick," she said, at last. "In my limited experience, she seems very loyal to you – I don't think she's going to go blabbing to Superintendant Rushwick. In any event, if Clive is eventually going to discover your 'terrible mistake', whatever it was, then wouldn't it be better for you to tell me now? Better to confide in me informally over a mug of coffee and a piece of chocolate cake than make a formal confession in a police interview room with the inevitable consequences." She looked across at the still slumped figure of Dick Beauregard and tried to offer a reassuring smile. "You know, Dick, I'm sure that Clive is going to want your involvement, he was most insistent on that when he spoke to me earlier, and I don't think it'll do you any good sitting around this pokey flat all day brooding and getting depressed."

Slowly and shakily, Dick Beauregard adopted a more upright posture and cut two slices of cake, taking the larger slice and placing it neatly on his plate. "No, no, I can see that. Yes, I can see that."

"Well?" Clare asked, with a hint of impatience in her voice. "Are you going to get this thing, this 'terrible mistake' off your chest?"

For what felt like several minutes but was, in fact, no more than a few seconds, Inspector Beauregard stared at Clare with heavy eyes. Clare responded with a gentle, understanding smile. "Alright, I think I can trust you," he finally conceded, albeit grudgingly. "Someone's got to know sometime. You remember one of the girls who went missing, Catherine Duffield, was on her way back from the village stores in Swincroft when she disappeared?"

Clare nodded.

"Well, Swincroft is a very small, close-knit village where people keep themselves to themselves. We were not getting anywhere with our house-to-house enquiries, so Inspector Rushwick, as he was then, asked me to go and talk to the staff and residents of Mallowcrest – it's a care home for the elderly. Catherine Duffield would almost certainly have walked past it on her way to and from the stores before she disappeared. Anyway, I went along to take statements but it was a frustrating and, frankly, depressing experience. All of the staff were too busy to have noticed a teenage girl walking past outside and the residents were either asleep or watching the television in the lounge, or too gaga to remember anything. Then I spoke to this very frail old lady called Doris. Her room overlooked the front of the building and she remembered looking out of the window and seeing a teenage girl with a bag of shopping get into a car right outside the home. She couldn't give me much of a description of the girl, only that she had fair hair, and she remembered the car as being 'dark'. She said she thought she recognised the driver – he sometimes came to the home – but didn't know his name or who he came to see. I tried to get a description of him from her but she was getting very tired and seemed quite confused.

"Anyway, when I'd finished there, I got into my car, put my notebook on the front seat and started to drive home. As I was nearly home, I remembered I needed to stock up on a couple of items – milk and bread, I think – so I stopped outside my local corner shop – it's just around the corner from here – and went inside to buy the stuff. I was only in there for a couple of minutes but I must've forgotten to lock my car because, when I came back to it, my notebook had disappeared – someone must've deliberately taken it, nothing else was missing. I asked around but nobody had seen anything unusual or suspicious. And my notebook never turned up.

"I went back to Mallowcrest a couple of days later to see Doris again and take a fresh statement only to be told that she had died the previous day. Then I remembered that everyone who came in to the home had to sign the visitors' book when they arrived and

I thought, perhaps if I could look through it, I might be able to draw up a short list of regular visitors but, when I asked to see it, I was told that it had disappeared, just like my notebook. I tried asking the manager if she could make a list of regular visitors but she wasn't very helpful; she said the information was confidential and that I'd need to make an official request in writing. Well, after my cock-up, that was the last thing I wanted to do, so I just filed a brief report saying that nobody at Mallowcrest had seen anything useful and left it at that. But, you see, Clive will wonder why my notebook is missing from the case notes. And, more importantly, my stupid negligence could've let the abductor get away and now look what's happening and it's all my fault."

Dick Beauregard blinked a couple of times and bowed his head. Clare waited for him to say something more but he just sat motionless with his head bowed.

"Oh, good God!" Clare muttered eventually. "Poor you! What a mess!"

"What are you going to do now?" Dick Beauregard whispered without opening his eyes.

"I'm going to tell Clive," Clare replied breezily, "that your notebook somehow got mislaid but that you may have an important new lead for him to follow up."

"Thank you," Dick Beauregard muttered. "Thank you so much!"

"Before I go," Clare added. "Did you have any theories at the time about who was abducting the girls?"

Dick Beauregard emitted a loud pitiable-sounding sigh. "No, not really; only the obvious one, Lenny Cave, although there was a journalist – he worked for the *Carlow Valley Gazette*; he still does. He's the editor now. He wrote a number of articles at the time, most of which were very critical of our handling of the case, and he included a lot of information that hadn't been made public. Now we reckoned he could only have got that information from someone in the force, or from the abductor."

"Or he was the abductor himself," Clare added impulsively. "Did you tell anyone about your concerns at the time?"

"Yes, I mentioned them to Inspector Rushwick and he said he shared my concerns and would inform Chief Superintendant Mencham but I never heard anything more."

"How intriguing! And what was the name of this journalist?"

"He was called Guy Sharston."

*

Although it was only a few miles between Stowbrook and Morstock, Clive soon discovered that following Alison Pawlett's car as it darted in and out of the traffic at high speed and accelerated rapidly around blind bends, was no less stressful than being driven by her. He was, therefore, greatly relieved, and not a little surprised, to arrive outside the Ashursts' house unscathed. Anxious to avoid betraying her undercover status to anyone who might be covertly watching, Alison Pawlett barely acknowledged her uniformed colleague as he stepped aside to allow her and Clive to enter the house.

Alan Ashurst was a short, podgy man with closely cropped, untidy grey hair, cold blue eyes and a ruddy complexion. His nose had the kind of flattened, squashed look that suggested it might have been broken in the past. His wife, Tessa, was taller and thinner with long, fair hair, tinged with grey, an oval face, lightly tinted, round glasses and a solemn demeanour. Their home, a modern detached house on a small estate on the outskirts of Morstock, was unexceptional but it had been furnished to a standard that suggested that the Ashursts enjoyed a relatively comfortable lifestyle. Their spacious living room had cream walls, a three-piece suite in beige and brown fabric and a large rug covered in black and white geometric patterns. A sliding glass door led out into a lean-to conservatory which contained a couple of cane chairs and a matching, glass-topped table. From what Clive could see of the back garden, it was tidy and functional, though it lacked both flair and colour, an indication perhaps that neither Alan nor Tessa Ashurst was a keen gardener.

Alison Pawlett made the usual introductions. "I'm Detective Sergeant Pawlett and this is Clive Walsingham, our Investigation Liaison Officer." Clive grimaced again as he and Alison sat down in the two matching chairs facing Alan and Tessa Ashurst who had arranged themselves neatly on the sofa.

"It's good of you to see us at such short notice," Clive began. "This must all be very difficult for you."

Alan Ashurst shrugged philosophically. "It's no problem. The police have advised us to stay indoors for the moment, in case anyone out there is gunning for us, and we were getting a bit bored so it's nice to have someone to chat to."

"I've been asked to lend a hand with the police investigation. As you can imagine, it is taking a lot of time and effort."

"I can imagine. It certainly knocked the wind out of our sails when we heard what had happened."

"Is it true they found another body today?" Tessa Ashurst asked in a tremulous, high-pitched voice.

Clive and Alison exchanged glances. "We understand so," Alison replied cautiously. "But we don't have many details yet."

"But it's another one of the parents, isn't it?"

"We're still waiting for a positive identification but…"

"Oh, God, this is so awful!" Tessa Ashurst's quiet voice sounded strained.

"It must be," Clive agreed before turning to Alan Ashurst. "I understand you'd arranged to meet somebody on Friday but they didn't show up. Can you tell me about it?" he asked.

"Yes, that's right," Alan Ashurst replied in a rasping voice. "I'd agreed to meet this person, whoever he or she was, in the car park next to Framingford Common at twelve o'clock on Friday. I took an extended lunch break and drove over there. I waited for about an hour but nobody showed up or phoned so I gave up and went back to work. I just thought it was some kind of cruel hoax – that is until the police turned up yesterday…"

"I think you had a lucky escape," Clive said.

"It would seem so," Alan Ashurst agreed.

"We'd like to know who contacted you, how and when." Alison Pawlett's tone was peremptory.

Alan Ashurst scratched his head and exhaled sharply. "Let me think! I got a text right out of the blue – it must have been towards the end of July, I suppose."

"Yes, that's right," his wife agreed. "It was just after we'd got back from holiday."

"What did the text say?" Alison Pawlett asked.

"I can't remember the exact wording, I'm afraid. I deleted it after Friday's little fiasco. But it said something like 'I know what happened to your daughter. If you'd like to find out, let me know and we can meet, but don't involve anyone else.'"

"And who sent you the text?" Clive asked.

"It was from somebody calling themselves 'Circe.'"

"Circe?" Clive repeated, looking puzzled. "Are you sure it wasn't 'circus'?"

"No, no, it was definitely 'Circe'; C-I-R-C-E." Alan Ashurst spelt the name out.

"Oh well, that explains something." Clive turned his head towards Alison Pawlett, who nodded her agreement. "Have you any idea who Circe is?"

"Absolutely none! We've never heard the name before and it put the wind up us a bit when he, or she, first made contact but Tessa and I discussed it and we felt… you know… we obviously weren't expecting to hear that Emily was alive after all this time but we felt... you know... that we wanted to know; we wanted closure. So I replied to 'Circe' and said that we'd like to know what had happened and would be keen to meet up and then he, or she, texted back suggesting Framingford Common at noon either on Thursday or Friday. He, or she, asked me to keep both days clear and to confirm that they were convenient, which I did."

"And when did, errm, this person confirm that the meeting was going to be on Friday?" Clive asked.

"Oh, I got a brief text on Tuesday morning. It said something like 'Friday at noon, Framingford Common, as agreed. Come alone.'"

"Have you kept any of the texts?" Alison Pawlett asked.

Alan Ashurst pulled a face. "No! As I said, I thought it was all a cruel hoax when nobody turned up on Friday. I was so annoyed that I deleted all the texts I'd received."

"I see. Is there any significance to Framingford Common as a location – is it somewhere that you visited or Emily knew?" Clive enquired.

"No, no, not at all – not as far as I know."

Clive paused sensing that Tessa Ashurst wanted to say something, but she remained silent, though her hands, which had been resting primly in her lap, began to twitch and fidget. "And while you waited there, you saw no one arrive or anyone acting suspiciously."

"No, not a thing!"

"Mmmm. Your mobile number – would it be known by a lot of people?"

Alan Ashurst scratched his head again. "Quite a few; I have a lot of contacts through my work..."

"What do you do?"

"I'm a computer programmer and, of course, we have a good many social contacts and..."

"I expect, when your daughter disappeared, you made a few new contacts. Did you keep in touch with anyone?"

Alan Ashurst glanced quickly at his wife. "We made a few contacts, certainly. I was in touch with the headmaster at Polbury Manor School, Mr Highcliffe, and his deputy, Mrs Calshott, for a while, and a couple of the other fathers who lost their daughters, Keith Draycott and Robert Huxton, until he moved on and lost interest. And there was a nosey journalist who worked for the *Carlow Valley Gazette* and kept pestering us for a while – name of Guy Sharston – and your colleagues in the police, of course. But we're not in contact with any of them these days."

"Your daughter, Emily – did she have a mobile phone with her when she disappeared?"

"Yes, it was virtually brand-new. We kept trying to call the number after she, er, disappeared but it was always switched off."

"Have you kept the same mobile number for the past ten years?"

Alan Ashurst looked puzzled. "Yes, yes, I think so. I've upgraded my phone a couple of times but always kept the same number."

"So whoever abducted your daughter could have got your mobile number from her phone?"

"I guess so."

"Mr and Mrs Ashurst, I need to be frank with you," Clive spoke with what he hoped was the necessary gravitas. "We are pretty sure that three parents of the girls who went missing ten years ago have been murdered in the last few days and another one is missing. The same fate could have befallen you on Friday but, for some reason, it seems the murderer failed to show up. Now I must stress that it is vitally important that you cast your minds back to when your daughter disappeared, however painful and difficult that is for you both, and you must tell us of anything that happened, however trivial or irrelevant it seemed at the time, that might lead us to whoever has murdered these people. For a start, can I ask you to go over the events of the day when your daughter disappeared?"

"Yes, well... I was at work all day," Alan Ashurst replied rather dismissively. "When I got home in the evening, Emily had already left to do her babysitting stint, or so we thought."

"Then maybe your wife can help us." Clive turned towards Tessa Ashurst who had been maintaining a largely tight-lipped, meek silence. "Perhaps you could tell Sergeant Pawlett what happened that day?"

Tessa Ashurst bit her lip nervously, glanced at her husband, raised her glasses, dabbed at her moist eyes and began her account, quietly and hesitantly.

"I don't, er, remember that much about the first part of the day. I worked part-time in those days..."

"What as?" Alison Pawlett asked.

"I worked in the finance department of Carlow Valley Council – I still do. Anyway, when I got in around lunchtime, Emily was up in her room – I could hear her moving about. We exchanged 'hellos' and that was about it for a while. Then, a little later, she went to see her friend, Maxine, who lived a bit further down the road. They often used to meet up during the school holidays."

"I'll need Maxine's details," Alison Pawlett said abruptly.

"Yes, well, er, I gave your people all the information at the time. I'm sure you'll have it on file. Her name was Maxine Padfield. I've no idea where she is now. She got married and moved away some while ago. I don't know her married name. Anyway, Emily came back home around half-past four, I think, and went up to her room for a while. Then she came down and had a meal around sixish – I made her an omelette – and then she set off about 6.45 and we never saw her again..." Tessa Ashurst looked away and closed her eyes briefly.

"Who was she babysitting for?" Clive asked quietly.

"What? Or, er, my friend Rachel. She lived about half a mile away. She had a five-year-old daughter, Ellen. She and her husband, Roger, were going to some kind of social gathering connected with his work and asked Emily if she could babysit for her. Well Emily was quite keen; she adored Ellen and she got a bit of useful pocket money."

"Had she done that sort of thing before?"

"A couple of times, yes. She enjoyed it – I think she used to indulge Ellen a bit – and Roger would always bring her home at the end of the evening."

"So what happened on this occasion?"

"I got a call from Rachel, just after 7.30, asking where Emily was. Well, obviously we went frantic. It was only a ten-minute walk to Rachel's and Emily should have been there by seven. We kept trying her mobile, we followed the route she would have taken, we phoned her friends, we went around the town calling out for her but nothing – absolutely nothing."

"Who would have known that Emily was babysitting that evening?" Clive asked.

"Oh, er, apart from us and Rachel and Roger, I'm not sure. She probably told Maxine and maybe one or two of her other friends but I really don't know…"

"And was there anything unusual at all about Emily's behaviour that day? As I said earlier, anything, however small or insignificant it seemed at the time, might help."

"No, no," Alan Ashurst replied confidently. "As we told the police at the time, she was behaving as she usually did."

"Well, er, except, er, there was something…" Tessa Ashurst added, tentatively.

"What do you mean? What are you saying?" Alan Ashurst demanded, his ruddy complexion suddenly turning blotchy.

"I'm so sorry, Alan. I know I should have told you before but… I was all over the place at the time, so worried about Emily that I couldn't think straight. But, thinking about it all later, yes, there was something, something that might be important."

"Oh for God's sake – after all these years, you suddenly remember something!" Alan Ashurst exploded, perspiration breaking out freely on his broad forehead.

"I know, I know," Tessa Ashurst replied timidly, her bottom lip quavering as she tried to hold back the tears. "As I said, my emotions were shot to pieces and then the other girls started to disappear, and… oh, I don't know… But the more I thought about it, the more I began to think that something wasn't quite right. Emily had been behaving a bit strangely for two or three days – a bit withdrawn, not as communicative as usual – nothing especially unusual for a girl of her age, of course, and then, the day before she disappeared, I overheard her on her mobile. She had her door closed and I couldn't hear everything that she said but I remember her saying that she was worried about something and she asked if she could meet up and that's all I heard…"

"Oh, for God's sake!" Alan Ashurst stood up and started pacing the room, his heavy tread leaving indentations in the black and white rug. He clenched his fist and thumped it into the back of the sofa. "Why the hell have you waited ten bloody years before you mention this to anyone?"

"Well, I, er…" Tessa Ashurst hesitated.

"And you don't know who she was speaking to?" Alison asked quickly.

"No, I've no idea."

"Did she have a boyfriend?"

"No, no one serious; she knew a few boys at school, of course, but they were only casual acquaintances."

"And you've no idea what she was worried about?"

"No, no idea!" Tessa Ashurst bit her lip and looked at the floor as her husband continued to pace up and down, repeatedly thumping the clenched fist of one hand into the open palm of the other.

*

Clare found Beth Wroxham sitting on the terrace, with a cup of coffee on the table beside her, enjoying the last of the day's sun.

"Hello, Beth!" she said cheerfully as she walked over to where the young woman was sitting and pulled out a chair. "Do you mind if I join you?"

Beth Wroxham looked up at her uncertainly, half squinting in the low, late afternoon sunlight. There was a pink tinge in her hazel eyes. "Err, n-no, I suppose not. I'm just having my afternoon break."

Clare smiled reassuringly. "That's fine! I just wanted to know how you were feeling today."

"Oh, a bit better than I was yesterday," Beth replied with no great conviction. "I just find it all sooo sad, sooo tragic, what's happened to those poor girls and to their parents."

"Well, it's about that I wanted to chat to you."

"Omigod! No!" Beth gasped as she clapped both hands to her cheeks. "I can't…"

"Do you remember Edward Duffield?" Clare persisted. "He stayed in room 13 after Olivia Farringdon checked out."

"Omigod!" Beth repeated. "Has he been, you know, has he been…? Has anything happened to him?"

"He's gone missing and he was the father of Catherine Duffield, one of the girls—"

"Who went missing." Beth Wroxham finished Clare's sentence before busting into tears.

Clare slid her chair alongside Beth's, placed a protective arm around her shaking shoulders and whispered gently, "I wouldn't ask you, Beth, except that you serviced Edward Duffield's room while he was here and you might have seen something important – something that may help the police to track down who was responsible."

"What about the other parents?" Beth gasped between sobs. "Is there any news?"

Clare pulled a face and chewed her lip thoughtfully. She wasn't sure how much she should tell Beth especially as she was obviously in an extremely fragile emotional state. On the other hand, she did need to impress upon her the potential gravity of the situation.

"Edward Duffield is missing, as is the mother of one of the other girls, so you see it is important!"

"Omigod! I can't do this, I really can't!" Beth Wroxham lowered her head and sobbed, her long, light brown hair twitching with each violent sob.

"I just need to know what you saw in Edward Duffield's room," Clare persisted. "It is so very important."

Beth Wroxham glanced up at Clare, who still had a protective arm around her shoulders. Feeling Clare's grip tightening slightly, she realised that she was trapped. Clare was not going to leave until she gave her the information she was seeking. She took a couple of swigs of tepid coffee, breathed heavily a couple of times, brushed some moisture from her eyes and sniffed loudly before she spoke.

"I don't really remember that much about Edward Duffield or his room," she began slowly. "At the time, he just seemed like another anonymous businessman passing through. I-I do remember not much liking what I saw though. The room didn't, er, smell very nice, sort of stale and sweaty. And it was very untidy. There were a couple of newspapers thrown across the bed – copies of the *Racing Post*, I think – and some screwed-up betting slips on the floor. And there was a half-empty bottle of cheap scotch on his bedside table. And I remember that there were two mobile phones on the windowsill, both the same make but one was blue and the other was red. And I thought it strange that he'd gone out and left not one, but two mobiles behind. And… and…"

Beth Wroxham seemed to be struggling to speak. She swallowed hard a couple of times and tried to say something but, apart from a couple of small guttural noises, she remained quiet.

"Are you alright?" Clare asked.

"Actually, n-no, I'm not feeling at all well," Beth Wroxham spluttered. "I'm feeling quite dizzy. I-I t-think perhaps I'd better go and lie down for a while." She grasped the edge of the table while she struggled to her feet, took a couple of unsteady paces across the terrace, then swayed slightly and collapsed with a thump onto the ground.

*

Gary Beechwood's traditional Sunday roast had proved to be a little too substantial for Alison Pawlett. As Clive approached, she drained her wine glass, placed her serviette neatly on the table and sat back heavily in her chair. "I don't think I could eat another thing," she announced as she patted her stomach.

Clive smiled indulgently. "We don't like our guests to go hungry." He glanced at his watch. "Alison, I know it's getting late and all you probably want to do is get up to your room and rest after that meal, but I think we should adjourn briefly to the office and review the day's events before we all start to doze off. I've organised some coffee."

Nodding reluctantly, Alison rose slowly to her feet and plodded into the office where Clare was waiting. They just had time to indulge in a few bland pleasantries before Clive returned with a tray of coffee and closed the office door behind him. "So, have your colleagues confirmed that the body they found this morning is Edward Duffield?" he asked Alison casually as he poured the coffee and handed the cups round. Clare emitted an audible gasp at the news.

"Yes they have," Alison replied as she wedged herself uncomfortably into what suddenly felt like a particularly small office chair. "They found his body in Lannock Woods this morning. His car was in a nearby car park. The pathologist reckons he's been dead for about a week."

"His body was lying there for a week and nobody noticed?" Clive asked doubtfully.

Alison nodded. "It appears so. Lannock Woods is a pretty remote spot and not especially attractive at this time of the year – it can get very muddy underfoot. And the killer knows his territory pretty well. The spot where they found the body is pretty secluded and the killer had made a good job of hiding it. Besides, we only realised he was missing a couple of days ago, so nobody was looking for him until then."

"So he was probably murdered not long after he checked out of here, just like Olivia Farringdon. And was it the same modus operandi as the others?" Clive asked as he shuffled past a large box on his desk and perched precariously on his stool, banging his elbow against the wall as he did so.

"Yes; he had been battered over the head, half buried under some bracken and any personal belongings he had with him – wallet, phone – had been taken. There was nothing much in his car of any interest, just a suitcase with some clothes, probably the one he had with him when he checked out of here, and a nearly empty bottle of scotch. There were several sets of tyre tracks in the car park but, given that the body had been in the woods for about a week, it will be difficult to get anything positive. And there were some fairly indistinct footprints near where we found the body – but getting a match won't be easy."

"So, the same modus operandi as the others," Clive reflected aloud. "The victim is disposed of in some remote woodland, their body is found a few days later, they have been battered around the head and their car is found in a nearby car park. Only, whereas Olivia Farringdon and Edward Duffield both checked out of here and, we assume, drove off to meet with their killer,

Keith Draycott, who lived locally, crept out of his house early in the morning and probably walked to Stowbrook Forest for his fatal assignation."

"And somebody put a newspaper article in his pocket a couple of days after he was killed," Alison Pawlett added importantly.

"Mmmm, that remains a bit of a puzzle, so let's move on for the moment!" Clive replied. "Who is Edward Duffield's next of kin?"

"His wife, Sonia, has been informed. She's making arrangements to travel down here tomorrow."

"Good. I'd like to know what your colleagues find out – maybe I could have a word with her at some stage, if it is okay with Superintendant Rushwick and Mrs Duffield is up to it."

"I'll have a word," Alison Pawlett affirmed.

"My God, this is so awful!" Clare muttered. "I tried to talk to Beth earlier, you know, to see if there was anything in Edward Duffield's room that might help us, like the way she found the word 'circus' written on a piece of paper in Olivia Farringdon's room."

"And?" Clive asked.

Clare frowned. "Nothing much, unfortunately! It seems that our Mr Duffield was a gambler who drank quite heavily but Beth did mention that he left two mobile phones on the windowsill when he went out, which seemed odd and…"

"I suppose he could have had one for his work and one for his social life," Clive mused. "A lot of people do, but wouldn't he take at least one phone with him when he went out?"

"Unless he had a third phone," Alison ventured.

"Yes, that's a thought," Clive agreed. "Maybe our Mr Duffield was leading a particularly complex and tangled life." He turned to Clare. "Did Beth say anything else?"

"Well, er, no. She actually got very distressed when she started to talk about Edward Duffield – strangely so, I thought – and then she said she wasn't feeling well. She got up to leave and she fainted. She banged her head when she fell."

"Oh, that's dreadful," Clive replied. "How awful! How is she now?"

"Resting, I hope. She's got a bit of a bruise on her forehead but no serious damage done from the fall. Jamie and I got her to her room and sat with her for a few minutes while she recovered. I've told her to get some rest and, if she's still feeling faint and dizzy in the morning, she should see a doctor."

"Yes, she should," Clive agreed. "I can't believe that she'd get so upset about Edward Duffield; somebody who, as far as we know, she'd never met. I suspect there's something else going on. Meanwhile, is there any more news on Kate Huxton?"

Alison Pawlett wrinkled her nose and shook her head. "She's still listed as missing so the search continues. We've traced a taxi driver who says he drove a woman answering her description from Fleetdale station to Morstock on Saturday 6th September but there have been no positive sightings since."

"And what about Mr and Mrs Ashurst?" Clare asked. "Are they safe?"

"Yes, the police are looking after them. We spoke to them earlier," Clive confirmed. "They hadn't got very much of interest to tell us about their daughter's disappearance except that Mrs Ashurst thought her daughter was worried about something shortly before she disappeared and that she might have arranged to meet someone. I sensed she wanted to say more but was feeling intimidated by her husband, who clearly has a bit of a temper."

"Didn't she mention that at the time her daughter disappeared?"

"Apparently not! She claimed that she was confused and not thinking straight at the time but I'm pretty sure she knows more than she's saying."

"And did they tell you what happened on Friday?"

Clive exhaled. "Yes, that was quite interesting. I suspect that our killer contacted all of his victims in a similar way. He sent each of them a text telling them that he knew what had happened to their daughter and suggesting that they arranged to meet. Then he suggested two, maybe more, possible dates, probably on consecutive days and didn't confirm which one it was going to be until no more than a couple of days in advance, probably to keep his victims guessing until almost the last minute. Maybe that explains why Olivia Farringdon and Edward Duffield both decided to make a reservation for several nights. It seems our killer deliberately chose somewhere pretty remote for each meeting — and there are quite a few to choose from around here — so I suspect he's local. And then, when they met, he bludgeoned each one to death, except for Alan Ashurst who says he arrived on time for his meeting, waited for an hour but no one turned up."

"So the murderer could try again?" Clare asked while increasingly struggling to keep hold of her turbulent emotions.

"That's our thinking," Alison Pawlett confirmed. "But, as Clive said, we're giving Mr and Mrs Ashurst round-the-clock protection."

"The other interesting thing about the way Alan Ashurst was contacted is that the individual used the name 'Circe'. I suspect that's what Olivia Farringdon had written down — Beth probably misread it — but I'm afraid it means nothing to me."

Alison gave Clive a smug look. "Ah, well, I looked that up when we got back and apparently Circe is a goddess of magic in Greek mythology. She is a sorceress who uses magic and potions to transform her enemies, usually men, into beasts."

"Wow! Excellent work!" Clive exclaimed appreciatively. "That might explain why Olivia Farringdon and Keith Draycott both had books about Greek and Roman mythology. Unfortunately, it doesn't tell us who our murderer is or why he's calling himself 'Circe.'"

"Except that it could be a woman," Clare suggested. "You said Circe was a sorceress."

"Possibly," Clive agreed reluctantly. In his experience, the nature of the murders suggested the killer was a man but he didn't want to dampen Clare's enthusiasm. "And how did you get on with Detective Inspector Beauregard?"

Clare looked perplexed. "Well it was a very strange visit. For a start, Dick lives in a pokey, dingy flat; it's what I can only describe as a rather squalid bachelor pad, and the decor is truly dreadful – it's no wonder he keeps the curtains closed. He said his partner had been called away for a few days but there was no sign of a female presence around the place. I reckon he's been living on his own there for quite some time, existing on takeaway meals and flat beer."

"Do you know anything about Dick's personal circumstances?" Clive asked Alison.

"No, not really!" Alison replied. "Dick never wants to talk about his private life. He's mentioned a 'partner' occasionally but I don't recall seeing her… or him. And he's never invited me to his place."

"Count yourself lucky!" Clare remarked with some feeling. "Anyway I did manage to drag out of him that there had been a bit of a cock-up with his notebook during the original investigation and he's now worried that it'll come to light and he'll be in trouble."

"What happened?" Clive asked.

"Well, I'm not too clear about the details," Clare replied, slightly mendaciously. "Apparently, Dick was tasked with taking statements from the staff and residents at this residential care home for the elderly – Mallowcrest – in Swincroft, which Catherine Duffield probably walked past on the morning she went missing. Anyway, there was one elderly resident called Doris who thought she saw a girl with fair hair getting into a car outside the home on that particular morning. She couldn't identify the car and she didn't know the name of the driver but she thought he was someone who used to visit the home. Anyway, Dick's notebook went missing somehow and, when he went back to the home to talk to the old lady again, he was told that she had died the previous day and, on top of that, the visitors' book had disappeared. I think he feels responsible for screwing up what might have been an important lead."

"Oh shit – so near and yet so far! I can certainly see now why Dick is feeling stressed. If it emerges that his carelessness caused the kidnapper to avoid arrest, you can imagine what the reaction will be," Clive observed ruefully. "I think it might be worth paying another visit to Mallowcrest. Ten years is a long time and there won't be any residents who were there then but, maybe, there'll be a member of staff or two?"

"It's a long shot but I'll do it," Alison replied enthusiastically, clearly disenchanted with her undercover role and keen to do some proper police work. "I'll give them a call in the morning."

"So what are we going to do about Dick now?" Clive asked Clare.

"Well, I told him that you'd be the one looking over the original case notes and that you were not obliged to tell Superintendant Rushwick everything you found and—"

"Yes, that reminds me," Clive interrupted. "Superintendant Rushwick was going to send me all the original case notes but I haven't seen them."

Clare threw back her head and laughed. "Now, remind me, Clive. You were once a detective inspector who was famous for his powers of observation?"

"Yes, I suppose I was," Clive replied warily, suspecting a trap. "Although I wasn't infallible and that was a little while ago."

"So you haven't noticed that then?" Still laughing, Clare pointed to a large cardboard box, positioned on the office desk just behind Alison's head. "You walked past it on your way in. It came by special police courier a couple of hours ago."

After a moment or two of embarrassed silence, Clive joined in the laughter. "There, you see! I said I wasn't infallible."

"Now I don't want to push myself forward or anything," Clare spoke diffidently. "But you and Alison are going to be out there talking to people and doing the official police stuff and, well, I couldn't do that, but I would be quite happy to stay here and take a look through these notes to see, you know, if anything strikes me as odd or might be worth following up."

Clive tugged his earlobe and looked quizzically at Alison.

"It would be highly irregular," Alison replied in her formal police voice. "But then there's a lot about this case that is already highly irregular so, I suppose…"

"Good," Clare replied enthusiastically. "I'll make a start tomorrow. And I think you'll find that Dick would be quite receptive if you were to contact him and ask if he could help you both in some small, unofficial way that Superintendant Rushwick need not know about."

"Excellent!" Clive enthused. "I'll talk to him tomorrow. And, talking of tomorrow—"

"There is—" Clare tried to interrupt but her husband was in full flow.

"Tomorrow, I'd like to talk to Kenneth Highcliffe, if he can be traced and—"

"Dick said something else—" Clare tried to interrupt again but with no more success than on her previous attempt.

"And I'd like to see ex-Chief Superintendant Mencham if we can track him down and he's amenable – I'd better do that one on my own because I'm told he won't speak to anyone in the police, and—"

"Can I just—" Clare tried and failed for the third time, thumping her fist on the desk in frustration.

"Alison, are you happy to contact the people at Mallowcrest and can you try and found out what your colleagues have been able to glean from Sonia Duffield and whether it would be in order for me to speak to her?"

Alison Pawlett nodded a little wearily. Tired and a little bloated following a long, difficult day and a substantial meal, she felt somewhat overwhelmed by Clive's seemingly boundless energy and organisational talents. "I'll do what I can," she replied weakly. "But I've already made arrangements for you to see Kenneth Highcliffe, I've got a phone number for Ian Mencham and I'm in touch with headquarters about Sonia Duffield and…"

"Good," Clive replied rubbing his hands together enthusiastically. "And Clare, you'll be happy to start looking through all the old case notes?"

"I will if you give me a chance to say something else first."

Clive recognised the frisson of anger in Clare's voice. "Of course, darling, I'm sorry, I didn't realise…"

"You're starting to sound like Superintendant Rushwick," Alison observed caustically. "You're not listening!"

Clive was about to say something more but Alison's remark stopped him abruptly. "Oh shit, you're right, Alison. I'm so sorry! You want to tell us something, Clare?"

"Well, I would quite like to. You see, when I was talking to Dick, he mentioned that, during the original investigation, there was a local journalist who worked for the *Carlow Valley Gazette*. Apparently he wrote a number of articles which contained facts of some kind, he didn't say what they were, that the police had not released to anyone. Dick was pretty sure he was getting inside information from someone but, it seems, nobody was prepared to take any action."

"Mmm; that's interesting. Maybe I'll raise that with Ian Mencham if I get to speak with him. Did Dick say who this journalist was?"

"Yes, he said his name was Guy Sharston."

"Guy Sharston?" Clive replied quickly. "That's the second time I've heard that name today. Hang on, where's that newspaper article we found in Keith Draycott's pocket?" He scrambled over to his desk, leaned across Alison and rummaged through a heap of untidy papers until he found what he was looking for. "Yes, here we are," he cried triumphantly. "*Carlow Valley Prepares for Arts Festival* by Guy Sharston!"

Eight

Clive grabbed an empty plate, glanced guiltily over his shoulder and quickly loaded it with a fried egg, two rashers of bacon, a couple of sausages, a tomato and some mushrooms. He then crept stealthily from the kitchen, juggling the hot plate in one hand and clutching a mug of coffee in the other and, looking sheepish, tiptoed into the office. Clare was waiting for him.

"Starting the day with a light, healthy breakfast?" Clare teased, her grey-green eyes glowing with mischief.

Clive jumped, his jaw dropped and a contrite look quickly spread across his face. He was only too aware that Clare had been trying to wean him away from the full English breakfast, of which he was so fond, onto something a little healthier and lighter and, every time he succumbed, he felt ashamed. "Ah well, I, er…" he stuttered. "This is my detective's breakfast. My brain seems to function better when I've had a full English breakfast. Besides I've got a busy day today and I don't know whether I'll have time for any lunch."

Clare smiled benevolently as she glanced down at Clive's yellow trousers. "I'll believe you! Let's just hope that this case doesn't drag on too long or your waistline will expand and you'll need to replace all your trousers. For myself, I wouldn't mind about those yellow ones, or the pink ones, the orange ones, the turquoise ones, even the red ones, but I quite like some of your less colourful trousers. Anyway, what's the plan for today?"

Clive sat down, speared a piece of sausage with his fork and thrust it quickly into his mouth as though fearing that Clare was about to snatch it away. "Well, Alison has tracked down ex-head teacher Kenneth Highcliffe. He lives in Swincroft apparently. So I'm going to get through a bit of work here over breakfast, because I am very much aware that we are still trying to run a hotel, and then I'm driving over to Swincroft to talk to Mr Highcliffe."

"Is Alison going with you?" Clare asked, with the hint of a smirk.

Clive half choked on his piece of sausage. "Alison? No, definitely not! She'll insist on driving. No, no, Alison is going to keep in touch with her headquarters to find out as much as she can about Sonia Duffield and ask if I can talk to her later on and then she's going to try and speak to ex-Chief Superintendant Ian Mencham and sound him out about me paying him a visit and, after that, if all goes well, she's going to contact Mallowcrest to talk to the staff there and…"

"Isn't Mallowcrest in Swincroft?" Clare asked, deliberately sounding a little suspicious.

"That's right!" Clive replied smiling. "And then Alison and I might meet up over a sandwich and…"

"So you are going to find time for lunch!" Clare retorted, teasingly.

"Possibly," Clive conceded grudgingly. "But it's by no means certain – either of us could get delayed. Oh, and I'll try and make contact with Dick. I think I might have a job for him if he's interested."

"That's a good idea," Clare agreed. "He needs to get out of that awful flat."

"And you'll be going through the old case notes?" Clive asked.

"Yes, I'm quite looking forward to it. Is there anything in particular that I should be looking out for?"

Clive tugged his earlobe while quickly demolishing some more of his breakfast. "I'm really curious about how the girls who disappeared were selected by our abductor and what his motives were. Most often, when teenage girls are abducted, the motive is clearly sexual but it is unusual for five girls to be abducted in such a short period of time – no more than a few weeks – and then for the abductions to suddenly stop, assuming that Lennie Cave was not the abductor. It makes me wonder if there might have been another reason. And why these particular girls? Did the abductor happen to stumble across them or were they deliberately selected and, if so, why? I suppose it would have been possible to mingle with the parents outside Polbury Manor School and select a couple of girls who looked vulnerable, maybe, or who he might already have known for some reason; but what about the others? Did he hang around the campsite at Corwood waiting for the right girl to wander into the shower block? Surely someone would have noticed. How did he know that Emily Ashurst was going to a babysitting assignment that night in Stowbrook? Was he the person she had secretly arranged to meet? And then what about Catherine Duffield? Was it just a chance encounter outside Mallowcrest, or did he know her as well?"

"So you don't want much then?"

Clive smiled. "No, no; just make a note of anything you come across that seems strange or that you think might be worth following up and we can talk it through when I get back later. By the way, have you heard anything from Beth this morning? I haven't seen her around."

Clare frowned. "Yes, she popped down a bit earlier. She looked very pale and delicate and quite down, which isn't like her. She said she was feeling a bit better but she hadn't slept very well and was still feeling a bit dizzy. I thought she ought to see a doctor so I arranged a taxi for her. I haven't seen her come back yet!"

*

Alison Pawlett had ordered a poached egg for breakfast, which was duly served with a flamboyant flourish by Jamie Coulton, who gave her the benefit of a sly wink as he placed the food in front of her. Alison had selected a table by a window overlooking the rear gardens of the hotel. She figured that gazing out across the lawn to the rose gardens beyond and the herbaceous borders that ran in front of the old walled kitchen garden would somehow be more entertaining and rewarding than trying to spy on the hotel's guests as they wandered in and out of the dining room. If any of them had some kind of guilty secret, then they were certainly concealing it well.

As she ate her way methodically through her poached egg, washed down with plenty of coffee, Alison noticed a grey van pull slowly into the hotel car park and stop. The driver's door opened and a short stocky man with wavy dark hair emerged, walked round to the rear of the van, opened the doors and hauled out several gardening implements including a spade, a hoe and a rake, together with a wooden toolbox with a carrying handle, which Alison presumed contained some smaller gardening accoutrements.

Alison watched the man intently as he wandered into the herbaceous border and began pottering. Most of the time, he was working with his back to the car park and, every two or three minutes, he would turn round and study it as though he was expecting someone to arrive. On a couple of occasions, a vehicle drove into the car park – the first was a guest arriving in his car and the second was a van making a delivery to the hotel – and, on each occasion, as soon as he heard the vehicle arrive and a door slam, the man abandoned what he was doing and, with a quick nervous glance over his shoulder, ran towards the shed, which stood against the wall of the kitchen garden, and went inside, closing the door firmly behind him. In both instances, he remained inside for several minutes, finally emerging, slowly and cautiously, only when he was satisfied that the driver had either disappeared into the hotel or had driven away.

A little later, as she was draining the dregs of her third cup of coffee, Alison noticed Clive striding quickly towards his car, clutching a black leather briefcase in one hand and brandishing his car key on a plastic fob in the other. Casually throwing his briefcase onto the passenger seat, he got into the driver's seat and slammed the door. Immediately, the gardener, who had been working on his hands and knees in a flower bed, leapt to his feet, raced to the shed and disappeared inside.

*

Kenneth Highcliffe greeted Clive warmly enough as he opened the front door of his white-painted cottage. He was of medium height with wavy grey hair, heavily rimmed glasses, dark brown eyes and an avuncular expression. The scruffiness of his clothes, in assorted shades of brown and grey, together with the fact that he was wearing gloves, suggested that he had recently been working in his garden.

"I've arranged for us to sit in the garden, if that's acceptable," Kenneth Highcliffe announced in a quiet voice and with what Clive thought was the hint of a Yorkshire accent. "Only my wife is, erm, indoors and she's quite frail these days and I don't want her getting agitated or flustered and besides, it's a pleasant enough day."

Clive glanced towards the heavens, where small patches of insipid blue sky were being overrun by swathes of heavy, grey clouds. He shivered. "Yes that's fine," he announced uncertainly. "Lead on!"

Kenneth Highcliffe opened a white-painted side gate and led Clive along the side of the cottage into his rear garden. It was not especially big but was full of mature plants and shrubs. An elderly wisteria, well past its best by mid-September, climbed erratically up the cottage wall, meandered above the upstairs window frames and cascaded down both sides of the back door. The borders were crammed with roses of various hues and perfumes, many of them still in full bloom. A few late summer bees flitted contentedly among the flowers and any number of small garden birds regularly fluttered to and from a couple of feeders hanging from a heavily laden apple tree. Kenneth Highcliffe wandered over to a rustic seat close to one of his lovingly cultivated flower borders and sat down with a heavy sigh.

"It's good of you to see me," Clive gushed as he sat down, realising immediately that the rustic seat was more pleasing to the eye than it was to the buttocks. "I imagine Sergeant Pawlett told you why I'm here."

"Is that her name?" Kenneth Highcliffe asked. "I'm not very good with names these days and she was a little abrupt. But yes, I know why you are here. I had hoped never to hear or speak about that awful business again, but I understand you've reopened the case."

"Sadly, yes. There have been some recent developments. The police thought at the time that a known sex offender called Lennie Cave was responsible but now it seems that might not be the case."

"Ah, yes, I remember Lennie Cave – a most unpleasant individual. Occasionally, he'd hang around the school gates in the afternoon, as all the pupils were leaving. We had to call the police a couple of times to remove him."

"It must have been a very difficult time for you, when the girls disappeared."

Kenneth Highcliffe shook his head sadly. "It was truly dreadful. We had the police crawling all over the place, talking to the staff and the students, we had a media scrum outside, hounding us wherever we went, we had angry parents demanding to know why we had allowed this… this business to occur and pointing accusing fingers at all kinds of perfectly innocent people and we had a bit of hysteria amongst some of the girls. It was unbelievably awful."

"Were accusing fingers pointed at you?" Clive asked pointedly.

"Oh yes, some were. I was called a filthy pervert by more than one angry parent," Kenneth Highcliffe replied with a sad shake of his head.

"Any particular reason?"

"I was head teacher at a school which three of the missing girls attended and lived in the village where another one disappeared so I was deemed to be guilty by association, I suppose. And, of course, because I was head teacher and in a position of authority, it was assumed that I was well placed to take advantage of the girls. Do you know, I'd been head teacher of Polbury Manor for nearly twelve years when all of this happened and there hadn't been a hint of scandal or inappropriate behaviour in all of that time? It was all very sad… In the end, you know, I became a virtual prisoner in my own school. Every time I stepped outside, I got accosted by an angry parent or some unpleasant journalist determined to get a story, even if the truth had to be sacrificed along the way. But Christine was marvellous…"

"Christine?"

"Christine Calshott, my deputy head. She was brilliant. She seemed far better able to talk to the press and placate the parents than I ever could; she always knew exactly what to say. And it helped being a woman, of course – everyone assumed the kidnapper was a man – so she was above suspicion. In the end, I'm afraid I took the line of least resistance, a decision of which I am not proud. I retreated more and more to my office and let Christine run the show."

"What happened to her?"

"When I retired, she expected to become the new head but she was overlooked for some reason, I don't know why, and resigned in a bit of a huff. She still lives locally, I believe, but I haven't had any contact with her for a long time. I don't know what she's doing with herself these days."

"Mmm, I see," Clive replied though, in truth, he wasn't seeing anything particularly clearly. He decided on a change of tack. "Did you actually teach any of the girls yourself?"

"What me? Good gracious, no!" Kenneth Highcliffe looked astonished. "I mean, I taught when I was much younger but that was before I came to Polbury Manor."

"What was your subject?"

"History – ancient history mainly – and classics, although there's not much call for…"

"So you would have known a lot about Greek and Roman mythology?"

"Quite a bit I suppose, but that was a long time ago. I don't think I could remember much now. Why do you ask?"

"We think the girls' abductor may have known a bit about ancient myths…"

"I hope you're not accusing me of…" For the first time, Kenneth Highcliffe showed a flash of anger.

"No, no!" Clive was quick to reassure him. "Not at all! I'm not accusing you of anything. I'm just trying to get a fuller picture. Tell me, how well did you know the girls who disappeared?"

Kenneth Highcliffe puffed out his cheeks. "Well, it was ten years ago and, as I said, my memory isn't quite what it used to be. I didn't know Emily Ashurst that well. She was in the same class as Charlotte Huxton and I think the two were quite good friends for a while – they both went to the same youth club, together with another girl, Maxine Padfield – but I'm told they'd fallen out over something at the end of the summer term. I don't know what caused the rift; boys, probably – it usually was. I think Emily's class teacher thought she might have been the victim of some domestic violence – she turned up with bruises on her face a couple of times – but she said it was just an accident and no further action was taken."

"And Charlotte Huxton?"

"Ah, Charlotte!" Kenneth Highcliffe stopped talking for a moment and gazed thoughtfully at the ground. "Yes, I knew Charlotte Huxton. She was quite bright but she wasted her talents. She was a bit of a troublemaker, you see. She was the middle one of three sisters and I think her parents were finding it a bit difficult to cope with three teenage daughters. Charlotte could be spiteful and she could be rebellious. She quite often stayed at a friend's house overnight because she couldn't face going back home."

"Any particular friend?" Clive asked while shifting his position on the seat to alleviate some numbness in his right buttock.

"Well, the friend her mother thought she was staying with on the day she disappeared was Karen; what was her surname? Let me think, er," Kenneth Highcliffe tapped his temple with his forefinger. "Yes that's right, it was Beechwood – Karen Beechwood. I understood that Charlotte's elder sister, Victoria, was quite friendly with Karen's elder brother, if you know what I mean."

"And do you know the name of Karen Beechwood's brother?"

"Yes, he was called Gary. He was a sixth-former at Polbury Manor at the time the girls disappeared. He fancied himself as a bit of a charmer by all accounts. In my view, he should have spent a bit more time studying and a bit less time flirting."

"Gary Beechwood?" Clive repeated slowly. "Bloody hell!"

"Everything alright?" Kenneth Highcliffe asked solicitously.

"What? Oh yes, it's just that I've come across Gary Beechwood in another context as it were. Tell me about Isabel Draycott."

"Ah, Isabel, or Issy, as everyone called her! I felt quite sorry for her. She was a very bright girl but, as I'm sure you know, she lost her mother in a motoring accident and her father, Keith, struggled to bring her up on his own. He was working full-time and didn't really give Issy the attention she needed. She became quite withdrawn and, I think, quite lonely. She had difficulty settling into her new class at the start of term and started to take time off. She claimed she was sick, but I suspect her symptoms were more emotional than physical. She'd been off school the two days before she disappeared and when she didn't show up on that fateful Wednesday morning, her teachers assumed that she was still off sick. It was only when her father phoned to check that she was okay that we realised something was wrong. Very sad!" Once again, Kenneth Highcliffe shook his head sadly.

"How well did you know the parents of the missing girls?"

"Mr and Mrs Ashurst? Hardly at all – they came to parents' evenings and that's about all we saw of them. I didn't really know Mrs Huxton at all until her daughter disappeared. I think she got quite a hard time from people who thought she should have been keeping a closer eye on her daughter under the circumstances. Funnily enough, I knew Robert Huxton quite well. We were having a new science wing built that summer and Robert was the architect – he often dropped by to check that the building was going okay."

"So you had builders on site that summer?" Clive asked quickly, sensing a new line of inquiry opening up.

"Yes, during the holidays mainly; the aim was to get the work finished by the start of the new term, which we almost did. I think it was mainly the electricians who were still working on site when we reopened but I don't think..."

"And who were the electricians?"

"A local company called Finnarts – they're still around; you may have heard of them."

"Bloody hell!" Clive exclaimed for the second time. "Yes, I've certainly heard of them."

Kenneth Highcliffe bowed his head and Clive thought he closed his eyes briefly as though the effort of recalling the events of a decade ago was proving too gruelling.

"And how well did you know Keith Draycott?" Clive resumed after a brief, respectful silence.

"I knew Keith quite well – he was a lovely man. Occasionally, he'd come and talk to the pupils at assembly. I don't think he made many converts but he was usually quite entertaining. And he helped me and Christine a lot when all this business blew up – he was very supportive. He was never quite the same after his daughter disappeared, of course, but in public he always put on a brave face. I had nothing but admiration for the manner in which he coped."

"Did you talk to him about his daughter and the other missing girls?"

"No, no, it was far too painful."

"And did you encounter Catherine Duffield at all? She was the girl who went missing in Swincroft."

Kenneth Highcliffe scratched his head. "Not that I recall," he announced after a brief silence. "I gather she only came to Swincroft on holiday and I don't think our paths crossed and…"

Kenneth Highcliffe closed his eyes again and seemed to doze momentarily.

"I've just a couple more questions," Clive said loudly, "and then I'll leave you in peace. We've been told that there was an art teacher at Polbury Manor at the time of the disappearances who was suspected of getting a bit too close to some of the girls – name of Russell."

Kenneth Highcliffe nodded and smiled. "Ah, that was Russell Chalbury."

"Chalbury, you say?" Clive asked quickly, recalling the name from somewhere.

"Yes, that's right. He was a good art teacher, quite talented, but his 'extra-curricular' activities certainly raised questions. He was an artist in his spare time – I think he wanted to make a living out of his painting but he didn't find it easy – and one of his favourite subjects was… er, well, was the female nude. There had been rumours for a while that he was paying some of the older girls to model for him at weekends and during the holidays but there were no formal complaints. I challenged him about the rumours once and he just laughed them off. He acknowledged that he used models but said he usually hired them from a reputable agency. He did admit, however, that one or two former pupils modelled for him occasionally, but he insisted that it was purely a working arrangement and there was never any physical contact. The thing is, Mr Walsingham, he'd resigned at the end of the summer term so he wasn't actually a teacher at the school when Charlotte and Issy disappeared. I heard that he moved away from this area and set up home with a former pupil but I don't know any details, I'm afraid."

"Mmmm, I rather think he's moved back into the area," Clive replied, recalling something he'd seen recently. "And I'm told there were rumours at the time of the disappearances about a groundsman, who was apparently fond of watching the girls change for hockey."

"Yes that was most unpleasant. He certainly used to hang around the changing rooms, leering and making the odd provocative comment, and he made a lot of the girls feel uneasy. We didn't employ him; he worked for the contractors who maintained our grounds – Harvey and something…"

"Harvey and Holford?"

"Yes, that was it. We had to ask them not to send him anymore."

"Can you remember his name?"

"Yes, I can; it was Raymond Gulliver!"

"Bloody hell!" Clive exclaimed for the third time.

*

The Cricketers was an attractive, well-maintained pub on the road leading out of Swincroft. It had white painted walls, some black, wooden beams of indeterminate vintage and a pleasant beer garden nestling behind a neat, white picket fence. The cricket field from which it took its name had long since disappeared and the pub now found itself at the edge of a small, select housing development. Monday lunchtime appeared to be a quiet time for the pub – several elderly regulars were grouped around the bar in animated conversation, and a couple of passing motorists and three businessmen, snatching a hurried lunch, made up the remainder of the clientele. Clive ordered a mineral water and a prawn sandwich and made his way over to a solid, round table in a panelled niche beside a window through which he had an uninterrupted view of the car park. There was no need for him to look out of the window, however, because, as he was taking his first bite from the sandwich, he heard a familiar squealing of tyres in the car park. Sergeant Alison Pawlett had arrived.

"Sorry I'm late," she shouted across the room as she rushed in rather breathlessly. "Bit of a busy morning…" Before Clive had time to react, Alison had marched over to the bar, ordered a diet Coke and a smoked salmon sandwich, demanded a receipt from the bored young woman behind the bar and strode over to where Clive was sitting.

"Any news?" Clive asked, sensing from her bustling demeanour that Alison Pawlett had plenty.

"Sonia Duffield has arrived at the police station and is currently being interviewed," Alison announced as she sat down opposite Clive. "She seems to have taken the murder of her husband remarkably well and I'm told that if I phone later this afternoon, we should be able to arrange for you to speak to her. And I've spoken to Ian Mencham. Before he hung up on me, I explained that you were a civilian helping us with our investigation, that you have only recently moved into this area and that you were very discreet, and he grouched and growled a bit but eventually agreed that if you call him on this number," Alison Pawlett pulled a creased scrap of paper from the pocket of her denim trousers and handed it to Clive, "and if you can convince him that you are not a journalist or anyone else with a vested interest, he'll give you half an hour of his time later on today."

"Oh well, that's very generous of him," Clive replied sarcastically. "And how did you get on at Mallowcrest?"

Alison Pawlett pulled a face. "Not very well! I spoke to Jackie Bembridge, the manager. Unfortunately, none of the present staff were working there ten years ago, so nobody could tell me about the resident, Doris, who spoke to Dick, er, Inspector Beauregard. I asked her about the visitors' book that Inspector Beauregard said had vanished and she confirmed that one was missing from their archives but she didn't know anything more."

"Mmm. It does sound a bit fishy," Clive mused. "Was there anything else?"

"No, not really! As I said, none of the present staff were there ten years ago and there's been a change of ownership since then, so a lot of the old records have disappeared."

"Any idea who the owners were ten years ago?"

"Yes, it was a company called Stewarton Care Services. As the name suggests, they specialised in providing care services for the elderly but they went bust about five years ago, so it might be difficult to track down anyone who can tell us anything."

Clive raised an eyebrow as he chewed on his sandwich. "But you'll have a go, won't you?"

"Of course," Alison replied reluctantly. "And how did you get on with Kenneth Highcliffe?"

"I'm a bit puzzled if I'm being honest," Clive replied. "Oh, Kenneth Highcliffe was pleasant enough but there were things that weren't quite right. For example, he said, on a couple of occasions, that his memory wasn't very good these days and yet he seemed to recall the incidents of ten years ago and the people involved as though it all happened yesterday. And he more or less admitted that he shut himself away in his office when the balloon went up and the press arrived in their shoals. It seems that it was his deputy, Christine Calshott, who fielded most of the enquiries from the press and faced up to the wrath of the angry parents. We need to track her down. And he made me sit in the garden because his wife was in the house and she was quite frail and he didn't want to stress her. It all seemed a bit strange."

"Did you get any new leads, apart from Christine Calshott?"

Clive tugged at his earlobe. "A few; Kenneth Highcliffe used to teach ancient history and classics so he had a good working knowledge of classical mythology and he got a bit prickly when I asked him about it."

"So he would know all about Circe."

"Exactly! He also said that Emily Ashurst may have been the victim of some domestic violence and that she and Charlotte Huxton were quite friendly for a while but had fallen out for some reason. He said that Charlotte Huxton was a bit of a rebel and often spent the night away at a friend's house and…" Clive hesitated, wondering whether he should mention Gary Beechwood at this stage but, on reflection, decided to make some further discreet enquiries first. "And I have a couple of names I'm following up on. And Isabel Draycott had some problems at home and at school and was becoming withdrawn and lonely and—"

"But none of this gets us any nearer to finding out who abducted them," Alison Pawlett interrupted impatiently.

"Maybe not but I also discovered that, around about the time of the disappearances, Polbury Manor was having a new science wing built, and the architect was none other than Robert Huxton, so he's got to be worth talking to. Do we know where he is at the moment?"

"I gather he's out in Dubai working on some prestigious project. He is aware that his ex-wife has gone missing though."

"Do we know when he went to Dubai?"

"He flew out last Thursday."

"Did he? The day after Keith Draycott was murdered and the day before Alan Ashurst's planned meeting that never happened – that's interesting. I also discovered that the electricians who were working on the new science wing were a local firm called Finnarts. They're a family firm. Debbie's son works for them now, although he was still at school ten years ago."

"Wow! That might be a bit awkward for you but it is a new lead of sorts."

"Yes and one that we need to follow up. I'd really like to know what Mr Finnart senior can remember about the work that he did at the school. Does he remember any gossip or did he see or hear anything that might be relevant? And just out of interest, I'd quite like to know where Finnarts have been working during the last couple of weeks and whether they've been close to any of the places where bodies have been found. Perhaps it's something you could look into?"

"Yes, but…" Alison Pawlett began, sounding increasingly piqued at Clive's remorseless demands for information but, after a brief hesitation, she chose to adopt a more conciliatory tone. "Of course, I'll do what I can but it might take a little while."

"Of course, of course!" Clive agreed. "But I fear it won't be too long before Superintendant Rushwick starts taking a keener interest in what we're doing and then we may not get much of a chance. I also asked Kenneth Highcliffe about two people who were identified as possible suspects at the time. One was the art teacher who, according to Kenneth Highcliffe, had a penchant for painting some of his older female students with their kit off – no complaints were ever made and, as far as I can establish, there was never a full investigation but he seems to have left Polbury Manor quite suddenly at the end of the summer term and moved away. Does the name Russell Chalbury mean anything to you?"

"Chalbury, Chalbury?" Alison Pawlett repeated the name while she desperately tried to recall it.

"Have you got a copy of the newspaper article that was found in Keith Draycott's pocket?"

"Yes, I've got a copy here somewhere." Alison Pawlett rummaged in her denim bag and produced a piece of paper which she studied briefly under Clive's forensic gaze. "Yes, here it is. Russell Chalbury is referred to as the coordinator of the Carlow Valley Arts Festival. So he must have moved back into the area."

"It certainly looks like it. Intriguing, isn't it, that he was around this area when the girls were abducted, he then moved away under mysterious circumstances and the abductions stopped? And now he's returned to this area and people are getting murdered. If you can find me an address, I think we'll pay him a visit."

"I'll get somebody to dig around. You said there were two people you asked Kenneth Highcliffe about."

Clive tugged his earlobe again. "Yes, I mentioned a groundsman, or groundsperson if you prefer, who looked after the school playing fields and seemed to be taking an unhealthy interest in the girls who were playing hockey. And it turns out that he worked for Harvey and Holford and his name was Raymond Gulliver!"

"Omigod, he's your gardener!" Alison exclaimed.

"Afraid so," Clive replied sheepishly, remembering all too painfully what had happened to Simon, his previous gardener. "For obvious reasons, I'd prefer it if you spoke to him first."

"Oh God, yes of course! Actually, I was watching him out of the dining room window while I was having breakfast this morning and he was behaving very strangely. Every time a vehicle pulled up in your car park, he jumped and ran for cover. I'll —"

Her reply was interrupted by her phone ringing. Excusing herself, she got up from the table and marched outside with her phone clasped to her ear. She returned a few moments later with an expression that told Clive immediately that she had bad news.

"It's headquarters," she announced grimly. "They've found a body on the old railway embankment near Morstock. They're pretty sure it's Kate Huxton."

*

The solid front door creaked open very slowly and not very far. In the half light, Clive could just detect a bald head and a pair of suspicious eyes peering out at him.

"Er, ahem," Clive began tentatively. "We spoke earlier on the phone. I'm following up on Detective Sergeant Pawlett's earlier call."

"And you are Mr Walsingham, I assume. Have you got any ID?"

Clive patted his pockets. "Well, er, nothing official, no. I'm not employed by the police. All I've got is a letter of authorisation and my business card."

The man tutted and his eyes peered nervously beyond Clive as though expecting that he had not come alone, or had been followed. "You'd better come in," he replied tersely.

Though no great expert on architectural styles, Clive reckoned that the detached house, constructed in solid red brick with elegant bay windows, had probably been built in the early years of the twentieth century. The living room had a high ceiling, moulded cornices ran along the tops of the walls, which were decorated with striped silver wallpaper, there was a substantial fireplace with brick surround and a polished wooden floor which was partially covered by a fussily patterned maroon carpet. The brown furniture and partially drawn curtains gave the room a gloomy feel. Ian Mencham sat down heavily in one of two brown armchairs. He was slightly above medium height with a noticeable paunch. What little hair he had was grey, his face was furrowed and careworn, and his dark eyes were alert and suspicious. He wore a pale yellow shirt, open at the neck and tightly stretched across his stomach. His grey trousers were of uncertain vintage but their threadbare, creased appearance suggested that they were well-worn favourites.

"May I?" Clive gestured towards an empty chair. Ian Mencham gave the slightest of nods.

"You didn't see any newspaper men outside, did you?" Ian Mencham asked nervously as Clive settled his long frame into the chair.

"No, no one!"

"Only they've been hanging around, even peering in the windows, wanting to know if I had any comments to make on the current investigations, asking me to admit that I got it wrong ten years ago."

"And did you get it wrong?" Clive asked, rather more directly than he had planned.

"Oh, yes, we got it wrong," Ian Mencham replied quietly, laying emphasis on the word 'we'. "Rather spectacularly, as it turned out, but all of this is off the record. This is not an official statement I'm making."

Clive nodded. "My only interest is trying to find out what happened to those girls ten years ago and who was responsible."

"Huh! I wish you well," Ian Mencham replied with a trace of bitterness in his slightly croaky voice.

"I take it you were never convinced about Lennie Cave's guilt."

"Good heavens, no! Lennie Cave was a very unpleasant man with a number of convictions for minor offences and a couple of sexual assaults, but abducting teenage girls was way out of his league – it wasn't his style. Granted, he'd been seen hanging around outside Polbury Manor School but nobody came forward to say he had even so much as touched one of the girls – and we couldn't link him to the other abductions. And whatever the reason for throwing himself to his death, I doubt that it had anything to do with the missing girls. Apart from anything else, Lennie Cave was as thick as two short planks. He wasn't capable of planning those abductions. Whoever abducted those girls was clever – very clever."

"But you brought Lennie Cave in for questioning."

"Of course we did – we had to. He was a known sex offender who had been seen hanging around outside the school where a couple of the abductions took place, but we had no evidence." Ian Mencham looked around as though expecting a reporter to suddenly spring up from behind the sofa, leaned forward and spoke in a conspiratorial whisper. "The thing is, Mr Walsingham – and this is very definitely off the record – we hadn't got the manpower or the experience to cope with such a high-profile case. We had five girls disappear without trace in less than eight weeks. No sooner had we started investigating one disappearance than we had another and another and… We were getting bogged down, we logged all the phone calls we got but we had no time to follow them up, we ran out of officers to do house-to-house enquiries, we tried to search patches of waste ground and derelict buildings but we were swamped. Meanwhile, we had the Chief Constable and the Police Authority jumping up and down demanding results. So when Lennie Cave turned up dead, leaving a note behind that said he was sorry, and the abductions stopped, they had their result."

"So they were happy?"

"Were they hell?" Ian Mencham replied angrily, slapping his open hand on the arm of the chair. "The Chief Constable made it perfectly clear that he didn't have much confidence in me. Oh, he didn't say so publicly – he made all the right noises about having the utmost confidence in me and my team – but he had Inspector Neil bloody Rushwick bleating in his ear all the time about how I was stifling the investigation and wasn't prepared to let him use his initiative."

"And that wasn't fair?"

"I played that investigation by the book," Ian Mencham replied, slapping his hand on the arm of the chair again. "Every time a girl disappeared, we spoke to all her known friends and family, we did house-to-house enquiries, we recreated their last known journey, we combed the immediate area looking for clues, we appealed for witnesses, we posted pictures of the missing girls everywhere we could think of, but we drew a complete blank. It was as if the girls had vanished into thin air. The Chief Constable knew we were badly under-resourced and understaffed and he went through the motions of trying to get us some more manpower but nothing much happened. But Neil Rushwick wasn't happy and he said so. I think he thought we spent too much time gathering information and not enough time being 'creative'. He liked using the word 'creative'; I think it was his way of saying 'let's tear up the rule book and do whatever is necessary to get a confession.'"

"Violence, intimidation?" Clive asked.

"Who knows?" Ian Mencham shrugged. "But there was an oily reporter called Guy Sharston working for the *Carlow Valley Gazette* – he still does – and I'm damned sure Neil Rushwick was feeding him confidential information about the investigation, who we suspected and what we were doing about it, and encouraging him to criticise me for not pursuing certain lines of inquiry."

"Could you prove it was Neil Rushwick?"

"No, he was far too clever for that and, like generations of journalists, Guy Sharston refused to disclose his sources."

"Did you have any suspicions at the time about who the abductor might be?"

Ian Mencham sighed heavily. "That was the problem. We had loads of information coming in – far too much to sift through and analyse properly – but nothing that pointed strongly to any one individual. There were plenty of people with theories and suspicions about who might have been responsible but there was nothing of much substance. Whoever it was, he was very clever. I think the abductions were very carefully planned, no clues were left behind and the girls all disappeared without trace. And whoever is carrying out the murders now is also very clever – I'll bet Superintendant Rushwick and his merry band have no more clues about who the murderer is now than I had about the abductor ten years ago."

"Have you ever heard of anyone calling themselves 'Circe'?" Clive asked suddenly.

"Circe?" Ian Mencham looked puzzled. "No, not that I remember! Why do you ask?"

"We think at least one victim and one intended victim were contacted by someone calling themselves 'Circe'. Circe was apparently a goddess of magic in Greek mythology."

"It all sounds very mysterious. And I tell you something else that was mysterious. On two or three occasions during our investigation, my phone rang and when I answered it, all I heard was a piece of music. I recall that one was an extract from Mozart's Requiem and another was Chopin's Funeral March. I'm pretty sure that it was somebody trying to warn me off but

I couldn't trace the caller. I tell you, whoever abducted those girls and whoever is murdering their parents is very clever, very calculating, very devious and very, very dangerous and you need to be very careful. I just hope you have better luck tracking them – him or her – down than I did!"

*

Alison Pawlett caught up with Raymond Gulliver as he was loading his lawnmower and a collection of garden implements into the back of his grey van. His face was stained in sweat, his wavy dark hair was dishevelled and grubby and his muscular hands were caked in soil. He was breathing heavily. Noticing her out of the corner of his eye, he stopped and gazed at her suspiciously.

"Hello," he said cautiously. "I know you from somewhere, don't I?"

"N-no, I don't think we've, er…" Alison Pawlett replied unconvincingly.

Raymond Gulliver chuckled. "I remember where I've seen you – I never forget a pretty face. I've seen you coming and going from the Follycombe Hotel. Don't say you haven't noticed me!"

"I'm Detective Sergeant Pawlett," Alison announced stiffly.

Raymond Gulliver took a step backwards. "Blimey! Do the police pay you to stay in good-quality hotels these days?"

"It's, er, just a temporary arrangement, which we needn't go into."

Raymond Gulliver leered. "This temporary arrangement; it wouldn't have anything to do with Jamie Coulton, would it?"

Alison Pawlett could feel her cheeks burning. "I'm, er, g-glad I've caught you," she floundered. "Are you finishing for the day?"

Raymond Gulliver glanced at his watch and ran the back of his hand across his sweaty forehead. "I wish! I've got one more job to do today. If the weather's dry, see, we have to cram as much work as we can into the day. It'll be autumn soon, see! You're welcome to come with me if you like. I could use a bit of female company, as long as Jamie doesn't mind!" Raymond Gulliver gave her a mischievous wink.

"Where is your last job?" Alison asked, taking an involuntary step backwards.

"I've got to mow the lawn in front of the library at Stowbrook. You could wait for me in the library if you like…"

"This isn't a social call," Alison replied primly. "I've got some questions to ask you in connection with the murder of Olivia Farringdon."

"Oh, yeah, I heard you've found some bodies. How many is it now? I hear one of them is Keith Draycott. Is that right?"

"We're investigating a link with the disappearance of five schoolgirls ten years ago," Alison Pawlett pressed on, ignoring Raymond Gulliver's question.

Raymond Gulliver's shoulders suddenly slumped. "Yeah, I remember that – terrible, it was! But surely you found the bloke who took those girls. Lennie Cave, wasn't it?"

"We have some new information," Alison said enigmatically.

Raymond Gulliver's eyes widened. "Don't say that, please don't say that!" Alison thought she detected a brief look of fear on his weathered face.

"Why do you ask?" she asked.

Raymond Gulliver hesitated for a moment or two before replying. "Oh, errm nothing really; it's just, it's just so, errm, upsetting isn't it, for everyone? Those poor families!" He shook his head.

"We understand that you looked after the Polbury Manor School playing fields back then?"

"Who says?" Raymond Gulliver asked, his eyes suddenly alert and suspicious.

"Do you deny it, then?"

"Course not, there'd be no point, would there?"

"There were rumours at the time that you were taking too keen an interest in the girls when they played hockey, 'accidentally' wandering into the changing rooms when the girls were in there, leering at them from the side of the pitch when they were playing, making suggestive comments…"

"Yeah, I heard those rumours too but they weren't true, see! I'll admit there was a bit of banter sometimes. One or two of the girls could be a bit flirtatious, see! They used to say things to me sometimes – sort of deliberately provocative – and I used to respond but there was never anything serious."

"And did you wander into the changing rooms?"

"There was one incident, see! Someone – one of the girls – complained that the showers weren't working and they asked me if I could take a look. I mean, I'm a gardener, not a plumber, but there was no one else around at the time, so I said I'd take a look. I honestly thought there weren't any girls in the shower room at the time but I walked straight into the trap they'd laid for me. Once the screaming stopped and the girls had got dressed and left, I had a look at the showers and I couldn't find anything wrong with them."

"Did you suspect any of the girls as being the ringleader?"

"Oh yes! Charlotte Huxton was the ringleader," Raymond Gulliver agreed with an emphatic nod. "She was a devious little madam, always causing trouble in one form or another and always trying to provoke me. She had a nice body though! A nice pair of—"

"I see," Alison Pawlett interrupted sniffily. "And after that incident, the company you work for were asked not to send you there again?"

"S'right! Somebody must've complained – I don't know who, but it was probably Mrs Calshott, the deputy head. She never liked me. She'd told me before to stay away from her girls."

"So were you interviewed by the police at the time the girls disappeared?"

"Oh yeah, a very self-important policeman came to see me. I forget his name but I think he was an inspector. He virtually accused me of kidnapping the girls. He got quite stroppy with me. I thought he was going to hit me at one point but he had to let me go in the end because, like I say, nothing happened between me and the girls – just a bit of banter!"

"Whereabouts do you work these days?"

Raymond Gulliver scratched his head again and looked around nervously. "Oh, all over the place; I find it best to keep moving around. You'd have to ask them in the office if you want a complete list – I don't remember them all. I mean, I obviously spend quite a bit of time at the Follycombe Hotel, but my bosses are subcontracted by the council so I get to do municipal parks and gardens, bowling greens, village greens, open spaces – that kind of thing."

*

Detective Inspector Beauregard's voice sounded strangely slurred and indistinct as he answered the phone. Clive wasn't sure whether he had been drinking or had just woken up from a deep sleep but, either way, it was not a promising start to their conversation.

"Hello, Dick – it's Clive!" Clive boomed unnecessarily loudly down the phone.

"Clive? W… w… why are you shouting?" Dick Beauregard stuttered.

"Am I? I'm sorry, I didn't mean to," Clive lied. "How are you? Alison and Clare are both worried about you."

"Oh, I'm alright, I suppose. It was good of Clare to come round yesterday. Did she tell you about our conversation?" Dick Beauregard asked nervously.

"A bit, but that's not really why I'm calling."

"Oh? But…"

"I was wondering if you'd like to rejoin our investigation. We've got some interesting new leads to follow up and you were, after all, part of the original investigation."

Dick Beauregard groaned. "I can't, Clive! You know that. I'm no longer part of the investigation team. Superintendant Rushwick has stood me down." There was a long silence, but Clive could hear Dick Beauregard breathing heavily.

"Well, that's true, I suppose," Clive conceded. "Technically you are no longer part of Superintendant Rushwick's team. But I'm a civilian and until I sign his contract which, incidentally, I have no intention of doing, I'm not part of his team and not directly answerable to him, so I reckon I can ask who I like to help me and I really do need your help."

"It's kind of you to offer, Clive, and I do appreciate it but, however you try and dress it up, I am still basically disobeying a senior officer and…"

"Well at least let me explain what I think you could do."

"Go on then!"

"The journalist that you mentioned when you spoke to Clare, Guy Sharston, keeps coming up in conversation. You've mentioned him, Ian Mencham has mentioned him and he was the author of the article your team found in Keith Draycott's pocket. Now, as part of my investigation into the original disappearance of the five girls, I would be negligent if I didn't suggest that someone should go and interview him – he obviously knows a lot. Now, Alison – er, Sergeant Pawlett – and I are supposed to be operating under the radar. That means that we can follow up on a few leads and talk to a few people because the press don't yet know that we're involved. But, as soon as we talk to Guy Sharston, our cover is blown, whereas you are already known to him so he won't be especially surprised when you ask to speak to him."

"Yes, but I bet he knows, Clive. I bet he knows that I'm off the case and I bet he knows that you're on it."

"Oh, really? And who would've told him?" Clive asked with a tone of feigned innocence.

"Rushwick, of course!"

"Exactly, and then you'll know for certain, won't you? If you go and see Guy Sharston and he says he knows that you're off the case and he knows that I'm part of the investigation, you can be pretty sure that Superintendant Rushwick has been feeding him information. And if word gets back to Superintendant Rushwick that you've been to see Guy Sharston, I imagine you could make life a bit uncomfortable for him. You could innocently ask if the Chief Constable knows that he's passing information to a journalist, if you see what I mean."

"I don't know, Clive," Dick Beauregard whimpered. "Even if Guy Sharston does know about me and you, it's still no proof. Guy Sharston will refuse to divulge his sources and Superintendant Rushwick will deny everything and Guy Sharston will just take the piss out of me and make all kinds of unwarranted accusations about police incompetence and…"

"The thing is Dick, during the original investigation, Mr Rushwick might have been quite keen to provide Guy Sharston with confidential information, particularly if it could be used to discredit and undermine Chief Superintendant Mencham, who he obviously didn't rate, but now he's in charge, why would he want to confide in a critical and provocative local journalist? What would be the point?"

"Well, I , er, I…"

"Why don't you sleep on it?" Clive urged. "And then maybe tomorrow we can meet up somewhere and you can tell me how you'd like to be involved – or not!"

*

The dining room was not yet open for dinner, so Clive, Clare and Alison were able to find a quiet corner in which they could sit, unobserved, in less cramped surroundings than the office, and review the day's events. As was becoming the custom, Clive had organised some coffee.

"Have they confirmed the body that they found earlier is that of Kate Huxton?" Clive asked Alison as he handed around the cups.

"They're sure it is," Alison replied, lounging back in her chair. "Although they're waiting for Robert Huxton to fly in from Dubai, sometime tomorrow, to do the formal identification."

"The same modus operandi as the others, I assume."

"Yup! Taken to somewhere remote and then beaten repeatedly over the head. The pathologist reckons the body could have been there over a week, possibly around nine days or so. The old railway embankment is very overgrown and on the edge of some waste ground – hardly anyone goes there. And, as with the other murders, there was no sign of a phone or a laptop or tablet or anything that might have yielded a few clues."

"Who found the body?"

"It was one of the police search teams – they were combing all the areas of woodland and waste ground in the area and finally stumbled upon her."

"Mmmm; so of the parents of the five missing girls," Clive began to count on his fingers, "Howard Edwyn committed suicide some years ago and Olivia Edwyn, now Farringdon, has been murdered. Laura Draycott was killed in a motoring accident and Keith Draycott has been murdered. Edward Duffield has been murdered and Sonia Duffield is, I assume, being looked after by your colleagues. Kate Huxton has been murdered and Robert Huxton is flying back from Dubai and will be met at the airport by the police. And Alan Ashurst had an appointment with someone who would probably have murdered him had he shown up and he and his wife, Tessa, are also receiving police protection."

"Correct!" Alison Pawlett nodded. "There is something else you should know, though. Somebody who used to know Robert Huxton when he lived round here contacted us. He is sure he saw him in Morstock on Saturday 6th September."

"Wasn't that the day a taxi driver said he'd taken somebody who looked like Kate Huxton to Morstock?" Clive asked.

"It was," Alison Pawlett confirmed. "According to our informant, Robert Huxton went into a restaurant just off Morstock High Street. He says he dined with a woman who was waiting for him in the restaurant. He didn't know her, but from the description he gave, it could have been Kate Huxton."

"Really? Your informant is very observant. Oh well, that'll be a fascinating line of questioning when Sir Robert returns from Dubai. Meanwhile, if we assume for the moment that the murderer isn't any of the surviving parents – Robert Huxton, or Sonia Duffield, or Alan or Tessa Ashurst, all of whom are, or will be, receiving police protection – then it's possible that the recent spate of murders has come to an end."

"It's possible," Alison Pawlett agreed uncertainly. "But we don't know what the killer's next move will be."

"No, quite, but assuming that there are no more bodies discovered in the next day or two, that nothing is discovered at the murder sites that leads to an early arrest and that nobody comes forward with important new information, then I'd expect Superintendant Rushwick to be back in touch soon to find out what we've uncovered. If necessary, I may have to distract him. Meanwhile, have you any more information on Sonia Duffield?"

"Obviously, she's had a bit of a gruelling day, but I'm told that it will be alright for you to speak to her tomorrow. She is very confused, though. While her husband was staying here, she thought he was away somewhere on business. Apparently, he often went away for a few days – he told her it was on business but, according to his boss, he transferred to head office a couple of years ago and didn't travel around on business anymore. He also confirmed that Edward Duffield often requested a few days leave – sometimes at fairly short notice – but he didn't know where he went. Nor apparently does his wife."

"Oh well, that should make for another interesting interview tomorrow. If Edward Duffield was leading a complicated private life, it could explain why he had two, possibly more, mobile phones. And perhaps you'd be kind enough to ask if I could speak to Robert Huxton, once Superintendant Rushwick has finished with him! I think he might have a bit of explaining to do."

Alison Pawlett suppressed a yawn. "I'll do my best. Oh and one more thing; I've been trying to find out a bit more about Stewarton Care Services who were managing Mallowcrest Care Home until the company went bust about five years ago." Alison Pawlett reached into her denim bag and produced a sheet of paper which she brandished triumphantly. "I've got a list of the board of directors when the company went bust. We're trying to trace them to see if they can help. There is one name that might be of interest."

Clive perused the names on the piece of paper which Alison handed to him. "No, I can't see any names that mean anything to me except possibly this one." He jabbed at the name with his long index finger. "Gordon Calshott – any relation to Christine Calshott?"

"We think he's her ex-husband; we're trying to trace him," Alison spoke slowly before she stopped and yawned again. "Oh, do excuse me. It's been a long day."

Concluding from Alison Pawlett's demeanour that she'd rather not have any more work to do that evening, Clive turned to Clare.

"And how has your day been?" he asked.

Clare sighed. "Unfortunately, I've had quite a few interruptions during the day and I've had to cover for Beth."

"Any news?" Clive asked.

"Sadly, she's still not very well. The doctor is running some tests and she should have the results in the next day or two. Meanwhile, we've got to cover for her absence. Debbie and Jamie have worked some extra hours today and I've got some agency staff booked for tomorrow."

"Oh dear, that's not good news about Beth," Clive replied. "Would it help if I had a word with her?"

"Huh, I doubt it," Clare mocked. "What Beth needs is a bit of understanding and sympathy, not an interrogation. Anyway, I did get an opportunity to look at some of the original case notes this afternoon for a while, when things were quiet. I confess I found most of them totally impenetrable, but I've been looking at Emily Ashurst's disappearance and there are a couple of things that don't quite add up."

"Do tell!"

"Well, according to the family that she was going to babysit for, Rachel and Roger Firbeck, she was expected to be at their house by 7.30pm but she told her parents that she had to be there by seven. She left home at 6.45 and the walk would only have taken her ten minutes, fifteen minutes at most."

Clive rubbed his hands together. "So maybe Tessa Ashurst was right; maybe Emily was planning to meet someone on her way to the Firbecks. You said there were a couple of things that didn't add up?"

"I did. I've been looking at a map of Stowbrook and there's more than one route that Emily could have taken to get to the Firbecks' house but the most direct route would have taken her past Stowbrook library. Now the library was open until eight o'clock on a Friday evening so you'd have thought that somebody might have remembered seeing her walk past, given all the publicity that the case had, but there were no reported sightings of any kind."

Alison Pawlett, whose attention had been wandering a bit, suddenly sat bolt upright. "When I spoke to Raymond Gulliver earlier, he said he was on his way to mow the lawn outside Stowbrook library. Maybe he was there when Emily Ashurst walked past."

"Possibly," Clive agreed warily. "But it was a long time ago and I doubt he was working there at seven o'clock on a Friday evening."

"And, according to the case notes, it was raining at the time," Clare added.

"Fair point," Alison agreed grudgingly. "But I'm planning to get his work schedules from Harvey and Holford so I'll take a look anyway."

*

Alison Pawlett reluctantly dined alone again that evening. Feeling fatigued and sleepy, but needing to keep an eye out for any of her fellow diners betraying the merest hint of suspicious behaviour, she opted for a light seafood salad. Jamie Coulton waited on her with more than usual attentiveness, frequently bending over and whispering something in her ear, occasionally causing her to giggle and, on a couple of occasions, to blush. At the end of the meal, feeling markedly less enervated, she left the table in some haste and strode briskly towards her room.

Clive and Clare had snatched a brief meal in the kitchen and, as he was ambling slowly to the office, Clive's mobile phone rang. It was Tessa Ashurst, sounding twitchy and nervous.

"I hope you don't mind me ringing you so late in the evening but I had to wait for Alan to go out," Tessa Ashurst said, breathlessly. "He can get so aggressive sometimes."

"No problem," Clive reassured her with his eyes raised skywards and his teeth clenched. "Do you have some information for me?"

"I do. You remember me saying that I heard Emily talking to someone on the phone the day before she disappeared?"

Clive exhaled. "I do indeed; as I recall, you heard her say she was worried about something."

"That's right." Tessa Ashurst hesitated for a moment, as though uncertain whether she should continue but after a couple of audible gulps, she spoke again. "I couldn't say any more with Alan around but I heard a bit more of Emily's conversation than I let on."

"And?"

"And… I… I heard her s-say that she thought she might be pregnant and that she needed to meet whoever she was talking to. I, I couldn't say anything to Alan. If he had known, he would have got angry with me for being a bad mother. He would have 'sorted out' whoever it was who had made her pregnant and he would have made life absolute hell for Emily."

Clive thought he could hear Tessa Ashurst sobbing at the other end of the phone. "And do you know who your daughter thought had got her pregnant?"

"Yes, I think so," Tessa Ashurst whimpered between sobs. "She was very friendly with a sixth-former at Polbury Manor. Alan didn't know anything about it – he wasn't always that observant."

"And who was the sixth-former?" Clive asked, slightly impatiently.

"His name was Gary Beechwood."

"Bloody hell!" Clive muttered when his conversation with Tessa Ashurst ended and he put his phone back in his pocket. "Something new has come up," he called across to Clare as he strode through the foyer and began to climb the stairs, his long stride enabling him to take them two at a time. "I need to tell Alison!"

"Clive, can't it wait?" Clare called back. "You saw how tired Alison looked earlier. She might be asleep."

"I'll knock!" Clive shouted back.

The door to room 13 was slightly open and Clive could see, through the crack, that a pale, subdued light was on. Anxious not to wake Alison if she was asleep, Clive knocked gently on the door.

"Come in!" Alison's reply sounded strangely sultry.

"I'm sorry to bother you…" Clive announced as he walked in. "Bloody hell!" he exclaimed as he was stopped dead in his tracks by the sight that greeted him. Alison Pawlett was lying on her back on the bed, with her eyes closed. She was naked. On her stomach, she had drawn, in what looked like red lipstick, an arrow pointing towards a triangle of neatly trimmed pubic hair.

"Clive! Jesus!" Alison shouted as she tried to roll over onto her front. Unfortunately, her momentum was such that she rolled off the bed and ended up in an untidy, naked heap at Clive's feet.

"God, I'm so sorry," Clive replied as he instinctively held out a hand to help Alison up. "When I knocked, you said 'come in' so I… I… I didn't expect to find you like this. I'm so sorry!" he repeated.

"I… I thought you were… Jamie," Alison blurted out as she tried to wrap herself in the duvet. "I, I didn't realise…"

"I'm so sorry. I'll catch you in the morning," Clive stuttered as he turned and fled hastily from the room. As he was nearly at the bottom of the stairs, he passed Jamie who was climbing the stairs, also two at a time, with a lascivious glint in his eyes.

"I'd go easy if I were you, Jamie," Clive spoke softly. "Alison has just had a bit of a shock."

Perspiring freely, Clive raced into the office, closed the door firmly behind him, sat down heavily in the chair and spent several minutes trying to recover his breath and his usual sangfroid. He was about to set off in search of Clare when his mobile rang. When he answered it, there was no voice at the other end – just a piece of music which he recognised instantly as Mozart's Requiem.

Nine

Clare half-stirred and briefly opened her eyes. In the blackness of the room, she could see nothing, but the bed felt strangely chilled and unwelcoming. Instinctively, she turned over and reached out for the reassuring warmth of Clive's body but the bedclothes were flat, cold and unresponsive.

Opening her eyes a little further, Clare squinted at her bedside clock; it was just after three o'clock. Switching on her bedside light, she blinked several times, sat up and cast her eyes around the room – there was no sign of Clive. Looking perplexed, Clare rose quietly from the bed, wrapped herself in her dressing gown and went off to search for her errant spouse. After a brief search of the reception area and the bar, she found him in the office. He too was wearing a dressing gown. His head was bent over, his thinning pate highlighted by the glow of the desk lamp. His downturned face looked drawn and weary. On the desk, there were numerous sheets of notepaper spread out and Clive was scribbling, almost manically, on one. The wastepaper basket on the floor was surrounded by screwed-up, cast-off sheets of paper. Archie the cat, pleased to see someone up and about at such an early hour, was relaxing sphinx-like at the opposite end of the desk and staring inscrutably at him as though trying to work out the machinations of his troubled mind.

Clive didn't look up when Clare entered the room. Instead, he carried on writing at a frenetic pace.

"Clive! Are you alright?" Clare asked, her wavering voice betraying her anxiety. "I wondered where you were."

Clive looked up – his eyes were heavy and bloodshot. "I couldn't sleep," he replied quietly. "So I thought I'd come in here. I didn't want to disturb you."

"What's troubling you?" Clare asked as she sat down, knowing full well what was troubling him.

"It's this bloody case!" Clive replied, predictably. "The answer must be here somewhere – it's got to be. Five teenage girls don't go missing in broad daylight without someone, somewhere, noticing something and yet…" Frustrated, Clive thumped the desk with the side of his hand, causing Archie to pin his ears back and stare at Clive with ill-concealed anger. "It's making no sense and the more I think about it, the less sense it makes."

"I've never seen a case get to you like this before," Clare spoke softly as she stretched out a comforting hand and gently touched Clive's arm.

"Mmmm. No, well, as you'll recall, I left the police not long after we met, and Inglemouth was not exactly noted as the murder capital of the south coast."

"Nevertheless," Clare persisted. "You've had a few thorny investigations to deal with."

"Yes and that's the problem," Clive replied tetchily. "I pride myself on being quite good at solving problems. I can usually think my way through them calmly and logically but this bloody case defies logic."

"Would it help to talk about it?" Clare asked, suddenly longing for a return to her cold, unfriendly bed.

"It might," Clive acknowledged, slightly grudgingly.

"Shall I go and make some coffee?"

"Coffee? Definitely not! I don't need anything to wake me up. There'll be some milk in the fridge – a glass of milk will be fine."

Clare disappeared, followed by Archie whose calm inscrutability had been disturbed by Clive's petulance and who sensed the possibility, albeit remote, of an unexpected meal. She returned a couple of minutes later, without Archie but with two glasses of milk, one of which she placed beside Clive's hyperactive right hand. "So, fire away!"

Clive smacked the desk with the side of his hand again. "So, I've been looking at the girls' disappearances again, writing down what happened, how it happened, where it happened and when it happened and there's just no pattern or common theme. For example, three of the girls were local and all went to the same school, so they could have known someone who lived locally and who took advantage of them, but the other two were visitors to the area – they were strangers. Two disappeared on a Friday but the others vanished on different days of the week. Three disappeared in the morning, one in the afternoon and one in the early evening. Two were on a regular route where someone might have been lying in wait for them, but the other three weren't. And they all disappeared in broad daylight, yet nobody apparently saw anything unusual or heard anything untoward – there were no screams or the squealing of tyres or anything. And, despite an extensive search of the area, appeals in the press and on the television, there has been no sign of any of them since."

"So what are you saying?"

Clive took a swig of milk from his glass and swilled it round his mouth before swallowing it. "I don't know what I'm saying really, except that there is no obvious pattern to the disappearances. It's just so puzzling! I mean, when Emily Ashurst disappeared, it was reasonable to assume that she'd run away. It's likely that she had problems at home and, if her mother is to be believed, was worried that she might be pregnant. But then, when Catherine Duffield and Rosemary Edwyn vanished, everybody would have assumed that the disappearances were connected and that there was somebody out there who had taken them. And so, people would have become vigilant and watchful. Anybody acting remotely suspiciously would have been noticed straight away – Lennie Cave was. And yet it seems our abductor chose to take the next two girls, Charlotte Huxton and Isabel Draycott, while they were on their way to or from school. There would have been hundreds of watchful pupils and parents in the vicinity and yet nobody saw or heard a thing."

"But what if they weren't taken on their way to or from school?" Clare asked as she reached for a pen and a piece of paper and started scribbling.

"How do you mean?"

"Well, Charlotte Huxton disappeared sometime after she left school on that Tuesday afternoon but we don't know where or when. She could have been almost anywhere when she was abducted. And Issy Draycott wasn't dropped at the school gates. She was dropped a couple of hundred yards away, so she could easily have turned round and headed in another direction once her father had driven off. She wasn't happy at school and had been unwell so maybe she just ran off. You said earlier that there were no screams…"

"Yes, well, Dick and Alison haven't mentioned any screams and I'm assuming you found no mention of screams in the case notes that you've looked at…"

"No, mind you, I've hardly started…"

"So maybe the girls went off to meet someone they knew and trusted, for whatever reason."

"Which rules out Lennie Cave, for example."

"Exactly, but one of the many things that's nagging at me is that two of the parents, Olivia Farringdon and Edward

Duffield stayed here before they were killed and another one, Keith Draycott, dined here on more than one occasion. And two members of our team keep cropping up – Gary Beechwood and Raymond Gulliver. They seem to have been 'close to the action' when one or two of the girls disappeared. Is that just a coincidence?"

"My God!" Clare gasped as she clamped her hand to her mouth. "You don't think they stayed here because they knew Gary or Raymond was involved? Or did Gary or Raymond suggest they stayed here so that they could…?"

Clive held up his hands in a gesture of surrender. "Frankly, I don't know what I think but I must have a chat with Gary when he arrives. And then, of course, there's the added mystery of Alan Ashurst's planned meeting with the murderer who never turned up."

"The mystery being that the murderer didn't show up?"

"Exactly! According to Alan Ashurst, all the necessary arrangements were in place; he'd had a text confirming the place, date and time of the rendezvous and he was there in good time. But, when you think about it, we've actually only got Alan Ashurst's word that a meeting was planned. He said he'd deleted all the relevant texts so there's no evidence. What if he just invented the meeting to throw us off the scent?"

"You mean it was Alan Ashurst who's been killing the other parents? But why?"

"I've no idea really, but let's just suppose that he accidentally killed his daughter, Emily. There were rumours that he had a bit of temper and Emily had turned up at school a couple of times with bruises on her face. Maybe he'd discovered that she was pregnant and got violent and it went too far. So when he realised what he'd done, he panicked. He hid his daughter's body somewhere and decided to cover up his actions by faking her disappearance and then randomly abducting some other girls to make it look as though a serial kidnapper was on the loose. And then suppose that, all these years later, one of the parents somehow found out what he'd done and contacted him anonymously."

"So, not knowing the name of the parent, he set out on a mission to murder them all? It sounds a bit far-fetched to me, Clive," Clare replied doubtfully. "Sounds like the sort of thing you might read in a dodgy crime novel."

Clive sighed and half-smiled. "Yes, you're probably right. I'm just a bit tired, but I still think it might be worth checking the case notes to see how seriously Alan and Tessa Ashurst were regarded as suspects after their daughter disappeared and if they had alibis for the times when the other girls vanished."

"I'll do my best, but let's not forget that it was Alan Ashurst who first mentioned the name 'Circe' to you and both Olivia Farringdon and Keith Draycott had books on ancient myths so it's quite probable that they were both contacted by 'Circe' as well."

"Yes, true, but supposing Alan Ashurst was 'Circe'. Supposing he used that name to contact the other parents." Clive took another swig of milk. "I think I'm going to have to satisfy my curiosity by doing a bit more digging on our friend, Mr Ashurst. Meanwhile, I'm no closer to understanding why the abductions suddenly stopped. Was it just coincidence that they stopped once Lennie Cave's body was found? Did the kidnapper's circumstances suddenly change? Nor have I worked out the significance of the newspaper cutting in Keith Draycott's pocket and why somebody would take the trouble to put it there." Clive rubbed his eyes. "You know, I think once I've spoken to Gary, my first priority is to go and have a look at the exact locations where the girls disappeared and retrace their steps. There must be something out there somewhere that links them, something that's been overlooked."

"Omigod!" Clare suddenly exclaimed as she studied the piece of paper on which she had been doodling. She sat bolt upright. "Omigod! I think I might have solved part of your puzzle."

"Which part?" Clive asked guardedly.

"Well, while you've been talking, I just started to casually write down the names of the girls who disappeared – Emily, Catherine, Rosemary, Charlotte and Issy. And then I looked at their initials – E, C, R, C, I – and then I rearranged them."

"CIRCE!" Clive shouted. "Clare, you're brilliant! So, if Alan Ashurst is to be believed and somebody contacted him using the name 'Circe', then we're not looking for a tenuous link to a mythological goddess. The person who contacted the parents was using the girls' initials as a kind of code. I suspect Ian Mencham was right when he said there is somebody out there who is playing a game – and a very dangerous game it is too!"

Ten

As had become her reluctant custom, Alison Pawlett had sat alone and partaken of a light breakfast in the dining room, while surreptitiously trying to observe the hotel guests as they arrived and left and, all the while, being served attentively and with a knowing grin by Jamie Coulton. She was just taking a final swig of coffee and staring blankly out at the damp lawn when Clive passed through on his way from the kitchen, having had an illuminating and thought-provoking conversation with Gary Beechwood. Unable to make eye contact with Clive, Alison stared into her nearly empty cup of coffee and fidgeted nervously with a chain pendant around her neck.

Clive stopped, looked sheepishly across at Alison and gave a nervous smile.

"You alright?" he asked vaguely.

"Yup!" Alison replied tersely without looking up.

An embarrassing silence followed, during which Clive clasped his hands together behind his back and shifted uneasily from one foot to the other while Alison continued to study the dregs in her coffee cup with unusual interest. The silence was eventually broken by Clive.

"I'm, errm, really sorry about what happened last night, Alison. I had no idea you were…"

"It's okay, Clive – after all you did knock! I just didn't expect you. I thought Jamie was… Anyway, I'm sure we've got work to do."

"Plenty! Can you spare a few minutes in the office?"

Clive led the way into the cramped office where they were joined almost immediately by Clare. Although no words were exchanged, the strained atmosphere and evasive body language didn't go unnoticed.

"You two okay?" Clare asked innocently.

"Yeah! As you know, I had a bad night," Clive replied.

"Me too," Alison confirmed without further elaboration.

"Oh well, that's alright then," Clare observed sardonically. "We're obviously all on top form this morning. So, while I'm sitting here trying to make some sense of the case notes, what are your plans? Do they include going back to bed and catching up on your sleep?"

Alison exchanged the merest of glances with Clive and puffed out her cheeks. "I'm going to pay a visit to the offices of Harvey and Holford. I'm going to see if I can lay my hands on an up-to-date work schedule for Raymond Gulliver and find out if they've got records going back ten years. Then I'm going to track down Finnarts, the electricians, and find out what they've been up to recently and whether they've got records going back ten years. And I'm going to make the necessary arrangements for Clive to talk to Sonia Duffield and Sir Robert Huxton and, if I have any time left, I shall try to have a look at Keith Draycott's computer."

Clive coughed self-consciously. "You, errm, haven't had a chance to look at his computer yet then?"

"Nope! I had a brief look but couldn't get into his files. I'll talk to our technical people later."

"Good," Clive replied without much enthusiasm. "And I thought I'd start the day by visiting the places where our five girls were last seen and retrace their steps – I'm sure we're missing something there. And, as you said, Alison, if you can make the necessary arrangements, I'm going to talk to Sonia Duffield and Robert Huxton. And I want to try and speak to Christine Calshott and I expect, at some point, to be talking to Dick and to Superintendant Rushwick. And perhaps, Clare, you could update Alison on your research into the name 'Circe' and what you've discovered, which was brilliant, but I'm afraid I'll have to dash."

Clive exhaled. He was finding the atmosphere in the cramped confines of the office a little too strained. He stood up, glanced at his watch, gave Clare a cursory peck on the cheek and, without looking across at Alison, strode briskly out of the office.

*

It was a dull, dank morning and a dispiriting shroud of dampness hung in the air. The roads and pavements were wet and glistening, while cool droplets of moisture dripped persistently from the overhanging branches of the nearby trees. Feeling as cheerless as the weather, Clive drove to Polbury Manor School. The school day had already started by the time he arrived and he was able to park in the near-deserted approach road, not far from the imposing wrought iron entrance gates. With his collar turned up and his hands thrust deep into the pockets of his waterproof jacket, he wandered up and down the road a couple of times pausing at the point where he imagined Keith Draycott had dropped his daughter on that fateful morning and tried to visualise possible scenarios in which Charlotte Huxton and Issy Draycott might have disappeared. He looked around as he recalled his earlier discussion with Clare. It would surely have been impossible for either Charlotte Huxton or Issy Draycott to have been abducted while they were in the approach road – they would have been surrounded by hundreds of other alert pupils and anxious, vigilant parents and there were no obvious hiding places for a would-be kidnapper. He wandered back to the point where the approach road intersected with the main through road to Stowbrook and looked both ways, beyond the steady stream of traffic. There was a bus stop nearby and a labyrinthine network of lanes and alleys leading off the main road, any of which the missing girls could have taken.

Feeling cold, damp and frustrated that his visit had probably been a waste of time, Clive returned to the relative comfort of his car, made a few notes and then drove the few miles to Stowbrook, passing St Mary's church and vicarage en route. Starting from Emily Ashurst's old house, he traced the two potential routes that she would have followed to the Firbecks' house for her babysitting assignment although, he reminded himself, if she had arranged to meet someone first, she could have taken an entirely different route. Recalling that it was raining on the evening that Emily Ashurst disappeared, rather as it was now, Clive imagined her walk, in whatever direction she went, would have been mundane and uninteresting. There would not, for example, have been many people casually strolling on the suburban pavements that Emily trudged down, nor too many drivers paying much attention to the occasional huddled figure hurrying to an unknown destination. As Clare had concluded, one of Emily Ashurst's possible routes would have taken her past Stowbrook library and, as Clive approached the library, something struck him as odd. He stopped for a moment and studied the small area of lush, wet lawn, either side of the path leading to the front of the building. The grass had not been mown for some time.

Having wasted little time in returning to the cosy interior of his car, Clive made a few more notes before driving on to Corwood campsite. The site itself still existed, pretty much as he imagined it had done ten years ago, with two or three hedged fields of carefully delineated pitches, although there was little evidence of much use on this particularly inhospitable mid-September morning. Some of its surroundings, however, had undoubtedly changed since the time of Rosemary Edwyn's disappearance. Where once, the campsite would have stood in largely unspoilt bucolic countryside, a smattering of recently built housing complexes had transformed much of the setting into a functional semi-rural environment of little intrinsic character or beauty. Clive had no trouble locating the shower block that he assumed Rosemary Edwyn was intending to visit on the day she disappeared – there was only one on the site – although it had clearly been recently renovated, with smart new brickwork and a gleaming roof, and he stood sheltering beneath a venerable oak tree and gazed thoughtfully around. On the opposite side of the road from the shower block, there was a small development of a dozen or so newish houses which, he was pretty sure, would not have been there ten years ago. He made some more notes before a drop of cool rain water from an overhanging branch dripped onto the back of his neck and trickled slowly down the inside of his collar, prompting a timely return to his car.

Clive's final visit was to the small village of Swincroft. He parked in the quiet road where Kenneth Highcliffe lived and made a point of walking past his cottage on his way to the house which Catherine Duffield's cousins occupied at the time of her disappearance. He couldn't be sure but, as he walked past Kenneth Highcliffe's cottage, he thought he saw the net curtain in one of the front windows twitch. The walk from the substantial former home of Catherine Duffield's cousins to the general store took no more than ten minutes along a narrow road where most of the houses were shielded from prying eyes by tall hedges, mature trees or high fences. The only building that offered some kind of open entrance was Mallowcrest Residential Home for the Elderly. As he stood and surveyed the front of the building, he noticed that an extension to one side seemed considerably more recent in its construction than the rest of the building. After a moment's hesitation and, acting on no more than what he used to call "a copper's whim", he went inside.

He was greeted by a brusquely efficient, uniformed, female member of staff. He explained that he was following up on a recent visit that had been paid by Sergeant Pawlett and asked if the manager was available to answer a couple of further questions that had arisen. Having signed the visitors' book and while he was waiting for the manager to appear, he decided to explore. He tried to give the impression of sauntering casually in the direction of the newer end of the building, though his progress was, in truth, more of a furtive scuttle which took him past an anodyne lounge where a few residents were spending their time in somnolent recreation and along a gloomy corridor whose institutionalised, magnolia walls were interspersed at regular intervals by solid, closed wooden doors, each bearing a number. A slight whiff of boiled cabbage permeated the air. At the end of the corridor, another door, half-open this time, led into a dining room, where a number of neatly aligned tables with white tablecloths and matching crockery were being prepared and laid for lunch.

"You're not really supposed to be in this area," a stern voice behind him suddenly boomed.

Clive started and turned round to face a tall, big-boned, middle-aged woman with a surly expression. "I'm so sorry, I didn't realise. You must be the manager?"

"Yes. I'm Jackie Bembridge. And you are?"

"Clive Walsingham. I'm the police Investigation Liaison Officer." As usual, Clive grimaced as he announced his title.

"I see!" Jackie Bembridge announced fiercely. "If it's the same matter that I spoke to your detective sergeant about yesterday, I'm sorry but I don't think there's anything more that I can add and I'm really very busy—"

"Well, there might be, actually," Clive interrupted quickly. "I was passing and I couldn't help noticing that this part of the building is newer than the rest of it and I was wondering how old it is."

"I don't see how that's relevant," Jackie Bembridge snapped. "But if you must know, it's about eleven years old."

"And do you know who the architects were?"

"I certainly do. We're quite proud of it! It was an early commission by Robert Huxton, now Sir Robert Huxton."

"Was it really? I don't suppose you have any information about who built it or anything like that."

"I wasn't here at the time, of course, as I explained to your sergeant yesterday, but they did have an opening ceremony of sorts and produced a little brochure about it. I think I've got one on file."

"I'd like to see it if I may."

"It's in my office." Jackie Bembridge stared at Clive as though hoping that he might decide not to pursue the matter but he just smiled and nodded his head gently. "I'll go and get it, then," she announced grudgingly.

"I'll come with you, if I may."

Jackie Bembridge turned and marched briskly along the corridor followed, at a more leisurely amble, by Clive. Her office was small but, to Clive's trained eye, appeared well organised. She went over to a row of grey filing cabinets running along the wall opposite her desk and, after a couple of moments of purposeful rummaging, emerged clutching the aforementioned brochure.

Sensing from Jackie Bembridge's severe demeanour that his continued presence constituted an unwelcome intrusion, Clive thanked her profusely and took the brochure into the entrance foyer where there were a couple of empty armchairs. Sitting down, he flicked quickly through the pages. He confirmed that Jackie Bembridge was correct when she said the extension was eleven years old and that the architect was indeed Robert

Huxton but then he saw another name that he recognised. The electricians were Finnarts. He phoned Sergeant Pawlett.

Returning the brochure to the formidable Jackie Bembridge, Clive hastily retraced his steps back to the relative comfort of his car. Once inside, he sat for a few minutes quietly mulling over the morning's events. As he did so, a combination of lack of sleep and the relative warmth of his surroundings caused a sudden drowsiness to overwhelm him. Within a few seconds, he had drifted off to sleep. It was some twenty minutes later when he was woken with a start by his phone ringing.

"Hello," he muttered sleepily.

"Hello, Clive! Rushwick here," the businesslike voice announced importantly. "I haven't had your contract of employment returned to me yet. Is there a problem of some kind?"

Clive smiled to himself. "No, no, there's no problem. It's just that I've been a bit busy and it keeps slipping my mind but I'm definitely going to be putting pen to paper today." As he spoke, Clive opened his notebook, removed a pen from his pocket and began doodling on a blank page.

"Excellent!" Superintendant Rushwick replied. "I expect you've heard that our body count has now reached four."

"Yes, of course. Obviously…"

"And I was wondering how your investigation was coming along, whether you've got any new leads that might help us track down the killer."

"We're making a bit of progress," Clive tried to sound optimistic though he suspected that Superintendant Rushwick was not fooled. "I've just been to look at the spots where the girls disappeared and Sergeant Pawlett is going to…"

"And have you drawn any conclusions yet?" Superintendant Rushwick asked impatiently.

"Not as such but there are a few new leads we'll be following up during the day and…"

"Only unless we have any important new leads today, which frankly I doubt, I might be able to release some resources to pick up your end of the investigation."

"What exactly are you saying?" Clive asked as calmly as he could, though he was inwardly angry at what he perceived to be the superintendant's overbearing attitude.

"What I'm saying," Superintendant Rushwick replied curtly, "is that we appreciate your help but unless you make some kind of breakthrough today, I expect to be taking over the investigation from you in the next day or two."

*

The offices of Harvey and Holford were located in a modern, utilitarian annexe to one of the old barns which Richard Edgton had converted into offices when he acquired Carlow Bridge farm and turned it into a "championship" golf course. There were two offices – a small, neat outer one, with two matching upholstered chairs and a couple of token houseplants on a shelf, which was presided over by a smartly dressed receptionist-cum-secretary, and a larger but very much more cluttered inner office which housed two men, neither of whom was called Harvey or Holford. One of the men, who introduced himself as Andrew Roderick, the managing director, rose to greet Sergeant Pawlett. He was a large, scruffy man, substantially overweight, with a double chin and a wheezing chest. The other man, smaller but equally scruffy and smelling strongly of nicotine, remained seated with his back half turned away from the visitor while studying something with obvious fascination on his computer screen. From his side profile, Sergeant Pawlett could just make out an ugly scar on his cheek.

"To what do we owe the pleasure," Andrew Roderick began with mock joviality as he pulled out a battered metal-framed chair for Alison Pawlett to sit on. Dispensing with any pleasantries, she went straight to the nub of her investigation.

"We've spoken to one of your employees in connection with a series of offences, some of which date back ten years. His name is Raymond Gulliver."

"Oh shit," Andrew Roderick replied before emitting a heavy, chesty sigh. "What's he done now?"

Alison Pawlett noticed the shoulders of the other man slump and his fingers slip from the computer keyboard.

"We don't know that he's done anything," she replied guardedly. "But we'd like—"

"Only that man is bloody trouble!" Andrew Roderick interrupted. "Oh, don't get me wrong – he gets the job done alright; he's quite conscientious in fact. It's just that, well, there are certain places that we can't really send him to."

"Such as?"

"Anywhere where he comes into close contact with females – women, teenage girls! He just has this habit of saying the wrong thing. I don't think he means any harm, it's just his way, but he makes them feel uncomfortable."

"I gather he was made unwelcome at Polbury Manor School, ten years ago, when a number of girls disappeared."

Andrew Roderick gave a weary nod. "That's right. There were complaints he'd been hanging around the changing rooms and chatting up some of the girls so we had to move him onto other duties."

"Were the complaints justified?"

Andrew Roderick shrugged his hefty shoulders. "Who knows? The deputy head, name escapes me, a bit of a dragon, was adamant that Raymond posed a threat to her girls so we had no choice but to move him."

"And have there been any other, more recent problems?"

"A few; he used to do some work in the municipal gardens

in Morstock but he kept chatting up the female dog walkers and joggers. There were more complaints. I don't think he, you know, touched any of the women or did anything, but he made them feel uncomfortable."

"But you haven't sacked him."

"No, but he's had a couple of warnings. As I said, he does a good job when he concentrates on what he's paid to do and, to be honest, we struggle to recruit good-quality people on what we can afford to pay. We can't afford to be too choosy."

"I don't suppose you'd have any schedules of the work that he undertook ten years ago?"

Andrew Roderick threw back his head and laughed – it was a throaty, wheezy laugh and the effort made him cough. "Hardly! We weren't even computerised then. We just had a list of outstanding jobs pinned to the noticeboard and allocated them to whoever was available."

"I see! And have you got a schedule or timetable of his current jobs?"

"Yes, we can print one out for you. Raymond actually spends a lot of his time working on the gardens and grounds at the Follycombe Hotel. Do you know it?"

"Oh, er, vaguely," Alison replied vaguely.

"It's a nice place, apparently, and Raymond does a good job although I think it's fairly cushy – the owners don't supervise him very closely. We just have to make sure that he has no dealings with the guests or any of the female staff."

"But that's not all he does, surely!"

"Oh no! We're subcontracted by the local council so he gets to do a bit of work on a few flower beds, a couple of bowling greens, grass verges, that kind of thing. Mind you, we know that he does a bit of freelance work – you know, looking after people's gardens for them; that kind of thing. He does it in his own time so I've no idea who he works for and what he does."

While Andrew Roderick had been talking, his colleague had printed out Raymond Gulliver's schedule of jobs which he thrust at Alison without looking up from his screen. She quickly ran her eye down the list until one particular entry caught her attention.

"Ah, I see he does some work at Mallowcrest Residential Home in Swincroft."

"Yes that's right. He looks after the garden and if you've met the manager you'll know that he's not allowed anywhere near the residents or staff."

*

To avoid arousing the unwelcome and persistent attention of the reporters who were still loitering in some numbers outside the police headquarters, Clive had arranged to talk to Sonia Duffield in a quiet cafe just around the corner.

She was a short, plump woman with spiky blonde hair, a round face and sad, dark eyes. Clive asked for two coffees at the counter and carried them back to the table.

"It's good of you to see me," Clive began solicitously, as he placed the coffees on the table. "I realise it can't be very easy for you."

Sonia Duffield sniffed. As Clive was to discover, it was something she did rather a lot. "No, it's fine, honestly. I find it helps, you know, to talk to people at the moment."

Clive recoiled slightly. Sonia Duffield's voice was louder and more shrill than was ideal for a confidential and potentially delicate discussion in a public place. "Good," he replied, deliberately muting his voice in the hope that Sonia Duffield would follow his example. "I'll try not to make things too distressing for you but I do need to talk to you about what happened ten years ago when your daughter, Catherine, disappeared. It does seem likely that your husband's, er, death, is related to what happened then."

"Yes, yes, of course. They told me you were looking into those disappearances."

"So what can you tell me about your daughter's disappearance?"

Sonia Duffield took a sip of coffee, pulled a face and sniffed. "Disgusting coffee!" she announced embarrassingly loudly.

"Your daughter's disappearance?" Clive prompted quietly.

"Ah, yes, yes! I'm sorry! But I don't think I can tell you that much, to be honest. Catherine was an only child… I had a miscarriage a couple of years after Catherine was born, there were complications and, basically, I couldn't have any more children. But Ted and I both came from quite large families and we were keen for Catherine to mix with kids of her own age… that's why she used to spend time here in the summer. My sister, Jo, had a couple of kids about the same age as Catherine… she lived in Swincroft. She had quite a big house with a spare room, so Catherine used to spend some time with her cousins during the holidays. They all seemed to get on well with each other and that summer – the summer when she disappeared – was the third time she'd been down to Swincroft. Everything seemed to be going well, as far as we could tell, and then, suddenly, we got this phone call to tell us that, you know, Catherine had disappeared. Well, we dropped everything and came dashing down here. We joined in the search, spoke to the police, made an appeal for her safe return but… well, you know, nothing happened…" Sonia Duffield sniffed and her eyes filled with moisture.

"Tell me about your sister's children – Catherine's cousins."

"How do you mean?" Sonia Duffield looked puzzled.

"Well, what were they like? How did they get on with Catherine?"

"Oh, er, I didn't really know them that well. They lived some distance away from us, so I didn't really see them that much." Sonia Duffield sounded strangely flustered.

"Didn't you visit your sister much?"

"Not as much as I would've liked. Oh, Jo was fine – she was always asking me to visit – but her husband, David, didn't like me for some reason. He was too polite to say anything but he was always very, er, very offhand, I suppose. So I tried to avoid him whenever I could."

"I see! So what can you tell me about Catherine's cousins?"

"Not much really; Ben was the older of the two. I'd guess he was about sixteen when Catherine, you know, disappeared. He seemed like a nice lad; a bit shy, not very communicative, like his father, but quite friendly, unlike his father. His younger sister was Sophie; she was very slightly younger than Catherine – only by a few months – and she looked quite like Catherine with her fair hair. Jo often said they could pass for sisters. Sophie was more like her mother. She was more outgoing than her brother and a bit scatty but very friendly. Catherine seemed to get on well with both of them and…"

"Which school did they attend?"

Sonia Duffield was unexpectedly quiet for a moment or two before she answered. "Oh Polbury Manor – they both went there."

"So they might have known the girls who went missing, or one or two of them at least."

"Ooooh, no, I don't think so; nothing was said," Sonia Duffield replied vaguely.

"What about their parents? What did they do?"

"Jo was a nurse. She worked at Carlow Valley Hospital – that's where she met her husband, David. He was a junior doctor back then."

"Were they questioned about Catherine's disappearance at the time?"

"I expect so but you'd have to ask them. Surely you're not suggesting they had anything to do with Catherine's disappearance."

"No, of course not! No, I'm just trying to fill in some background, like where they were at the time."

"So you *are* suggesting they had something to do with Catherine's disappearance." Sonia Duffield's voice was becoming embarrassingly piercing.

"No, no," Clive replied in little more than a whisper. "But it would help if we could eliminate them from our inquiries."

"Oh, I see! Well, Jo was at home. She always took a bit of time off during the school holidays. But David was working – at least that's what I was told."

"You sound doubtful," Clive persisted.

"Do I?" Sonia Duffield replied doubtfully. "It's just that, well, David worked long hours and nobody said he was at home so I kind of assumed he was working. I expect the police checked where he was at the time."

"Yes I'm sure they did." It was Clive's turn to sound doubtful. "What happened to your sister and her family? Where are they now?"

Sonia Duffield sighed. "They live in Kent now. David is a consultant gynaecologist these days. He works at the local hospital where, no doubt, he charms all the mothers-to-be with his friendly bedside manner! Jo works part-time in a private nursing home. Ben joined the army about four years ago – he's serving somewhere abroad at the moment. And Sophie and her partner have just had a baby girl – their second daughter – both delivered by her father!"

Clive sat back in his chair and exhaled. He looked anxiously around the room to make sure that no one was obviously listening to Sonia Duffield's high-pitched and intimate narrative. She was clearly willing enough and resilient enough to talk even if her rapid, staccato style of speech was difficult to keep up with and her account was oddly vague and unquestioning in places.

"Did your daughter know anyone else around here, apart from your sister and her children?" he asked after taking a sip of bitter coffee.

Sonia Duffield sniffed and her bottom lip wobbled. "No, no one was ever mentioned. I expect her cousins had a few friends that she mixed with when she was here. I think there might have been a youth club that Ben and Sophie went to occasionally, but I don't really think she was close to anyone else… she never got a Christmas card from anyone."

"Did she have a boyfriend at all?"

Sonia Duffield looked shocked at the suggestion. "What? Catherine? No… she didn't seem that interested… she had a few friends but they were all girls…"

"And what hobbies did she have?"

"Oh, the usual ones a fourteen-year-old girl would have, I suppose. She liked pop music, she liked hanging around with her friends. She read quite a lot, mainly teenage magazines…"

"Mmmm. Tell me about you and your husband."

Sonia Duffield looked puzzled. "In what way?"

"What did you both do for a living, for example?"

"Well Ted works, sorry, worked for a company that sells and installs central heating systems. He was a sort of salesman, I suppose. And I worked at the local school… I was a dinner lady… not very glamorous but it brought in a bit of money and it meant I was always home when Catherine came back from school each day."

"Is that what you still do?"

"What? Oh, no! After Catherine disappeared, I couldn't face working in a school… too many bad memories. These days I help out at a local cafe – a bit like this one, but the coffee's much better – and cheaper. I do a bit of food preparation, a bit of waiting at tables, that sort of thing."

"I see. We think someone must have contacted your husband, probably by text, and probably towards the end of July. We think that person might have used the name 'Circe' and probably told your husband that he had some information about your daughter's disappearance. We think that's why your husband travelled down here."

"Yes, that's what the police told me, although they didn't say anything about 'Circe'... that's a strange name isn't it?"

"So did your husband mention that someone had contacted him?"

"No, not at all... He didn't say a thing! He was always very secretive; I didn't realise why at the time, although I do now, of course! I mean, he was always going away for a few days. He used to go to trade conventions or to talk to potential customers... at least that's what he told me. That's certainly what he told me when he left on 4th September... Of course, I've now found out that he'd been in a new job at head office for about two years and didn't have to travel around anymore so..." Sonia Duffield fell silent briefly and stared into the distance as though deep in thought.

"So, do you know where your husband actually went when he told you he was going away for a few days on business?"

Sonia Duffield sniffed again. "I didn't, but I do now... Apparently somebody else has reported him missing – a lady who lives a few miles away from us. According to the police, she said that Ted used to spend a few days with her 'whenever he could get away' – the bastard!"

"So he was having an affair? Do you know the lady's name?"

"Huh! No, I don't and I don't want to. But I'd recognise her perfume... Ted used to reek of it sometimes when he got home... He told me a girl in the office used to wear it and, like a fool, I believed him... The police have got the details about his... his... mistress if you want them."

Clive tugged at his earlobe. "No I don't think that will be necessary. Would your husband have left any notes behind about who might have contacted him?"

"I certainly don't remember him leaving any notes lying around... As I say, he was always quite secretive... I can see why now!"

"Do you know how many mobile phones he had?"

Sonia Duffield looked puzzled. "I, er, think he had the two. One was paid for by his company – he used that one just for business – and the other one which he used for his social calls."

"Might he have had a third mobile?"

"Quite honestly, he could have had half a dozen for all I know. I mean, he could have had more than one mistress for all I know!"

"I assume he had a computer?"

"Yes, he had a laptop, or rather a tablet, I think it's called, but he always took it with him whenever he went away."

Sonia Duffield sniffed again and took a swig of coffee. "God, this coffee is foul!" she exclaimed so loudly that the woman serving behind the counter tutted and stared directly at her.

"Yes, ahem, well, thank you for the information," Clive announced while quickly tidying away his notes. "I think we'll leave it there..."

*

The cramped, shabby offices of the *Carlow Valley Gazette* were located above a chemist's shop in the older part of Morstock. They were reached via a rickety, wooden staircase. Guy Sharston, as befitting the status of editor, had a small office of his own, while the rest of his small, underpaid team occupied the slightly bigger adjoining office.

Guy Sharston had his back to the door and was talking loudly and animatedly into his phone when Inspector Beauregard wandered sheepishly into his cluttered office and sat down. Guy Sharston was fatter and his short-cropped hair was greyer than when Dick Beauregard had last seen him, although, as he was shortly to discover, the penetrating stare was exactly as he remembered it. The half-rimmed spectacles perched on the end of his bulbous nose, however, seemed to be a recent addition to his accoutrements.

When Guy Sharston had finished his phone call, which, from what he could hear, Dick Beauregard suspected was from a journalist working for a national daily who was pumping him for information about the murders, he swore quietly, slammed his phone down and pivoted in his chair so that he was now facing the inspector across his substantial, untidy desk.

"Well, well, well!" Guy Sharston chortled. "Detective Inspector Beauregard – Carlow Valley's very own sleeping policeman! And to what do I owe this dubious pleasure?"

Inspector Beauregard gave a self-conscious cough. "We're reinvestigating the disappearance of the five schoolgirls that took place ten years ago."

Guy Sharston stared intently at the inspector over the top of his spectacles – it was an intimidating stare. His pale blue eyes were cold and piercing. "Are you really?" he asked slowly. "Because I heard you'd been taken off that case."

"Well, your information is incorrect," Dick Beauregard replied unconvincingly.

Guy Sharston gave a supercilious smile. "I could make a phone call to find out." He picked up his phone and looked quizzically at the inspector as though challenging him to retract his denial.

Dick Beauregard returned his smile. "Be my guest! I'd like to know where you're getting your information from."

Guy Sharston hesitated momentarily while continuing to stare at the inspector. "I'll make it later," he announced at last, replacing the phone. "So how can I help?"

"Well, you seemed very well informed during our original investigation, so I wondered if you had gleaned anything that might help us find out what happened to those poor girls."

"Ah well, of course, Inspector, you know very well that I can't disclose my sources."

"Your sources? There was more than one?"

Guy Sharston leaned forward in his chair and glowered at the inspector. "I really can't tell you," he replied firmly.

"But you must have had some theories about who was responsible."

Guy Sharston's supercilious grin returned. "Oh, I'm just a humble journalist, Inspector. I just report on the facts. You guys are the ones who are supposed to have the theories."

"Nevertheless, you might have picked up some information that wouldn't necessarily reach our ears. People might be more comfortable talking to a journalist than a policeman."

Guy Sharston continued to glare at Dick Beauregard while he decided how to respond.

"I think we all want to catch the bastard responsible, so I'll tell you a couple of things," he replied, eventually. "Firstly, I don't think anybody really thought Lennie Cave was responsible. He was well known for being a bit of a perv so I don't imagine for one moment that any of the girls who attended Polbury Manor would have gone anywhere near him. And apart from anything else, I don't think he had a car at the time and I imagine him trying to abduct a screaming, wriggling girl from near the school entrance on foot or on his bicycle might have been noticed."

Inspector Beauregard nodded. "Unless he had an accomplice! You said there were a couple of things."

Guy Sharston sat back and folded his arms across his substantial girth. "My guess is the abductor was probably someone they knew and trusted – someone who didn't arouse suspicions; a family friend, a schoolmate maybe, a teacher even – or possibly a policeman!"

"Or a journalist, perhaps?" Inspector Beauregard countered quickly. Feeling rashly emboldened by the verbal jousting, the inspector immediately feared that he might have gone too far. He was right. Guy Sharston leaned forward, rested his podgy elbows on the desk and subjected the inspector to his most sinister, penetrating gaze.

"Would you like me to make that phone call now?" His voice, calm until that moment, suddenly sounded full of menace.

"I'd like to go back to what you said about the girls going with someone they trusted," the inspector replied, trying hard not to be intimidated by the journalist's hectoring attitude. "Two of the girls didn't live near here; they were only here on holiday, so they wouldn't have known many people round here."

Guy Sharston sat back in his chair which creaked under the sudden pressure. He too was rather enjoying the verbal sparring. "Y'know, it's always been assumed that all five girls were abducted, but what if one or two of them were just runaways? We know that all of them had problems in some shape or form."

"Are you thinking of anyone in particular?"

The journalist shrugged. "Who knows? Rosemary Edwyn was being overprotected by her mother, Catherine Duffield was probably quite lonely, Emily Ashurst had problems with her father, as did Issy Draycott, and Charlotte Huxton's home life was pretty chaotic…"

"You are well informed," Inspector Beauregard replied.

"It's my job!"

"You said earlier that a teacher could have been involved."

"I've got no evidence, if that's what you mean, but Polbury Manor is a big school with lots of teachers…"

"Russell Chalbury's name was mentioned at the time."

"Ah, Russell, yes! Now he's an interesting character. Did you know he's back in the area? He's one of the leading lights in the Carlow Valley Arts Festival. I've spoken to him a couple of times. He's doing up one of the old derelict boathouses down by the river as a studio-cum-gallery. But tell me, Inspector, why do you always assume that the perpetrator was a man? The girls would have been far more likely to trust a woman than a man, don't you think?"

*

The woman who answered the door was pale, gaunt and very twitchy. Her face, lacking any cosmetic enhancement, was heavily lined and her grey hair was greasy and unkempt. She studied her visitor with haunted, blue, almost violet, eyes.

"Are you Christine Calshott?" Clive asked uncertainly.

"Who's asking," the woman replied suspiciously.

"I'm Clive Walsingham. I'm working with the police. I phoned earlier."

"Oh yes, I remember. You'd better come in."

Christine Calshott led the way into the living room of her small flat. It felt cold and damp. The walls were covered in pale, flowery wallpaper which, Clive hazarded, had probably been fashionable twenty or thirty years ago, and, on the floor, there was a dusky blue, slightly faded carpet. A lopsided bookcase, propped precariously against one wall, contained a number of worthy tomes of English literature, though Clive imagined that, if he were to run his finger over the tops of them, he would discover a generous layer of dust. A small, dented electric fire occupied a disproportionately large grate and, on the mantelshelf above, there was a framed picture of a teenage girl with fair hair.

Clive cleared his throat self-consciously as he sat down on one of two threadbare armchairs. "Have you, errm, lived here long?"

"Longer than I wanted to or expected to," Christine Calshott replied bitterly. "I don't know how much you know about me, Mr Walsingham, but the last few years have been a bit of a struggle for me."

"Oh, I'm so sorry to hear that," Clive replied in what he hoped was a suitably sympathetic voice, though he was always prepared to admit that administering sympathy was not a particular forte of his, unlike Clare, whose genuinely compassionate nature he constantly admired. "Can I ask what happened?"

There was a long, funereal silence during which Christine Calshott reached for a tissue with an unsteady hand, wiped some moisture from both eyes, and stared resolutely at the floor.

"Is it relevant?" she asked quietly, her voice cracking with emotion.

Clive puffed out his cheeks. He had been unprepared for Christine Calshott's fragile appearance and impoverished circumstances and felt extremely discomfited.

"Errm, well, as you may be aware, in the light of some, errm, recent events, we are reinvestigating the disappearance of five girls that took place ten years ago."

Christine Calshott nodded gently. "Good. About time! Those girls deserve justice."

"But the things is," Clive continued hesitantly. "From everything I've read and everything I've been told, you were one of the major driving forces behind the success of Polbury Manor School – the power behind the throne. Everyone speaks very highly of you, your energy, your dynamism and your professionalism. For example, I heard that you went out of your way to support and console the parents of the missing girls and to reassure some of your more impressionable female students. And yet," Clive looked around searching for the right words, "and yet," he repeated, "what went wrong?"

By now, Christine Calshott was crying uncontrollably, her skeletal frame heaving with emotion. Eventually, after what felt to Clive like several minutes, she wiped the tears from her eyes and took a number of deep breaths as she tried to compose herself. "It was all going so well," she said, at last. "We – me and my husband, Gordon – had good jobs, a lovely house, a nice garden and two wonderful children, Jacob and Amy. And then gradually, bit by bit, everything fell apart. Gordon got made redundant and it hit him hard. And then I was overlooked for the post of head when Kenneth Highcliffe retired, which came as a bit of a shock. And then Gordon decided he'd had enough and walked out on me, by which time it was patently obvious that I couldn't work with the new head, so I resigned. And then, poor Amy, who was always a bit anxious, and who I subsequently discovered was being bullied at school, got herself into a state over her A levels and took a fatal overdose. Jacob tried to comfort me through it all, but he'd met a girl and had his own life to lead. And so..." Christine Calshott bowed her head and began to sob.

Embarrassed by Christine Calshott's unrestrained display of raw emotion, Clive shuffled his papers and waited for her to compose herself. "You mentioned your husband, Gordon. It seems he was on the Board of Directors of a company called Stewarton Care Services. They were involved in the management of a number of care homes for the elderly until they went bust about five years ago."

Christine Calshott shrugged. "I don't know anything much about that. Gordon was always a bit of a chancer and when he got his redundancy money, he invested it in some highly risky ventures that were being set up by a couple of so-called friends. I imagine Stewarton Care Services was one of them but he wasn't really part of my life by then."

"So you didn't know about his involvement with Mallowcrest Care Home?"

"Mallowcrest? I think I've heard of it but, no, as I say, Gordon wasn't part of my life then."

"Do you know where he lives these days?"

Christine Calshott shrugged again. "The last I heard, he was living in the West Country, somewhere near Exeter, I believe, but that's all I know."

Clive sensed it was time to change the subject. "Is that your daughter, Amy?" he asked, pointing to the picture on the mantelshelf.

Christine Calshott snuffled and nodded. "Yes; she got her looks from her father. I'd no idea how troubled she'd become. I should have spotted the warning signs, of course, but I didn't."

"She went to Polbury Manor?"

"Oh, no, no! That would've been too difficult for both of us – too much of a conflict of interest. No, no, we lived within the catchment area of Penheath School, so both our children went there. It had a good reputation and Jacob seemed to thrive but it didn't suit poor Amy. I think some of the teachers pushed her harder than was good for her."

"I see. I'm so sorry! You said you resigned from Polbury Manor after the new head was appointed?"

Christine Calshott buried her head in her hands and began to tremble. "Yes," she replied falteringly. "I'd been given to understand that I had a good chance of taking over as head when Kenneth retired but it didn't happen. The Board of Governors seemed to want some fresh blood so they appointed a young man called Nick Anslow. He was a very self-confident young man, full of trendy jargon and had his own very clear ideas about how he wanted to run the school, but they weren't my ideas and he made it very clear that he had no time for some of the old guard like me, so I left."

"And then what did you do?"

"I did a bit of supply teaching for a while but, by then, I was a bit of a wreck. My life had fallen apart, Amy had taken her own life, Jacob had moved out and I became hooked on antidepressants. I haven't worked for four years now – I haven't been well enough. I got a bit of money from the divorce settlement – that was when Gordon still had a bit of money – so I've been getting by but I don't know for how much longer…"

Christine Calshott stopped talking and began sobbing again, her shoulders heaving violently as she grappled with her emotions.

Clive shuffled the same set of papers for a second time. "I'm, errm, obviously sorry to have caused you so much distress," he said, quietly, when Christine Calshott finally stopped sobbing. "I really wanted to talk about the disappearance of the five girls and, as you were deputy head at Polbury Manor School at the time, I wondered if you might recall anything that happened, that seemed odd, or any staffroom gossip about who might have been responsible."

"Have you spoken to Kenneth?" Christine Calshott asked anxiously, biting her bottom lip.

"Yes, yes I have," Clive replied warily. He didn't want to divulge the contents of his conversation with Kenneth Highcliffe.

"And what did he say?"

"I'm afraid I can't answer that, except to say that he obviously thought highly of you."

"Huh! I bet he didn't tell you about his interest in teenage girls," Christine Calshott observed bitterly.

"I'm not sure I follow."

"Oh, we used to make a bit of a joke of it – that is until the disappearances started. Kenneth always seemed to find an excuse to summon the prettiest girls to his study for a 'confidential chat'. It might be because a girl had turned up late for school a couple of times, or hadn't done as well as expected in her exams, or he wanted to offer some careers advice. You name it…"

"I see." Clive tugged at his earlobe. "Did he… I mean… Were any complaints made?"

"None that I was aware of and it may have been no more than a middle-aged man with an eye for a pretty girl, but it makes you wonder."

"Did you say anything to the police at the time?"

"No, they were a pretty hopeless bunch, endlessly chasing shadows and turning prevarication into a fine art. In any event, I had no proof of anything untoward. And I felt a bit sorry for Kenneth in a way, I suppose. He was starting to suffer from narcolepsy – that's really why he had to retire – so he was finding it all quite difficult and…" Her voice tailed off.

"Mmm. Well, as I said, everyone, including Kenneth Highcliffe, seemed to have had nothing but praise for you at the time," Clive repeated, hoping to lift Christine Calshott's sagging spirits. "You did a lot to comfort the female students and reassure their parents."

Christine Calshott wiped away some more moisture from the sides of her eyes. "Oh, it was all such a long time ago, Mr Walsingham. I did what I could as deputy head, you know, especially as Kenneth tended to hide away in his office. I tried to issue a few words of advice to the girls – you know, the usual kind of stuff; don't go talking to strangers and let the police know if you see anyone behaving suspiciously. And, of course, I offered my sympathies to the affected parents. And I tried to reassure everyone that we were taking every conceivable precaution to ensure our girls' safety – that kind of thing. Me and dear Keith – Keith Daycott, bless him – became a bit of a double act, I suppose. He offered spiritual guidance and I tried to offer a bit of secular help. It's really terrible what happened to Keith, by the way – such a nice man!"

"So did you have any theories at the time about what had happened to the girls and who might have abducted them?"

Christine Calshott shrugged and sniffed. "Not that I recall. You have to remember, Mr Walsingham, that two of the five girls had no connection with Polbury Manor and the other three didn't vanish on school premises, so we didn't really believe that the disappearances were an inside job. Of course, fingers were being pointed in all directions – quite a few of the male teachers became suspects, as did some of the older boys, as did some of the shadier parents, as did the very unpleasant groundsman, as did Lennie Cave, but there didn't seem to be much substance to any of it. So, no, I really have no idea who was responsible. I'm really sorry I can't help."

"I've heard the name Russell Chalbury mentioned a couple of times."

Christine Calshott's hand suddenly twitched and she dropped her tissue. "Ah, Russell – now he was definitely very strange. I don't know why it was, but he seemed to be something of a Svengali figure to some of the more impressionable girls. They worshipped him and seemed to admire his unorthodox Bohemian lifestyle. I suspect, knowing him, he took advantage of some of the more vulnerable girls but nothing was ever proved and Kenneth, for whatever reason, was reluctant to take any action. As I recall, Russell left at the end of the summer term and there were rumours that he recruited a small harem of female followers from among the sixth-formers who had just left, but we heard nothing more from him or them. He didn't strike me as a kidnapper though. Girls seem to throw themselves at him without him even trying."

"I understand that you'd recently had a new science wing built and that the architect, Robert Huxton, was a frequent visitor."

Christine Calshott's hand twitched again, more violently this time. "Why? What has he been saying?"

"Oh, errm, nothing yet; I'm hoping to talk to him later on today."

"I see. Yes, well Robert did pay us a visit from time to time. He was quite diligent and wanted to make sure that his design was going well."

"Who did he see when he visited?"

Christine Calshott swallowed hard. "To start with, it was Kenneth but Kenneth wasn't very good with creative arty people so, after the first couple of visits, it was me that he saw." Christine Calshott suddenly stood up, tottered slightly and started to pace the floor. "You know, you mustn't believe everything that Robert tells you," she declared defensively. "Whatever he might say, we were close for a while, closer than perhaps we should have been, but there was never anything serious. It was just something that happened…"

"I'm not sure I understand," Clive replied with a feigned obliqueness.

Christine Calshott stopped pacing and held both hands up in a defensive gesture.

"No, no, I'm sorry, Mr Walsingham but I've said too much already – far too much. And our little chat has brought back too many painful memories. I, I really don't think I can cope with any more questions, so I'm going to have to ask you to leave."

As Clive made his way slowly down the stairs and back to his car, still slightly stunned by Christine Calshott's final admission, he reflected on the way that she and Keith Draycott had both suffered serious personal tragedies and how differently they had coped.

Eleven

Steady drizzle continued to fall unremittingly from a louring sky. Alison Pawlett's car screeched to a halt. She got out and strode across the damp road to where a red van was parked. The words *Finnarts Electricians* were embossed in white lettering down the side. The double doors at the rear of the van were open and a large, tall man with a mop of dark hair and several days' growth of beard was putting something inside. He stood up and studied Sergeant Pawlett suspiciously as she approached.

"Detective Sergeant Pawlett," Alison announced importantly. "I phoned earlier."

"Ah, you'll be wanting my uncle," the man replied slowly as he towered over the detective. "He's inside. I'll go and get him." Leaving Alison Pawlett standing restlessly in the drizzle, the man ambled slowly towards the house, which was in the final stages of completion, and went inside. A few moments later he emerged with an older, thinner, smaller man wandering slowly in his wake.

"This is my uncle Tommy," the man announced. "Tommy Finnart."

Alison Pawlett introduced herself with a cursory nod and scrutinised the older man. He seemed so different from his big, bulky nephew. He had a slight stoop when he walked, a long, narrow face, thinning light brown hair, lopsided glasses, and a vague demeanour. When he spoke, his voice was quiet and hesitant, with the hint of a stutter.

"As I mentioned when I called," Alison began in her usual brisk, businesslike fashion, "we're reinvestigating the disappearance of five schoolgirls ten years ago."

Tommy Finnart removed his glasses and absently polished them on the sleeve of his creased, sweaty shirt. "Yes, I'd heard. A t-terrible business!"

"I was at school with three of the girls," Danny Oxton confided as though betraying some vital secret.

"Yes, er, anyway," Alison Pawlett continued. "We think you'd been doing some work at Polbury Manor School around the time that two of the girls disappeared."

Tommy Finnart replaced his glasses and squinted at the sergeant. "Was I? I d-don't remember; it was a long t-time ago."

"It was a new science wing that had been designed by Robert Huxton – there was a lot of publicity about it."

Tommy Finnart swallowed hard. It was clear that Sergeant Pawlett was not going to be deflected by his airy denial. "Ah, yes, I remember now," he conceded. "I was employed to put all the electrics in. It was quite a d-difficult job, it being a science lab."

"We were wondering whether you might have seen or heard anything suspicious, or maybe overheard some of the pupils or teachers discussing the girls' disappearances."

Tommy Finnart leaned casually against the side of his van and scratched his thinning pate. "I remember the disappearances, of course, and I remember there was a lot of chat going on about what had happened and who might be responsible but I d-don't remember any detail, I'm afraid. It's a long time ago."

"What about you, Danny?" Sergeant Pawlett turned to Tommy's nephew who had been standing a few feet away, smirking at his uncle's discomfort under interrogation. "You said you were a pupil at Polbury Manor at the time. There must have been all kinds of stories going around. You must have heard something."

"I, I didn't know any of the girls," Danny Oxton protested vehemently. "I was a couple of years younger than them. But I do remember there was a lot of people who thought Lennie Cave was the man. He was often hanging around leering at the girls and making silly remarks."

"Was anyone else mentioned?"

Danny Oxton giggled. "Yeah, there was 'Hands-on Highcliffe.'"

"The headmaster? Is that what you used to call him?"

"Yeah, well, no, not me! But I heard some of the girls… And then there was 'Randy Ray', the groundsperson."

"Raymond Gulliver?"

"Yeah, that was his name, I think. He used to hang around the dressing rooms when the girls were changing – lucky bastard!"

"I would remind you that we're investigating some very serious offences and it would be appreciated if you could take things a bit more seriously," Alison Pawlett reprimanded Danny primly.

"Yeah, yeah, of course – sorry! I did hear that a couple of the girls who disappeared were quite friendly with a sixth-former but I forget his name. It might have been Barry someone."

Alison Pawlett swept some beads of drizzle out of her hair with the palm of her hand as she tried to control her frustration. "So your list of suspects consists of the headmaster, a randy groundsperson and a sixth-former who might have been called Barry?"

Danny Oxton gave a smug grin. "Yeah, that's about right!"

Alison Pawlett tutted loudly and turned to face the older man who was still leaning casually against the side of the van.

"And can you remember anywhere else you were working at the time the girls disappeared?"

"Hang on!" Tommy Finnart replied with sudden, unexpected passion as he propelled himself forward from his leaning position. "What are you suggesting?"

"I'm not suggesting anything. It's just that we believe you were doing some work at Mallowcrest Care Home in Swincroft shortly before one of the girls, Catherine Duffield, disappeared from right outside and I wondered whether you may have noticed something – anything – unusual or suspicious."

"I know where you're going with this," Tommy Finnart replied angrily, jabbing the air with his index finger. "And for your information, I d-don't remember working at Mallowcrest, I d-don't recall seeing anything suspicious and I certainly had nothing to do with the girl's d-disappearance. Now it's raining quite steadily, I'm getting wet and I've got work to do, so if you'll excuse me…"

Tommy Finnart turned and marched towards the front door of the house.

"Where have you been working in the last couple of weeks, Mr Finnart?" Alison called after him.

Tommy Finnart stopped and spun round. "If you must know we've done three or four emergency call-outs – Danny will have the details – we've been wiring up the property here and we've been working on an old boathouse down by the river. A guy called Russell Chalbury has been converting it into a studio and gallery and we've been installing all the electrics."

*

While Superintendant Rushwick was conducting his daily briefing session with the assembled media ranks at the front of the police headquarters – outlining the progress of his investigations without saying anything specific and skilfully defending the continued lack of arrests – Clive Walsingham was allowed to slip unnoticed into the building via the back door.

Sir Robert Huxton was sitting quietly in the interview room reading the brief for the next prestigious project that he was hoping to get involved with. From time to time, he would underline a word or two, or a complete sentence, and occasionally scrawl something in the margin. He had a wide, chubby face with tired-looking, light brown eyes. His hair was short, grey and well groomed. His brow was heavily furrowed, making him look rather older than his 51 years. He wore a plain white, expensively tailored shirt, unbuttoned at the collar and sported a pair of gold cufflinks. As Clive walked into the room, he stood up, revealing a solid, heavy frame, and proffered his hand. The handshake that followed was firm and lengthy.

"Thank you for agreeing to see me," Clive began. "I know this must be very difficult for you but, as I think you know, I've been asked to look into the events surrounding the historic disappearance of five girls, including your daughter, and I was hoping that you might be able to provide some useful background information."

Sir Robert Huxton sat down heavily and glanced at his expensive-looking watch. "I'll do what I can, obviously," he replied. "I'd like to see you nail the bastard, but I'm expecting to fly back to Dubai later this evening so I'm hoping this won't take too long."

"I'll do my best," Clive responded amiably. "What can you tell me about your daughter's disappearance?"

Sir Robert Huxton shrugged his broad shoulders and his brow furrowed. "Unfortunately, I'm not sure I can tell you very much. On the day in question, I'd left for work before Charlotte was ready. She was still in her room – she shared it with her sister Becky, er, Rebecca – so I called goodbye, she replied and I left. I got home quite late that evening, probably around nine o'clock. Charlotte wasn't around but that wasn't especially unusual. She and Vicky – Victoria, my eldest daughter – were often out in the evening. Kate told me that she was staying with a friend overnight; that wasn't especially unusual either. Charlotte often stayed with a friend overnight – she seemed to prefer her friend's company to ours. I left for work as usual the following morning and then I got a call from Kate around ten o'clock. She said that the school had phoned because Charlotte hadn't turned up and when Kate made further enquiries, it transpired that she hadn't stayed with her friend at all. And we never saw her again."

Clive exhaled. "Given that three other girls of about the same age as your daughter had disappeared from the area over the preceding few weeks, weren't you surprised that your wife hadn't checked to see if your daughter had arrived safely at her friend's house and kept in touch with her?"

Sir Robert Huxton spread out his large hands, palms upwards, on the desk in front of him. "I was not in the least surprised, Mr Walsingham, since you ask. I'm afraid Kate was not the most responsible or reliable of mothers. Oh, when the girls were younger, she was fine but once they developed into, shall we say, more challenging teenagers, Kate couldn't really cope. She started to drink. It was just the occasional glass of white wine to start with but, over time, one glass became two and two became a bottle. And I confess, Mr Walsingham, to my eternal shame, that I was no help either. My career was beginning to take off, I was working longer and longer hours and I was neglecting my family. With me at work and my wife seeking solace in increasing quantities of 'vino blanco', there was no one around to look after the girls, so they pretty well did as they pleased."

"Did your wife go out to work?"

"She was a music teacher; that's the other tragedy. When she was younger, Kate was an excellent violinist. Her teachers thought she could probably have made a career out of it but then we got married and, when Victoria came along, she gave it all up. For a while, she made some money out of teaching the violin to the reluctant offspring of pushy parents, but once the drinking started, the work dried up... Ironically, Charlotte herself was a good violinist when she was younger – much more talented than her sisters – but she gave it up when she got into her teens. Apparently it wasn't considered 'cool' to be a violinist..."

Sir Robert Huxton appeared momentarily to choke on his words. He gave a cough and fell silent.

"Tell me about Charlotte, if you can," Clive suggested after a moment or two's hesitation. "What kind of girl was she?"

Sir Robert Huxton cleared his throat noisily. "Wilful, truculent, deceitful; she was a nightmare, if I'm honest. I think it was to do with being the middle one of three girls. She was jealous of Victoria for being brighter than her and, because she was a couple of years older, for bagging the best boyfriends and she resented Rebecca because she was spoilt rotten by her mother. Charlotte was very pretty with lovely blonde hair and she knew it. When she was in one of her more wilful moods, she'd deliberately try flirting with Vicky's boyfriend of the moment, which, as you can imagine, didn't go down too well."

"Do you know anything about the friend she was supposed to be staying with on the day she disappeared?"

"Kate assumed it was her friend Karen. She often stayed overnight with her but Karen always maintained that Charlotte hadn't made any arrangements to stay with her on that particular occasion and hadn't seen her since they left school that afternoon."

"Can you remember Karen's surname?"

"Yes, I can – it was Beechwood. Karen had an older brother, Gary, who was very friendly with Vicky for a time. There was a small group of them, Vicky, Gary, Karen, Charlotte, Emily, one of the other girls who went missing, and a couple of others – one was called Maxine, I think. They all went to the same youth club for a while but then there was a big falling out over something – boyfriends, probably."

"I'd like to speak to your daughters, Victoria and Rebecca, if possible."

Sir Robert Huxton shook his head sadly. "I can give you contact details for Becky although she's taken the news about her mother very badly, so you'll need to be gentle. She always remained close to her mother, who still spoilt her until the very end, and is very distressed about all of this, but I've no idea where Vicky is. She walked out on us just after she left school and has not been in touch since."

"Do you know why she walked out?"

"She never said, obviously, but Kate and I were going through a messy divorce, I was out of the country a lot, Kate was hitting the bottle, Charlotte had gone missing and Becky was very obviously Kate's favourite. I guess there wasn't much incentive for Vicky to hang around really! I always hoped that she'd get back in touch one day, but she never has."

"Did you report her as a missing person?"

"What? No, no – it never occurred to us. No, she just walked out. I think her last words to us were something like 'I can't stand any more of this shit!'. Becky had this fanciful theory that she'd run off with her art teacher, with whom she was apparently quite friendly, but we never attached much importance to it. Becky has a vivid imagination sometimes."

"I see; thank you! I understand you designed the new science wing at Polbury Manor School?"

"Yes, that's right. It was the project that first got me noticed, ironically."

"So you were a regular visitor to the school for a while."

"Yes, I suppose I was, but I don't see…"

"I just wondered if you might have heard or seen anything that could be helpful to us. Any of the staff or pupils acting strangely – any gossip, maybe?"

"Oh, er, I didn't really mingle much with the staff or pupils. Whenever I visited, it was always to see Kenneth, the head teacher, or his deputy, Christine."

"What did you think of Mr Highcliffe?"

Sir Robert Huxton's brow furrowed. "He struck me as a strange man. He was very serious and very correct but he never seemed that interested in my designs, which I found surprising. He seemed to be a man under a lot of pressure, for whatever reason, and he didn't seem especially proactive. In the end, I took to meeting with his deputy, Christine Calshott. She was much more energetic and creative. I liked her – she was always very visible, unlike Kenneth, and always very supportive and helpful to the girls and their parents during those awful times. I tried to recruit her to join my team at one stage but it, er, never happened."

"Christine Calshott hinted that you and she were involved rather more than just professionally for a time."

Sir Robert Huxton snorted. "Christine Calshott and I spent quite a bit of time together during the construction of the science wing and, after work, we'd occasionally have a social drink together. And when we got talking, we realised that we were both experiencing problems at home and we cried on each other's shoulder and yes, we did have a very brief fling. But, as far as I was concerned, that was all it was – a 'no strings attached' liaison. When I moved on to my next project, I tried to end it but Christine wouldn't let go. She kept calling me out of the blue to try and set up a meeting, she'd follow me in the street, she'd hang around outside my house. She became so obsessed, in fact, that I needed a court injunction in the end to get her off my back."

"Do you think your wife or daughters were aware of what was going on?"

"Kate? Almost certainly not! She was too sozzled most of the time. Vicky? Probably; she didn't miss much that was going on and, if I'm being honest, my behaviour probably contributed to her decision to walk out. And I expect she told Becky but, again, nothing was said."

"Christine Calshott seems to be in a bad way these days. Do you think your behaviour contributed in some way?"

Throughout the interview, Sir Robert Huxton had been civil and courteous but now, suddenly, his demeanour changed. Now he was ruffled and angry. "I have no idea, Mr Walsingham, and I resent your impertinence. What went on between Christine Calshott and I is our affair and is not remotely connected to the disappearance of the girls. I suggest we move on. As I said, I've got a plane to catch."

"Of course! I believe you also designed an extension to Mallowcrest Care Home in Swincroft?"

Clive thought he saw Sir Robert Huxton blink momentarily at the mention of Mallowcrest. "Did I?" he replied vaguely.

"You did. We have the brochure that was produced at the time. It was about a year before the girls went missing, one of whom probably disappeared from right outside Mallowcrest. I imagine you were a regular visitor for a while?"

Sir Robert Huxton waved his hand dismissively. "I doubt it. I don't remember the project that well, but it sounds fairly straightforward. I imagine I only visited the place a couple of times." He glanced impatiently at his watch. "I do hope this won't take much longer."

"Ah yes, of course. I expect the visitors' book at Mallowcrest will tell us when you visited. As a matter of interest, when did you fly out to Dubai?"

"If you must know, it was last Thursday." Sir Robert Huxton was sounding increasingly prickly.

"That's Thursday 11th September?"

"That's right, but I don't see…"

"Had the trip been planned in advance or was it a last-minute thing?"

"Actually, it was a last-minute thing. I'm working on a high-profile development and one of the main financial backers wanted to make some changes – it happens quite often."

"When did you find out that your ex-wife was missing?"

"I got a text from Becky sometime last Saturday. You must understand, Mr Walsingham, that Kate and I divorced a few years ago and we lead, or rather led, entirely separate lives."

"So when did you last see your ex-wife?" Clive tried to make his question sound innocent.

"Let me see, let me see. It must have been about eighteen months ago – we met up for Becky's twenty-first. We took her out for a meal and then we went our separate ways."

Clive smiled. "That's strange because we have an eye witness who said he saw you and your ex-wife dining together in a restaurant in Morstock on Saturday 6th September. That's the day your ex-wife disappeared and was murdered."

Sir Robert blinked again, more slowly than before.

"Ah, I think you must be mistaken there, Mr Walsingham. I was nowhere near Morstock on that Saturday."

"So I imagine you won't mind if we speak to the restaurant owner. If you paid by credit card, which I suspect you did, then the details of your payment will be recorded. And then, of course, we could always look at the CCTV images from the cameras positioned in the High Street. That might—"

"Alright!" Sir Robert Huxton snapped. "If you must know, Kate and I had been in touch for a little while. We got on surprisingly well at Becky's twenty-first and kept in touch. Kate had stopped drinking, apart from the occasional lapse, and seemed to be more in control of her life and Becky was always nagging us to get back together. We'd spoken on the phone a few times and agreed to meet up again but it was so difficult to find a mutually suitable opportunity. And then Kate said that she'd got to come down to Morstock on Saturday 6th; she said she had an appointment but she didn't tell me the nature of the appointment and I didn't ask. And it so happened that I had a rare free weekend. Now I own a small cottage out near Buckham; or to be precise, my company owns the cottage. We allow some of our employees to use it occasionally for a long weekend. Anyway, it was empty that weekend so I decided to come down and stay overnight. I've always liked it around here, so it was a pleasure to pay my old hunting ground a visit. And I met with Kate and we had a pleasant lunch but then Kate announced that she had to rush off for her mystery appointment and she left. I paid the bill and eventually went back to my cottage."

"So did your ex-wife say anything to you about who she was going to meet and where?"

"I've just told you," Sir Robert Huxton replied tetchily. "She said nothing at all about it."

"But were you planning to invite her, errm, back to your cottage for…?"

"If you must know, I was planning to take her to a concert in the evening – the Carlow Valley Symphony Orchestra. I'd obtained a couple of tickets."

"And then?"

"You are straying way beyond your brief, Mr Walsingham. That is absolutely no concern of yours and I resent the intrusion…"

"But it is my concern," Clive persisted. "Especially as we think she was murdered shortly after she left you."

"As I understand your role, Mr Walsingham, you are helping the police investigation. Is that right?"

"That's correct."

"But as you're not a serving police officer, you have no power to arrest me."

"That's also correct."

"And by the same token, you have no power to keep me here. So I think it's time I left. As I said, I've got a plane to catch."

Over many years of encounters with mercurial and unpredictable clients, Sir Robert Huxton had largely learnt to control his emotions but it was clear that he was very angry. He placed the document he had been reading into his expensive-looking leather briefcase, stood up, knocked his chair over with a sweep of his muscular arm and marched towards the door. It was only as he was striding towards the door that Clive could see what a big bear-like man he was. Just before he reached the door, he turned and advanced a couple of steps towards Clive who was still sitting.

"I understand that you run a hotel locally; is that right, Mr Walsingham?" He barked the words with a snarl.

"Yes but..."

"And I bet your business would suffer if it suddenly started getting poor reviews on all of these travel and holiday websites."

"I hope you're not trying to intimidate—" Clive began before Sir Robert interrupted.

"Oh, I'm not trying to do anything, Mr Walsingham, apart from offering you a bit of advice. Let's hope you're sensible enough to heed it."

*

Clive was feeling drained of all energy. A combination of a sleepless night, Superintendant Rushwick's perfunctory phone call, about which he was still seething some hours later, difficult, sometimes painful, interviews with Sonia Duffield and Christine Calshott and the bullying threats made by Sir Robert Huxton had left him variously frustrated, bewildered and angry. On top of which, he had nagging doubts that Gary Beechwood, his chef, might have been more involved with the missing girls than he had let on. As he was wandering slowly through the reception area holding a glass of cold milk, Alison Pawlett bustled up. "Clive, I think we need to talk."

Clive emitted a sigh which, in the monastic atmosphere of the empty reception area, proved to be more audible than he expected.

"Have I said something wrong?" Alison asked in typically bullish tones.

"No, not at all," Clive replied wearily. "I'm just feeling a bit tired and frustrated, but you're right, we need to talk. I've got a couple of phone calls to make and then I'll find Clare and we can assemble in the office."

*

"Hello, Dick? Are you alright?" Clive asked as the phone was finally answered.

Dick Beauregard's voice sounded so distant and disembodied that Clive wasn't sure at first that it was him.

"Yes, I'm okay, I suppose," the inspector replied in his familiar, morose fashion.

"Have I called at a bad time?" Clive asked. He was concerned that Dick had taken a long time to answer the phone and, now that he had finally answered, he sounded as though he was being distracted by something or someone.

"It's as good a time as any, I suppose."

"Only I was wondering if you managed to see Guy Sharston today."

"Yes, I did see him and he didn't throw me out, although he knew that I'd been taken off the case – he took great delight in telling me so! He didn't actually say so, but it was pretty clear that he's in regular touch with Superintendant Rushwick and I'm pretty sure he will have phoned him as soon as I left."

"Mmmm – that's interesting. And did you get any useful information from him?"

"Not a lot! As always, he wasn't giving much away. He made a big thing out of not disclosing his sources. He was pretty scathing about our original interest in Lennie Cave. He said he was too well known as a 'perv' for any of the girls at Polbury Manor to go anywhere near him and, in any event, he probably didn't have access to a car. He said the abductor was almost certainly someone the girls trusted – he even went so far as to suggest it might be a woman – and he did confirm that Russell Chalbury has moved back into the area and is currently doing up an old boathouse as a sort of studio-cum-gallery."

"Yes, I think it's about time I paid Russell Chalbury a visit. Incidentally, Dick, I had your Superintendant Rushwick on the phone this morning. He didn't say so in as many words but he's effectively given me twenty-four hours to crack the case or he's going to stand me down as well."

"Oh, well, that's that then," Dick Beauregard responded gloomily. He sighed heavily.

"Not necessarily," Clive replied, trying to sound more optimistic than he felt. "I think I might have a way of distracting him for a while, but tomorrow is almost certainly going to be our last chance. I take it you're still willing to help?"

"Absolutely! I don't seem to have any other pressing engagements."

"Good! I'd like us to go and see Alan and Tessa Ashurst in the morning."

*

In the background, Clive could hear an animated, though indistinct, conversation between at least two female voices.

"Have I called at a bad time?" he asked anxiously.

"No, it's okay," Becky Huxton replied, half shouting to make herself heard above the cacophony of voices. "I share a flat with another couple of girls and this is the time of day when we all get back from work and catch up on the day's gossip."

"I spoke to your father a little earlier and he gave me your details. I hope you don't mind."

Becky Huxton giggled. "Yes, he phoned to tell me. It sounds as though you might have upset him, Mr Walsingham, which was a silly thing to do. It doesn't pay to upset the very important Sir Robert Huxton, you know."

"Yes, he certainly seemed a bit miffed," Clive confided. "Does he get angry a lot?"

"He has his moments," Becky Huxton agreed, though Clive wondered if she might have been holding something back. "Let's put it this way – he doesn't like to be contradicted, or challenged in any way, although I suppose having a forceful personality is one of the reasons he's been so successful."

"What sort of a father has he been?"

"Absent mainly. When he's not been in touch for a while, he sometimes suffers from guilt feelings and he buys me expensive presents or takes me out somewhere nice, so I suppose it's not all bad."

"I get the impression that you've been pretty close to your mother over the years."

"I have." Clive detected a tremor in Becky Huxton's voice. "It was such a shock to hear what had happened to her. She may have had a few failings over the years, mainly alcohol related, but she didn't deserve that. I hope you catch the bastard."

"We're doing our best and that's really what I wanted to talk to you about. We're pretty sure there's a link between your mother's, erm, murder and the disappearance of the five girls, including your sister, ten years ago. According to your father, you shared a room with your sister, Charlotte."

"Yeah, that's right. Vicky, my eldest sister had her own room – the perks of being the first born, I suppose – and Charlie and I shared."

"Did you get on well?"

"Listen," Becky Huxton lowered her voice to a conspiratorial whisper. "I don't know what my father told you but Charlie was well… erm, not that easy to get on with."

"In what way?"

"In every way, pretty much! She seemed to have a permanent chip on her shoulder about something or other. She resented Vicky for being older and more mature, she resented me for being 'mummy's pet' as she put it, she resented her father for never being at home, she resented her mother for being, well, pretty hopeless, she resented her teachers for picking on her, or so she thought, and she resented most of her friends for a whole variety of reasons, but mainly to do with boyfriends."

"So it would be fair to conclude that your relationship was strained?" Clive asked diplomatically.

"Oh, we rubbed along most of the time – we had to really as we were sharing a room – but she was two years older than me so, inevitably, we had our own friends and our own interests."

"I see! And was there anything unusual or strange about your sister's behaviour in the days, weeks even, before she disappeared?"

"Not strange exactly but she had changed. She'd found out – we both had – that our father was screwing the deputy head at Polbury Manor, Christine Calshott, and she began to feel sorry for our mother. I certainly think she was beginning to regret not being as close to her as she should have been. I think she was making an effort to curb her rebellious ways a bit. For example, she started playing the violin again. She'd been very promising as a youngster – a talent she'd obviously inherited from her mother – but she'd given it up when she started to develop other interests. And then suddenly, a few weeks before she disappeared, around the time she found out about our father and Christine Calshott, she told me in the strictest confidence that she had started to play again. She used to smuggle the violin out of the house. Our mother was never very observant and, after school, Charlie would go off and rehearse somewhere; I don't know where or who with, I'm afraid, but her plan was to put on a little informal recital for our mother when she felt she was good enough – it was going to be a surprise. Sadly, she never got the chance…"

"What about the day she disappeared. Your mother seemed to think that she was spending the night with her friend Karen Beechwood, but Karen denied any knowledge."

"Yes, that was odd. I mean, Charlie would often decide to spend the night with Karen – usually when she'd had a bit of a spat with our mother – but the arrangement was that Charlie would always phone and let us know that she was at Karen's. She wasn't terribly reliable, of course – something else she'd inherited from her mother – so sometimes she'd forget to phone but nobody seemed to worry that much; she always turned up the next day. On the day that she disappeared, she'd had a bit of a falling out with our mother over breakfast – I can't remember the details – so it was no great surprise when she didn't show up after school. I thought, at the time, that our mother got a phone call from her during the evening, but I was up in my room so I didn't hear the conversation. All I know is that, later on, our mother announced that Charlie wouldn't be coming home that night and nothing more was said. I just assumed – we all did – that Charlie was at Karen's but, of course, we now know…"

"And yet, when your mother was first interviewed by the police, she said that she'd had no contact with Charlotte, er

Charlie, that evening but that she just assumed she had spent the night with her friend, Karen."

"I know," Becky Huxton agreed. "It's very strange isn't it? We, Vicky and I, challenged her about it later but she got very defensive and said she must have got confused. It's possible that Charlie did phone to say she wouldn't be home that night and my mother just assumed she was with Karen, or maybe the phone call my mother got wasn't from Charlie at all…"

"So do you have any theories about where Charlie might have gone?"

"No, absolutely none; she just vanished," Becky Huxton replied firmly. "We realised later that her violin was missing but no one could remember when they last saw it, so we didn't think it desperately important or relevant."

"Mmmm. Are you in touch with your sister, Victoria?"

"Not what you'd call 'in touch'. I expect my father told you that she walked out on us when she was eighteen and I haven't seen her since. I know she's alive and out there somewhere because I get a text from her every Christmas and on my birthday, but I've no idea where she is or what she's doing."

"Were you surprised when Victoria walked out?"

"Not surprised, exactly, but bloody angry. I mean, we didn't have the easiest of times with our parents and I know Vicky got pretty frustrated but, when she walked out, I felt as though she'd abandoned me. Losing both your sisters in the space of a couple of years is bloody hard to take especially when your father is an absentee and your mother is an alcoholic…"

"Have you tried to meet up with Victoria?"

"Tried for a while; I used to reply to her texts suggesting we meet up but never got a reply, so I gave up in the end."

"You stayed close to your mother though."

"Somebody had to. She was in a terrible mess."

"We understand she had a job at Craigbridge School but she resigned at the end of the summer term. Do you know why?"

"She had the occasional lapse, Mr Walsingham. Most of the time she was fine but, every so often, when she got stressed, she'd seek solace in copious quantities of wine. It doesn't do to turn up for work drunk so she had to go."

"Do you know why she was so stressed?"

"Mmm, I'm not really sure. I think she'd had some contact with my father – I don't know what about – but she seemed quite agitated."

"Did you know that she met your father for lunch in Morstock on the day we think she was murdered?"

"What? You're joking! Surely you're joking!"

"No! Your father told us and we have an eye witness and CCTV images. Your father said they were considering getting back together."

"Really? Well I'd been encouraging her to try to and make a go of it with my father for a while but I didn't think she'd been taking me seriously. Wow, that is a shock! Hang on a minute though, are you suggesting that my father was involved in her murder?"

"I've no idea who murdered your mother. All I know is that your father was very evasive when I challenged him about it."

"Huh! It's no wonder he got angry then."

"But let me be clear about something. We're pretty sure your mother was murdered on that Saturday, 6th September, but you didn't report her missing for another week. Why is that?"

"I didn't know she'd been murdered, for God's sake! I don't live, sorry, didn't live with my mother. I work during the week so didn't have a lot of contact with her apart from weekends. I did try to phone her during the week, Wednesday I think, to arrange to meet at the weekend but there was no answer. That wasn't especially unusual – she sometimes went out in the evening even if it was only to the off-licence – but when I still couldn't get a reply by Friday I was getting worried so I phoned her neighbour. She said she hadn't seen her during the week at all, so I went round to her place and it was obvious that she hadn't been there all week; there was a pile of post on the doormat. So I spent the rest of Friday evening phoning anyone that my mother might have been in touch with – relatives and friends – but I drew a complete blank – so, on Saturday morning, I reported her missing and then I sent a text to my father who was out of the country, as usual."

"I see. Thank you for your time," Clive replied solicitously. "I'm sure this has all been very difficult for you. I have just one final question and then I'll let you go. Did your mother own a computer?"

Becky Huxton hesitated for a moment or two before responding. "She had a computer but she hardly ever used it. She did have a smartphone which she used all the time. I think her entire life was on there – her messages, her appointments, her list of contacts, her photographs, her—"

"Her photographs!" Clive interrupted. "I wonder!"

*

Clive, Clare and Alison had once again assembled in the tiny office, each manoeuvring themselves carefully into their allocated chair. Clive had arranged for a selection of reviving drinks to be provided. As Alison sat down, she sighed heavily.

"You alright, Alison?" Clare asked, with her uncanny knack of sensing a person's mood even before they had uttered a word.

"What? Oh, yeah! It's just that I'm not looking forward to dining on my own again this evening. I mean, don't get me wrong, your chef, Gary, produces some great food. It's just that the dining room is usually half empty and none of the diners –

residents or guests – ever look remotely suspicious. I'm sure I could be doing something more useful."

"Well, I rather think your days of undercover surveillance have come to an end, as it happens," Clive replied gloomily. "I got a call from Superintendant Rushwick this morning. We agreed that he is unlikely to find any more bodies so…"

"You haven't heard about the latest body then?" Alison asked.

My God! Another body!" Clare shrieked excitedly. Clive's reaction was more circumspect. There was something casual, almost flippant about Alison's announcement, as though the latest discovery was not one of critical significance.

"You've found another body?" Clive asked. "Where? When?"

"Earlier today, washed up on a beach near Marbella. The local police think it's the body of Derek Farringdon."

"Had he been murdered?" Clare asked, her grey-green eyes sparkling with excitement.

"They're not treating his death as suspicious. We know he had serious financial problems…"

"So he threw himself into the sea," Clive mused.

"It certainly looks that way."

"So probably not directly connected to our investigation?"

"No, probably not," Alison agreed reluctantly.

"Okay," Clive continued. "So, as I was saying, of the ten parents of the girls who disappeared, six are already dead, three are receiving police protection and one is already on his way to the airport with a police escort. Now, Mr Rushwick and his team are no doubt working hard studying all the forensic evidence, appealing for witnesses, talking to relatives and friends of the victims, all that sort of stuff, but the impression I'm getting is that they're getting nowhere, rather like the original investigation ten years ago. So, unless he gets lucky and turns up a new lead or two overnight, I suspect he will shortly be switching his attention to the work that we've been doing. Under those circumstances,

"Alison, I reckon it'll be safe for you to join us – me and Clare – for dinner this evening. Among Gary's dishes tonight is salmon fillet which I can heartily recommend."

Alison smiled. "That's very kind of you, Clive, and I accept your invitation."

"But what about our investigation?" Clare asked, her strained voice betraying signs of anger and frustration. "Is that it? Are we just going to hand over the case to Superintendant Rushwick and walk away?"

Clive winked at Clare. "Not yet! Now I reckon that I can give him a bit of a distraction for a few hours tomorrow but after that, I'm pretty sure he's going to take us off the case, especially when he finds out that I asked Dick to pay Guy Sharston a visit today."

Clare narrowed her eyes and stared at Clive. "You're up to something, aren't you?"

Clive smiled mischievously. "I might have something up my sleeve, but I'd rather not say any more at the moment. All I know for certain is that we haven't got much time left if we're going to solve this case. So I suggest we share all that we've found out today and agree what we're going to do tomorrow. But before we go any further, Alison, do you mind if I ask you a question?"

Clive turned towards Alison Pawlett who started slightly, as though not expecting Clive's immediate attention. "Is it about the case?" she asked uneasily. The previous evening's embarrassing encounter with Clive was still painfully fresh in her memory.

"Of course," Clive replied with what he hoped was a reassuring smile. "When you first went to Olivia Farringdon's flat, I imagine you removed anything financial that you thought might be helpful; bank statements, bills and receipts – that kind of thing."

"Naturally!"

"Would it be possible to have a look at them? I'd rather not say why just at the moment but it might be important."

Alison looked at Clive suspiciously. "Of course, I'll, errm, get somebody in the office to email copies of them over to you."

"Thank you, Alison. And I also have a question for Clare."

Clare glanced nervously across to Clive. "Do you? What have I done?"

"Nothing," Clive reassured her. "I just wondered, when you get a moment, could you have a little search on the internet for anyone locally who gives private violin lessons? I'll explain why later."

Keen to play her full part in the investigation, Clare replied enthusiastically. "I'll have a go, if it'll help."

"Good, thanks. So, Alison, I imagine you want to tell us what you've been up to today?"

"Ah, er, y-yes, I s-suppose so," Alison Pawlett stuttered as she reached for her notebook and turned over several pages. "I paid a visit to Harvey and Holford's offices and spoke to the so-called Managing Director, a rather sleazy character called Andrew Roderick. He's confirmed that Raymond Gulliver works for them but, interestingly, he's had several warnings for inappropriate remarks or behaviour in the presence of women. They don't want to sack him because he's quite good at his job so they turn a bit of a blind eye to his misdemeanours and try to regulate his work so that he doesn't have much contact with women."

"I noticed, by the way, that the lawn outside Stowbrook library hasn't been mown for some time," Clive observed.

"And Raymond Gulliver told me, yesterday afternoon, that he was on his way there so…"

"And I haven't seen him around here today, either," Clare interjected. "I know it's been a bit of a damp day but he usually puts in an appearance of some kind during the day, if only to potter in his shed."

"Mmm, it sounds as though you might have to speak to your friend Mr Roderick again in the morning to see if

Raymond has reported for duty." Clive made his comments sound like a command.

Alison wrinkled her nose. "Yes, thanks! Love to! My friend, Mr Roderick, did say a couple of things that might interest you, though. Firstly, Raymond Gulliver does some freelance work, in his own time. Mr Roderick thought it might be just looking after a few people's gardens but he didn't really know. So Raymond Gulliver could be working for anybody, anywhere, for all we know. And I was given a copy of his work schedule and guess where one of the locations is – Mallowcrest!" Alison concluded triumphantly.

"Oh, God, oh, God!" Clare exclaimed. "Gary and Raymond's names keep cropping up. That's two of our staff well and truly implicated!"

Clive frowned. "Yes that is a bugger!" he said, quietly. "Oh and that reminds me," he snapped his fingers in frustration. "I meant to ask how Beth is today. Have you seen her?"

"I put my head around her door this morning," Clare affirmed. "She was very tearful and she seemed quite frightened about something, but she didn't say what. She's still waiting for the results of the tests that the doctor carried out so maybe she's frightened about what they might reveal. Gary's been very good though. When he came in this afternoon, he went up to Beth's room and spent some time with her before he started preparing dinner. He said he thought he'd cheered her up a bit but he didn't go into details."

In the momentary silence that followed, Alison Pawlett gave an embarrassed cough. "And if I may continue," she continued, "I tracked down Finnarts the electricians. I spoke to Danny and his uncle Tommy – I didn't much care for either of them, if I'm being honest. They were behaving quite strangely, a bit evasive at times and a bit cocky at other times. They confirmed that they had worked at Polbury Manor School when the science wing was being built but claimed to have no recollection of working at Mallowcrest. They did say—"

"Hang on a minute," Clare interrupted. "Did you think they'd been working at Mallowcrest?"

"Y-yes," Alison replied, tentatively. "Clive phoned me earlier to tell me about the extension to Mallowcrest and how Finnarts were the electricians. Didn't he tell you?"

"I haven't had a chance yet," Clive replied quickly before Clare could say anything more. "I was going to mention it later but, since it's come up, I'll tell you now. I paid a visit to Mallowcrest this morning and discovered that they had an extension built around eleven years ago. The architect was Sir Robert Huxton and the electricians on the project were Finnarts."

Clare gasped. "Oh God, that's terrible. So not only do we have Gary Beechwood and Raymond Gulliver potentially implicated, we now also have Debbie Oxton's brother-in-law! It's no wonder the police have been paying so much attention to this place – half the people who work here are mixed up in this sordid business in some shape or form. If any of this gets out, we'll be finished here. Nobody will want anything to do with us and…"

"Hang on, hang on!" Clive admonished. "Let's try and keep things in perspective. We have no proof that Gary or Raymond or Tommy Finnart are involved in anything illegal, certainly not mass murder, so let's just calm down!"

"Yes but—" Clare began before Clive quickly interrupted.

"Let's just give Alison a chance to finish her account and then we'll mull over what we've learned."

"Yes, yes, I'm sorry," Clare conceded. "I'm just very tired and finding this whole business a bit stressful. Carry on, Alison."

"Thank you," Alison replied politely enough although her expression made her frustration clear. "As I was saying, the Finnarts are spending quite a bit of time installing the electrics at a boathouse that Russell Chalbury is converting."

"Yes, Dick, er, Inspector Beauregard found out about Russell Chalbury's boathouse from Guy Sharston," Clive added. "So Mr Chalbury will be receiving a visit from us tomorrow."

"Oh that reminds me," Clare chimed in while rummaging through some notes in front of her. "I came across this item in the original case notes. I thought you might find it interesting." She thrust a piece of paper under Clive's nose. He studied it briefly before emitting a low whistle.

"It's a note about a conversation with Lennie Cave!" Clive sounded excited. "Was it followed up at all?"

"Not that I can see."

"Ah, well no, it wouldn't be," Clive replied enigmatically before returning the note to Clare. "This could be very important – we'll need to follow it up."

"And what else have you both discovered?" Alison asked, somewhat piqued that Clive already knew about Russell Chalbury and the boathouse and annoyed that he had returned the note to Clare without letting her see it first.

Clive tugged at his earlobe and exhaled sharply. "Well, for a start, I don't think Charlotte Huxton and Isabel Draycott could have been abducted on their way into or out of school. The road outside would have been full of pupils and parents and there are no blind alleys or dark corners in which a potential abductor could lurk unseen."

"What if the abductor was a woman?" Clare suddenly asked.

"How do you mean?" Clive asked, immediately realising the inanity of his question.

"Well everyone has been looking for a man – after all it's usually a man who abducts young girls – but somebody mentioned that the abductor was probably someone the girls trusted and a woman would not seem nearly so suspicious, especially if she was known to the girls."

Clive took a large swig from the glass of milk that he had just poured out. "You know that's exactly what Dick said when I spoke to him earlier. He'd had the same conversation with Guy Sharston. Mind you, I'm not sure what a woman's motive would be; it's less likely to be sexual."

"Yes, true," Clare replied, excitedly. "But she could have been working for a man, you know, selecting the victims for him, or it could be jealously or rage or… who knows?"

"Trouble is we haven't got many female suspects."

"That's because we haven't been looking for them. There must be plenty of female teachers at Polbury Manor and loads of mums collecting their kids."

"True, but we've probably not got very long before Superintendant Rushwick calls us off, so we haven't got time to start too many new lines of inquiry. It might be worth speaking to Christine Calshott again, though. Sir Robert Huxton mentioned her; he seemed to have had a particularly soft spot for her, if you get my meaning – and I did hear something today about Tessa Ashurst that made me sit up."

"What was that?"

"I'd rather not say until tomorrow but I'm just wondering, Clare, if you found out whether Tessa Ashurst was ever regarded as a serious suspect in the original investigation."

Still determined to play her full part in the investigation, Clare quickly thumbed through her neatly compiled notes. "Well, from what I can glean from the case notes, Tessa and Alan Ashurst were originally both treated as suspects when their daughter disappeared but no evidence was found and, once other girls started to go missing, the police lost interest in them. It's interesting though that both Alan and Tessa were given compassionate leave by their respective employers and Tessa didn't actually return to work until the end of August and even then, it was only part-time so…"

"So she may not have an alibi for the dates that the girls disappeared. Alison, I wonder if you'd mind phoning Carlow

Valley Council tomorrow and find out what hours Tessa Ashurst works and whether she's had any leave recently."

Alison nodded wearily. "I'll look into it. Meanwhile, what did you make of Sir Robert Huxton?"

Clive exhaled sharply again. "He seemed quite pleasant to start with, but he became very defensive whenever I tried to probe a bit more deeply. He did say that his wife, Kate, became an alcoholic and, basically, lost control of their three daughters. He admitted to having had a brief affair with Christine Calshott and he also said that his daughter Charlotte's behaviour was especially difficult. Interestingly, he said that Kate thought that the friend Charlotte was staying with on the night she disappeared was called Karen Beechwood…"

"Oh, God! Not Gary again!" Clare muttered under her breath.

"He also said," Clive continued, "that their eldest daughter, Victoria, walked out on them many years ago and hasn't been in touch since."

"Wow, another missing girl!" Clare exclaimed.

"Possibly," Clive conceded with little conviction. "Although she's had some limited contact with her sister Rebecca. As I said, I also discovered that Sir Robert designed an extension at Mallowcrest. It was completed at least a year before Catherine Duffield went missing but it does at least give him a connection with the building – something that he was trying to deny, for some reason – and he's bound to have visited the place occasionally. He also got quite angry when I pointed out that he'd been having lunch with his ex-wife on the day she was murdered. He tried to deny it at first but then admitted that he had met Kate for lunch. He said they were thinking about getting back together but Kate had to rush off and that's the last he saw of her. It was then that he started to threaten me."

A look of panic spread across Clare's face. "My God, what did he do?"

Clive shrugged dismissively. "Oh, nothing important; he just likes to bully people, I think. He also confirmed that his flight to Dubai last week was a last-minute thing."

"Is that important?" Alison asked, sounding mystified.

"Probably not," Clive conceded, "unless he felt he had to leave the country in a hurry. If he had been going around murdering the parents of these girls, including his ex-wife, his sudden departure would explain why he didn't turn up on Friday to meet with Alan Ashurst. Talking of which, I've been taking another look at the sequence of the recent murders. We've tended to focus on them in the order in which their bodies were discovered but, based on the pathologist's findings, I've made a list of when they were actually murdered."

"And?"

Clive rummaged amongst a wad of papers on his desk before he found the one he wanted, which he brandished with an air of satisfaction. "And, based on the pathologist's conclusions, Olivia Farringdon was murdered on Thursday 4th September, the day she checked out of here, Kate Huxton was murdered on Saturday 6th September, Edward Duffield was murdered on Monday 8th September, also the day he checked out of here, Keith Draycott was murdered on Wednesday 10th September and it is possible that Alan Ashurst was due to be murdered on Friday 12th September. Can you see a pattern?"

"Each murder was two days after the previous one," Clare cried triumphantly.

"Exactly! I don't know what it proves, except that our murderer had planned his executions very precisely. After each murder, he gave himself forty-eight hours to hide the body, dispose of all the victim's personal effects, cover his tracks and prepare himself for the next murder."

"Phew, you have been busy," Alison observed before yawning heavily.

"Well, as I said earlier, I don't think we're going to be given much more time. But I do have another couple of observations to make," Clive continued.

"Oh, good!" Alison muttered sardonically as she glanced surreptitiously at her watch.

"I spoke with Sonia Duffield for quite a while earlier, or rather, I listened to her for quite a while. I don't think she's directly connected with our kidnappings or our murders but it appears that Edward Duffield was having an affair – that's why he spent so much time away from home. She says she's only just found out."

"But that would give her a motive for murdering him," Clare suggested.

"Yes it would, but not any of the other parents as far as we can tell. And when I went to look at Corwood campsite, it's obvious that a group of new houses has been built on some land that was close to the shower block that Rosemary Edwyn was heading for when she disappeared. I'd like to know what was there at the time."

"I remember seeing a map in the case notes," Clare announced excitedly. "I'll have a look at it. Oh and incidentally, when I had a look at the statements that were taken at the time, there seemed to be a bit of a discrepancy."

"How do you mean?"

"Well, the official line is that Rosemary Edwyn was kept on a pretty tight leash by her parents and that she was only allowed out of their sight when she went to the shower block; that's certainly what her mother said at the time. But in Howard Edwyn's statement, he said that Rosemary had made a couple of friends on the campsite and that she spent a bit of time with them – unfortunately he didn't say who the friends were or when and where Rosemary spent time with them, but it does suggest that Rosemary wandered off on her own a bit more than we thought."

"Mmm, it certainly does; well done! And did you find out anything else of interest today?"

Clare hesitated briefly and ran her hand through her hair. "I'm not sure," she replied uncertainly. "It may be just a quirk, but I've been looking at the photographs of the five girls and there's something a bit odd. I mean, it might be coincidence, of course, but four of the five girls had fair hair – look!"

She handed over the relevant file to Clive who subjected the photographs to his normal thorough scrutiny. "So they have," he agreed at last. "So did our abductor have a penchant for girls with fair hair? And if so, why does one of them have dark hair? I'm not—" Clive was interrupted by the sight of Alison Pawlett's head suddenly falling forward and the thud of it hitting the desk in front of her."

"My God, Alison, are you okay?" Attentive as usual, Clare was quickly on her feet and at Alison's side as the sergeant slowly lifted her head and rubbed it thoughtfully.

"I'm so sorry," Alison said quietly and slowly, while still rubbing her head. "I must have dozed off. I'm terribly sorry – it's just I didn't have a very good night and it's been a busy day and I've been trying and failing to access Keith Draycott's computer." She shot a quick glance at Clive.

"Alison, I'd no idea you were still trying to access Keith Draycott's computer." Clive's tone was apologetic. "You should have said. I just assumed you'd looked at it and found nothing of interest."

"I wish! I've tried all the obvious passwords – names, birthdays, mother's maiden name – you know, the usual things, but nothing…" She was interrupted by the loud click of Clive snapping his fingers.

"Bordeaux 1991!" he exclaimed.

"I beg your pardon?" Alison replied, wrinkling her nose and looking bemused.

"Bordeaux 1991," Clive repeated. "You remember that book about vintage wines we found on Keith Draycott's desk?"

"Yes, I've still got it in my room."

"Well, he'd been through the book and marked some of the wines. And, from what I know, they were all the best vintages except one. 'Bordeaux 1991' is known to be, shall we say, an ordinary wine compared to the rest that he'd marked. I couldn't work out at the time why he'd marked that one – it made no sense – but it would make perfect sense if he was using it as a password. It's a bit of a long shot, but…"

"Yes, right, thanks. I'll get straight on to it," Alison replied.

"No you won't. You need to get some sleep. It can wait until the morning." Clive looked at his watch. "Look, it's seven o'clock. Let's forget about all of this for a while and go and have dinner."

As she was nearest to the door, Clare led the way briskly, followed more lethargically by Alison, still rubbing her forehead, with Clive bringing up the rear. As they entered the dining room and walked over to their allotted table, Clare glanced casually out of the window across the lawn, its colour fading fast in the dusky half-light, stopped and gasped.

"My God!" she shrieked. "There's a fire, down by the walled garden!"

"That's Raymond's shed," Clive shouted as he hurtled through the conservatory door, dashed across the decking and sprinted across the lawn. As he got nearer, he was half-blinded by the orange flames, brilliant against the dark background, spewing from the collapsing timbers of the shed. He had closed to within a few feet when he was driven back by the heat of the fire.

"My God!" Clare shrieked again, as she caught up with Clive, and pointed to the adjoining car park. "That's Raymond's van over there, isn't it?"

"Yes it is," Clive called over his shoulder as he raced towards the grey van parked neatly in a corner of the car park. "Raymond, are you in there?" he shouted as he banged on the doors of the van.

"There's no sign of him out here," Clare wailed. "I thought he might be trying to put the fire out but there's no sign!"

"Oh shit, no, no!" Clive exclaimed. "Please say he's not got trapped inside!"

"I've called the fire brigade," Alison announced importantly as she joined Clive and Clare.

"Good work, Alison," Clive called. "Let's hope they're quick. We think Raymond might be trapped inside!"

At that moment, Clive's phone rang. Thinking the call might be related in some way to the fire, he answered it quickly, but all he could hear were the first unmistakeable bars of Chopin's Funeral March.

"Oh for God's sake, just sod off!" Clive shouted.

Twelve

Clive couldn't sleep. As soon as he noticed the first signs of watery daylight penetrating a small gap between the bedroom curtains, he rose silently, so as not to disturb Clare, crept into the bathroom where he dressed quietly, wandered on tiptoe through the hotel, nearly tripping over Archie the cat who had, for some reason, chosen to sleep in the middle of the main corridor, opened the conservatory door and marched across the dew-laden lawn towards the still-smouldering embers of the gardener's shed. As he approached, discovering rather belatedly that the casual shoes that he had put on were not waterproof, he could discern, amongst the blackened, charred timbers, the burnt residue of some garden implements but, mercifully, there were no signs of human remains.

As he was studying the scorched debris, he failed to notice Alison Pawlett arriving silently at his shoulder.

"It was obviously started deliberately," Alison suddenly announced, causing Clive to recoil in surprise.

"Bloody hell, Alison, you startled me!" Clive exclaimed.

"Sorry, I didn't mean to, I…" Alison spluttered, her breath forming a cloud of vapour in the cold, damp air.

"You should be in bed," Clive admonished her gently. "Couldn't you sleep?"

"Nah! I've been taking a look at Keith Draycott's computer. I looked out of my window and saw you walking across the lawn so I thought… Anyway, you were absolutely right about 'Bordeaux 1991' being the password. As soon as I tried it, I got into all of his files."

"That's brilliant, Alison! And what have you found?"

"Nothing very exciting, unfortunately; the files that I've looked at so far are mainly to do with rather boring church business and there's a bit on the Carlow Valley Arts Festival, with which he was obviously involved, but there's nothing there about the disappearance of his daughter or any of the other girls or the recent murders or anything that might help us. I had hoped that there might be an email or something from 'Circe' which would have given us a lead, but sadly not. I'm going to let our technical experts take a look in case there are any recently deleted files that they can retrieve. I did find this though. I printed it off for you."

Alison Pawlett rummaged in the pocket of her denim trousers and produced a crumpled piece of paper which she handed to Clive who studied it carefully for a moment or two before he spoke.

"Mmmm. This is a newspaper account of the car accident that killed his wife, Laura. I see it took place in Penheath. I wonder, Alison, if you can track down the police record of this accident. It must be on file somewhere."

I'll have a go," Alison affirmed.

Clive sniffed the air thoughtfully.

"Gosh, there is a strong smell of petrol."

"Exactly," Alison agreed. "As I said, this fire was started deliberately. Somebody doused the shed in petrol before they set fire to it."

"Mmmm," Clive replied thoughtfully as he rubbed his hands together. He was feeling the cold. "All very intriguing! Any news of Raymond yet?"

"No, none at all. There's nothing to suggest that he was in the shed when it went up and he's not in his van." She nodded towards Raymond Gulliver's deserted van in the hotel car park. "His mobile is switched off and there's no sign of him at his usual address. I'll give Andrew Roderick a call when his office opens."

"Maybe Raymond took fright and legged it when his shed went up in flames though God knows where he's gone. Unless of course…" Clive fell silent as he mulled over another possible scenario.

"So was this just a random arson attack or was Raymond being targeted?" Alison asked a still reflective and silent Clive.

Clive shrugged. "I can't be sure, but Raymond's mysterious disappearance suggests that it wasn't random. Of course, this could be a warning to me – you know, 'this time it's your shed, next time it'll be you'. Somebody played a funeral march down the phone at me yesterday evening and there are a few people who definitely don't like us poking around. Sir Robert Huxton, for example, was certainly making threats when I saw him yesterday. Maybe we're getting too close to the truth for somebody's liking." Clive turned to face Alison, bent his knees slightly so that he was at the same height as his colleague and peered into her eyes.

"The thing is, Alison," he confided. "You have made a huge contribution to our investigation over the last few days but I've got a feeling that things are about to get quite dangerous and you could be put at some risk if you continue with your inquiries. I wouldn't blame you one jot if you pulled out now and asked Superintendant Rushwick for your duties to be reassigned."

Alison Pawlett's reaction was predictably brusque. "Bugger that, Clive! Just when things are getting really interesting? No way!"

"Okay, that's fine," Clive replied. "But for God's sake, look after yourself."

*

Although his early start had been unplanned, Clive had used the opportunity to talk to Gary Beechwood before his chef's attention focused on the preparations for breakfast. It had been time well spent. Feeling pleased with himself, he was returning from the kitchen with an invigorating, steaming mug of coffee in his hand when he bumped into Beth Wroxham. She was dressed for work and, although a little pale, seemed contented and relaxed. Her easy smile had returned.

"Hello, Beth," Clive chirped. "I didn't expect to see you up and about this morning; how are you?"

"Oh, I'm much better this morning," Beth gushed. "I'm ready to get back to work today and I'm sooo, sooo sorry for the problems I've caused you and Clare over the past couple of days. You've been so kind and…"

"Well it's good to see you looking so much better," Clive replied. "But don't try and do too much too soon. I'm sure Clare will understand."

"Yes, but I would like to explain to you both why I've been out of sorts and behaving strangely. I owe it to you both and—" She was interrupted by Clive's mobile phone ringing.

"Sorry Beth, I think this call might be important," Clive announced grimly as he marched towards his office. "Try and catch me later."

"Hello, Clive! Rushwick here," the brusque voice at the other end of the phone boomed. "It has been drawn to my attention that Detective Inspector Beauregard was helping you with your investigations yesterday."

Clive smiled to himself as he wandered into the office. Guy

Sharston had obviously been in touch. "Yes, that's right," he replied casually.

"Well, I'm very disappointed in you, Clive. You came with such a good reputation but you must realise that deliberately bringing Inspector Beauregard into your investigation was contrary to my express instructions and I will therefore have to consider your future—"

"The thing is," Clive interrupted, though he wasn't sure that Superintendant Rushwick was listening. "Sergeant Pawlett and I are supposed to be operating under the radar – that was the brief you gave us – but we felt that someone needed to talk to Guy Sharston. He seemed to know an awful lot about the original investigation ten years ago and, after all, his job is to root out stories, so we thought he might have some useful information for us. The trouble is, we felt that our cover would be well and truly blown if we turned up at Guy Sharston's office asking questions, so I suggested to Dick, er, Inspector Beauregard, that he went along instead. There was no one else that I could ask and it was important that someone spoke to him."

"Nevertheless…"

"So I presume that Guy Sharston phoned you."

"Yes, er, well, yes." For the first time, Superintendant Rushwick sounded discomfited. "Be that as it may, your investigation doesn't seem to be getting anywhere. I'm grateful for your help, but I think it's time…"

"Ah well, that's not quite true – I do have a name for you. It's a name that's cropped up quite a lot in connection with the girls' disappearances and I suggest you take him in and find out what he knows. Oh, and there have been sightings of a blue Toyota."

*

Detective Inspector Beauregard appeared to be clutching a half-eaten jam doughnut as he clambered inelegantly into Clive's car.

"Thanks for helping me out," Clive said cautiously, as he recalled the inspector's accident-prone tendencies and hoped that the doughnut would not suddenly explode its contents over his recently cleaned upholstery.

"S'alright," the inspector replied, unenthusiastically, whilst chewing. "Things can't get much worse, after all. I mean, I haven't got much to lose and there's just the chance that we can crack this case before I'm formally suspended."

"You know, I've so missed your positive, up and at 'em, devil-may-care attitude," Clive observed sarcastically.

"I'm sorry," the inspector replied sourly. "But I haven't really got much to be cheerful about at the moment. Anyway, you'd better tell me what you want me to do."

Clive chuckled to himself. For a moment, he thought of introducing Dick Beauregard to the equally doom-laden Christine Calshott and taking them both to Beachy Head for an al fresco picnic lunch, but he relented.

"It's very important that I get to speak to Tessa Ashurst alone. So, when we arrive, I'd like you to take Alan Ashurst into a different part of the house and ask him some questions. Perhaps you can start by asking about the meeting that never took place with his would-be murderer. Ask him who contacted him and when. Ask him if he's remembered seeing or hearing anything remotely suspicious or unusual while he was waiting. Ask him, for example, if he saw a blue Toyota while he was waiting on Framingford Common. We've been through it all with him before, of course, but he might have remembered something new. Alternatively, his account might differ from the one he gave us last time, which could be illuminating. And, if you think it worthwhile, you might like to ask him where he was last Wednesday when Keith Draycott was murdered – that might get him rattled. And then you might want to talk to him about the death of his daughter, maybe suggesting that he is known to have a quick temper. You could say the school was worried about some bruises on his daughter's face. Ask him if he had a row with his daughter, lost his temper and hit her so hard that he killed her. Suggest that he could have hatched the idea of murdering some other schoolgirls to deflect police interest away from himself. You're a detective inspector, I'm sure you know what to ask."

"I'll do my best of course," Inspector Beauregard announced with little conviction. "But I'm not sure how far I'm going to be able to go. Meanwhile, aren't you going to tell me why you want to get Tessa Ashurst on her own?"

"No, best not," Clive replied firmly. "Remember, you're not really supposed to be here, so the less you know about what I'm doing, the better."

While they were waiting for the door to be opened, Clive had the misfortune to glance across at his colleague and found himself transfixed by a large dollop of jam which had lodged neatly in the middle of his grey tie. He was about to point it out to the inspector when the door opened a fraction and Tessa Ashurst peered apprehensively around it. Her facial expression, initially formal and solemn, transformed into one of nervous anxiety as soon as she recognised Clive.

"Ah, er, hello," she said twitchily. "I didn't expect to see you again. You'd, er, better come in." She led the detectives into the living room and gestured towards the beige and brown three-piece suite. "I expect you'll be wanting to speak to Alan," she announced over her shoulder. "He's upstairs – we've converted the spare bedroom into an office so that Alan can work from home. The police are, erm, still advising us not to leave the house. I'll go and get him."

"No need," Inspector Beauregard interrupted, suddenly sounding confident. "I'll go upstairs and introduce myself and ask him a few questions. Why don't you, erm, wait here with my colleague, Mr Walsingham?"

"Oh! I hope everything's alright," Tessa Ashurst muttered uncertainly as she sat down opposite Clive, while Inspector Beauregard's heavy footsteps thundered up the stairs. "I thought we'd told you everything we know already."

"Oh, it's nothing to worry about," Clive replied, trying to mollify her. "I just wanted to follow up on a couple of things you mentioned when you phoned me."

"Oh, I see!" Tessa Ashurst spoke in little more than a whisper as she turned her head to check that the living room door was firmly closed. "But I don't think…"

"Only I've managed to track down Gary Beechwood."

Tessa Ashurst's face twitched. "Have you? Does he still live round here?"

"He does – not far away from me actually. Anyway, I've spoken to him and I mentioned what you told me about your daughter, Emily, thinking that she might be pregnant and that he might be the father."

"I had no proof," Tessa Ashurst announced defensively. "It was just what you detectives like to call supposition."

"Anyway," Clive continued, smiling, "Gary told me a rather different story. Oh, he didn't deny that he had been friendly with your daughter and he didn't deny that he quite fancied her, but he insisted that he was never, err, intimate with her. He reminded me, quite forcibly, that your daughter was only thirteen at the time. On the other hand, he did tell me that he was frequently intimate with you."

"What? How dare he? He's got no right to say that and you've got no proof," Tessa Ashurst protested with some vehemence, until she realised that she had raised her voice so much that her husband might hear her.

"There are some photographs, apparently," Clive added, disingenuously. He couldn't be sure that there was any photographic record of the illicit liaison – merely a throwaway remark that Gary Beechwood had made, possibly in jest – but he thought it was worth a gamble. It was!

"That's not true, there are no photographs," Tessa Ashurst protested. "He promised me he'd destroyed them. Oh God, I mean…"

"Gary told me in quite some detail – surprising detail, actually – how you often used to entertain him here during the afternoon. When your husband was out at work and your daughter was round at a friend's house, you'd invite Gary over here for a bit of, er, horizontal recreation. And it wasn't your daughter who thought she was pregnant, it was you, wasn't it Mrs Ashurst?"

Tessa Ashurst's face, normally pallid, had turned pink and blotchy. She fidgeted almost uncontrollably as she struggled to compose herself sufficiently to say something coherent.

"I, er… It was… Does Alan have to know?" she asked, weakly. "He can be so… intolerant."

"I can't give you any promises at this stage, but we are investigating abduction and murder, so it is very important that you're honest with me now. We don't want you being accused of misleading the police, do we?"

Tessa Ashurst swallowed hard. "No, no, I suppose not. It, er… it all started as a bit of harmless fun, you see. Gary called round one afternoon for Emily but she wasn't in. I told him she wouldn't be long and invited him to wait. And I made him a drink, and we got talking and I found him quite entertaining in a slightly immature, cocky sort of way. And he seemed quite interested in me and what I had to say, which made a refreshing change. Alan was always working late and, when he did come home, he was always tired and usually in a bad mood. So, anyway, I started inviting Gary around when the coast was clear and, well, one thing led to another and we kind of developed a bit of an understanding. I mean, it was just sex, nothing more than that, but it was good sex. And then, one afternoon, Emily came home unexpectedly and caught us in bed together. And, as you can imagine, she hit the roof. She started screaming and slamming doors and then she shut herself in her room and sobbed for about three hours. It was the next day when I heard her talking on the phone to someone – I really don't know who. I heard her say she was worried about something and wanted to meet up. I assumed she was worried about what she'd seen when she burst in on me and Gary." Tessa Ashurst shrugged. "But I never got the chance to find out."

"Why didn't you tell me this to start with?" Clive asked firmly.

"In front of my husband?"

"You could have mentioned it when you phoned."

"I don't know – I guess I was feeling so ashamed and so embarrassed and so… stupid. And Gary never saw me again after, er, you know, what happened and that hurt. So I suppose part of me wanted to get back at him, in a way. That's why I lied to you. I've been pretty stupid, haven't I?"

"Yes, you have, Mrs Ashurst. If you'd told the police this at the outset, they would have had a better chance of being able to track down whoever it was who abducted your daughter. I don't suppose you have any idea who Emily phoned and who she wanted to meet?"

"Not really, although I can think of a couple of people she might have confided in."

"I'm going to need some names, Mrs Ashurst. Let me…" He was interrupted by the sound of a commotion upstairs.

Inspector Beauregard's interview with Alan Ashurst had been fractious from the start. He was clearly annoyed at being interrupted while he was trying to work and became quite heated when the inspector kept asking about his abortive rendezvous with "Circe".

"I've already told your colleagues what happened at least twice and I see no point in going over it all again," he repeated at least twice. "Now I really am very busy…"

"Tell me about the day your daughter disappeared," Inspector Beauregard persisted.

"Oh, for God's sake, this is bloody ridiculous. I've been through this all before – several times. You know what happened. I came home from work to discover that Emily had gone missing. And that's all I can tell you."

Inspector Beauregard permitted himself a rare smile. Convinced that he had no future with Carlow Valley Police, he was feeling strangely emboldened. "It seems likely that your daughter had arranged to meet somebody on the way to her babysitting appointment. We don't know who it was, but it was almost certainly somebody she trusted. Like her father, for instance?"

"And just what are you implying?" Alan Ashurst got to his feet and began to pace up and down the small room.

"And it is well known that you've got a quick temper."

"You're way out of order, Inspector," Alan Ashurst shouted as he clenched and unclenched his fists.

"After all, we know that Emily's teachers at school were concerned by some bruising on her face."

"Now just…"

"Maybe, when you met her, you got angry and you lashed out. Only you hit her harder than you meant to. Maybe she fell and hit her head and…"

"This constitutes harassment, my friend. I shall be in touch with your superiors about this. Meanwhile, I must ask…"

"And when you realised you'd killed your daughter, you panicked. You hid her body somewhere and hatched an elaborate plan to divert the inevitable police interest away from you. You decided you'd kill a few other schoolgirls to make it look as though a serial killer was responsible and…"

"I've had enough of this rubbish!" Alan Ashurst marched over to where the inspector was sitting, grabbed him by the lapels and hauled him to his feet.

"Where did you hide the bodies?" were the last words Inspector Beauregard uttered before a swinging fist thumped into his face.

When Dick Beauregard stumbled into the living room he was holding a bloodstained handkerchief to his nose.

"Dick, are you alright? What happened?" Clive asked, suspecting he knew the answers.

"Mr Ashurst has just punched me on the nose," the inspector mumbled.

"Oh, God, no!" Tessa Ashurst shrieked. "Let me take a look…"

"Stay away!" Inspector Beauregard shouted. "Come on Clive, we're leaving!"

*

Clive found Clare and Alison sitting by a window in the otherwise deserted conservatory dining room. In front of them, on a table, was a percolator of coffee, a plate of biscuits, countless sheets of paper and Alison's laptop. In a nearby chair, Archie the cat was snoozing contentedly.

"Guess who I found," Clive chirped as Dick Beauregard followed lugubriously behind his host, still holding a bloodstained handkerchief to his damaged nose.

Clare looked up. "Dick! What's happened? Who did this?"

She rushed over to the injured inspector intent on examining the injury, but Dick Beauregard backed away.

"It's, it's okay – no need to fuss," the inspector replied quietly through the handkerchief. "No serious damage done."

"I'm afraid Dick had a bit of a disagreement with Alan Ashurst," Clive announced solemnly. "I don't think Mr Ashurst entirely approved of Dick's line of questioning."

"Huh!" Clare replied with an affronted expression. "I hope you arrested him for assaulting a police officer."

Dick shook his head, pulled up a chair and sat down. "No, I couldn't do that," he said dejectedly as he dabbed gently at his sore nose. "I'm not supposed to be on duty at the moment – I've been suspended, remember – so I had no authority to arrest him." He shook his head again, more emphatically than before. "No, no, I wouldn't be surprised if Mr Ashurst reports me for harassment and that really will be my career, or what's left of it, down the drain."

Clare exchanged quizzical glances with Clive, who shrugged. She was about to say something when her eyes were drawn to a large red stain on Dick's tie. "Oh, Dick, your tie – there's blood on your tie. Would you like me to wash it for you?"

"I think you'll find that's congealed jam," Clive suggested with a smirk that he could barely conceal.

Clare exchanged more quizzical glances with Clive and ran her hand through her hair as though momentarily uncertain what to say or do. She seemed strangely flustered. "Yes, well, I think I'll go and get some cakes," she announced eventually as she turned on her heels and marched out of the room before returning moments later. "It's okay, Jamie's on the case. He'll bring some cakes along in a few minutes. Meanwhile, Clive, I'd like an explanation."

Although Clare was doing her best to keep her emotions in check, in deference to her guests, Clive had no doubt that she was angry; he knew the signs – the pinkness in her cheeks, the fire in her grey-green eyes, the slight pout. He tried to feign innocence but knew that Clare was too perceptive to be fooled.

"An explanation about what?" Clive ventured, with a look of injured innocence.

"You know very well! Gary has been arrested. Apparently Superintendant Rushwick had a tip-off."

"Did he?" Clive asked, still feigning innocence, and moving his chair slightly so that he was just out of striking range.

"You? You tipped off Superintendant Rushwick?" Clare exploded.

Clive gave a rueful smile. "Yes, I'm ashamed to say I did, Clare. You see, I needed to distract Mr Rushwick, otherwise I suspect that, by now, he would've started to trample all over our investigation."

"But, Gary? You shopped your own member of staff!"

Clive poured himself a cup of coffee, just as Jamie arrived with a plate brimming with cakes, which he placed on the table in such a way that he had to reach across Alison, deliberately brushing against her arm as he did so. "I did," Clive continued. "And I think I might also have let slip that a blue Toyota had been seen near a couple of the murder sites."

"Has it? But Gary drives a blue Toyota."

"Yes I believe he does, now you mention it," Clive agreed. "Might I be allowed to explain?"

"This had better be good," Clare replied, her anger showing no sign of abating, as she sat down with a flounce.

"Okay. What I'd like you to do – all of you – is hear me out. Let me tell you what is going on and then, when I've finished, you can tell me what you think. Is that fair?"

"Huh! It depends on what you have to say." Clare half-turned away from Clive as she spoke.

"Alright, here goes! Now, unfortunately, while we've been poking around, Gary's name has come up rather a lot. He was in the sixth form at Polbury Manor shortly before the girls started to disappear and he had a bit of a reputation for chasing the girls. He knew and was friendly with Emily Ashurst and, as Dick and I discovered earlier, he was even more friendly with Tessa Ashurst."

"He was what?" Alison Pawlett spluttered.

"You said you'd let me finish," Clive chided gently.

"Yes, of course, sorry! But Tessa Ashurst and Gary Beechwood? They were having it off? You're not serious!" Alison sounded incredulous.

"Deadly serious! Tessa Ashurst has admitted to regular afternoon trysts with Gary. Then, one day, her daughter came home unexpectedly and caught them at it and that was the end of that! Anyway, as I was saying, the afternoon that Charlotte Huxton disappeared, her mother Kate thought that she was going to spend the night with her friend, Karen Beechwood, the younger sister of Gary. Now, Emily, Charlotte and Gary were part of a group that regularly attended a local youth club. So, when Superintendant Rushwick asked me if I had any names, I mentioned Gary. I also lied and told him that a blue Toyata had been identified as a suspect vehicle."

"But, but…" Clare protested, gesturing animatedly with her hands. "You can't do that… You can't! You have no proof! He might be innocent!"

"Anyway," Clive continued, ignoring Clare's intervention. "I went and had a word with Gary while he was preparing breakfast this morning and told him what I was planning to do and he roared with laughter! You see, whatever his reputation as a bit of a charmer and however close his friendship with some of the girls and Tessa Ashurst was, I know that Gary had absolutely nothing to do with their disappearance."

"Can you be sure?"

"Well, you may remember when he applied for the job here, he came with an extensive CV which included details of where he'd worked previously and a series of glowing testimonials. Now, Gary left Polbury Manor at the end of the summer term, just before the first of the girls disappeared, and went abroad on his travels. We know that he was working in a restaurant in Paris from the start of August right through until October. The head chef at the restaurant has provided a detailed testimonial and will confirm that Gary was there the whole time. And there are other people; people who worked in the restaurant, friends he made while he worked there, his landlord in Paris, who can vouch for him. So, in exchange for a favour, as yet unspecified, that I owe him, Gary has agreed to hold out for as long as possible under Superintendant Rushwick's intensive, razor-sharp interrogation but, eventually, when it's time for him to get back here and start preparing dinner, he will give in and provide Mr Rushwick with his cast-iron alibi and Mr Rushwick will have to let him go. He will then have to make a slightly uncomfortable admission to the media that he's arrested the wrong man."

"Hang on though, Clive," Alison interjected. "When Superintendant Rushwick realises what's happened and that you've been playing games with him, he's going to be gunning for you and, take it from me, you don't want to get on the wrong side of him."

"You certainly don't!" Dick Beauregard agreed, managing to fill his mouth with chocolate cake while still occasionally dabbing his injured nose.

Clive puffed out his cheeks. "Well, I still haven't signed Superintendant Rushwick's contract of employment so he can't fire me and I'm rather hoping that we'll have got this case pretty well sewn up by the time he has tracked me down."

"You seem very confident," Alison said. "Have you been holding out on us?"

Clive permitted himself a smug smile. "I think some of the pieces are coming together, but there's still a lot to do. Has anyone got any more revelations to make before we go our separate ways?"

"I haven't got very far with violin teachers," Clare announced, her anger slowly abating and her enthusiasm gradually returning. "I've got one or two names but no one I recognise. I'll keep searching. There is one thing, though; I said I remembered seeing a map of the area around Corwood campsite at the time of Rosemary Edwyn's disappearance, and I came across this." She opened a file, pushed it across the table towards Clive and pointed at a map.

Clive studied the map carefully before he spoke.

"Bloody hell! You have done well! There's a building on that site that's not there now. We need to find out all we can about it."

"I'll do it," Dick Beauregard said quickly, spraying his colleagues in cake crumbs. "It doesn't sound too dangerous!"

"And I've tracked down the boathouse that Russell Chalbury is renovating," Alison added. "It's just down on the river; you can walk it from here in ten minutes."

"The boathouse! I wonder," Clive replied enigmatically. "Definitely time we paid Russell Chalbury a visit!"

*

The dank, melancholic weather of the previous day had given way, at least temporarily, to a bright, crisp, early autumnal day and Clive wasted little time in declining Alison's offer to drive him to the boathouse. Instead, he donned a pair of waterproof shoes and set off briskly across the hotel lawn to a rustic gate from which a path meandered through a gap in the trees down to the River Carlow, snaking its way gently through the bucolic rural valley below. As he walked, he sniffed the air appreciatively and reflected on the investigation and the progress made. He knew that he was running out of time and that Superintendant Rushwick could take the investigation out of his hands at any time. As he considered that prospect, his pace quickened and his stride lengthened.

The boathouse was about half a mile along the towpath. It was a calm, quiet, relatively unfrequented stretch of the river where an occasional family of swans would drift by or a moorhen would explode noisily from some rushes at the water's edge. Clive smiled and nodded as an unknown cyclist rode by and he paused briefly to allow a shapely female jogger to speed past, but otherwise, he was on his own, alone with his thoughts.

Alison Pawlett was waiting for him as he strode, frowning, towards the boathouse, her fidgety body language suggesting that she was getting impatient. The boathouse itself, one of several scattered along that particular stretch of the river, was a two-storey timber building, with double doors opening out onto the towpath. The brambles and ivy that smothered the sides of the building and some splintering in the timber cladding hinted at a long period of neglect.

Alison hammered aggressively on the double doors, one of which was soon opened by a man of medium build with short, light brown hair brushed forward over his scalp, an abundant beard and a languid expression. He was wearing a paint-stained green shirt, a scruffy pair of jeans and sandals on his otherwise bare feet.

"Russell Chalbury?" Alison asked, somewhat superfluously. "I'm Detective Sergeant Pawlett and this is my colleague, Clive Walsingham. He's working with the police as—"

"A consultant," Clive butted in before Alison could announce the pompous and largely meaningless title that had been conferred upon him by Superintendant Rushwick.

"We are investigating the disappearance of five schoolgirls in this area ten years ago and a number of recent murders that we think are connected."

"Yes, I've heard a lot about it all," Russell Chalbury replied pleasantly. "It's a terrible business! You'd better come in."

He led the way through the ground floor, which was unfurnished apart from a couple of venerable wooden oars, some bits and pieces of old boating equipment, which were gathered to one side, and a pair of bicycles leaning against a wall. A slight smell of damp mingled with the somewhat fresher aromas of new timber and recently applied paint. Clive and Alison followed Russell Chalbury up some creaky wooden stairs to the first floor, which he was obviously using as a studio. A number of plain, white canvasses were propped up against the walls and a half-completed portrait of a female nude took centre stage on a solid easel. Next to the easel was a low table with numerous tubes of paint strewn randomly across it, a pot containing a variety of brushes and a palette bedecked in a kaleidoscope of dried, flaky colours.

"Please excuse the chaos," Russell Chalbury talked over his shoulder as he led his guests to a corner of his studio where dust sheets covered what appeared to be four upright chairs. "I only bought this place a few months ago and it had been derelict for a number of years so there was a huge amount of work to do – there still is. I'm planning to turn the ground floor into a gallery – if you can have a gallery on the ground floor – where I can display and, hopefully, sell some of my paintings. I'm hoping to be ready for the start of the Arts Festival. And this first floor area is my studio. The light through these big old windows will be magnificent when we've finished."

"Who owned this place before you bought it?" Clive asked as he sat down gingerly on a dust sheet-covered chair and looked around. The "big old windows" that Russell Chalbury spoke so highly of were grimy, some of the panes were cracked and much of the light was obscured by ivy, its growth clearly uncontrolled for many years, which covered the walls and straggled across the windows. Whatever Russell Chalbury might claim, Clive reflected, his apparent penchant for painting the female nude had less to do with "magnificent" light and more to do with the secluded, private location that the old boathouse offered.

"It belonged to Polbury Manor School," Russell Chalbury announced casually as he balanced precariously on another of the chairs. "The school had an active rowing section for many years but then a lot of Health and Safety crap came along and they closed it down. I don't think anyone had been inside it for many years."

Russell Chalbury looked up as a wooden door at the rear of the studio flew open and a statuesque young woman wandered in holding a mug with a steaming beverage inside. She was quite tall and slim and, when she walked, she was lithe and graceful. She had a stud in the side of her nose and long flowing dark hair interspersed with bright blue highlights. But it wasn't her hair that was the most striking thing about her — it was the fact that she was completely naked.

"Oh, sorry, Russ! I didn't know you had visitors. Hi, I'm Belinda," the young lady announced nonchalantly as, still naked, she wandered slowly past the two guests and sat down on another one of the dust-sheet-covered chairs.

"Bel, these people are Detective Sergeant Pawlett and, er, Mr Walsingham from the police."

"Oh, I see!" the young lady's tone, so affable a moment or two ago, became suddenly frosty and her erstwhile lissom body became stiff and awkward.

Clive's eyes darted backwards and forwards between the unadorned and clearly unashamed young lady sitting no more than a few feet away and the half-finished nude on the canvas. He was pretty sure that they were the same person, but allowing his eyes to wander without being accused of voyeurism was proving difficult.

"Er," Clive suggested. "As this is an official police matter, I wonder if you'd mind putting some clothes on."

The young lady stared sullenly at him and spread her legs provocatively. "What's the matter, Mr Walsingham? Are you shy? Have you never seen a naked woman before?" She turned her attention to Alison, who was sitting next to Clive and bristling with prim indignation, and studied her closely for a second or two. "Huh, look at Miss Prissy Pants over there!" the young lady continued scornfully. "I bet you've never seen her with her kit off, have you, Mr Walsingham? I wonder if anyone has."

"Well—" Clive began, before he was swiftly cut off by Sergeant Pawlett.

"Of course, we could make this official and continue our discussions down at the station," Alison announced officiously.

"Better go and put something on, Bel," Russell Chalbury urged quietly.

The young lady stood up and stared at Clive again, before flouncing off towards the door at the rear of the studio muttering something about "fascist lackeys". She disappeared briefly and re-emerged wearing a sulky expression and a grubby dressing gown. When she sat down, she deliberately turned away as though she was resentful of the police presence, and stared fixedly out of one of the grimy, ivy-covered windows.

"We'd like to ask you some questions about the disappearance of five schoolgirls ten years ago," Alison continued, apparently oblivious to the young lady's petulant antics. "Three of the girls were pupils at Polbury Manor School, where you were employed as an art teacher."

Russell Chalbury stroked his beard thoughtfully. "Yes, I remember it all, of course. I'd taught all three girls at some stage – such a tragedy. I hope you find out what happened. But, before we go any further, I must stress that I had left the school before the disappearances started."

"Yes," Clive interjected. "I'm curious to know why you left when you did. Nobody we've spoken to can give us a reason."

Russell Chalbury looked pensive for a moment. "Two reasons actually. Firstly, Christine Calshott, the deputy head, had been gunning for me for a while and she was not somebody you wanted to mess with…"

"Why was she gunning for you?" Clive asked.

"She thought I was a bad influence on some of the girls. Oh, there was nothing untoward, I promise you, but she thought I was being overfamiliar and advised me to 'consider my position' –

I think those were the words she used. She was, let us say, a very conventional, straight-laced kind of teacher and I wasn't."

"There were rumours at the time," Clive persisted, "that you were using some of the girls as models."

"Those rumours, though a little exaggerated, were basically true, Mr Walsingham. Yes, some of the older girls did model for me occasionally – at weekends and during the holidays – but they were all volunteers; nobody forced them to do it. They all received a fee for their time and there was nothing untoward going on. I was very strict about there being no physical contact of any kind and they were always allowed to bring a friend with them as a kind of chaperone. Oh, one or two parents got a bit angry when they found out – they said they didn't want their daughters spending time out of school hours with a bad influence like me – but most people seemed fine about it."

Clive looked quickly towards the pouting figure of Belinda. "And were you, Belinda, one of those girls? Were you a pupil at Polbury Manor?"

"They tried to indoctrinate me, you know," Belinda replied huffily while continuing to stare out of the window. "With their middle-class, bourgeois attitudes and their petty rules and restrictions but Russ was different. He wanted to change things."

"I'll take that as a yes, then," Clive observed sardonically. "Errm, I don't think I caught your surname earlier?"

"That's because I didn't tell you! I'm just called Belinda."

"We're going to need to know," Alison interceded firmly.

Belinda exchanged the merest of glances with Russell Chalbury. "It's, errm, Fairhead," she replied after a little hesitation.

"So you were Belinda Fairhead when you attended Polbury Manor?"

Belinda exchanged another brief glance with Russell Chalbury. "Yes, obviously!"

"You said there were two reasons why you left. What was the other one?" Clive asked, turning his attention back to Russell Chalbury in an attempt to move the conversation on.

"Yes, that's right," Russell Chalbury replied. "Teaching was a way of earning some money but my heart wasn't really in it. I really wanted to be an artist, full-time. And then I got lucky. I inherited a bit of money – it wasn't a vast sum but it was enough for me give up my job and rent an old stables building which I converted into a studio."

"But that wasn't around here, was it? We understood you had moved away from this area."

"Yes, I decided to make a clean break. There was no reason to stay around here, especially with Christine Calshott and one or two irate parents breathing down my neck, so I decided to move to Norfolk where property is a bit cheaper, the air is clean, the light is good and there is plenty of sky."

"At the time, nobody seemed to know where you'd gone," Clive added. "Did you use your own name when you rented the stables?"

There was yet another exchange of subtle glances with Belinda. "Ah, errm, no, actually. I called myself Carlo Russell."

Clive looked puzzled. "That's a bit odd, isn't it? Why did you feel the need to change your name? You hadn't done anything wrong. You weren't on the run from anyone, were you?"

Russell Chalbury stroked his beard. "I, err, had my reasons. But I assure you those reasons had absolutely nothing to do with the disappearance of those poor girls."

"And did Belinda go with you?"

"I couldn't wait to go, if you must know," Belinda replied, moodily. "We set up home together. Russ rented a flat and I helped him a bit in the studio and did some temporary work to help pay the bills."

Clive tugged at his earlobe. "I'm getting the strong impression that you were both pretty keen to move out of the area, for whatever reason, and yet here you are, ten years later, back where you started. What happened?"

Russell Chalbury gave a mannered laugh. "It's a funny thing but for some reason I never felt as creative living under an assumed name in deepest Norfolk. The area where we lived was a bit too rustic at times and a bit too bourgeois at others and I didn't really fit in. I felt as though I was a fugitive; that I was running away, although I had no genuine reason to do so. And when I found out that Christine Calshott had left Polbury Manor, we began thinking it might be good to return. And, although she'll probably deny it, Bel was getting a bit homesick. Alright, she'd fallen out with her immediate family, but she grew up around here, she knew the area well and she'd made a few good friends around here. So, first of all, we came back for a long weekend, in the spring, just to see if everything was as we remembered it and we immediately felt at home, so we started looking around to see if we could find some suitable cheap premises and we stumbled upon this place. Polbury Manor weren't asking much for a run-down, ramshackle old boathouse. To be honest, they were grateful to me for taking it off their hands, so we got a good deal and, well, here we are."

"And no sooner had you moved back than someone starts murdering the parents of the girls who disappeared ten years ago," Alison Pawlett observed acidly.

"I've had enough of this," Belinda announced loudly as she stood up, removed her dressing gown, flung it petulantly onto the floor, walked slowly past Clive and flounced towards the door. "Russ is the nicest, kindest, gentlest man I know – he wouldn't hurt a fly and I resent your insinuations. I'll be in the kitchen if you need me."

Russell Chalbury sat calmly while he watched Belinda stomp off. "I'm sorry about that," he said quietly, after she had slammed the creaky, wooden door behind her. "Despite all the bravado and defiance, she's quite vulnerable, deep down. She hasn't had the easiest of lives in some ways and she feels very threatened sometimes if she…" Russell Chalbury fell silent and pensive.

Clive coughed self-consciously. He thought it time to change the subject again. "I see you're the coordinator of the Carlow Valley Arts Festival, so it looks as though you've been welcomed back after all these years."

Russell Chalbury permitted himself a shy smile. "Mmm, it's funny isn't it? Everyone loves the Carlow Valley Arts Festival – it has a very good reputation – but nobody wants to take on the work of making it happen. The previous coordinator, Douglas Hammerton, had to give it up – he was over eighty and in poor health – and the Festival Committee wanted someone a bit younger and more energetic with a few fresh ideas. One or two of them had heard about my new venture here and one of them, Keith Draycott, came to see me to ask if I'd be interested in taking on the role. Well, I jumped at the chance – a perfect opportunity to do something positive for the community and get a bit of free publicity at the same time, I thought."

"I find that quite interesting, Mr Chalbury. Keith Draycott's daughter was one of those who disappeared and he must have known who you are and the reputation that you had ten years ago."

Russell Chalbury permitted himself another smile, more smug this time. "Oh yes, Keith Draycott knew who I was all right, but, unlike some, he also knew that I had nothing to do with his, errm, with the disappearance of those girls. He had a lot of confidence in me."

"I see. Keith Draycott's wife, er, widow mentioned that he was heavily involved with the Arts Festival. She said he was always dashing off to committee meetings."

Russell Chalbury looked surprised. "Is that what she said? Oh, he attended the first two or three but then he seemed to lose interest. As I recall, he didn't turn up to our last three meetings."

"Oh really? Have you got the dates of those meetings?"

"Yes, somewhere. You'll have to excuse me; as you can see things are a bit chaotic." Russell Chalbury stood up and sauntered across to a table by the far wall. In a pile of papers, he located his diary and flicked quickly through the pages. "Ah yes, here we are," he announced with some satisfaction. "The last meeting was on Thursday 11th September – I think we now know why he didn't attend that one, poor bugger. The previous two were on Monday 8th September and Thursday 4th September. He didn't send his apologies or anything; he just didn't turn up."

*

"What did you make of all that?" Clive asked as he climbed nervously into Alison Pawlett's car, having glanced up at the gathering clouds and reluctantly accepted her offer of a lift back to the hotel.

"It felt like an act that was being staged for our benefit," Alison replied cynically. "Did you actually manage to get a good look at Belinda's face?"

"Er, well, no, erm, I er, found it difficult to concentrate, you know…"

"Exactly! First of all, she distracted us by deliberately wandering around naked, no more than a few feet away, and then later, after we made her put something on, she deliberately turned away. We were supposed to think she was being huffy with us, but I reckon it was just a way of hiding her face."

"Yes, I see what you mean," Clive agreed, flinching and jamming his right foot on the floor as Alison Pawlett drove round a narrow bend at a disconcertingly high speed. "And she wasn't even prepared to tell us what her real name was."

"Added to which, Russell Chalbury used an assumed name when he moved to Norfolk. It feels like they'd something to hide, despite his denials."

"Yes, quite! Belinda Fairhead, or whatever her real name is, more or less admitted she was at Polbury Manor at the time the girls went missing but didn't want to give us her real name. I suspect those two know a lot more about what went on ten years ago than they're telling us. Alison, I believe we're getting quite near to the truth now and that means that things might start to get a bit dangerous. I'd like you to go snooping around a bit – I'll tell you where in a minute – but if you do, you could be putting yourself at risk and I'd quite understand—"

"Nah, Clive, it's alright," Alison interrupted. "I know how to handle myself."

Clive gave her a doubtful look. He could recall only too vividly the night she got her nose broken by her violent ex-partner, while she was supposed to be on a low-risk surveillance mission. He was about to remind her of that incident when his mobile phone rang. When he answered, the voice at the other end sounded uncharacteristically jaunty.

"Clive! Dick here!"

"Hello, Dick – you sound very pleased with yourself. How's your nose?"

"My nose is fine, more or less, and so am I. I've been looking into the history of that building that used to overlook the Corwood campsite, you know, the one that Clare found on that old map. As we thought, it was a youth club and guess who owned and ran it."

Though Clive had his own suspicions, he didn't want to steal Dick's thunder. "Go on, tell me!" he urged.

"It was run by the Church of England and one of the organisers and leading lights was Keith Draycott."

"Great work, Dick!" Clive observed encouragingly. "I wonder if I can ask you a favour. It shouldn't result in you getting hurt again!"

*

Clive stopped briefly before ringing the doorbell. He had just noticed something which, to his annoyance, he hadn't spotted on his previous visit. At the bottom of the doorstep, there was a small grating. Clive bent down and studied it briefly before finally ringing the bell.

Vanessa Draycott seemed surprised, shocked even, to see Clive standing on her doorstep and her mouth fell open momentarily before she regained her usual serene composure.

"Mr Walsingham! This is a surprise!" she announced calmly.

Clive smiled. "Yes, I'm really sorry to bother you again but one or two things have cropped up since my last visit and I was hoping to have a quick word, you know, if it's convenient."

"Oh, I see!" Vanessa Draycott glanced around. "Are you on your own?"

"Yes, Sergeant Pawlett, who you met last time, is following a different line of inquiry. This is all very informal. I hope you don't mind."

Vanessa Draycott nodded slightly and smiled. "Yes, well, I suppose you'd better come in." She led the way through the neatly proportioned, tastefully decorated entrance hall into the spacious lounge, which Clive remembered well from his previous visit, and waved a hand airily towards one of the two beige sofas placed precisely at right angles to each other.

"Actually, I was wondering if we could go into the study – your husband's study?" Clive asked politely as he sneaked a surreptitious glance at the photograph on the mantel shelf. "I take it you've not touched anything in there?"

"Oh, er, no, I don't think so. I've not really ventured in there. It's all still very raw emotionally, you understand, and everything there belonged to Keith. But Sergeant Pawlett has removed certain items – Keith's computer and some of his books," Vanessa Draycott replied. Though courteous, her comments lacked any warmth. Clive sensed that she did not welcome his intrusion nor Alison Pawlett's removal of some of her husband's personal effects. "I don't know why you'd want to go in there again," she added, defensively.

"There's something I'd like to take a look at," Clive replied, enigmatically.

Vanessa Draycott shrugged. "Very well; I'll lead the way."

The study was much as Clive remembered it – small and gloomy with a plethora of walnut bookshelves and a studious feel. Several miscellaneous items, including a camera, a pair of binoculars and a violin, which Clive recalled from his previous visit, were still there. The grandfather clock which Clive remembered ticking loudly, now stood silent and brooding in the corner.

Clive looked slowly around, subjecting the room to a thorough visual examination. "I was hoping to find your husband's diary. I don't remember seeing it last time we came."

"Isn't it here?" Vanessa Draycott asked. "That's very strange! Keith normally kept it on his desk. He always claimed it was his second most important book, after the Bible, of course."

"I take it you haven't needed to use it since your husband, er, passed away."

Vanessa Draycott smiled gently. "Oh, no; I've discovered that most of his parishioners knew much more about what was in Keith's diary than I ever did. No, now you come to mention it, I don't recall seeing his diary, er, since, well, you know. It has a maroon binding, if that's any help."

Clive nodded sympathetically. "Oh well, never mind," he replied, casually. "Perhaps you can help me with another matter.

You may remember, when we spoke before, that you said your husband was always rushing off to attend the meetings of the Carlow Valley Arts Festival committee."

"Yes that's right," Vanessa Draycott affirmed. "He was a great supporter of the festival and was always very keen to make a contribution."

"And yet we understand that he didn't show up for either the meeting on 4th September or the one on 8th September."

"Didn't he? That was most unlike him. I'm sure he said he was going to attend them and I'm afraid I don't know why he didn't. I don't recall there being any emergencies or anything."

Clive smiled again. "I was hoping his diary might help us, but never mind. Maybe your husband's computer can shed some light. I understand Sergeant Pawlett has now got access to all his files." Although Vanessa Draycott's expression remained calm, and her smile polite, Clive thought he sensed a momentary flicker of alarm in her eyes. "Meanwhile," he continued, "I have one more question for you. Do you know how old this house is?"

Vanessa Draycott seemed suddenly flustered. She started running her hand through her hair. "What? Er, I'm not sure! Is that relevant? Keith would've known, of course – he knew everything about this house. I think it dates back to around 1750ish, but I'm no expert."

"Yes, that's roughly what I thought," Clive agreed. "I remember you saying, when we last spoke, that your husband maintained a small collection of vintage wines under the stairs."

"Yes, that's right – there's a cupboard there. It's only a small collection – he couldn't afford to buy very much – but you're welcome to take a look if you're interested. It's of no use to me, I'm afraid."

"Thank you, but I'm curious. Most wine connoisseurs that I know – and I confess I don't know many – prefer to keep their wines in the cellar where they have one. I'm told wines tend to mature better and more slowly in dark, dank, cool conditions where the temperature doesn't vary very much. And I bet this house has a cellar. Most large houses of this type and vintage were built with a cellar – at the time, it was the only way to store and preserve food. Cellars only really disappeared at the end of the nineteenth century. And I noticed a telltale grating by the front door; that's usually a sign that the house has got a cellar."

Vanessa Draycott's arched eyebrows gave her a permanently surprised expression, but she still contrived to look slightly startled at Clive's enquiry. "You're very knowledgeable on such matters, Mr Walsingham. Yes it does have a cellar," she agreed reluctantly. "But I've hardly ever been down there. Keith used to go down there sometimes but I don't think he was very impressed. He said it was very dark and damp and not at all pleasant."

"Nevertheless," Clive persisted. "I wonder if I could take a look – just to satisfy my curiosity."

"I really don't…" Vanessa Draycott began to protest.

"It might be important," Clive persevered.

"I don't suppose you've got a search warrant?" Vanessa Draycott asked, suddenly sounding formal.

"Er, no," Clive replied. He was surprised at Vanessa Draycott's question and suspected that she might be trying to hide something. "I only want to take a peek in the cellar. Do I need one?"

"No, no, I suppose you don't," Vanessa Draycott conceded. "But we'll need a torch – I'll go and get one."

Muttering under her breath, Vanessa Draycott marched out of the study, closing the door firmly behind her. It was the opportunity Clive had been waiting for. He strode over to the shelf where a camera nestled on top of a heap of church pamphlets – he had noticed it on his previous visit and it had aroused his curiosity. He reached it down, examined it carefully, switched it on and, after a moment or two of uncertainty caused by a lack of familiarity with its functions, found the "playback" facility. As the first image flashed onto the small, built-in screen, he whistled quietly to himself then, as he flicked quickly through a few more images, he smiled contentedly. When Vanessa Draycott had failed to return after a couple of minutes, Clive tiptoed over to the study door, still clutching the camera, and opened it slightly. He thought he could hear Vanessa Draycott talking animatedly to someone on the phone but he couldn't make out what was being said. After a minute or so, she stopped talking and Clive quietly closed the door. He was idly peering at a shelf of untidily stacked religious tomes when she returned carrying a torch. He looked up and smiled.

"I hope you don't mind," he said, apologetically, as he held up the camera. "I've just been having a look at this – it's quite new and expensive. I didn't realise your husband was a keen photographer."

Vanessa Draycott gave a nervous laugh. "Neither did I, but it seems there's quite a lot about my husband that I don't know."

"I'd like to borrow it if I may."

"Of course – it's no good to me. Might it help you with your inquiries?"

"I hope so," Clive replied enigmatically. "There are some interesting pictures on the card – a couple of my hotel, the Follycombe, which is curious, and some shots of some woods, which might offer up a clue or two. One or two look like they might have been taken on the edge of Carlow Woods, not that I know them that well."

"Really? Well, as I said, there's quite a lot about Keith that I don't pretend to know. Anyway, I've got the torch," Vanessa Draycott announced a little breathlessly. "I couldn't remember where I'd left it for a moment or two. It's this way."

Vanessa Draycott led the way out of the study along a small corridor lined with framed prints of ecclesiastical scenes, towards the entrance hall, where Clive placed the camera on a convenient table. She then went down a couple of steps to a solid wooden door which she opened with some effort. "Be careful, these steps are steep and might be quite slippery," she cautioned as she went ahead slowly, shining the torch onto a flight of solid stone steps, each of which had been worn down in the middle, suggesting generations of regular use. As Vanessa Draycott shuffled slowly and reluctantly down the stairs, regularly placing her left hand against the wall for support, a beam of light from her erratically aimed torch picked out a switch on the wall. Clive spotted it immediately, flicked the switch and immediately bathed the stairs and cellar below in a bright, flickering, yellow light.

"Good heavens! I didn't know there was a light switch there," Vanessa Draycott explained with no great conviction, prompting Clive to wonder whether her errand to retrieve a torch had simply been an excuse to make an urgent phone call, or whether she might have been planning to abort their descent into the inky black depths of the cellar by switching the torch off and claiming that its batteries had failed. He paused for a moment and looked around. The stone steps, perhaps twenty in number, descended into a square room with an uneven, damp, stone floor and brick-lined walls. Against one of the walls, and apparently fixed to it, was a tall, solid-looking grey, slightly rusty, metal cupboard and, to one side, there was a small metal table and fold-up chair. From the ceiling, a fluorescent light flickered intermittently. Clive shivered; the atmosphere was dank, chill and eerie.

"Do you know what's in the cupboard?" Clive asked.

"No, I'm afraid not," Vanessa Draycott replied quietly, though her voice resonated around the cellar, making it sound louder and stronger than usual. "Keith used to come down here occasionally and put things in the cupboard – I got the impression he stored some parish records in it — but he always kept it locked."

"Parish records? In this damp cellar?" Clive asked sceptically. Without waiting for an answer, he walked over to the cupboard, his footsteps reverberating on the stone floor, and pulled at the handle on the door but it wouldn't turn. "It's locked! Where's the key?"

"I have no idea, I'm afraid. Keith was very secretive sometimes; he never told me where the key was and, to be honest, I never asked."

"That's a pity — still never mind!" Clive sensed Vanessa Draycott sighing quietly with relief as he turned and headed back up the steps. When he reached the door at the top, he suddenly stopped and spoke.

"Thank you very much for your time, Mrs Draycott. It's been most interesting, although not quite as useful as I had hoped. I wonder if I could ask one small favour before I go. Running a hotel, I take a bit of an interest in good wines and I know your husband was something of an expert. I wonder if I could have a quick look at his collection. Earlier on, you said I would be welcome to take a look."

"Did I? Well, yes, yes, I suppose so," Vanessa Draycott replied with little enthusiasm. She squeezed past Clive and led him back into the entrance hall where she opened a wooden door that led into the void beneath the stairs. "His collection is in there; as I said, it's not very big — it'll be a bit of a squeeze for a tall man like you."

Clive stooped uncomfortably, exhaled slightly, and peered into the cupboard. "Yes, I see what you mean," he grunted as he examined a rack of bottles lining one wall. "May I borrow your torch? It's very dark in here."

"Yes, of course." Vanessa Draycott handed the torch to Clive, who switched it on and scanned the interior of the cupboard with its beam. Either side of the door, against the walls, were neatly stacked racks, each full of bottles, most of them covered in a generous layer of grey dust. Clive deployed the torch beam to highlight the label on each bottle and, after a moment or two, his attention was drawn to one particular bottle, the only one that lacked any obvious coating of dust. He carefully lifted it from the rack.

"Now, that's interesting," he announced, as he studied the label. "We have here a bottle of Bordeaux, 1991 vintage."

"Is that good?" Vanessa Draycott asked, innocently. "I'm no expert on wines, I'm afraid."

"Not especially; quite the reverse really," Clive replied. "Which is why I'm puzzled. But if you look carefully, you can see that there is no dust on this bottle, unlike all the others, and this bottle has been opened. I wonder!"

Clive shook the bottle gently and heard a rattling sound coming from within. With the practised wrist movement of someone used to serving behind a bar, he removed the cork and turned the bottle upside down. Two keys fell out onto the floor. Clive bent down, picked up the keys and examined them. "Did you know these keys were here?" he asked in a more aggressive tone than he had hitherto adopted.

"No, I, errm, I-I had no idea," Vanessa Draycott stuttered.

"So you don't know what the keys are for?"

"No, I, I don't remember seeing them before. I, erm, didn't know they were there."

"One looks like it might be a padlock key and the other one is, well, I think we need to visit the cellar again." This time it was Clive who led the way. As he descended, he switched the light on.

Vanessa Draycott hung back in the shadows of the cellar as Clive walked over to the metal cupboard, inserted the key in the lock and slowly turned the handle. The cupboard door opened with a judder. The sight that greeted him caused Clive to step back and catch his breath. In the background, Vanessa Draycott gasped.

"Jesus!" Clive exclaimed as he leaned against the open cupboard door while he struggled to comprehend the awful sight that greeted him. Inside the cupboard, there were half a dozen metal shelves and, on each shelf, there was a neatly arranged collection of objects. He wheeled round angrily and addressed Vanessa Draycott.

"Did you know all this was here?" he demanded aggressively.

Vanessa Draycott had backed into a corner of the room and hidden her face in her hands – she was shaking.

"No, no! I had no idea," she protested. "Not Keith – not this! It can't be..."

Clive, meanwhile, had moved back to the cupboard and, using just his fingertips, he began to examine the contents of each shelf, speaking aloud as he did so.

"This is like some gruesome trophy cabinet. We've got several mobile phones; I'd guess some of them would be about ten or eleven years old. We've got laptops, we've got little bits of jewellery, no doubt belonging to one poor victim or another. We've got a school bag, with the initials 'CH' on it, a violin and some sheet music – I'll bet these all belonged to Charlotte Huxton. We've got a wash bag, probably the one that Rosemary Edwyn was carrying when she went to the shower block. And we've got a shopping bag, most likely the one that Catherine Duffield was carrying when your husband came out of Mallowcrest Care Home, saw her and offered her a lift. And talking of Mallowcrest, what have we here?" Clive reached to the back of one of the shelves and, still using only his fingertips, carefully removed what looked like a simulated leather-bound ledger. "This looks like the visitors' book to Mallowcrest, the one that went missing, under mysterious circumstances, ten years ago when your husband was a regular visitor, offering spiritual comfort to those nearing the end of their lives. Ah, and here we have what looks like Inspector Beauregard's missing notebook – the one that he lost shortly after visiting Mallowcrest. And then, down here on the lower shelves, we've got some more recent additions, several quite modern mobile phones, including three identical ones, but in different colours – red, blue and black – probably all belonging to Edward Duffield, and a couple of laptops. And there's a space just here where I expect he was planning to put Olivia Farringdon's camera – the new one I found in his study – except that he didn't, for some reason. And, ah, here it is! We have your husband's missing diary, at least I assume it is." He held up the maroon-covered diary and looked at Vanessa Draycott who was sitting on the bottom step with her head buried in her hands, sobbing. "This should make interesting reading. And, oh my God, I don't believe this, it's just too…"

Clive broke off, unable to say anything for the moment, as he reached into the darkest recess of the cupboard and retrieved an exercise book which he started to thumb through. "This is really quite shocking!" Clive gasped when he finally felt able to speak. "This exercise book appears to record, in his own handwriting, the details of the murders your husband carried out; all in cold, detached detail." Clive turned the pages slowly, swallowing hard as he did so. "Emily Ashurst, Catherine Duffield, Rosemary Edwyn and so it goes on. There's even a mention of Doris, the frail old lady at Mallowcrest, who he murdered to prevent her from saying anything that could implicate him and – yes, here we are – he mentions pushing Lennie Cave over the balcony of his flat. And then, later on, in fresher ink, we've got descriptions of what he did to Olivia Farringdon, Kate Huxton, Edward Duffield…"

Barely able to control his emotions, Clive turned angrily to face Vanessa Draycott. "I don't think I need to spell it out to you, but it is obvious that your husband was a mass murderer of horrific, monstrous proportions and this cupboard looks like… well, like some kind of macabre collection of souvenirs from his revolting activities. And what's this on the bottom shelf?"

While Clive had been berating Vanessa Draycott, he had

noticed something on the bottom shelf, protruding from a plastic bag. He knelt down for a closer look. "Oh my God!" he repeated. "That is a claw hammer and there are blood stains all over it!"

"I don't know anything about all this… stuff," Vanessa Draycott protested lamely, as she continued to sob. "I can't believe Keith could do such evil things – there was so much goodness in him. I can't believe it."

By now, Clive too was shaking, partly with rage and partly with utter disbelief. When he spoke, his voice cracked with emotion. "So the questions remain; why did your husband abduct and murder five schoolgirls, including his own daughter, why did he murder three of their parents and, most crucially of all, who murdered your husband?"

"Oh, God! This is dreadful! This is too dreadful! I can't stay down here…" Vanessa Draycott sobbed before running up the stairs and disappearing.

Clive didn't bother to race after her. He sensed that she wouldn't be far away when he needed to speak to her. Instead, he just sat on the chair next to the cupboard and stared incredulously at its contents while tears began to trickle down his cheeks. Eventually, he stood up, a little shakily, carefully removed Keith Draycott's diary and notebook, locked the cupboard, pocketed the key and slowly climbed the stairs. He had just reached the top and closed the door behind him, when his phone rang.

"Hello, Clive, it's Alison here," an excited, breathless voice announced. "Three things; firstly, the pathologist has left a message for me. She said she's got some important new information for me – I'll call her back as soon as I can. Secondly, our technical people have been taking a look at Keith Draycott's computer and found something very interesting which I'll tell you about later. And thirdly, I'm in the churchyard at St. Giles in Crowdale and I think I've found something. It's…" Her excited report was cut short by what sounded like a gunshot and the phone went dead.

Thirteen

The church of St Giles nestled between a wooded escarpment and a gentle bend in the River Carlow. At one time, when the river was faster and more freely flowing, it provided the village of Crowdale with a modest degree of prosperity. Along both banks of the river, there was once a lively community of people, living in basic cottages, whose livelihood was mainly water-based – fishermen, millers, merchants and boatmen of one kind or another.

These days, there was no real sign of the cottages, save for a few bricks that occasionally protruded from the water during extended periods of dry weather. Nowadays, the heart of the village was nearly a mile away where a pub, the King's Arms, a general store and a scattering of cottages were clustered around the village green. Although the church continued to provide occasional succour to the villagers, its picturesque setting and slightly decrepit appearance was, nowadays, more of a magnet for local artists and walkers.

The church itself was of a typical medieval design. Constructed from local limestone quarried at Fearnley, it had a squat, square tower at one end and an entrance porch along one side. Inside, there was an arched window, above the altar, with a later, Victorian stained-glass depiction of little merit, an organ so in need of repair that it was no longer playable, cracked wooden pews and a strong musty smell. The churchyard, separated from the old towpath by a crumbling stone wall and surrounded on three sides by a straggly yew hedge, was reasonably well maintained either side of the footpath leading to the church but, towards its furthest extremities, was badly overgrown, with just the occasional lopsided gravestone protruding from the long grass and brambles.

Wishing, for the first and probably only time in his life, that Alison Pawlett had been driving him, Clive screeched to a halt in the small gravel car park by the lychgate and half tumbled out of his car, paying uncharacteristically scant attention to the two other cars already parked there. As the odd, heavy drop of rain began to fall from a suddenly sombre sky, he raced into the churchyard and looked anxiously around. There was an ominous silence, broken only by several crows screeching to each other from a pair of nearby trees and the rustle of leaves, whipped up by the gathering breeze. There was no sign of anyone.

Fearing that there might be a dangerous gunman at large somewhere nearby, Clive crept gingerly towards the church, his head forever turning and his eyes wide and alert. Then he looked down and noticed some fresh spots of blood on the path which, on closer inspection, seemed to form part of a trail that led towards the church door. Eschewing his previous caution, Clive rushed up to the door, which was slightly ajar, and ran inside. Sitting in the musty-smelling porch, on a stone bench in an alcove, was the familiar denim-clad figure of Sergeant Alison Pawlett with a bloodstained handkerchief covering the left side of her face.

"My God, Alison, what's happened? Are you okay?" Clive shouted as he ran towards her.

Alison Pawlett slowly turned her head and looked at Clive with anxious eyes. "More or less, I think!" Although she was trying to sound calm and reassuring, there was a pronounced tremor in her voice. "My mobile's been shot to pieces but the bullet only grazed my ear. There's quite a bit of blood but I don't think there's any serious damage, fortunately. Mind you, it was just as well that Dick turned up when he did. If the gunman had managed to fire a second shot I don't think I would have been so lucky."

"Bloody hell!" Clive exclaimed as he sat down on the stone bench next to Sergeant Pawlett, gently eased the handkerchief away from her ear and examined the wound.

"Yes, you're right; it's just a flesh wound on the earlobe but I'd advise you to have it checked out when you can – just to be on the safe side."

"Well you warned me it might get dangerous," Alison observed ruefully as, wincing slightly, she reapplied the handkerchief to her ear. "Dick tells me that you asked him to follow me to the churchyard. You obviously thought something like this might happen."

"I guessed something might happen but I didn't expect anybody to take a shot at you. Do we know who fired the shot?"

"Oh, yes. It was our fugitive friend Raymond Gulliver, although I don't yet know why. I didn't hear him or see him. I just heard a shot and my mobile flew out of my hand."

"So where is he now?"

Alison Pawlett pointed, a little shakily, towards a pair of open wooden doors that divided the entrance lobby from the nave of the church. "Oh he's in there. Dick has handcuffed him to the stair rail leading up to the pulpit and is standing guard over him."

"Have you called for backup?"

"No! No need – I reckon we've got everything under control. Besides, we didn't think you'd want a detachment from police headquarters turning up at the moment."

Clive smiled at Alison and winked. "Quite right! Well done! I'd better go and take a look. Are you going to be alright for a few minutes?" Alison wrinkled her nose and nodded.

"Well, well, well," Clive exuded a false cheerfulness as he approached the pulpit, his footsteps echoing on the cold stone floor, and studied the scene that confronted him. Raymond Gulliver was sitting on one of the steps leading up to the pulpit, his head bowed and his wrist manacled to the rail, while Inspector Beauregard was standing over him, holding a gun in one hand and a bloodstained handkerchief up to his nose with the other. Below the handkerchief, Clive thought he detected the hint of a self-satisfied smile that seemed oddly out of place on the inspector's normally saturnine features.

"Well done, Dick! Excellent work! It sounds as though you got here just in time," Clive enthused.

"Thank you, yes," Dick Beauregard agreed, while trying to sound nonchalant although he could feel his heart pounding. "I'd followed Alison to the church, as we agreed, and was just going into the churchyard when I heard a shot. Fortunately, Mr Gulliver was so intent on firing at Alison for a second time that he didn't hear me creep up behind him. I caught him off guard and knocked him to the ground, the gun flew out of his hand and I managed to get some cuffs on him. Mind you, he caught my nose with his elbow and made it bleed again." Dick Beauregard dabbed at his sore nose. "So are you going to tell me what the hell is going on?" he asked.

Clive smiled. "Firstly, I think Mr Gulliver needs to explain why he fled the scene of the fire last night, where he's been since then and why he was firing at Detective Sergeant Pawlett," Clive paused and looked across questioningly at the hunched, sullen figure of Raymond Gulliver.

"I've got nothing to say," Raymond Gulliver replied defiantly.

"Oh, really? Then you might be interested to know that I've just come from the vicarage in Stowbrook where I had a really interesting chat with Vanessa Draycott. And after our little chat, we went down into the cellar and we found a large cupboard down there which we opened up."

"You're lying!" Raymond Gulliver exploded. "Reverend Draycott had the only key and only he knew where it was hidden and..." Raymond Gulliver stopped abruptly, quickly realising that he had just admitted far too much.

Still smiling, Clive reached into his pocket and produced the key to the cupboard which he brandished in Raymond Gulliver's surly face. "Maybe Keith Draycott didn't hide it as well as you thought he had. Anyway, I've had a good look in that cupboard, though frankly what I found made me feel sick. And amongst other things, I've found Keith Draycott's diary together with a notebook in which he has recorded, in some horribly graphic detail, the abduction of the girls and their subsequent murder. Your name also appears from time to time – it seems you were quite a willing accomplice..."

"I never touched the girls," Raymond Gulliver protested. "I might have... er... assisted the Reverend Draycott here and there but I never laid a finger on those girls."

"We'll see! But at the very least, we know you fired a gun at Sergeant Pawlett so a charge of attempted murder should give you something to think about."

"I wasn't trying to kill her!" Raymond Gulliver protested again. "I was just trying to defend myself."

Clive laughed incredulously. "You were trying to defend yourself by firing on an unarmed policewoman who had her back to you?"

"You don't understand, you don't understand," Raymond Gulliver replied, his shrill voice betraying his rising hysteria. "There's somebody after me, I don't know who but I reckon they've found out about me and what I may have done. They've already killed the Reverend Draycott and I reckon that I'm next on their list. So, after they torched my shed last night, I wasn't taking any chances. I keep this gun in my van, see, with my gardening equipment—"

"Do you have a licence for it?" Inspector Beauregard interrupted.

Raymond Gulliver looked scornfully at the inspector. "What do you think? The Reverend Draycott gave it to me when… when all this business started. I didn't ask where he got it from. He said I might need it one day and he was bloody right. When I saw the shed was on fire, I didn't hang around. I took the gun from my van, see, and legged it through the woods, along the side of the river and hid myself here in the church. I was pretty sure that someone would come looking for me so, when I heard a car pull up outside and a door slam, I crept out and… Look, I didn't mean to hurt her, I just wanted to warn her off!" Raymond Gulliver shut his eyes, bowed his head and rocked slowly backwards and forwards.

"What did you want to warn her off about?" Clive asked sternly. "My guess is that she'd found something in the churchyard that you didn't want her to see, hadn't she?"

"I, er, I… don't want to say anything more. I want my solicitor."

Clive turned to Inspector Beauregard and handed him the key to the cupboard. "Dick, I'm just going to make a quick call and then I suggest you arrange for Mr Gulliver to be taken into custody. Then I suggest you clean yourself up and go over to the vicarage in Stowbrook and have a look at the contents of the cupboard in the cellar – prepare yourself for a thoroughly unpleasant experience. That should tell you all you need to know about Keith Draycott's role in the murder of the schoolgirls and three of their parents. You'll also find your notebook in there – the one that went missing during the original investigation. Oh, and I've got Keith Draycott's diary and notebook and what is probably the murder weapon – there's a chance that Vanessa Draycott does have another key and

I wouldn't want her trying to protect her late husband's reputation by destroying all the evidence. I'll fetch them from the car. And, incidentally, when news about what you've found and who you've arrested gets out, I'm happy for you to take all the credit. This is no time for false modesty!"

"Thanks, Clive; I really appreciate this. I've been such a…"

"Yes, well, I'll leave you to make the necessary arrangements. I'll make my call and get the items that I mentioned from the car and then I'm going to look after Alison."

*

"You've got something to show me?" Clive asked as he approached Alison Pawlett who was still sitting in the porch of the church dabbing at her ear.

"How did you get on with Vanessa Draycott?" Alison asked as she rose, slightly unsteadily, to her feet and led Clive through the churchyard.

"Pretty well, thanks," Clive replied. "In a gruesome sort of way. There is a welter of macabre evidence in the cellar of the vicarage that proves that Keith Draycott was responsible for the kidnapping of the schoolgirls and the subsequent murders of Olivia Farringdon, Kate Huxton and Edward Duffield. I have to tell you that there is a very, very sick collection of some of their personal possessions in a cupboard in the cellar, displayed as trophies. It doesn't make for pleasant viewing." Clive shuddered as he mentioned it.

Alison Pawlett stopped dead in her tracks, she seemed to stagger momentarily and her jaw fell open. "What are you saying, Clive? Are you saying that it was Keith Draycott who was responsible for all this mayhem and bloodshed?"

"I'm afraid so."

"Oh well, that at least helps to explain what our technician found on his computer."

"Go on!"

"Well, apparently somebody recently made a pretty clumsy attempt to delete a lot of files but they didn't do the job very well. Our technician has recovered a lot of files – very unpleasant files." Alison paused briefly, unsure whether she could continue. But, after a moment or two, she swallowed hard, took a couple of deep breaths and resumed her narrative. "I haven't seen them for myself, and I don't want to, but apparently there are loads of sexually explicit images of young girls and…" Alison paused again and closed her eyes.

"I get the message," Clive replied quickly. "You don't need to say any more. Keith Draycott was clearly a monster. But it was so easy for him, you see. He was such a trusted well-respected member of the community that he could go pretty well anywhere and talk to anyone without raising even a hint of suspicion. The girls all trusted him, some knew him through the youth club he was involved with, and so did their parents, when he subsequently contacted them claiming to know what had happened to their respective daughters."

"And obviously, that would explain why nobody turned to up to meet Alan Ashurst – Keith Draycott was already dead. But, if he was responsible for all this, then who murdered him?" Clearly Alison had sufficiently recovered from her traumatic experiences to begin firing questions at Clive.

"Good question!"

"Was it Raymond Gulliver?" Alison Pawlett fired another question.

"No, I don't think he was the murderer although he had a devious, unpleasant role to play in the abduction of the girls. And I suspect that once he heard that Keith Draycott had been murdered, he was fearing for his own life – that's why he's been running scared."

"But, but, surely Keith Draycott didn't kidnap and murder his own daughter?"

Clive shrugged. "Ah, we don't know exactly what happened to each of the poor girls yet."

"Now there, I might be able to help," Alison Pawlett announced proudly as she walked over to a gravestone in one of the oldest, least visible parts of the churchyard. "This is what I found."

Clive crouched down, parted some long grass that was partially obscuring the front of the gravestone and read the inscription:

IN LOVING MEMORY OF BELLA FAIRHEAD WHO FELL ASLEEP 12 SEPTEMBER 1752.

And below the inscription, in the same italic letters was the word "*CIRCE*".

"Bloody hell!" Clive exclaimed. "The girls are buried here! "That's why the young woman at the boathouse was calling herself Belinda Fairhead! She knew about this!"

"Yes, that's what I thought," Alison agreed doubtfully. "But why bury the girls in an old grave?"

Clive emitted a rather smug chuckle. "You remember that book we found on Keith Draycott's desk – the one about time and calendars?"

"Yes, but I couldn't really understand it," Alison confessed, wrinkling her nose.

"Yes, it is a bit abstruse but Keith Draycott had been inadvertently helpful by underlining the relevant passage. You see, we adopted the Gregorian calendar in 1752 and, as a result, a number of days in September were lost, including 12th September – there was no such date, so nobody could've died on that date and… yes, of course!" Clive suddenly slapped his hand against his forehead. "You remember that newspaper cutting that we found on Keith Draycott's body?"

"Yes, but…"

"We studied the article from all angles and decided there might be a connection between Keith Draycott and the Carlow Valley Arts Festival or with Russell Chalbury or with Guy Sharston, but it wasn't the article that was important – it was the date. The article was dated 12th September – somebody was trying to tell us, in a strange, convoluted way, where we'd find the bodies and… Oh, bloody hell, I've just realised something! Excuse me a minute, I've just got to make another phone call, it's very urgent."

Clive turned and dashed back to his car where he sat with his phone to his ear for a minute or two before returning to the churchyard where Alison still stood, motionless, staring dolefully at the gravestone. Clive knelt down, reached forward and scrabbled away at the tangle of grass and weeds that was obscuring part of the gravestone. "You see, this gravestone isn't very old." He beckoned to Alison who crouched down beside him. "Oh, it's been placed deliberately in the oldest part of the cemetery and at a wonky angle and somebody's had a go at making it look old – they've hacked lumps out of it, probably with a chisel or some such implement, and rubbed away at the surface, but the stone is quite new and the lettering far too sharp and crisp for something that purports to be over 250 years old. I reckon it might be worth asking around at local monumental masons to see if we can trace who commissioned this stone, probably around ten years ago."

Alison wrinkled her nose again. "Yes, I'll have a go and I think I understand what you've said, but I don't quite understand who Bella Fairhead was."

Clive chuckled again. "You know, aside from being a mass murderer and a sexual predator, Keith Draycott loved his little games and puzzles. 'Bella' is an abbreviated form of Isabella, or Isabel, and Fairhead is a description. You remember Clare pointed out that four of the five girls who disappeared had blonde or fair hair?"

"Yes, and one didn't – the odd one out."

"Exactly! Now I can't be sure – we'd have to arrange for an exhumation – but I reckon we'll find the bodies of four fair-haired girls down there."

"There's no need to arrange an exhumation," a voice behind them broke the silence. "I can tell you that there are four bodies down there – Catherine Duffield, Rosemary Edwyn, Charlotte Huxton and Emily Ashurst."

Alarmed, Clive and Alison spun round to find Belinda Fairhead standing over them. She was wearing a red baseball cap, which covered the blue highlights in her hair, white T-shirt, black leggings and pink trainers and was holding something behind her back. Her feet were planted firmly apart, giving her an intimidating posture, and her voice carried a hint of menace.

"And you, I assume, are Isabel Draycott," Clive announced calmly.

"Correct! Well done!" The woman's tone was patronising.

"When we paid you a visit at the boathouse, I must admit I was surprised at the extreme lengths you went to, to prove to us that you were not a natural blonde."

Isabel Draycott laughed. "Yes, that was something of a triumph, wasn't it? I did especially enjoy the look on Sergeant Pawlett's face!"

"How did you know we were here?" Clive asked.

"Oh, Vanessa – Mrs Draycott – telephoned me. She said you were at the vicarage and that you had asked to see the cellar and that once you had looked in the cupboard and seen my father's grotesque collection, you were bound to come snooping around the graveyard, so I came straight over."

"So that's who Mrs Draycott phoned. She knew who you really were?"

"Oh, yeah," Isabel Draycott replied, casually.

"And you and Mrs Draycott knew all about the contents of the cellar?"

"Oh yeah! She took me down there one day and showed me. It made me feel sick!"

"She had a key?"

"She knew where to find one. It was in the cupboard under the stairs."

"Did you know about the cupboard in the cellar when you were living at the vicarage?" Alison asked.

"No, of course not!" Isabel Draycott replied scornfully. "My father only moved into that vicarage when he transferred to Stowbrook. I've never lived there. When I lived at home, it was in quite a modest little house up near Crowdale green."

"And did it have a cellar?"

"God, no! My father must have been assembling his macabre collection of trophies while I lived there, but I never saw any of them. Mind you, he kept a lot of things under lock and key in various drawers and cupboards and he was very secretive about what he stored in the garage, so he probably stashed them well away from where I was likely to see them."

At that moment, a police car screeched into the car park, its siren blaring. Isabel Draycott glanced over her shoulder and looked startled. "A police car?" she asked nervously. "What's a police car doing here? I noticed there were three vehicles in the car park and yet there are only two of you, so something's going on. Tell me what's going on."

"Ah, yes," Clive replied. "Well, one of the cars belongs to Dick, er, Detective Inspector Beauregard. He came here to arrest Raymond Gulliver who fired a gun at Alison, er, Sergeant Pawlett. The police have come to take Mr Gulliver away."

"Ah, yes, Randy Ray, the gravedigger! He dug this grave you know; it was one of his freelance commissions. It's all recorded in my father's notebook which, I imagine, you have both now seen."

"Not yet, but I am aware of it," Alison Pawlett replied. "I think Clive has seen it, though." She turned towards Clive who nodded. "So are you responsible for your father's death?" Alison Pawlett asked in her familiarly abrupt, bristling fashion.

By now, the odd heavy raindrop that had greeted Clive on his arrival at the church had transformed into steady, dispiriting rain. "Look, can we go somewhere to talk?" Isabel Draycott asked as she glanced up at the brooding sky. "This place gives me the creeps and it's starting to rain."

"I'm not going anywhere until I know what you're hiding behind your back," Clive said firmly.

"Oh, what, this?" Isabel Draycott suddenly whipped her hand out from behind her back. In the same instant, Alison Pawlett, fearing that Isabel was wielding a weapon, threw herself at her and brought her crashing to the ground. Isabel Draycott screamed.

"What the f...! What the hell are you doing, you stupid cow?" Isabel Draycott screeched as Alison Pawlett landed on top of her, causing the bunch of flowers she was holding to fall from her grasp.

"It's okay, Alison," Clive shouted as he rushed forward to help both women to their feet. "I'm sorry, Isabel, but you must understand that if you play games like that with us, this kind of thing will happen. Alison's already been shot at once today. You can't blame her for not taking any chances. Why carry a harmless bunch of flowers behind your back?"

"They're for the grave," Isabel Draycott muttered as she brushed some imaginary dirt from her leggings. "I am ashamed to say that I may, inadvertently, have caused all this mayhem in the first place."

"I think we'd better go and sit in the church," Clive said as he watched Raymond Gulliver being escorted away, accompanied by Inspector Beauregard. He led the way along the path through the entrance door and into the nave, where he located a pew beneath a side window. Isabel Draycott sat between Alison and Clive. The bolshie, belligerent facade that she had displayed when they first met her in the boathouse had completely vanished, to be replaced by a snuffling, frightened one.

"I can't help noticing that your T-shirt smells quite strongly of petrol," Alison observed as she gave Isabel a quizzical look.

"Does it?" Isabel replied innocently. "It's probably turpentine or white spirit – Russ uses quite a lot of it when he's painting."

"So you had nothing to do with Raymond Gulliver's shed burning down last night," Alison persisted.

"Oh yeah, I burned the bastard's shed down. I wanted to frighten him in the same way that he must've frightened those poor girls. I wanted him to know that we were onto him."

"We'll be charging you with criminal damage and—"

Clive decided to intervene. "Perhaps we can come back to the question of Raymond's shed later. What I'd really like to know is where did all this start?" he asked.

"It started with the car accident, I suppose," Isabel Draycott whimpered.

"When your mother was killed?"

Isabel Draycott nodded and wiped some moisture from her cheeks. "I remember it was a late afternoon in January and it was freezing. My mother and father had been to some important church function which had overrun for some reason. I wasn't with them; they'd left me with a neighbour but they were worried because they were late and feared that I might have played up and outstayed my welcome – it was something, apparently, that I had done before. Anyway, it seems that my father was driving a bit quicker than he should. They were driving through Penheath when, according to my father, a fair-haired girl, about the same age as me, ran out in front of the car without looking. My father slammed on the brakes to avoid her, skidded on some ice and crashed into a roadside tree. My mother was killed instantly but my father escaped with a few cuts and bruises. The accident happened after dark and there were no street lights in Penheath, so my father didn't get a clear view of the girl, just a brief glimpse in his headlights. As I say, all he knew was that she was blonde and, he reckoned, about the same age as me."

"I've checked out the police report of the accident," Alison added importantly. "And although there are references to a girl with fair hair, the official conclusion was that Keith Draycott was driving far too fast for the conditions. If he hadn't been driving so fast he wouldn't have needed to brake so hard and the accident would've been avoided."

"Was the fair-haired girl ever traced?" Clive asked.

"No she wasn't – there were no witnesses and no one came forward."

"I see," Clive replied before turning to Isabel Draycott. "I'm sorry if all this is upsetting for you, but we do need to understand what happened."

"No, no, it's alright," Isabel Draycott sniffed as she brushed away some more tears. "Anyway, as you can imagine, the accident had a terrible effect on my father – on both of us really. Oh, my father was fine in public, he carried on with his job as professionally as he could, but when he was alone in the house he was always so bitter and angry. That's why, I think, he didn't spend as much time with me as I thought he should. I mean, my mother had just been killed in a road accident and he was hardly ever around to comfort me, or encourage me, or even just sit with me. He just immersed himself in his work because it gave him something to focus on, I suppose, and stopped him getting too sullen and moody. I thought things might get a bit better over time, but they didn't; in fact they got worse. I was getting increasingly pissed off because he was never around when I needed him and he just seemed to be getting more and more angry and behaving more and more erratically. And then he started going out on his own at strange times – quite often, it was after dark and he'd take a torch with him. He never said where he was going or why or how long he'd be and, quite often, he left his car behind and went out on foot."

"Anyway, eventually, curiosity got the better of me and, one evening, I followed him. I remember it had been a nice summer's evening and it was dusk. I followed him as he headed down to the river and started to walk along the towpath. He even stopped to pass the time of day with a couple of his parishioners who were walking their dog. He looked round a couple of times, rather furtively I thought, but, each time, I managed to slip behind a tree before he noticed me. Anyway, he eventually came to the old boathouse which, at that time, belonged to the school. I didn't see whether he had a key or not – it was getting dark – but he opened the door and went inside."

"Oh, that reminds me," Clive interrupted as he rummaged in his trouser pocket. "As well as the key to the cupboard in the cellar, I found this key in your father's wine cupboard. It looks like it might be a key to a padlock. Do you recognise it?" He showed the key to Isabel Draycott who briefly glanced at it before looking away.

"I'm, er, not sure. There was a padlock on the boathouse door and that might have been the key but I really don't…"

"No, no, I quite understand and I'm sorry to have interrupted you," Clive replied solicitously. "You were saying…"

"Yes er, well, I waited until my father had gone inside the boathouse and then I crept as close as I dared. I could see the light from his torch flickering as he waved it about. And I could hear voices – one was my father's but I was sure there was another male voice, probably Raymond Gulliver from what I now know. And then I could hear a young female voice kind of crying and whimpering and then I heard these muffled screams – terrible screams and I just turned and ran back to the house. God, it was awful!" Isabel Draycott shuddered as she recalled what she had seen and heard.

"Did you tell anyone what you had witnessed?" Alison asked.

"God, no!" Isabel Draycott replied. "I mean, after all, he was still my father and I tried to convince myself that there was an innocent explanation for what I had witnessed. You have to understand that I'd lost my mother and I was terrified that if something happened to my father, I'd be put into care or something, so I just tried to pretend that nothing had happened. And then the story of the missing girls hit the headlines and I started to put two and two together and then I saw what my father did to poor Charlotte Huxton."

"You saw him murder her?" Alison asked incredulously.

"No, I didn't but… The thing was that Charlotte had fallen out with her parents – her mother mainly, because her father wasn't around much – and she wanted to get back into her good books. She told me that, when she was younger, her mother had encouraged her to learn the violin, but she threw a strop and stopped practising. Now a few of us used to go to the local youth club, which my father helped to run, and Charlotte found out that my father played the violin, so she asked him if he would give her some secret lessons – it was meant to be a surprise for her mother so we were all sworn to secrecy. Anyway, I came home earlier than expected one afternoon – I can't remember why – and I caught my father and Charlotte in his bedroom and they were… well, you can guess. As Charlotte had no money to pay for her lessons, my father had obviously decided he would extract a payment in kind. God, it still makes me feel sick, even after all this time. But it was then that I decided I'd had enough!

"I used to enjoy my art lessons at school and I was one of the girls that Russ took a bit of a shine to. I often used to wander down to the river with my sketch pad and pencils and record the scene and Russ, I think, spotted that I might have a bit of talent so he kind of took me under his wing. He became a kind of surrogate father figure in a way. Sometimes, after school, we'd go round to his place and we'd talk about art and he'd look at my sketches and offer some advice. And then, one day, out of the blue, he asked if I would model for him. I was quite flattered, I suppose, that he asked and he paid me a small fee for my time. And then, on one occasion, he asked me if I would take my top off for him – I mean, I know I should have said no and I know that he shouldn't have asked, but I was so desperate for a bit of attention that I agreed and well, things went from there.

"I can remember being so upset when he announced that he would be leaving at the end of the summer term. He knew how unhappy I was at home and so he suggested that I run away with him and we'd make a fresh start miles away where nobody knew us. To be honest, I think it was just bravado on his part – he never expected me to say yes – but I jumped at the chance. So I finished school, as usual, on the Friday afternoon, went home to pack – my father wasn't around, as usual – and, on the Saturday morning, I phoned Russ to let him know the coast was clear. He came round to pick me up and we drove off into the sunset – not literally, you understand. We stopped off en route somewhere to buy some things so that I could change my appearance a bit and look older than I was – a wig, some cosmetics and some different clothes and we drove to this pokey little flat in Norfolk which Russ had just taken out a lease on."

"But as I recall, your father didn't report you missing until the following Wednesday," Clive said.

"That's right! I left him a note saying I'd left home and not to come looking for me, but I think he was still expecting me to come creeping back with my tail between my legs so, on the following Monday morning, I gather he just told the school that I was sick. Apparently, he finally reported me missing on the

Wednesday morning — the same morning that poor Charlotte was reported missing. I don't know exactly what happened to her, whether she resisted my father's advances or threatened to report him, but I know she was never seen again."

"Were you aware, at the time, that your father had reported you missing?" Alison Pawlett asked in a reproachful tone.

"Of course — I could hardly avoid it. My name and picture were all over the telly and in the papers. It felt quite spooky actually. I hardly dared set foot outside Russ's flat until everything had died down a bit."

"And you spent the next ten years in Norfolk, living with Russell Chalbury?"

"Yup! My real Christian names are Isabel Linda so I started calling myself Belinda Carlow — a bit pretentious maybe but nobody worked out who I really was. Russ changed his name to Carlo Russell — even more pretentious — and we lived a life of Bohemian anonymity in rural Norfolk. We took a variety of temporary jobs to keep some money coming in and Russ started to sell some of his paintings so we got by."

"So what prompted you to come back to this area after all that time?" Clive asked.

Isabel Draycott fell silent for a moment or two before she replied. "For a start, we didn't really know anybody in Norfolk and, as we were both using aliases, it was kind of difficult to take anyone into our confidence. We felt as though we were fugitives on the run, holed up in a pokey flat, jumping every time there was a knock at the door. Oh, that kind of lifestyle can be exciting for a while but, eventually, it becomes really, really tiresome. And I think we both began to hanker after a return to this area. It was, after all, where I was born and brought up and, despite all that had happened, I still had a soft spot for it. And Russ had lived around here for several years and was keen to return. And, after ten years, I finally felt brave enough to come home and confront my father."

"And did you?"

"No, I never got the chance! I knew that my father had been transferred to Stowbrook and that he had remarried – you can find out so much on the internet these days – but I wasn't in too much of a hurry to confront him. Russ and I had been down here for a long weekend to have a quiet look around and then Russ came back later to see if he could find somewhere suitable for his studio. Well, you can imagine my shock when he came home and said that he could buy the old boathouse from Polbury Manor for next to nothing. I hadn't told Russ what I'd seen and heard all those years ago, so I tried to sound pleased but I didn't really want to have anything to do with the boathouse – I felt sick at the prospect. But Russ was so keen on it and, having thought about it for a bit, I began to think that it really might help to confront my demons and lay a few ghosts, if you'll pardon my mixed metaphor, so we went ahead. We took it over in May but there was so much to do that I didn't have any time or energy to think about my father or anything. I know he paid Russ a visit at one point to talk about the music festival but I kept out of the way; I wasn't ready for a confrontation.

"Anyway the boathouse hadn't been used for years, a lot of the timber was rotten, the roof leaked, we had nearly as much plant life inside as we did outside. And then, when we started to remove some of the old timber floorboards, I got really spooked. We found lots of what looked like bloodstains and, trapped between two boards, we found a rusty locket which looked very much like one I'd seen Charlotte wearing. I'm afraid that just about freaked me out. Well obviously, at that stage, I had to tell Russ about the history of the boathouse and what I'd witnessed. He was brilliant about it. He said that he'd stop using the boathouse if I was finding it too stressful, but I really wanted to continue what we'd started. He did suggest, quite forcibly for Russ, that I should tell the police who I was and what I knew but I was just too frightened – I don't think I could've coped with it all coming out into the open – and Russ was quite understanding. Anyway, it was not long afterwards that I made a really, really, stupid mistake and I am so, so very sorry."

"Your mistake?" Alison asked, wrinkling her nose again. "I don't understand."

"Let me explain. One day, I'd had enough of being an unpaid lackey and handywoman at the boathouse – my hands were blistered and my muscles were aching – so I took a wander along the towpath back here to St. Giles and I strolled into the churchyard. It might seem an odd thing to say, but I had some happy times in the churchyard. It was peaceful, it was calm, it was secluded. I often used to sit in a quiet corner and do a bit of sketching or just sit and think. There was one particular corner of the churchyard that I used to go to – it was the oldest part and the easiest part to hide away in – but when I went back, I found that it was much more neglected and overgrown than I remembered when I was a kid. And then I saw it, this gravestone. It talked about someone called Fairhead who was supposed to have died in 1752 or something and had an inscription that read 'Circe'. I was sure it hadn't been there when I was a kid – I knew that part of the churchyard like the back of my hand – so there was obviously something not right. And then I remembered what my father had said about the fair-haired girl and the accident and things started to fall into place. I couldn't work out the significance of 'Circe' for a while. It was Russ who suggested it might be the initials of the five missing girls, including me. And when I realised that this was almost certainly where they were buried, I felt I needed to pay my respects so I left a bunch of flowers on the grave."

"And that was your mistake?"

"Russ called it a grave error. Two or three weeks later, I finally summoned up the bottle to meet Vanessa. I sent her a letter to start with, explaining who I was and asking her if we could meet up and she seemed quite keen. We met in a tearoom in Morstock and had a pleasant little chat and I told her about my suspicions. I don't know how much she already knew, but she seemed quite horrified. And then she remembered that my father had come home one day, quite agitated about something, and all he would say was 'somebody knows something'. And she reckoned it was probably a day or two after I'd put the flowers on the grave. We think he must have visited the churchyard for some reason and seen the flowers. And he must have concluded that somebody knew about the grave and who was in it. In his own demented, unravelling mind, he must have figured that a parent of one of his victims had somehow stumbled on the truth, but he had no way of knowing who it was so he set out to eliminate them all. And it was all my fault..."

"So are you responsible for your father's death?" Alison Pawlett repeated her earlier question.

"Oh, yes, I killed him," Isabel Draycott replied, her voice trembling with emotion. "I sent him a note explaining that I was back in the area and asking if we could meet and he replied saying he would like to. It was Vanessa who suggested we arrange to meet in Stowbrook Forest – a quiet, secluded spot – and she very kindly agreed to come along as moral support, in case things got unpleasant. But she had nothing to do with his death. It was me who hit him, again and again. I was so angry..."

At this point, Isabel Draycott burst into floods of uncontrollable tears and Clive, who disliked displays of raw emotion and who was, in any event, growing restless, decided to draw matters to a temporary close.

"Alison, I think we should take a break. Perhaps you can take Isabel somewhere safe and look after her for a while. And you need to get someone to take a look at your ear and get yourself a replacement mobile."

"What about you?" Alison asked.

"I need to track Vanessa Draycott down. Earlier on, I asked Clare to go off and search for her but I'm beginning to think she might need some help. You'd better let me know when you've got a working mobile because I think I might need your help as well."

Fourteen

Clive had last seen Vanessa Draycott, in considerable distress, scampering up the stairs away from the cellar in the vicarage but he guessed she wouldn't have gone far so he decided to head back towards Stowbrook. He had nearly reached the vicarage when his phone rang. Recognising the caller, he pulled sharply over to the side of the road and took the call.

"Clare! What news?"

"Clive, you'd better come quick!" Clare shrieked. "I've found Vanessa Draycott. She's on the roof of the tower of St Mary's church and is threatening to throw herself off!"

"Bloody hell! I'll be there in a couple of minutes! Don't do anything daft!"

For the second time that day, Clive found himself wishing that Alison Pawlett was at the wheel as he screeched and skidded his way to the church causing the occasional passing pedestrian to gawp in amazement as he sped past. He slewed across the church car park before lurching to a sudden halt. Then he raced from his car and looked up towards the tall grey stone tower, its silhouette highlighted against the brooding, rain-laden sky. Shielding his eyes from the stinging drops of cascading rain, he could just discern a small figure – he assumed that it was Vanessa Draycott – perched precariously on the parapet and looking down, but there was no obvious sign of Clare.

On the path leading from the car park to the church entrance, a small group of interested bystanders had gathered beneath several umbrellas and were peering up to the top of the tower in a hushed, expectant silence. Clive wasn't sure whether they were hoping that Vanessa Draycott would jump or that she would be rescued. Either way, their interest, though riveted, seemed entirely passive.

"Do you know what's going on?" Clive asked the first bystander that he came to, an elderly lady wearing a beige raincoat and headscarf.

"It's the vicar's wife, er, widow. I think she's threatening to jump."

"Is there anybody else up there?"

The elderly lady shook her head vaguely. "I'm not sure. There was a lady who rushed into the church a few minutes ago but I haven't seen her since. I'm afraid I didn't recognise her, but she looked a bit panic-stricken. She did tell me her name. What was it? What was it? Carol, I think she said."

"Clare?" Clive corrected her impatiently.

"Yes, Clare, that was it; well done!"

"And have the emergency services been called?"

The elderly lady looked around doubtfully. "Oh, er, no, I don't think so. The lady, er Clare, said we were to leave it to her."

"Shit!" Not entirely confident of the elderly lady's ability to act decisively, if at all, Clive turned and addressed the whole group. "Look, I'm working with the police. I'm going to go up the tower. Give me five minutes and if we haven't got Mrs Draycott down, can somebody please dial 999?"

The assembled heads beneath the umbrellas nodded in unison and there was much animated murmuring.

Access to the belfry, near the top of the tower, was by a steep, winding stone staircase but, from the belfry, the roof could only be reached by a rickety wooden ladder secured, none too firmly, to the wall. Having clambered breathlessly up to the top of the tower, Clare slowly opened the creaky wooden trapdoor that led out onto the tower roof. It was an impulse, born out of a deep-seated desire to help, that had made Clare climb the tower but, now she was there, she wasn't sure what to do. She was scared. On the opposite side, Vanessa Draycott was straddling the crenellations with one foot on the roof and the other on the parapet. As she heard the trapdoor open, she looked round at Clare, her eyes open even wider than usual.

"Who are you? Do I know you?" Vanessa Draycott demanded crossly, before suddenly shouting, "Keep away, whoever you are!"

Clare slowly hauled herself onto the roof and stopped to take some deep breaths. The arduous climb up to the top of the tower had left her panting, on top of which, her mouth had become uncomfortably dry. She was not a great fan of heights at the best of times and she certainly didn't relish the prospect of some kind of confrontation on the slippery parapet edge, especially with steady rain falling.

"Er, no, you don't know me," Clare gasped. "I was here, at this church, for the memorial service for your husband, but you wouldn't remember me. You'll remember my husband, Clive, though. He came to see you earlier today."

"Ah yes, I remember him. He's a lot smarter and a lot more persistent than I gave him credit for, damn him!"

With her heart pounding, Clare took a couple of tentative steps towards Vanessa Draycott, who immediately sounded an agitated warning. "I've warned you once. Don't come any nearer or I will jump. I'm serious you know."

"Yes, I'm sure you are," Clare agreed in as calm a voice as she could manage. "Although, I don't know why you would want to jump."

"Because I killed my husband," Vanessa Draycott wailed. "I bludgeoned him to death with his hammer. So ask yourself, you interfering do-gooder, what sort of future do you imagine I've got to look forward to?"

"But your husband was a monster. He murdered innocent teenage girls. I think a lot of people will sympathise with what you did. You stopped him from murdering any more innocent people. I suppose you could…" Clare stopped herself from saying any more, suddenly realising that the merest hint of disapproval could be the trigger for Vanessa Draycott to throw herself from the tower.

"I could have informed the police – that's what you were going to say, wasn't it? And yes, you're right, I could have informed the police but then my husband would still be alive – which he didn't deserve to be – and there would have been a trial which would have been a dreadfully harrowing ordeal for the friends and family of all his victims. No, no, I couldn't have that."

"You might have killed your husband," Clare acknowledged as she shuffled almost imperceptibly towards Vanessa Draycott, "but you almost certainly saved at least one life. If your husband had lived, he would probably have killed Alan Ashurst; he certainly planned to do so. And who knows where it would have ended."

"Maybe, but it doesn't make any difference. I'm still a murderer." With that, Vanessa Draycott turned away from Clare, elevated herself to her full height, looked briefly down at the ground and raised her arms, as though about to jump. At that point, she was momentarily distracted by the sound of the heavy trapdoor creaking open and, as she looked round, Clare sensed that she had a split second in which to act.

Wiping the rainwater from her eyes and shouting "no!" Clare raced towards Vanessa Draycott, grabbed her around the waist and tried to haul her away from the parapet edge. The lead roof of the tower had become wet and treacherous and, as Clare's feet slipped from under her, Vanessa Draycott shouted, "Let go of me, you stupid woman," and wriggled fiercely in a bid to escape from Clare's tenacious grip. As the struggle continued, and the rain became heavier, both women, locked together in a writhing clinch, lurched towards the parapet edge. With a surprising show of strength for a woman of her slight build, Vanessa Draycott managed to extricate one of her arms from Clare's tight embrace and used her bony elbow to dig her adversary in the ribs. Surprised and hurt, Clare lost her grip on her quarry, staggered back, slipped, lost her footing again and began to teeter over the edge of the parapet.

Clive's arrival had been delayed slightly as he was making the final ascent up the ladder from the belfry. His long legs, often a useful asset, were not designed for the short steps that the ladder required and, in his haste, he too had lost his footing and had cracked his shin on a rung.

He was still rubbing his leg when he opened the trapdoor, peered out and observed the desperate struggle being played out before him. As Clare began to wobble on the parapet edge, her arms flailing desperately, Clive propelled himself across the roof, his long legs again proving to be an asset, and made a desperate lunge for the first part of Clare's unsteady anatomy that he could reach – her left thigh. Summoning up every sinew of strength, he hauled his screaming wife back from the edge of the tower and eased her gently to the floor where she lay for a moment or two, panting and sobbing. Meanwhile, Vanessa Draycott, now free from Clare's clutches, had headed back to the parapet and was about to leap when she was momentarily startled, for a second time, this time by a loud clap of thunder from close by. Her temporary distraction offered Clive the opportunity he needed. He hurtled towards her, grabbed her by the throat and, half-throttling her, bundled her to the floor next to Clare.

"Nobody goes anywhere near the edge," Clive shouted as he struggled to recover his breath. While Vanessa Draycott hauled herself up into a sitting position and gingerly fingered her bruised throat, Clare slowly rose to her feet and embraced Clive.

"Boy, am I glad to see you," she exclaimed. "I thought I'd had it there for a moment."

"You okay?" Clive asked, attentively, as the rain continued to fall.

"I've got a bruised rib or two and a few scratches. I'm a bit shaky, I'm soaking wet and my hair's ruined but I'll live, which I didn't expect to be saying a moment or two ago."

"You were very brave," Clive remarked proudly.

"Oh, don't be silly! I didn't have time to think about being brave; I just acted on instinct really. I couldn't do nothing and watch her plummet to the ground, could I? I had to try. What are you going to do about her now she's confessed to murdering her husband?" Clare pointed to Vanessa Draycott who was beginning to rise unsteadily to her feet.

"Has she? That's odd. She's the second person, within the last hour or so, to confess to murdering Keith Draycott."

Clare's mouth fell open. "Really? Who else has confessed?"

"I'll tell you later. For the moment, if you are up to it, we are going to escort Vanessa Draycott down and, if necessary, summon some help. I asked the group of rubberneckers down there to call the emergency services but I doubt that anybody has."

They had completed over half of the descent down the winding staircase with Vanessa Draycott, sobbing profusely, sandwiched uncomfortably between Clare and Clive, when they encountered Sergeant Pawlett bounding up the stairs towards them.

"Alison! What are you doing here?" Clive asked.

"I heard on the police radio that someone had called for assistance at St Mary's and I had a feeling you might be involved and possibly in danger, so I turned round and raced over here."

Clive instinctively winced at the news that Alison had raced to the scene. "And where's Isabel Draycott?" he asked.

"She's locked in my car and handcuffed to the steering wheel," Alison announced proudly before studying, more closely, the bedraggled and badly shaken trio standing miserably in front of her. "Are you alright?" she enquired.

"Kind of," Clive replied. "Mrs Draycott was about to throw herself from the tower when Clare got to her and dragged her back."

"Blimey! Really? Well done!" Alison looked admiringly at Clare as the sound of a police siren drowned out any chance of further conversation.

When all four individuals had completed their descent and were making their way through the church, leaving a trail of water behind them, Clive turned to Alison and whispered to her.

"Alison, I think I should get Clare home as soon as possible. She's had a very nasty shock. She says she's okay at the moment but there can often be a reaction. Are you okay to take Vanessa and Isabel Draycott back to your HQ and start asking them a few questions? I'd really like to know when Vanessa first discovered what her husband had been up to and what role Isabel played in it all. I'll try and get in touch a bit later."

Clive and Clare stood and watched from beneath the partial shelter of an ancient yew tree as Isabel Draycott was transferred to a police car, where she was joined by Vanessa Draycott and they were driven off at speed. Clive then put his protective arm around Clare who was shaking uncontrollably. "Come on, let's get you home!"

As the rain continued to fall heavily, they dashed to Clive's car, splashing through several deep puddles en route, and Clare quickly hauled herself into the passenger seat. Clive was manoeuvring his angular frame into the driver's seat when another car screeched to a halt in the car park and a tall, self-important looking man with fair, gingery hair emerged, opened an umbrella and marched purposefully towards him.

"You must be Clive Walsingham," the man announced loudly as he approached. "I'm Superintendant Rushwick."

"Yes, I rather thought you might be," Clive replied enigmatically through the half-opened car door.

"I heard you were in a spot of bother here."

"Just a little local difficulty," Clive conceded. "But it's all been sorted out."

"I see!" Superintendant Rushwick sounded disappointed. He waited for Clive to say something more but Clive just smiled. He had become fascinated by the way Superintendant Rushwick kept tapping his right foot on the ground as he spoke.

"I had to let your Mr Beechwood go," the superintendant continued. "He had a cast-iron alibi for the time when the girls disappeared."

"Did he?" Clive tried to sound surprised. "I had no idea!"

"Yes and I have to say I'm very disappointed. I feel I've been wasting my time today, thanks to your misleading information. And on top of that, I've had Alan Ashurst complaining that he was assaulted by Inspector Beauregard earlier on today even though he was not supposed to be on duty. You know, you came with such a good reputation, Clive, but I have to say I feel you've let me down. So I'm ending your involvement in this case with immediate effect; best leave it to the professionals in future."

"You haven't heard then?" Clive asked innocently as he eased himself out of the car, flinched as the heavy rain began to pound his face and stood face to face with the foot-tapping superintendant. "You haven't spoken to Inspector Beauregard?"

"Him?" The superintendant almost spat the word out. "Why would I want to speak to him?"

"Well for a start, Detective Inspector Beauregard has irrefutable proof that Keith Draycott was responsible for the kidnapping and subsequent murder of four schoolgirls, ten years ago. He also has irrefutable proof that Keith Draycott was responsible for the murders of Olivia Farringdon, Kate Huxton and Edward Duffield. And he also has some evidence that links Keith Draycott to the death of Doris Milburn at Mallowcrest Care Home and to the death of Lennie Cave. Detective Inspector Beauregard has also taken Raymond Gulliver into custody where I imagine he will be charged with the attempted murder of Detective Sergeant Pawlett and other offences committed while assisting Keith Draycott in the abduction and murder of four schoolgirls. Meanwhile, two people have confessed to the murder of Keith Draycott and Sergeant Pawlett has taken them both into custody where they will be questioned further. One of the two is Isabel Draycott, who is alive and well and has recently returned to this area after an absence of nearly ten years. In connection with her disappearance, you may want to consider charging Russell Chalbury with having sex with a minor, although you might have some difficulty proving that one.

"Oh, and I also took the liberty of phoning Guy Sharston at the *Carlow Valley Gazette* – I reckoned that that was probably what you would have done. I told him what had happened and that Inspector Beauregard was to be congratulated on solving the case and I'm sure something along those lines will appear in the next edition of the *Gazette*. In fact, he may well be waiting at your HQ, together with a photographer, when Isabel and Vanessa Draycott arrive."

"But…" Superintendant Rushwick spluttered.

"And now, if you'll excuse me, I need to get my wife home – she's had a bit of a fright. I'll put my invoice in the post."

"Yes, but hang on!" Superintendant Rushwick called after Clive as he got into his car and drove quickly away.

*

"I could murder a large brandy!" Clare announced as she stepped shakily from the car.

"You could have phrased that better," Clive said with a wry smile as he placed an arm around his wife's sodden shoulders and led her swiftly into the hotel while the rain continued to cascade into the dark puddles that were rapidly engulfing the car park.

"You don't have to fuss me, Clive," Clare replied, gently easing herself from Clive's embrace. "Besides, my ribs are hurting a bit and I could do without your bear hug. I'll be fine once I've had that brandy and dried off. How is Alison, by the way? I noticed there was quite a bit of blood around her ear."

"Raymond Gulliver took a shot at her in the churchyard at St. Giles. Fortunately the bullet only grazed her earlobe."

"Omigod! Really? Poor Alison! Mind you, it's as well he didn't graze your earlobe – you'd have probably bled to death."

"Thanks for the compliment. I'll go and get that brandy for you. Then you can go and dry off and relax for a while."

Clive was just emerging from the bar with a full brandy glass in his hand when he almost bumped into Gary Beechwood, who was rushing towards the kitchen. His fair hair was more unkempt than usual and there were beads of perspiration on his forehead.

"Ah, I heard they let you go," Clive observed, rather obviously.

Gary Beechwood gave a wide grin and his brown eyes sparkled with mischief. "Yup, I gave them a good run for their money but when Superintendant Smug Bastard started to threaten me, I thought I should own up to being out of the country when the girls were abducted. He didn't seem too pleased and insisted on checking my alibi carefully before he let me go. I hope I bought you enough time."

"Yes thanks, you did – but only just! We'd just about tied it all up and Clare had stopped Vanessa Draycott from hurling herself off the church tower when your favourite superintendant turned up. I must say he didn't look too pleased. I really am very grateful, Gary, for what you did – it can't have been easy."

"S'alright," Gary Beechwood replied casually. "I quite enjoyed it really, knowing that I could play my trump card whenever I wanted. And I quite enjoyed seeing the look on Superintendant Smug Bastard's face when I threatened to sue him for wrongful arrest as I left. Mind you, I'm afraid dinner will have to be a pretty instant affair this evening – I haven't got much time."

"That's fine! And don't forget I owe you a favour."

Gary Beechwood laughed. "Oh, no, I won't forget. In fact, I'm probably going to ask you about that very soon."

*

Inspector Beauregard had shaved, brushed his hair, gently bathed his swollen nose, removed any traces of congealed blood from his face and changed into a freshly laundered shirt and stain-free tie. "Do you want to call your solicitor?" he asked as he strode, with unusual confidence, into the dingy interview room, with Sergeant Pawlett trailing in his wake. He pulled up a chair.

Vanessa Draycott looked across at the detectives with reddened, moist eyes and spoke quietly. "I don't think that will be necessary, thank you, Inspector."

"Can I take it that you are still admitting killing your husband, Keith Draycott?"

"You can."

"When did you first suspect that your husband was responsible for the deaths of those girls?"

Vanessa Draycott sighed. "I don't recall the exact date – it was sometime in early July, I should think. I got a letter, quite out of the blue, from someone claiming to be Issy Draycott and asking if we could meet. I must admit I thought it was a hoax of some kind at first but I was intrigued so I wrote back and asked her for more information about herself and, when she replied, she seemed genuine enough. So, eventually we met up in Morstock. And it was then that Issy told me about what happened all those years ago, what she suspected Keith had done to those poor girls, how she had run off with Russell Chalbury and how she had found the gravestone." Vanessa Draycott shuddered.

"So what did you do?" Inspector Beauregard asked.

"Nothing at first; I was mortified by what Issy had told me, of course, but I couldn't think straight enough to work out what to do. Keith had been acting a bit strangely for a while but I couldn't fathom why at first. And then I remembered him coming home one day, quite agitated, and saying 'somebody knows something' over and over again. Now Keith had always been a bit secretive – there were some things that I learned never to discuss with him – but he suddenly seemed to completely shut himself away. He would spend hours in his study – much more than usual – and he kept disappearing into the cellar."

"You knew about the cellar?" Sergeant Pawlett asked.

"I knew of the cellar but I didn't know what was down there at first. Keith told me that there were a lot of old parish records down there. I didn't think anything of it at the time but, on reflection, it would have been ludicrous to keep such important old documents in somewhere as damp as the cellar; your colleague Mr Walsingham realised that as well. So anyway, I started to follow him around the house."

"He didn't suspect anything?"

"Oh no, he was far too wrapped up in what he was doing and I have the advantage of being quite small and light on my feet. I noticed he kept going into the cupboard under the stairs before and after every visit to the cellar and, on one occasion, I saw him take something – I didn't know what – in a bag down with him. So, one day, when I knew he'd be out for a while, I went into the wine cupboard and had a nose round. It didn't take me long to realise that all of the bottles that he kept in there were covered in dust, apart from one, and, when I picked it up, something inside it rattled. I removed the cork and found a couple of keys inside, one of which turned out to be the key to the cupboard in the cellar. Well, when I looked inside, my blood ran cold. He had all these personal belongings from the girls – his trophies, I suppose – and his diaries and notes. I couldn't bear to read most of his notes – they were too triumphal and gloating and really quite nauseous – but they left me in no doubt as to what he had done. And then I noticed something that made me realise I had to do something pretty drastic."

"What was that?"

"It was a mobile phone that obviously belonged to one of his victims. Now, I'm no expert but it looked reasonably new and, when I switched it on, it powered up. It wouldn't have done that if it had been ten years old. And that was when I first realised that Keith had plumbed new depths – he had embarked on a new killing spree!"

"You didn't report your suspicions to us."

"No, I didn't," Vanessa Draycott replied with a chilling calm. "And perhaps I was wrong but I decided to take matters into my own hands; that way, I could be sure of the outcome. It was on the Monday morning – the Monday before last – that I decided to act. Keith had been behaving strangely over breakfast – he was on edge about something and was perspiring quite freely – much more than usual. And then he disappeared down into the cellar for about ten minutes and, when he came back, he announced that he'd got to go out for a while, so I decided to follow him. He took his car, which was quite unusual – he usually rode his bike if it was a local journey – so I followed him in mine. I had to hang back a bit to avoid him recognising me and my car in his rear-view mirror but, fortunately, he seemed very focused on where he was going and, because he didn't drive that often, he was quite slow, so I was easily able to keep him in my sights. I'm not sure he ever looked in his rear-view mirror! Anyway, he drove down the lane leading to Lannock Woods and parked in the small car park by one of the main paths. Obviously, I didn't want to be seen, so I parked a little further down the lane and walked back. There was another car in the car park which I didn't pay much attention to at first. I waited for a few minutes and then I glimpsed Keith walking back through the woods towards me so I hid behind a tree – there were plenty to choose from. He opened the boot of his car, reached inside for a large plastic bag of some kind and then he placed what looked like a hammer inside – it made me shudder. And then he went over to the other car, opened it, rummaged around inside and removed several items – I couldn't make out exactly what they were – and put them in the boot of his car. And then he looked round a bit furtively and drove off. Well, by now I was in no doubt what he had been up to in the woods and I decided that this couldn't go on any longer. He was going to have to meet the same fate before he killed anybody else."

"So what did you do next?"

Vanessa Draycott leaned forward in her chair and looked impishly at the detectives as though she was deriving some kind of pleasure from recounting what had happened. "When Keith was out on some parish business or other, I phoned Issy and explained what I'd witnessed and she agreed to help me, although I don't think she knew what I was planning. She agreed to contact Keith, explain who she was, say that she was anxious to get to know her father again and ask if they could meet up to bury the hatchet, as it were. Well, Keith seemed intrigued by Issy's phone call and he agreed to meet her in Stowbrook Forest on the Wednesday morning – that would be last Wednesday. I had got there earlier and was already lurking behind a tree when they met. And, while he was talking to Issy, I crept up behind him and despatched him with the same hammer he'd used to despatch his victims. Poor Issy seemed pretty shocked by what she had seen and it took her a few minutes to recover her composure, but then she seemed quite willing to help me hide his body in some dense undergrowth – mind you, I was holding a bloodstained hammer at the time! And then we went our separate ways. I must stress that Issy played no part in her father's murder – that was all down to me. All she did was help to make it possible – she was the bait to lure him in."

Detective Inspector Beauregard puffed out his cheeks. "And was it you who put the newspaper cutting in your husband's breast pocket?"

Vanessa Draycott threw back her head and laughed. "Oh, yes, it was me! I hadn't planned to do that but then, when I was looking through the *Carlow Valley Gazette* on the Friday morning, I noticed the date and the idea came to me. I thought, if I planted a cutting with the date on it, it might provide you – or Mr Walsingham, at least – with a clue that would lead you to the gravestone, the graves of the missing girls and the identity of your child abductor. It also gave me an opportunity to check to see if Keith's body had been found – it hadn't! I must admit that your colleague, Mr Walsingham, turned out to be a lot smarter and a lot more persistent than I gave him credit for. I thought it might be fun to phone him up and play something like a requiem or a march to the gallows just to scare him a bit and maybe even persuade him to stop his investigation. It was something that Keith had done during the original investigation, according to his notes. I tried it twice but it didn't seem to put him off at all. How is his wife, by the way? I didn't mean to subject her to that terrible ordeal on top of the church tower."

"She'll be alright," Alison Pawlett replied, acidly. "But naturally, she's a bit shaken up."

Vanessa Draycott sighed. "Yes, she's a lot tougher than I thought. You're right; she'll be fine, although I do wish people wouldn't interfere with other people's lives. It rarely does them any good."

"Well, thank you for your frankness," Inspector Beauregard said, politely. "We're nearly done, I think." He paused to observe Vanessa Draycott emit an audible sigh of relief. "There are just two more things that Sergeant Pawlett wants to mention."

"Yes, thank you," Alison Pawlett nodded dutifully. "You may remember, Mrs Draycott, that I took your husband's computer away with me. We hoped that we might find something on it that would help us."

"Yes, I do remember, of course," Vanessa Draycott replied warily. "But, as I said at the time, my husband would have used a password and I'm afraid I don't…"

"Oh, that was no problem," Alison Pawlett replied dismissively. "Clive was able to work out that little puzzle."

"So you've seen what, erm, files he had on there," Vanessa Draycott was sounding increasingly nervous. "I don't expect you found anything very interesting – just parish business."

"The thing is, Mrs Draycott, we've got technical people who are very good at recovering files that have been deleted. Now somebody had tried to delete some files from your husband's computer, but they hadn't done a very good job – it was a bit of an amateurish attempt, apparently."

"Oh, really? I wonder why…"

"But of course, you know what those files were, don't you? They've only been deleted recently – some time shortly after your husband died, we think. Despite all that he'd done, you were still trying to protect his reputation, or what little reputation he still had. You didn't want anyone to know about all that child pornography. You didn't want anyone to know that your husband was a paedophile, did you?"

Vanessa Draycott swallowed hard. "Surely, you don't think…"

"And I've been speaking with our pathologist who's also been in contact with our forensic team. She's been having a closer look at your husband's body. Normally, she would have done this earlier but, with the bodies piling up the way they have, it's taken a while. Anyway, she's now concluded that your husband was attacked with two different weapons; one was indeed the hammer that he'd used to murder his victims but there was another weapon, also metal, but flatter with a sharper, pointed end." She paused to observe Vanessa Draycott's reaction, which was one of increasing alarm. "Anyway, having carefully studied the wounds inflicted on your husband, she has come to a very interesting conclusion. She is pretty sure that the wounds inflicted by the hammer were made after your husband was already dead. She's estimated, in fact, that those wounds were probably made around two days after your husband died, which, interestingly, gives us a date of Friday 12th September."

"You see," Inspector Beauregard interjected. "My theory is that some time after your husband was murdered, you decided to make it look as though he'd been killed in the same way as all his victims, beaten to death with his hammer, so you went back to Stowbrook Forest on the Friday morning, found your husband's body and tried to cover up his original wounds by hitting him repeatedly with his hammer. And then, just for fun, you put the newspaper cutting in his pocket."

"That's preposterous," Vanessa Draycott protested. "Why on earth would I go to all that trouble and run the risk of being caught?"

"Because you were trying to protect the identity of the real murderer. The pathologist has been puzzling over what metal object was used to inflict the initial blows that killed your husband. Our forensics team have been doing a lot of research and they think they've come up with the answer –

the murder weapon was almost certainly a caulk removing tool."

"A what?" Vanessa Draycott asked with a look of bewilderment.

"A caulk removing tool," Inspector Beauregard explained, "is used in the repair and maintenance of boats – you'd find one in most old boathouses. In fact they found the very thing in Russell Chalbury's boathouse – and it had traces of blood on it."

"My God! Isabel? You think Isabel killed her father?"

"You confessed to the murder of your husband to protect Isabel Draycott, I assume because you felt sorry for her. It was Isabel who arranged the meeting with her father in Stowbrook Forest and it was Isabel who murdered him; your only role was to help her hide the body!"

"But—"

Inspector Beauregard held up his hand. "And before you say anything more, Isabel Draycott has already confessed to killing her father."

*

Clive had been reluctant to leave the hotel so soon after Clare's ordeal, but she was famously resilient and, as she promised, once she had downed her large brandy in commendably fast time, she seemed much better, although, in truth, she was shakier and more tearful than she would admit to her husband. After Clive left and, although her ribcage was sore, she decided to busy herself in the kitchen helping Gary prepare the evening meal and using the opportunity to share their respective experiences of an extraordinary day.

There was one more visit that Clive felt he needed to make. It wasn't a visit that he was looking forward to, but he was angry – very angry – and there were things that needed to be said. It would not be an easy encounter and, if he hadn't been driving, he would have been tempted to have had a large, fortifying brandy, like Clare, before he left. It was several minutes after he pulled up before he felt courageous enough to ring the bell.

Christine Calshott looked surprised, hostile even, as she opened the door to find Clive standing on her doorstep.

"Oh, it's you," she said, disdainfully. "I told you all I could yesterday when you came round. I do find it all rather distressing raking up the past and I'd rather not…"

"I have some news that you might be interested in," Clive announced solemnly. "May I come in?"

Christine Calshott hovered on the doorstep for several moments, seemingly uncertain how to respond. She opened her mouth several times, as though about to speak, but each time, she said nothing. Eventually, however, she said, "Oh, alright," and rather grudgingly stood aside to let Clive squeeze past her into the lobby of her small flat.

As before, she led the way into the living room and, as before, it felt cold, damp and uninviting. She guided Clive, with a limp wave of her hand, towards a decrepit, maroon armchair in the coldest, dampest corner of the room, before arranging herself on the edge of an equally decrepit, pale green armchair.

"Er, well, I'll get straight to the point," Clive said as he struggled to position himself comfortably on the lumpy chair. "I thought you should know that we now know who abducted and murdered those girls ten years ago – it was Keith Draycott."

"My God!" Christine Calshott clamped her hand to her mouth and started to tremble. "Keith? Are you sure? It can't be! I mean… I thought he'd been recently murdered!"

"Yes, that's right," Clive replied calmly. "His daughter has been arrested in connection with his murder."

"His daughter – Issy?" Christine Calshott asked incredulously. "But surely she was one of the girls who disappeared. I thought she was dead."

"So did we, originally!" Clive agreed. "But it turns out his daughter ran away from home when she realised what her father was doing. She spent the best part of ten years living with Russell Chalbury in Norfolk, but she's back in the area now. She and Russell are still together and they're doing up an old boathouse down by the river."

"My God!" Christine Calshott repeated as her trembling became more pronounced and she slumped back in her chair. "Keith Draycott? Are you absolutely sure?"

"There can be no doubt," Clive observed sombrely. "We have his notebook in which he made a full confession together with a mass of other evidence."

"But… but Keith was so helpful to the distraught parents and he made a point of coming into the school to support the girls who were getting so upset by what had happened and he was bloody brilliant! And we all rallied round him when Issy disappeared and…"

"He was operating in plain sight, as they tend to say these days. He was so trustworthy that nobody paid any attention to him mingling and chatting with the girls, or gave him a second glance if he offered one of them a lift. And talking of daughters, I wanted to ask you about your daughter, Amy."

"Amy?" Christine Calshott wiped her damp eyes with the back of her hand and sniffed. "I'd really rather not talk about Amy – I find it too distressing."

"Alright, well let me do the talking for a while," Clive replied. "You'll recall that Keith Draycott lost his first wife, Laura, in a car crash about twelve years ago."

"Ye-es, yes, I remember," Christine Calshott replied, guardedly. "Didn't Keith hit a tree?"

"He did; the road was icy and he skidded and hit a tree. The police investigated the accident and produced a report which concluded that he was driving too fast for the conditions. But

Keith Draycott always maintained that the reason he lost control of the car was because he had to brake sharply to avoid hitting a schoolgirl who had run out into the road. The girl was never traced and no one came forward but, from the description he gave at the time, the girl would have been about the same age as your daughter Amy. She had fair hair, like your daughter Amy and the accident took place in Penheath where you lived at the time."

"No, no!" Christine Calshott emitted a piercing shriek. She held her hands over her ears as though trying to obliterate what Clive was saying.

"Now I've got no proof," Clive continued, "but I reckon it was your daughter Amy who ran out in front of Keith Draycott's car and, when she realised what had happened, I expect she panicked, ran home and confessed to you."

"She was absolutely hysterical," Christine Calshott conceded, falteringly. "She admitted that she'd dashed across the road without looking and then, she said, a car came from nowhere, skidded and hit a tree. And I confess I didn't know what to do. Amy was screaming at me, begging me not to tell anyone what had happened and eventually I decided that I wouldn't say anything unless I was asked. I figured that if someone had seen Amy and identified her, the police would call round and I would have to tell them what I knew. But no one called. And then we heard on the news that poor Mrs Draycott had been killed in the accident and Amy became hysterical again and, when she finally started to calm down, she became so... depressed that I worried what she might do. So I kept quiet and did my best to live with my conscience, which wasn't easy. But Amy never really got over it – neither of us did, really! Amy became increasingly withdrawn – reclusive, I suppose – and fell into a deep, continuous depression. She was prescribed antidepressants but she became addicted to them over time. I tried everything I knew to snap her out of it and wean her off her dependency but nothing worked and eventually Amy could take no more..."

Christine Calshott began sobbing, her gaunt shoulders heaving with the effort and her head buried in her hands.

"And I don't expect your involvement with Sir Robert Huxton helped," Clive added quietly.

Christine Calshott looked up briefly, her eyes red with emotion and her lips quivering. "Robert Huxton? What the hell do you mean?"

"You said something when I was here before, so I spoke with Sir Robert and he told me about your affair and how he tried to end it but you got very upset – so upset that he had to take out an injunction against you. I don't imagine all of that going on helped your daughter at all…"

Christine Calshott chewed her bottom lip for a moment or two before replying. "It was a restraining order to be precise. Robert and I got on so well whenever he turned up at Polbury Manor with his latest plans. Occasionally, we'd meet outside school somewhere – a bar or a restaurant – where we could continue to chat about his plans in a, shall we say, less formal environment? And one thing led to another and…" Christine Calshott's voice tailed off and she buried her head in her hands again, while she tried to recover some composure. Eventually, after several deep breaths, she spoke again.

"You know, I really thought Robert and I could make a go of a long-term relationship but it soon became clear that he wasn't interested. It turned out I was just his local conquest – someone he could shag whenever he was in town. But what he did to me hurt so much that I couldn't let it go. I started behaving like some stupid teenage girl with a crush, but he made it clear he wanted nothing more to do with me. And, to cap it all, the bastard ruined my chances of succeeding Kenneth Highcliffe as head teacher. He got in touch with the Board of Governors, unofficially you understand, and told them that I was emotionally too unstable to be considered for the job and that was that. God, what a bloody awful mess!"

Clive fidgeted uncomfortably in his lumpy chair. Yet again, somebody was pouring out their emotional problems to him and, yet again, he felt totally unable to respond adequately.

"Ahem," he said, at last. "You told me that your husband, Gordon walked out on you. Did that have anything to do with your affair with Sir Robert Huxton?"

Christine Calshott nodded and wiped some more tears from her cheeks. "Gordon and I hadn't been hitting it off for a while but, when he found out about me and Robert, that was the last straw. He packed his bags and moved out."

"Which I assume only added to your daughter's, errm, emotional difficulties."

Christine Calshott nodded again but said nothing.

Clive's mouth felt dry and he could feel his heart pounding against his ribcage. The sight of Christine Calshott, so riddled with anguish and so emotionally fragile, was making him wonder whether he should say what he had come to say. Maybe, he reflected, he should terminate his visit and walk away, leaving things unsaid. Maybe, he should arrange to talk to her again when her emotions were calmer. But his anger wouldn't go away and he knew he would have to say something. He would try to choose his words carefully.

"The thing is," he continued, slowly and quietly, "as Keith Draycott's mind began to unravel, it seems he became obsessed by the fair-haired girl who he blamed for the accident and the death of his wife. He didn't know who she was, of course, but as his obsession grew, so did his desire for vengeance. So, over time, it seems he developed an irrational hatred of any fair-haired girl of the right age and appearance that he came across, with the most tragic of consequences. But, after his daughter had run away, I suppose Keith Draycott must have come to his senses and decided to end the killings. I suspect he was uneasy about how much his daughter might know about his activities and decided to lie low. I also suspect his final act of barbarity, at that time, was to murder Lennie Cave. He made it look like a suicide, so that the police would think that Lennie Cave, wracked with guilt, threw himself from the balcony of his flat to avoid arrest. And it seemed to work because the police thought they had their man and called off the search.

"And then, slowly and gradually, things returned to normal. Keith remarried and started to rebuild his life and the memory of the missing girls began to fade. But then, a couple of months ago, something happened, completely out of the blue, that led him to believe that someone knew something that linked him to the girls and their grisly fate. Suspecting that it must be a parent of one of the murdered girls, he set about eliminating them. He'd got as far as murdering Olivia Farringdon, nee Edwyn, Kate Huxton and Edward Duffield before he met his own grisly fate. So, by my calculations, we've had nine murders, two suicides and one attempted suicide, not to mention the appalling ramifications for all the relatives and friends of the victims – and all because you and your daughter tried to cover up her involvement in the accident that killed Laura Draycott. And the biggest irony is that the police didn't blame Amy for the accident in the first place. They even thought about charging Keith Draycott with dangerous driving but they didn't have any witnesses, so they dropped the case. Just think how so many lives would have been so very different if you had admitted your daughter's involvement at the outset. Oh, things wouldn't have been very easy for either of you for a while, but your daughter would have been exonerated, you would have come through and all those lives would have been spared."

After a further period of prolonged sobbing, Christine Calshott slowly wiped her eyes, blew her nose and rose unsteadily to her feet. "This has all been so dreadful and so unexpected. I hope you don't mind, but I need a glass of water," she stuttered as she wandered slowly into her kitchen.

Clive listened for the sound of Christine Calshott running water from the tap but instead, he heard a drawer being opened and then a strange muffled sound followed by a cry of pain. Dashing into the kitchen, Clive saw Christine Calshott standing by the sink, a bloodstained kitchen knife in her right hand and blood pouring from her left wrist.

"No!" Clive shouted as he dashed towards her, intent on wrestling the knife from her hand. But as he got close, Christine Calshott suddenly raised the knife in her hand and rushed towards him. Instinctively, Clive held up his hands to protect himself and let out a cry of pain as he felt the knife penetrate his flesh.

Fifteen

Clive was standing behind the hotel bar pouring the contents of a bottle of sparkling beverage into four glasses. He wasn't used to holding the bottle in his left hand and was concentrating so hard that he didn't immediately notice Clare marching briskly in, accompanied by their two guests.

"Look who I found at reception," Clare announced, grinning.

Clive put the bottle down and glanced at his watch. "And bang on time – I'm impressed!"

He moved out from behind the bar, walked towards his two visitors, proffered his left hand and shook their hands. Caspar Beauregard was wearing a smart charcoal-grey suit – smarter than anything Clive could remember seeing him in before – a startlingly bright turquoise shirt and, even more startling, a broad smile. Standing next to him, Alison Pawlett was also wearing a broad smile and a flowing lilac dress; it was only the second time Clive could remember seeing her in a dress.

"You're both looking well and, if I may say so, very smart this evening," Clive said, obsequiously.

"Sensational, I'd say!" Clare enthused.

"Thank you," Alison Pawlett replied demurely. She was not used to receiving such compliments. "I would've worn my best earrings for the occasion but, unfortunately…"

"How is your ear?" Clive asked.

"Still a bit sore but otherwise okay," Alison replied, fingering her earlobe gingerly and wrinkling her nose. "And how is your hand?"

Clive lifted his heavily bandaged right hand and looked thoughtfully at it. "Oh, it's nothing too serious, but it was quite a deep wound and it bled a lot. At least I was able to wrestle the knife out of Christine Calshott's hand before she did any more damage, either to herself or to me. But I'm okay – I've got quite a few stitches but no long-term damage has been done."

Clare smiled indulgently and gave a sly wink to Dick and Alison. "You've no idea how many jobs around the hotel Clive has put off, claiming his hand is too sore or too heavily bandaged. He claims he can't type properly, he can't pour drinks properly, he can't carry suitcases and he can't carry many plates to the kitchen, although I noticed that his injury didn't prevent him from cleaning his golf clubs yesterday."

"Yes, well, dinner will be ready in half an hour," Clive announced, clumsily changing the subject. "Gary is preparing a couple of his specialities for you but I thought you might like a glass of champagne each to start with, just to celebrate a job well done." He turned to Clare. "I wonder, darling, would you mind carrying the tray only—"

"Only you can't use your right hand." Clare completed the sentence with a look of resignation.

While Clive escorted their visitors to a neatly arranged table beneath the window, Clare went over to the bar and lifted down a tray with four full champagne glasses which she carefully carried to the table.

"I see you've made it to the national newspapers, Dick," Clive chortled as he handed round the champagne. "*Detective Inspector*

Caspar Beauregard, the arresting officer etc. Guy Sharston certainly gave you a good write-up and you looked suitably, er, solemn in the photograph."

"I know! It's a bit embarrassing really!" Dick Beauregard replied, modestly. "I mean, I didn't have that much to do with the investigation – it was all down to you really."

"Ah, but you did tackle Raymond Gulliver just as he was about to shoot at Alison – that's worthy of a mention on its own. And how is Superintendant Rushwick? I bet all that publicity has gone down well with him."

"Ah…" Dick Beauregard began before collapsing into giggles.

"You won't have heard," Alison took over. "Superintendant Rushwick is being transferred. He's going to work for South Humberside police."

Clive exhaled. "Is he? Is that out of choice?"

Alison wrinkled her nose and also started to giggle. "Nobody is saying anything, obviously, although everything seemed to happen surprisingly quickly. Superintendant Rushwick is claiming it's a good career move and that Carlow Valley isn't challenging enough for a detective of his ability, but there are those who think that Mr Rushwick couldn't bear the loss of face after Dick, who he removed from the investigation, made the vital arrests and got all the headlines. And there are some people close to the Chief Constable who seem to think Mr Rushwick was transferred because the Chief had lost confidence in his abilities."

"There were also some concerns about Superintendant Rushwick feeding confidential information to the press," Dick Beauregard added with a knowing smile, his attack of giggling having subsided.

"Oh dear! I expect you'll miss him," Clive added with a smirk.

"We will, of course, but we will try to soldier on stoically," Dick Beauregard replied, mischievously. "But enough of us!

What about you two? You're all over the papers: *Hotel owners foil two suicide bids in one day* was one headline I remember."

"It could have been phrased a little better," Clare reflected. "The headline made it sound as though two of our guests suddenly developed suicidal tendencies after staying here for a day, probably after they saw the size of their bill… or Clive's pink trousers!"

Clive fell silent for a moment as he swilled the champagne around in his glass. "Mmm, I can't pretend that we've enjoyed the publicity very much but I have to admit that it has been great for business," he announced proudly. "What with the publicity over the attempted suicides and Gary's 'wrongful arrest', people are flocking to book with us. We're twice as busy as we were this time last year, which is extremely welcome news after such a disappointing summer."

"You know, I'm not sure we ever did discover why Olivia Farringdon and Edward Duffield stayed here before they were killed," Dick Beauregard mused.

Clive shrugged. "No, but we do know that Keith Draycott dined here on a couple of occasions so, when he was in touch with his two intended victims, using his alter ego, 'Circe', he may have recommended this place to them."

"So there you have another glowing testimonial," Clare added. "Follycombe Hotel as recommended by mass murderer Keith Draycott."

"Mind you, our murder mystery weekends are fully booked well into next year," Clive said cheerfully, before tugging at his earlobe thoughtfully. "Incidentally, have you heard how Christine Calshott is? I can't help feeling that I was a bit too hard on her despite what she tried to do to me."

Briefly, Dick Beauregard's much practised woebegone expression returned. "You said what needed to be said, but she's not too good, I'm afraid. Oh, thanks to your prompt action,

Clive, she survived her suicide attempt and is currently staying with her son Jacob and his family, but I hear she is still very fragile, temperamentally, and someone has to be with her the whole time to stop her from trying to kill herself again. She may improve over time, but…" Dick reverted to his annoying habit of failing to finish his sentence.

"And how are you getting on with Isabel and Vanessa Draycott?"

"Oh, fine," Dick replied. "They're both very calm, serene in a way. Isabel has willingly confessed to murdering her father. She seems quite relieved, in a way, that all the deception and deceit has come to an end and she's quite prepared for her fate. I imagine the courts will treat her reasonably kindly under the circumstances."

"And Vanessa Draycott?"

"She's admitted to being present in the woods when Isabel killed Keith Draycott. She's admitted helping to hide his body and she's admitted going back to the scene a couple of days later and mutilating the body, but she's retracted her earlier confession to murder. She is now quite adamant that she didn't know Issy was planning to murder her father when they lured him into the woods. She said she thought the plan was to confront him about his crimes and then report him to the authorities. It's difficult to believe that she didn't know what Issy Draycott was planning to do, but it might be difficult to prove otherwise and there's certainly no great appetite for retribution in her case. Most people feel she's more of a victim than a villain."

"And talking of villains, what news of Raymond Gulliver?"

"He's been charged with attempting to murder a police officer and conspiracy to murder and—"

"And I've spoken with a local monumental mason," Alison interrupted eagerly. "And he's checked their records and confirmed that they were commissioned to produce the *ISABELLA FAIRHEAD* gravestone just under ten years ago. Of course, he couldn't remember who had placed the order, or what he looked like, or why he said he wanted the gravestone, but he's kept all his records and they confirm that the individual gave his name as Jonathan Swift."

"The author of *Gulliver's Travels!*" Clare exclaimed triumphantly.

"Exactly! Another one of Keith Draycott's little games, of which he seemed so fond."

"So what role do you think Raymond actually played in the girls' murders?" Clare asked Clive, her eyes agog with curiosity.

Clive exhaled. In his view, despite her frequent protestations, Clare still hadn't fully recovered, emotionally, from her life-threatening grapple with Vanessa Draycott and would not respond well to a harrowing recounting of Keith Draycott's graphic description of what had happened to the girls in the boathouse.

"I wonder if we'll ever know exactly what happened in the boathouse," he replied diplomatically. "But I've no doubt that Raymond Gulliver was there and knew what was going on. And according to Keith Draycott's written account, it seems likely that the girls were actually murdered in the boathouse and their bodies were transported along the river by boat to the graveyard after dark. We know that Keith Draycott was a good oarsman when he was younger. He used to coach some of the pupils at Polbury Manor – that's how he knew about the boathouse and how he acquired a key. And he knew the river well, but it would still have been a two-man operation to get the bodies into and out of the boat."

Clare gasped. "My God – the poor girls! Were they, you know, interfered with at all?"

Clive gave an involuntary nod. "I expect Raymond Gulliver would have wanted some incentive to participate but we don't really know for sure. And it is inconceivable, of course, that Keith Draycott really believed any of the girls was responsible for the crash that killed his wife – two of them, after all, were only on holiday in the area – so, despite what he might have claimed in his notes, he must have had other motives as well. Maybe it was some warped hatred of any teenage girl with fair hair, or maybe he was trying to find some justification for..." Clive fell silent and brooding.

"Our forensic team are going over the boathouse with a fine tooth comb," Dick Beauregard confirmed. "So we might know a bit more when they've finished. And they've also confirmed that the weapon they recovered from the boathouse was—"

Clare shook her head. "No, no, I think I've heard more than enough already!"

"Of course, one of the interesting things about Raymond Gulliver," Clive reflected, "is that he doesn't seem to have been involved in the second wave of killings at all – that was all Keith Draycott's work. But I imagine Raymond knew what Keith Draycott was up to and must have been terrified when he heard that he had been murdered, especially after his shed went up in flames. He probably figured that whoever had murdered Keith Draycott, would have known about his involvement with the girls and would come looking for him. That's why he armed himself with a gun. I don't know whether he recognised Alison in the churchyard, but if he stumbled across anybody taking an interest in that gravestone, he was going to panic."

Clive's revelations, though he spared his listeners some of the more shocking passages in Keith Draycott's narrative, were of sufficient gravity to bring about a temporary hiatus in the conversation. For a moment or two, there was an embarrassed shuffling of seats and adjusting of demeanours while his news was being fully digested. It was Dick Beauregard who finally broke the silence.

"I hope you don't mind me asking, Clive," he ventured. "But when was it that you began to suspect Keith Draycott?"

Clive smiled gently. Although he would never admit it, he found it quite satisfying when he could enjoy something of an intellectual advantage over the detective inspector.

"Lennie Cave!" Clive announced and then fell silent while he awaited the inevitable response.

"I beg your pardon!"

Clive rested his elbows on the table and leaned forward conspiratorially as though about to impart some dark state secret.

"You see," he continued, "Lennie Cave was one of the main suspects at the time of the girls' abductions, so, after they found his body and there were no more kidnappings, everybody assumed that he had killed himself because he couldn't live with the shame of what he'd done. The word 'SORRY', which Keith Draycott must have scribbled on the back of a betting slip in Lennie Cave's flat seemed to confirm the suicide theory. But, when the second wave of killings started, it seemed improbable that Lennie Cave had anything to do with the girls' disappearances all those years ago. If the second wave of killings was linked to the first, as it clearly was, then Lennie Cave couldn't have had anything to do with them. So, if he wasn't responsible for the girls' disappearances, then you have to ask yourself why he apparently committed suicide – there was no reason.

"And then Clare found the note in the original case files. It was buried amongst a lot of other notes and statements but it was quite clear. At some point during the original investigation, the police received a phone call from someone who said he had been fishing on the banks of the River Carlow late one evening. He said he had seen some flickering lights coming from the old boathouse. He thought he heard a scream and, a bit later, he had seen someone coming out carrying a torch and walking towards a boat that was moored there. Now, as far as I can make out, the details were passed to Detective Inspector Rushwick but no further action was taken. Maybe that was because the investigation team was under too much pressure to follow up on every phone call and every scrap of information that came their way, or maybe Inspector Rushwick didn't have any confidence in the veracity of the information, given that it had been provided by one of the main suspects..."

"Lennie Cave!" Clive's three table companions cried simultaneously.

"Exactly! And there you have it. Lennie Cave didn't name Keith Draycott when he phoned the police – all he said was that there were strange things going on at the boathouse – and no further action was taken. Now it is quite likely that Keith Draycott had seen Lennie Cave skulking about near the boathouse – he would have been very vigilant – and realised that he knew more than was good for him. Of course, he didn't know exactly how much Lennie Cave had seen or heard, or whether he had told the police, but he couldn't afford to take a risk, so he decided that Lennie Cave would have to be silenced. And, incidentally, we shouldn't discount the possibility that Lennie Cave had seen Keith Draycott up to no good at the boathouse and, being a petty criminal with few scruples, might have been trying to blackmail him – either way, he had to go. So I imagine Keith Draycott went to see him, on some pretext or other, killed him and made it look like suicide. And once it became clear that the police thought Lennie Cave was the abductor and weren't looking for anyone else, Keith Draycott knew he had to stop, especially as his daughter had run off and he had no idea how much she knew about his activities.

"Now I have to admit that what you've just heard is partly supposition but it got me thinking. After all, the boathouse was only a short distance downriver from St. Giles church. And then I realised that other bits and pieces of information were also pointing in the same direction. For example, Keith Draycott's murder was the only one where someone went back and placed a newspaper cutting in his pocket; why didn't that happen with any of the other murder victims? Of the five girls that were reported missing, Keith Draycott's daughter was the only one with dark hair. Keith Draycott had mysteriously missed two meetings of the Carlow Valley Arts Festival Committee meetings, one on 4th September, the day Olivia Farringdon was murdered, and the second on 8th September when Edward Duffield was murdered; no reason for his absence was given. And then, of course, once Keith Draycott himself had been murdered, the killings stopped.

"Once I began to suspect Keith Draycott, I needed to work out how he selected the four schoolgirls that he murdered. Two of the girls, Emily Ashurst and Charlotte Huxton sometimes visited the church youth club that he used to run and he obviously took them both into his confidence, so much so that Emily had arranged to meet him to express her concern that her mother was having a sexual relationship with one of her friends, Gary Beechwood. Charlotte Huxton asked him if he could give her some lessons on the violin so that she could impress her mother. I suspect he happened to see Rosemary Edwyn wandering to the shower block at Corwood campsite when he was organising activities at the outdoor youth club which, at that time, was just across the road. He probably found some excuse for engaging her in conversation and, for whatever reason, she was persuaded to get into his car. I think he literally bumped into Catherine Duffield. I suspect he was coming out of Mallowcrest where he had been offering succour and comfort to one of the terminally ill residents and chanced upon Catherine Duffield wandering past carrying a heavy bag of groceries. Of course, it's quite possible that he mistook Catherine for her cousin Sophie, with whom she was staying, and who was also an occasional visitor to his youth club; Catherine's mother remarked on how alike she and Sophie were. In any event, Keith Draycott played the Good Samaritan, offered her a lift and that's the last anyone saw of her.

Incidentally, I don't know how he found out that Dick had turned up at Mallowcrest and was talking to Doris Milburn. Maybe he happened to be there at the time or maybe Raymond Gulliver was working in the grounds and tipped him off. Either way, he knew he had to act in case old Doris had witnessed something out of her window. So he found himself at Mallowcrest when Dick left, and he followed him. And he took his notebook while Dick was in the shop. And then, the following day, he went back to Mallowcrest and murdered Doris. He was fit and strong and she was old and frail so I don't imagine she put up much of a fight when he smothered her with her pillow. And, on the way out, as a precaution, he took the visitors book so that no one would be able to see when and how often he had visited.

"Anyway, I digress. It was some time after Rosemary Edwyn went missing that Keith's daughter, Isabel, realised what he had been up to and decided to run away, in the company of Russell Chalbury. She had also caught her father in bed with Charlotte Huxton and I suspect that chance encounter sealed poor Charlotte's fate.

"But although everything was starting to fit together, what I really needed was some hard evidence to back up my suspicions. That's why I asked Alison to have a nose round St Giles church and graveyard. Obviously, I didn't expect Raymond Gulliver to come steaming out of the church firing a gun and I must apologise for that. And that's why I needed to get back into the vicarage. The day Alison and I first visited Vanessa Draycott, just after the memorial service for her husband, we were shown into his study and, amongst other things, I noticed a camera – quite high spec and quite new – and, for some reason, it looked a bit out of place amongst all the dusty tomes and venerable artefacts. I could remember being told about Olivia Farringdon and how she had enrolled on a photography course, but there had been no sign of her camera either at her flat or in her car. But Alison showed me the receipt she'd found in Olivia Farringdon's flat and the make and model seemed to tally with the one in Keith Draycott's study. So, when I went back to the vicarage, I checked the camera and there were pictures on the memory card that had obviously been taken by Mrs Farringdon. There were some of this hotel – no doubt taken when she stayed here – and even one or two of herself, probably taken for her by a willing passerby at places she had obviously visited on her walking holidays – the Lake District, Snowdonia, the Scottish Highlands. And ironically, the last couple of pictures were of Carlow Woods, almost certainly taken shortly before she was murdered. Keith Draycott must have claimed her camera as a trophy.

"And then, of course, there was the cellar. On our first visit to the vicarage, I looked carefully at the outside of the building. Its elevation and its vintage suggested that it should have a cellar and, when I went back, I noticed the telltale grating by the front doorstep. Then, as we walked around inside, you could hear the floorboards creaking a bit, which might also have indicated the presence of a cellar. And when I started to ask Vanessa Draycott about it, she immediately looked uneasy, so I just played a hunch. But I never expected to find anything as grisly as that awful, locked cupboard." Clive shuddered.

When Clive finished his account, the room again fell silent for a moment or two.

"Blimey!" Alison Pawlett muttered, eventually, before draining her glass.

Dick Beauregard's face broke into a broad smile, an expression that did not suit his naturally forlorn demeanour and seemed strangely at odds with the gravity of Clive's narrative. He turned to Clare. "I'm very impressed by what I've just heard. Your husband is really very clever!"

"Yes, a bit too clever for his own good, sometimes," Clare replied, waspishly. She glanced at her watch. "I reckon dinner should be ready about now and we don't want to keep Gary waiting. Why don't you all follow me into the dining room while Clive can still get his head through the doorway!"

"Wooah!" Clive admonished, throwing up a restraining, bandaged hand. "Before we go, I just want to put on record that it was Clare who found the note about Lennie Cave reporting his suspicions about Keith Draycott. It was Clare who deciphered the meaning of 'Circe', it was Clare who noticed that all of the girls who went missing had fair hair apart from Isabel Draycott, it was Clare who spotted the historic presence of a youth club opposite Corwood campsite and, above all, it was Clare who saved Vanessa Draycott's life. So if you've any champagne left in your glasses, I suggest we raise them to Clare, her intuition, her determination and her courage."

As glasses were raised, Clare turned bright pink, shouted, "Oh, shut up!" at Clive, turned and made a bolt for the door, calling "dinner's ready" over her shoulder as she hastily disappeared.

*

Clive had reserved a table for his three dining companions and himself in one of the many cosy alcoves which Clare had created, using ornamental screens with oriental motifs and trellis frameworks festooned with climbing indoor plants. As main course options, Gary Beechwood had prepared some of his favourite dishes and, as dinner progressed, Jamie Coulton waited on them solicitously, frequently pausing at Alison's shoulder to brush against her arm, while clearing the dishes, and whisper affectionate words in her ear at the same time.

At the end of the meal, Gary approached, more diffident and nervous than usual, ostensibly to check that the guests had enjoyed his specialities, which they were able to confirm with enthusiastic and vigorous nodding of heads.

"I hope you've recovered from Superintendant Rushwick's grilling," Dick Beauregard observed amiably. "He can be a bit of a bastard!"

Gary laughed and gave the inspector a sly wink. "Nah! Clive, er, Mr Walsingham had warned me what to expect and I was ready for him. To be honest, I had quite a bit of fun winding the pompous git up!"

"And it's turned Gary into a bit of a celebrity locally, thanks mainly to Guy Sharston's publicity," Clare added.

"Yes and I've created a new dish in his honour," Gary replied, still laughing. "I'm calling it 'Lobster Rushwick'. It's grilled for a long time, it's tough on the outside and hard to break but well worth it when you do." Gary's demeanour suddenly changed and a look of apprehension spread across his sweaty face. "Actually," he announced gravely, "I wonder if this might be a good time; there's something I want to ask." Without further explanation, he turned and strode out of the dining room, leaving the four diners looking quizzically at each other. When he returned, he was hand in hand with Beth Wroxham, whose round face had a bright scarlet hue, and followed, at a lively pace, by Archie the cat, who unfailingly associated Gary with food and tried to pursue him whenever he could. Gary turned towards Clive.

"You know you said you owed me a favour for subjecting myself to Superintendant Lobster's grilling?"

"Ye-es," Clive replied guardedly.

"Well, the thing is," Gary seemed suddenly strangely self-conscious, forever wiping his hands on his apron. "The thing is, would it be okay if Beth and I got married and had our wedding reception here in the hotel?"

Clive, who had been leaning back in his chair, easing the pressure on his full stomach and enjoying the last drops of wine in his glass, spluttered, temporarily unable to utter anything coherent, and almost fell off his chair. "You and, errm, Beth? Getting married? I mean, I had no idea that, errm you two were, errm—" Clive stammered.

"I think what my husband is trying to say," Clare interrupted excitedly, "is that we'd be delighted for you to use the hotel for your wedding and reception. It's just we didn't realise that you and Beth were engaged or, or, even seeing each other, or, or anything."

"Oooooh, we've tried to be discreet," Beth gushed, her large hazel eyes ablaze with excitement. "We're here to work and we try not to mix business with pleasure. We only meet up in our own time."

"Of course," Clare replied. "Quite right! But how long have you known each other? You haven't been here very long. Did you know each other before you started working here?"

Gary Beechwood and Beth Wroxham exchanged nervous glances before Gary spoke. "About twelve years, actually; we were at school together!"

"Hang on, hang on!" Clive interjected, his sleuthing instincts coming to the fore. "You were at Polbury Manor, Gary, and I know you were friendly with some of the girls who disappeared, but I don't recall anyone mentioning a girl called Beth Wroxham."

"That's because…" Gary Beechwood coughed nervously, wiped his hands on his apron again and exchanged a fleeting glance with his fiancée. "I need to tell them, Beth!" His fiancée nodded gently, squeezed his hand and gave a toothy smile. "Allow me to present Victoria Huxton," Gary announced to a stunned quartet.

Clive spluttered again. "Victoria Huxton? The elder sister of Charlotte Huxton? The one who left home at the age of eighteen and hasn't been heard of since?"

The girl shuffled uneasily. "Gosh, yes, that's me. At the time, I couldn't face being at home anymore. Obviously, the loss of Charlotte pretty well broke us up as a family. My mum turned to drink, my dad took to working long hours and was never home and Becky, er, my baby sister, Rebecca – well, let's just say Becky and I had an uneasy relationship. So when I finished school, I packed my bags and buggered off. I moved to a part of London where they don't ask too many questions, changed my name by sticking a pin in the local phone book and got a job working in a fairly seedy hotel where they didn't worry too much about references and employment history. But I kept in touch with Gary and we'd meet up whenever we could, but we were living and working in different parts of the country and it was becoming very difficult. Anyway, eventually we decided we wanted to move back to this part of the world and try and find jobs here so that we could spend more time together. As luck would have it, shortly after Gary got a job here, he found out that you wanted to recruit another receptionist, so, at his suggestion, I applied. Gary told me about you both and what sort of person you were looking for and what questions you might ask and, well, here I am!"

Clive gave a mannered cough. "And am I to assume, therefore, that parts of your CV were not factually correct?" he asked with deliberately exaggerated pomposity.

Victoria Huxton's face turned scarlet again, her mouth gaped open and she swallowed hard. "Gosh, err, n-no, some parts were, errm, not strictly true…"

"Minor things like your name and the school you attended?"

"No, that's right," Victoria Huxton replied earnestly. "But my employment history is accurate and the references I gave were real. Oh, please don't sack me! It's all been so difficult and Gary and me, or er, Gary and I, we're together at last."

Clive smiled benignly. "I must say, you've done very well while you've been here – you both have. I take it there are no more surprises?"

Victoria Huxton swallowed hard and fixed her gaze firmly on the floor. "I, errm, wanted to apologise for the last few days when I haven't, errm, been myself. I was pretty shaken up when I heard about my mother's murder. I mean, I hadn't been in touch with her for ages but she was still my mother and I wouldn't have wished that fate on her and I took it all very badly. And then, and then, I errm, discovered I was pregnant. That's when me and Gary, errm, or rather Gary and I, decided we wanted to bring the wedding forward. Originally, we were thinking of getting married in St Giles church but obviously that's no longer appropriate and so we thought of here. I, err, I, I just want to thank you for taking me on – for taking both of us on – you don't know what it means…"

"Oh shut up!" Clare found herself being embarrassed again. "So tell me about the wedding – I love a good wedding. Is it going to be a big affair? What about your family, Beth, er, sorry, Victoria?"

Victoria Huxton giggled. "I prefer to be called Vicky, and, yes, my family, or what's left of it, will be invited. I've lost my little sister Charlotte and I've lost my mother and I've spent far too long not talking to my dad or my baby sister, except by an occasional text message, and I think it's about time we got together, kissed and made up. So I shall be contacting them both, telling them about me and Gary and, hopefully, spend some time getting to know them better. And we'll be inviting some of our old school friends. It's a shame that Issy won't be able to, errm…"

Victoria Huxton broke off and wiped some tears from her eyes.

While the conversation with Gary and Vicky had been going on, Jamie Coulton had been secretly eavesdropping, clearing the table more slowly than was necessary and lingering unseen behind one of Clare's ornamental screens. Having heard about Gary and Vicky and their plans, he glided over to the table, leaned across Alison and whispered, "How about it? How about you and I...?" His words were cut short by a sharp elbow thrust into his ribcage with some force, causing him to gasp in pain and recoil backwards.

"That's a 'no' then is it?" He gulped as he staggered back towards the kitchen carrying a pile of empty plates.

*

Clare was in the conservatory dining room, busily preparing the tables for dinner while listening to one of her favourite CDs of organ music, when she happened to glance out of the window towards the car park just as Clive was lifting a flat square parcel from the boot of his car.

He was looking furtive as he scurried through reception and was clearly dismayed when he was intercepted by Clare.

"Hello, darling! What's that you've got there?" she asked cheerily.

Clive looked down at the brown paper parcel as though surprised to see it in his arms. "Oh, ah, errm, what, this? It's er, it's a painting. I, er commissioned it from Russell Chalbury. I gather he's decided to sell up and move on. However lightly the courts treat Issy, he knows she's going to be away for quite a while and it seems Dick's forensic team made a bit of a mess of the boathouse when they were looking for evidence, so he's put it on the market. He's going to make another fresh start somewhere, probably under another assumed name. You know, he's having such a rough time at the moment and he is really talented and I felt sorry for him and..."

"And what have you done, Clive?" Clare demanded, sensing that he was hiding something.

"I asked him to paint a portrait of you. I supplied him with a recent photograph of you and commissioned him to do the work. It's your birthday next week and it was, errm, going to be a bit of a surprise, but..."

"Oooh, can I see it now?" Clare asked excitedly.

"Well, errm, it hasn't turned out quite as I planned," Clive replied sheepishly. "Russell's interpretation isn't quite what I expected. It's not what I asked him to do."

"I'd still like to see it. Can I see it?" If anything, Clare's excitement had been heightened by Clive's prevarication.

"Oh, errm, yes, well I suppose... Let's go through to the office."

Still contriving to look furtive, Clive led the way into the office with Clare following excitedly behind and slowly unwrapped the painting which he nervously held up for Clare to inspect. It was a full-length study of a nude female.

"Oh, what...?" Clare spluttered in surprise before studying the painting closely for a moment or two. "Hang on a minute!" she exclaimed. "That bit's me! But those bits aren't. How did...?"

"The face is yours," Clive explained. "And, in my view, a good likeness. But for some reason, Russell has chosen to superimpose your face onto an incomplete painting of a nude that looks very like the one he was working on when Alison and I went to see him. From what I saw that day – and I saw a great deal – I'd say everything from the neck down belongs to Isabel Draycott. Maybe he didn't want to keep the canvas after what she did."

"Well, yes, I can see that it's not me," Clare agreed while trying to hide her disappointment. "It's actually quite flattering in a way, I suppose. The boobs are much bigger and firmer than mine, there are no wrinkles or creases and no evidence of the ravages of time or the impact of gravity. I must agree that the face is a good likeness though; he's done it well."

"I thought I might hang it over the bar," Clive suggested with a smirk.

"Oh no, you're not," Clare admonished with a wagging finger. "I'm not having a nude painting of myself hanging in the bar for everyone to see."

"Yes but it's only your face. The rest isn't of you."

"Yes, you and I know that, but our guests won't – they'll look at that and think it's me! They'll start mentally undressing me and…" She shuddered.

"Alright! I'll hang it in the dining room then."

"No!"

"In reception?"

"No!"

"Oh alright, I'll hang it in our bedroom then." Clive studied the painting closely for a moment or two and then eyed Clare up and down. "You know," he observed with a playful smile. "I'm not so sure there is that much difference between the body in the painting and yours. Mind you, I am getting a bit forgetful. I'd really need to compare them both, like for like, as it were, to be sure."

Clare gave him a flirtatious smile. "Mmm, yes, I do see what you mean. Well you leave me with no choice then. I'm just going up to the bedroom. I'll see you there in a minute, and don't forget to bring the painting with you!"